DOWN
RIVER

KAREN HARPER

DOWN RIVER

MIRA®

ISBN-13: 978-1-61664-092-7

DOWN RIVER

Printed in U.S.A.

To the wonderfully independent Alaskans
I met on our trip, and, as ever,
to my traveling companion through life, Don.

Part I

Fighting the Foam

Like the dew on the mountain,
Like the foam on the river,
Like the bubble on the fountain,
Thou art gone, and for ever!
—Sir Walter Scott

Prologue

Lisa Vaughn fought to pull her wrist loose from her mother's strong hand. "No, I'm afraid. I'm going to tell Grandma. No, Mommy, no, nooo!"

They were up on the deck where everyone had done the lifeboat drill but now no one else was around. Eight-year-old Lisa loved the big cruise ship she was on in the middle of the blue sea with Grandma, Mommy and baby Jani. But Grandma was taking a nap in their cabin, and Mommy was crying. So was Lisa's baby sister, maybe because Mommy was holding her so tight against her chest with only one arm. With the other hand she dragged Lisa toward the back railing of the ship with lots of bubbling white water underneath.

Walking around the deck with Mommy and Jani, Lisa had thought it was pretty at first, all that wild water like when you swished your hand real fast to make lots of bubbles in the bathtub. But Mommy kept saying something about "Getting away just like your father did, just getting away with my girls... peace forever..."

Lisa started to cry, too, when her mother put one leg up high over the railing. Still, she didn't let go of Lisa's wrist, dragging her closer. Jani cried and squirmed. Wet-faced from her own tears, Mommy kissed her little cheek, then looked back at Lisa.

"You have to come with us, Lisa. Stop struggling!"

She gave Lisa a huge tug, trying to lift her over the rail, scraping her stomach.

"No!" Lisa shouted as she pulled back and kind of shoved Mommy away at the same time.

Lisa fell hard on the deck, so surprised and scared as Mommy, still holding Jani, fell backward, down. Lisa jumped to her feet in time to see Mommy and Jani drop and disappear, sucked into the sea by the wild white water.

1

Despite the calm beauty of Duck Lake ten feet below the pine-tree-lined path, Lisa Vaughn felt compelled to watch the Wild River on the other side of the low ridge where she stood. Because the summer sun had warmed the snow-tipped Talkeetna Mountains for hours, the snowmelt river roared. When the temperature dropped at night, despite the fact the skies barely darkened, the river rumbled like distant thunder. She was amazed by the reddish-colored salmon as they battled the fierce current on their long journey upriver to their breeding grounds. It almost looked as if the river was bleeding.

But mostly the river awed Lisa because, exactly twenty-six years ago, she'd seen her mother and baby sister drown in the turbulent, foaming wake of a cruise ship. Since then, roiling water mesmerized her. And she had never seen anything like the rapids of the Wild River.

She pulled her gaze away and hurried along the ridge toward the cutoff to the lake landing where she and Mitch had agreed to paddle a kayak to a picnic spot. "I know you've never been in a kayak," he'd said when he suggested it, "but we'll be fine as long as you match your strokes to mine, so we don't slam our paddles together."

Match your strokes to mine. His words echoed in her head. Was it just she who was still furious about the death of their passion? Although their romance and future together had ended when they'd slammed their different goals into each other, the man still got to her in a dangerous way. This trip had to be all business for her, all about getting a promotion, not rehashing the wreck of their relationship. She'd been dreading this whole slippery situation, but maybe talking it out could help her to finally write the obituary for what she'd thought was mutual love. She let out a breath, then inhaled deeply, not to savor the fresh, pine-scented air, but to calm herself.

Mitch Braxton seemed a different man from a year ago when they'd broken their engagement and he'd left her and Fort Lauderdale for the heart of Alaska. He'd broken her heart, but she'd been so angry with him that she'd quickly patched herself back together, at least on the surface. She'd gone on with a vengeance, not looking back until her boss set up this command performance at Mitch's lodge.

Lisa had worked hard to pretend to get over her resentment of his shattering her prettily planned-out life. She had expected to be a skilled attorney, a wife, a working mother to their future children. Though she knew better, sometimes she felt that, at age thirty-four, her marital and biological clocks were not only ticking but clanging. Just when she'd thought never to see Mitch again, Graham Bonner, the managing partner of Carlisle, Bonner & Associates, had been adamant that he had a unique plan for screening the three candidates for the next senior partner of the prestigious law firm.

Graham and his wife, Ellie, insisted they were taking the three junior partners to participate in the family/corporate bonding program Mitch offered at the lodge he'd inherited in Alaska. Since they'd only arrived yesterday, all they'd done so far was walk blindfolded through an obstacle course by following vocal directions—but so much more was in store. Scheduled during the week were ziplining and whitewater rafting, all the while being observed by the Bonners to decide who would get the coveted senior partner position Mitch had abandoned.

Some of Lisa's friends had argued it was a crazy way to vet a lawyer, though it sounded like a great, free vacation. But Graham was clever and convincing. He'd learned the law-firm ropes from Ellie's father and her brother Merritt, who used to run the firm and had used it as a stepping stone to his fast-rising political career.

Come hell or high water, Lisa intended to be the new senior partner, but she knew her competitors Jonas and Vanessa were just as tenacious and ambitious. Maybe that was what the Bonners were judging them by anyway. She couldn't help but wonder if, as upset and betrayed as the Bonners had also felt by Mitch's defection, they hadn't still enlisted him to help them make the important decision. He'd always been the Bonners' golden boy. Once Lisa had even thought they were grooming him not only to take over the firm but to partner—in more ways than one—with their twenty-four-year-old only child, Claire, who was now in law school at Duke University, and would soon join the firm as its third-generation lawyer.

Stopping above another clearing where she could see the river, Lisa brushed several mosquitoes away, then put down the small plastic cooler she carried. The cooler had been beautifully packed, down to bright cloth napkins and a tablecloth by Mitch's lodge manager and chef, Christine. Like the lodge, Christine Tanaka seemed both down to earth, yet frontier elegant. Lisa had sensed something between Mitch and the striking, ebony-haired, high-cheekboned woman, and was annoyed that it bothered her.

While Christine knew where they were going, Lisa hoped they wouldn't be missed by the others during this three-to-five afternoon break, when everyone had some private time before gathering for pre-dinner appetizers and wine.

She sprayed herself lightly with the bug repellent she'd brought along. Close to the lodge they fogged the area and the brisk breeze today kept most of the mosquitoes away. She was used to them, being from South Florida, but the Alaska version seemed especially voracious. At least, in his introduction to them yesterday, Mitch had mentioned the bug season was waning.

She forced her gaze away from the river rapids and stuffed the small spray can back in the top of her sock, then rolled her jeans back down. She wore her running shoes and a life preserver over a light jacket and T-shirt, but the day seemed warm—too warm, if she kept thinking about Mitch.

Turning back to the river, Lisa fastened the Velcro straps of her orange PFD jacket. Mitch had warned them, "No one, not even Olympic swimmer Michael Phelps, if he shows up here, goes out on the lake or the river without a PFD!"

She and her colleagues had joked that an attorney, on the losing end of a lawsuit, must have named it a Personal Flotation Device, but then it wasn't a plain old life preserver. PFDs were made of sleek, contoured neoprene, a far cry from those old bulbous, canvas jackets the cruise ships had passengers wear during lifeboat drills. For all she knew, that drill had given her mother the idea to jump overboard.

If Lisa was getting in a kayak for the first time, she

was going prepared. She could swim like a fish, but since her family tragedy—though she tried not to let people know—churning water not only horrified her but lured her.

She picked up the cooler and glanced back down the path toward the sprawling two-story log lodge with its four rustic cabins huddled nearby like chicks around a mother hen. No sign of Mitch yet; he was busy here, king of his realm. But then, he'd seemed to be master of his fate in Florida, too, before the dam broke and their mutual future was swept away.

She heaved a huge sigh, staring down into the river. Mitch said he'd bring the drinks, and she wondered if it would be wine. Last year, the night they had broken up, she'd snapped her wine goblet off at the stem when he'd told her he had to get out of the rat race and leave Fort Lauderdale. Her hand had bled from a puncture wound; she still bore the scar—that and too many others as she went on with her high-flying career. That terrible night, she had tossed her engagement ring at him, and would have thrown the gold bracelet with the flying seagulls he'd bought her as well, except the clasp had stuck.

But now, when she looked back on that night, she knew she'd done things to upset him, too. She recalled Mitch's explosion when she'd told him she had volunteered both of them to testify at a state senate committee hearing. They were both under pressure then, working day and night on a high-profile money-laundering case. They'd been harassed, even stalked by someone, until Graham had suddenly taken them off the case for their safety. She was trying to find another way to keep them in what she thought of as "the local lawyer limelight." They were having drinks on the patio of her condo with its view of a golf course she'd never played.

"No way!" he'd shouted, shocking her. "I just can't take time to testify at some senate hearing! Leave that political stuff to Ellie's beloved brother, who will probably be our next senator or even president, for all I know!"

"Listen, I realize it will take time from your other cases, but it's great PR, and your name carries clout now," she'd insisted.

"I may be successful, but I'm so stressed I'm getting distracted—careless—when people's futures are in my hands. I'm scared I'll not only ruin someone else's life, but my own. Carelessness can lead to self-destruction. Sometimes I don't give a damn about things I need to care for, to control. Half the time, all I've worked for seems pointless."

"Including a future with me? Our love, our plans, both professional and personal?" she'd demanded in her best litigator's voice. "Mitch, we can have everything together, including our careers, helping people, not wasting time on something pointless!"

That was when he'd dropped the bomb that he'd inherited his uncle's land and lodge and wanted to move to Alaska. He'd been meaning to find the right time to tell her. Would she change her plans to go with him?

Shocked and angry, she'd refused, accused him of being self-centered. But she saw now she had been, too. Why couldn't he understand that no urban career woman who loved luscious, lively Fort Lauderdale needed a dropout who preferred the lonely wilds of Alaska? No, she couldn't risk loving someone who suddenly claimed to be nearly suicidal, not after all she'd been through.

Now, lost in her regrets, trembling again at the memory, she frowned at the raging river. Then something happened. Somehow, it was as if her rage at her past, at her mother, at Mitch, pushed her over some psychic edge. She tumbled headlong off the path, off her feet. The cooler went flying, hit her knee. She screamed, lost her balance, then rolled sideways down the ridge.

She landed on a spruce sapling, but before she could grab it, it bent under her weight to fling her forward. In the clearing, nothing else stopped her fall. Over, over she rolled, until she slammed into the rushing river, going under. The frigid water shocked her. She gasped and sucked some in. Choked. Her sinuses burned while her skin froze.

The PFD lifted and righted her, head up, but foam crested over her. Mother with Jani in her arms fell over the rail again. The boiling foam devoured them, devoured Lisa. Had Mommy pulled her in with them? How did this happen? She was horrified for her family, for herself. Terror screamed at her, in her, echoing the smashing water, clawing at her courage.

She was swept around, past jutting rocks. She pulled her hands and feet in close. She had to get out but found nothing to hold as she was tossed, whirled, pulled and yanked, bumped by boulders, cold and drowning, dragged downriver.

Though the two glasses Mitch had thrown in his backpack with the cans of ginger ale were plastic, they clanked as he walked the ridge path, their dissonant sound nearly drowned by the river's roar. If Lisa thought he'd cart wine out here for some sort of a lovey-dovey reunion, she was wrong. This was strictly a business meeting, he told himself.

So what if he still felt he wanted her? It was a pure physical reaction from hot memories. His body's reaction to being near Lisa again was something he could absolutely handle—had to.

When he moved to Alaska, he'd needed to cleanse himself of the dirty feeling of defending clients he knew damn well were guilty. He felt guilt-ridden by his own obscenely high fees and the busy schedule that left no time for pro bono work. Pressure, pressure, pressure—and for what? Prestige? Cruising Lauderdale's canals in his boat, chasing women or raising a future family he didn't have time for? Unlike Ellie Bonner's brother, Merritt Carlisle, he didn't want the power that came from a place in national or even state politics. Back home—though this was home now—he'd been fed up with convoluted power connections in the fast-fleeting fame lane. Thank

God, Alaska had helped to heal him. It was said people who came to Alaska from outside were either running from something or to something. He guessed, in his case, it was both.

He knew he had let a lot of people down when he'd come north, but helping other people's families, friends and coworkers to connect with each other was far more fulfilling than his old life. He'd continued his uncle's work here through his adventure-bonding program. At least Graham and Ellie bringing their three candidates here to decide who should fill Mitch's vacant position showed they still trusted his judgment and had forgiven him for leaving.

But golden-skinned, blonde, beach-baby Lisa Vaughn had never understood why he had to change his life, leave Florida for Alaska to keep his sanity, even if it meant changing the plans they'd made. They needed to just talk it out, this time briefly, unemotionally, objectively, then they could get back to the business at hand.

He wished Lisa well in her quest to make senior partner, but he wasn't playing favorites. He owed Graham that—Ellie, too, because her father had founded the firm, and the old man had eventually made his son-in-law Graham a full partner before he died. Graham had been Mitch's mentor, just as Mitch had tried to mentor Jonas, the candidate he actually favored, although both Lisa and Vanessa were excellent lawyers. No one worked at Carlisle, Bonner & Associates of Fort Lauderdale, Miami and Palm

Beach, if they weren't. Though Mitch didn't especially trust politicians, Merritt, who had still been a lawyer at the firm when Mitch first worked there, was someone who had managed to keep his nose clean.

Just before he cut off the ridge path onto the downward spur toward the lake landing where he'd told Lisa he'd meet her, he spotted the small, white cooler Christine had said she'd given to Lisa. It was open, with wrapped appetizers, bright plates and napkins, strewn down the ridge toward the river like a hand pointing toward the water. Had Lisa seen a bear and run? No, the bear wouldn't have left the food.

He stooped and squinted down toward the river. The drop-off over the ridge was fairly open. Surely she knew to turn right toward the lake, not left. Had she fallen toward the river? Dear God, please don't let her have fallen *in* the river!

"Lisa! Lisa!" he shouted, but he knew the roar of the river would cover his voice if she wasn't nearby. She was physically fit, an outdoors girl, but the kind who loved sunny skies and sand. Beach volleyball, at which she excelled, was her sport of choice.

"Lisa? Liiiisaa!"

Holding on to a couple of spruce saplings, Mitch went down the steep bank to the river. He gasped when he saw her in the foaming water, about ten yards away, clinging to a rock on the far side. He never would have spotted her, except she wore an orange PFD that showed up like a beacon in the rapids. If she let go, she'd be a goner, because not far beyond was a narrow gorge with a hairpin turn of boiling white water, and later, a series of small falls that didn't stop the salmon coming up but could kill her going down. Worse, exposed to water this cold, she'd go numb and hypothermic in twenty minutes, then die. His uncle had told him that feeling in the limbs went after about seven minutes, consciousness in the next seven, and life itself in the following seven or so. And a South Florida girl was hardly prepared for a snowmelt swim.

He waved his arms and shouted again but she was facing downriver and didn't see him. She was hanging on for dear life—literally.

He half climbed, half crawled back up the bank. A kayak! He needed the kayak that was on the other side of the ridge. There was no time to get help. No one at the lodge would hear him above the water if he shouted, nor could they see him from here. How long could she hold on?

He'd have to get her in the kayak without tipping it, shoot the next eddies, humps and holes to get them to a landing spot before the gorge where he could tend to her. But there was no easy way to return. They'd have to either hike back on the other side of the river or portage the kayak around the falls and ride the rapids all the way out of these mountains.

He yanked himself up from Sitka spruce sapling to sapling, digging his nails into the green moss and orange lichens. He scrabbled past where she'd dropped the cooler, over the ridge, then raced down the path to the red, two-person kayak sitting by the serene lake awaiting their easy trip across to one of his favorite picnic spots. Damn, why hadn't she fallen down this side of the ridge?

His heart pounded; adrenaline stoked his strength. Kayaks weren't overly heavy, but he had to get it up the path, then over the ridge to launch it without splitting the quarter-inch plastic. Yes, two paddles in it. Two PFDs, too. He glanced once across the lake to see if his friends Ginger or Spike might be somewhere in sight, but saw no one. Ginger's little motor boat was pulled up on the shore near the lodge, but she was nowhere around.

"No one but me," he grunted as he shoved the kayak before him up the path. *Please Lord,* he prayed, *let her hang on to that rock.*

Panting, his heart pounding and muscles screaming, he got the kayak up and over the ridge, now trying to keep it from crashing down into the river and taking off without him. Sweat burned his eyes as he squinted to see if Lisa was still hanging on. Yes!

He cursed the time it took him to get the spray skirt out of the fore dry storage well and tight around him while he hung on to a sapling so the kayak didn't take off from under him. Otherwise, if too much water got in, he could go hypothermic himself, or capsize. He fought the violent pull of the water—nothing like surfing offshore in South Florida.

Mitch realized he still wore his backpack when it

bumped against the kayak. He yanked it off and exchanged it for one of the PFDs in the front seat. He jammed the backpack into the well. He needed the neoprene wet suit he saw there, but no time, no time. He realized he had no helmet—hadn't put one in for a simple paddle across the lake. He was breaking the rules he'd laid out for safety, but this was life and death—Lisa's, and maybe his, too. "Be stupid and a kayak can be your coffin," he'd told more than one group of guests.

He felt a jab of anger at Lisa for being in the river, for getting them into this nightmare, when he'd thought things in his life were going so well. So well, that is, except that for the week hc had to be near the woman who loved her career and her sunny spot on the planet more than she had loved him.

He shoved off, stabbing the river with deep strokes, fighting for control and balance so he wouldn't shoot past her. He prayed he could get over to her and somehow get her on board without rolling them both under. "Don't let go! Don't let go!" he shouted, though he figured the roar of the water would keep her from hearing him.

He squinted through sun and spray to locate her by her orange PFD again, and, in that instant, saw her swept away, flailing in the foam.

2

Lisa tried to cling to the next rock she saw, even claw her way atop it, but the water pinned her against it. She couldn't breathe. Should she let go? Try to find a flatter rock to hold?

But the choice was not hers, caught in the cold current, being twisted and turned. Her shins scraped boulders on the riverbed; she pulled her legs up and arms in for warmth, for safety, but found neither. She saw bloodred salmon streak past her in the foam, going the other way. How could they fight this water? she wondered. It might be easier going deep down.

Deep down, deeper… Mommy and Jani had gone deeper, so deep. The wet, white arms of water and death had taken them away. It would be easier that way, to let it all go, let everything go.

Lisa tried to swim for the riverbank, but each time she neared a handhold, the river snatched her away. She knew enough to try to point her feet downstream, but she couldn't control that. When her numb legs bobbed up, she saw the water had ripped off her shoes.

She was doomed. Dead. Smashed by violent fists of water...her lungs burning to get a breath. Icy water surged up her nose into her sinuses. Get your head up! Take another breath! Hold the air in!

How had she fallen in? The water had looked so beautiful, even alluring. Did something trip her? Surely no one had pushed her. Had Mother and Jani pulled her in to be with them at last? Was this just her memories turning to a drowning, screaming nightmare again?

No, this was not some awful dream where she could will herself to wake up. She had to fight. To live. *Dear Lord, help me. Help me be safe and warm.*

But the force was brutal, banging her through waves like giant fists, slamming into rocks. Like a leaf going down a storm sewer...lost at sea. Her mother had lost her mind, Grandma said, postpartum depression or some sort of mental aberration made her kill herself. Daddy's desertion of the family might have caused it, too. That's what a psychiatrist had told her once.

Mother, I didn't know. I was only a child. I knew you were sad, but if I had known you were desperate, I could have helped you. At least I could have saved Jani for Grandma to raise along with me.... Someone once said you loved me, so you wanted to take me with you. But it's wrong to kill someone who hasn't had a chance to live....

But should she have drowned, too? Why had Lisa lived when Mother and Jani died? She was haunted by a thought she'd told no one, not even her psychiatrist. When she'd yanked back so hard from her mother's grasp, did that send her over? If she had not pulled back, maybe there was a split second where her mother would have changed her mind. In that last moment, had she sent them into the wild, white water?

So confused, so dizzy, so caught in a spin of water, of fears...

Whispers, loud ones, roared all around her, wet and cold in her ears. Stop it! Stop the memories! This was real. She had to find a place to get out. If only she'd told Mitch she was sorry. Not sorry she didn't go with him, but that she still cared, still wanted him in some sort of angry way, but now all she wanted was out of this forceful, freezing water. Fingers going numb, so cold. Keep your head. Keep your courage. Don't let go! She heard a voice in her head and heart shouting, "Don't let go!"

Mitch was getting panicky. Because Lisa was in the river and his kayak was on top of it, she was moving away from him faster and faster. And she had a head start.

At times he lost sight of the flash of orange that was his best chance of tracking her in the foaming rapids. On river right, he passed a big boulder, fighting hard not to be smashed into it. Unfortunately, he was in a wide, flat-water kayak best used on the lake, not the narrower white-water craft designed for mobility. It took much more strength and skill to maneuver this craft in white water. Yet, heedless of humps and holes and the danger of submerged rocks, he dug his paddle in faster, faster, trying to catch up.

Trying to catch up—the story of his life. He'd been raised in the shadow of an older brother who was brilliant, Superman, his parents' all in all. There was no mountain too high, no challenge too big for Brad Braxton. Eagle Scout. High school student body president. University of Miami Gators swim team, All-American. Couldn't try out for the Olympics because he was a Rhodes Scholar. Now a thoracic surgeon in Miami, with a gorgeous wife and two kids. Unreal expectations to keep up with…keep up with…

This was unreal. Could not be happening. How in hell had Lisa fallen in? No way to call for help. Cell phones didn't work in the Talkeetnas, and he needed both hands on the paddle. The snowmelt had the river up to at least a Category III with four-foot waves and a rocking roll with worse ahead in the tight turns of Hairpin Gorge. His friend Spike had told him that the old prospectors had called that part of the Wild River the Turn Back Gorge, but there was no way he could turn back now, even if he lost her.

Using the paddle, he braced himself away from another rock, then righted the kayak when it was yanked into a pivot point. Off to the races again, squinting through the spume, hoping to see that slash of orange. She had to be here somewhere, unless she'd been trapped in a snag or sieve underwater.

In the first twist of Hairpin Gorge, narrow, gray haystacks of constricted water piled up into standing waves on both sides of the bow. He saw the path through it was chaos. Lisa would never survive.

The crash of the water almost deafened him. He pointed the kayak toward the chute and plunged into it. He glimpsed red king salmon struggling to go the other way. He fought a force he felt he'd never conquer, but sometimes a narrow ribbon of white water was faster than other places in the river. He was chilled and sopped down to where the spray skirt gripped his waist. He braced his knees against the inside of the craft, working the foot rudders, praying he wouldn't capsize. When Uncle John had taught him kayaking years ago on his summer vacations, he'd joked it was really an underwater sport. He'd taught Mitch the Eskimo roll, but it would be a life-and-death combat roll if he flipped today.

Lisa knew she'd be dead already if she hadn't been wearing her PFD. To keep her arms and legs from being banged by rocks both above and below the surface, again she fought to wrap herself into a ball, knees pulled up, arms around them. But when the water rolled her head under, she had to let go to right herself. She tried to kick and paddle but she still got tossed aside and around out of control.

She saw the taller walls of the gorge ahead. The first turn into it nearly finished her. She held her breath until she thought her lungs would burst. For one wild moment the sun was in her eyes. She tried to think of hot days on the beach, the South Florida sun beating down on her, not the weight of all this water. She might suffocate before she'd drown.

On the next turn, she knew she had to make one last grab for something along the bank or she'd black out. She had to drag herself out of this water, hang on. Back at the lodge, Mitch would miss her, maybe figure out what happened. But what had happened to get her in this killer river?

She tried to grab a rock and was shocked to realize both arms had gone numb. What was that called when you got so cold you fell into a fatal sleep... drifted into death? She couldn't die of something she couldn't recall the name of... Lawyers always had the right terminology, whether in English or Latin. *Qui bono,* who would profit from a crime? Lawyers knew all about plea bargains...the way out...but there was no way out here.

Though Mitch was in great physical shape, the muscles in his arms and back not only ached but burned. He had to find her now or it would cease to be a rescue and become a body recovery, if he could even manage that. But a whirlpool snagged him, and when he freed himself, he shot into another chute. It was fast, very fast, suddenly a smoother ride than any of Spike's musher sleds on sleek snow with his huskies barking. He imagined he heard them now, heard voices in the roar of the current, heard a woman's screams, but it was all in his head.

After the second twist of the gorge, he saw her again, pinned against a busher—a fallen tree—caught like a salmon in a Yup'ik fish wheel. Danger! Bushers were deadly, because they could trap a kayak or smash its thin plastic hull to bits.

But he had to risk it and go after her. Maybe they could climb out onto the tree, make it to the rock ledge. Was she moving? She'd have to be hypothermic by now, but could it be even worse? The power of the water pinning her there must be brutal.

He tried to edge in next to her, but the kayak corkscrewed and the current capsized him. Praying he wouldn't hit his head on the trunk or a submerged rock, he held his breath as he went under. The frigid slap of water shocked him, and made him fear for Lisa even more.

"Eskimo roll!" He heard his uncle's voice, clear and crisp. "Paddle thrust, body twist! Up! Over and up!"

He fought to keep from panicking. His lack of helmet could kill him, too. Upside down, with his body submerged but buoyed by his PFD, he lifted his paddle above the water with both hands out, then swept his torso and paddle while he snapped his hips up. The rotation worked, though the thrust of the current slammed the kayak sideways against the tree trunk again, jarring his teeth as he shook his head and upper body like a dog to get the water off. The entire craft shuddered.

He sucked in a huge breath. Despite the warmth of the air and sun, he felt as if he was rolling in snow. Five feet away from him, Lisa lay sprawled, unmoving, draped over the tree trunk like a drenched rag doll, apparently not breathing as the water crested in white plumes over and around her back. At least it had stopped her before the rest of the sharp turns and then the series of small falls a couple of miles beyond. And, thank God, she was upright with her shoulders and head out of the water.

He tried to brace himself with the paddle to get close enough to at least touch her, pull her down into the kayak or get them both out onto the tree. But when he took another stroke, the washing-machine effect of the churning river flipped him back under again.

Christine Tanaka occasionally glanced out the kitchen window of the lodge, but she kept cutting smoked salmon strips with her small, sharp *ula.* She was readying plates of appetizers for their guests from Mitch's old law firm—his job in his past life, as he liked to put it.

"*Iah,* don't say it that way!" she'd told him more than once. "It sounds like you're a ghost come back from the dead!"

But really, Mitch could do no wrong in Christine's

eyes, including the fact he mispronounced her name in her Yup'ik tribal language when he called her *Cu'paq.* It was a tough language for a *kass'aq,* with its clacking sounds deep in the throat. But it always sounded like Mitch was saying Cupid, that little winged spirit who zinged arrows into people to make them fall in love. She knew too much about that and how dangerous it could be. But the thing with Mitch was he honored her people and was trying hard to become an Alaskan. She loved him for that and for so much more.

She jumped at the deep voice behind her and turned off the Yup'ik radio broadcast she often listened to in the summer when she worked, just to hear the language of her kin. One long, beaded earring snagged in her thick, shoulder-length hair, and she tugged it free.

It was Jonas Grant, the tall, African-American lawyer here with the Bonncrs. He was one of the attorneys vying for the senior partner position that used to belong to Mitch.

"Mind if I come into your kitchen?" he asked, holding the swinging door ajar. "Tell you the truth, I'm starved, and Mitch told us to see you if that was the case. All this fresh air or my jet lag's making me hungry."

She was surprised she hadn't heard him come in because she had sharp ears and usually sensed someone's presence, but this man moved so quietly. Jonas had a shaved head, which wasn't the wisest thing in

Alaska, but it probably worked well where it was hot and humid.

Mitch had joked, "I taught Jonas everything he knows, which means he's pretty smart." She thought the man's wide, dark eyes under his sleekly arched brows backed that up. Jonas was always watching others—keeping his own counsel, as Mitch had put it when he'd given her a pre-arrival rundown on their guests. Yes, she could see that Jonas Grant was always calculating what to say and do. Truth be told, she was wary, too, so she'd recognized that in him right away. And she liked the color of his skin, a lot like the Alaskan sun- and wind-burnished complexions of her people—that is, her former people, before so many turned their backs on her for what she had done.

"Sure thing," she told him with a nod. "I'm fixing salmon tenders with strawberry dip, moose enchiladas and squares of fresh-baked bread with black raspberry spread for appetizers. You want something to drink, too?"

"No, thanks—just hungry."

As she fixed him a hearty plate, she glanced out the window to note no Mitch, but no kayak either. She squinted into the sun to see Ginger Jackson getting in her motorboat for the across-lake trek home. Ginger made all of the baked goods for the lodge and brought them each afternoon, especially the array of yummies for the breakfast buffet the next morning. How she managed to bake all that with a bum right hand was beyond Christine. The only bad thing about Ginger's baking was that she fed her brother Spike too much. In the summer, when he wasn't running the dogs but was mostly taking tourists flightseeing, he put on weight around his middle.

Spike Jackson's red seaplane sat at the far end of the lake since some guests had complained about the early-morning noise when he took off near the lodge. If guests didn't want to drive or land at Talkeetna's airport, he flew them in from Anchorage. He also took people on what was called flightseeing. Earlier today he'd flown Mrs. Bonner, who had her own private pilot's license no less, to view the entire area from Talkeetna clear down to Wasilla. She'd said she wanted to see the little town where that spunky, ambitious Sarah Palin was from, who had come out of nowhere—though folks hereabouts didn't think of big-boom Wasilla or the capital, Juneau, as nowhere—to run for vice president of the United States. Mitch had mentioned that Mrs. Bonner had a brother who was big in Florida politics and aiming higher, so no wonder Mrs. Bonner was interested in Alaska's Governor Palin.

Christine handed the filled plate to Jonas. "Thanks," he said with a big smile that flaunted lots of straight, white teeth. "My boy would say this really rocks—not the smoked salmon but moose in an enchilada."

"How old is he?" Christine asked as she followed him toward the door to the big common room that comprised the living area and dining room. The lodge bedrooms were upstairs in two wings, guests to the east side, Mitch's suite to the west. Christine's room was at the back corner of the first floor, next to the small library loaded with books about Alaska and overlooking the stone patio with the barbecue, fire pit and Finnish wood-fired sauna and hot tub, and then the lake beyond.

Actually, the Duck Lake Lodge—the original name for the lake was *Dukhoe*—was the most beautiful home she had ever had. Made of rough-cut local spruce with pine-paneled walls, it boasted a seven-foot bubble window overlooking the lake. The entire building and the outlying cabins were heavily insulated, so in the winter it was like being in a thermos that held heat from the big, central stone fireplace.

The fourteen-foot cathedral ceiling above the common room had hand-hewn beams that soared above comfortable clusters of upholstered sofas and chairs interspersed with rocking chairs all set around woven area rugs in muted blues and greens. Snowshoes, quilts and antlers decorated the walls, except in the little library where Mitch had insisted she put the remnants of her collection of Yup'ik dolls on display. Her real realm, the kitchen, looked strictly modern, with new stainless steel appliances that would make a Fairbanks restaurant proud. Off and on, as needed, two women came in from Bear Bones to help with housekeeping chores.

"My boy's nine," Jonas was saying in answer to

her question. "He's been pretty sick. He's—" facing away from her, he either cleared his throat or swallowed something "—he's had chordoma, a malignant bone cancer in his spine, since he was five."

"Oh. I'm so sorry. How hard for a young kid who wants to run and play."

"Yeah," he said, turning back to face her at the bottom of the central staircase. "Doctors give about a seven-year life expectancy for that when it's first diagnosed. I'd love to have Emerson here to see Alaska—bears, moose and that rough river out there. Tell you the truth, I feel guilty spending even a few days away from him, but this big opportunity with Carlisle and Bonner..." Frowning, he cleared his throat. Christine saw his eyes were glassy with unshed tears. "'Course, I'd do *anything* to help him survive, and those massive medical bills keep piling up. Well, didn't mean to bend your ear, but Mitch said you're easy to talk to."

"Did he?" she asked, feeling warm clear to her belly. "It's because I don't say much myself. Now, you need anything else, you just let me know. And get some rest if you can because the summer nights not only come later here compared to where you're from, but the summer sun never quite goes down, even in these mountains."

"What's that they used to say? 'The sun never sets on the British Empire'?"

"Did they say that? Well, we gotta get all the sun and light we can this time of year."

"In the long, dark winters, I guess you pay the price."

"But that gives us the gift of the northern lights, the aurora borealis."

"Yeah, I'd like to see that. Like for Emerson to see that, too. Mitch said you have a lot of Japanese tourists here because they believe a child conceived under the northern lights will be fortunate." He shook his head and started upstairs before he turned back, looking down at her over the banister. "Do they, you know, conceive the child outside in the winter, really under the lights?"

Christine smiled and shook her head, suddenly feeling irrationally happy. She was very fortunate. She'd done what she had to do to protect herself. And she certainly sympathized with Jonas, because she understood doing anything to survive. "No," she told him. "In the winter, even the wildest Alaskans do that inside, in bed."

He smiled sheepishly, thanked her again and went up the stairs toward the east hall guest rooms. Though she had a meal to start for about eight people, counting Spike if he was staying, she stepped out the back door and glanced down the familiar ridge path toward the lake landing. Lisa Vaughn had been no good for Mitch before and wouldn't be now. *Iah,* if only that woman hadn't come with these other lawyers to this haven Mitch had made for the woman he called his Cupid.

3

Once Mitch managed to right the kayak again, he knew he had to abandon it. The current pinned the boat tight to the tree, though he knew it could capsize again. He had to get to Lisa, be sure she was breathing, then get her—both of them—warm. But he'd need some of the supplies that were stowed in the kayak for them to survive out here. They were going to have to hike back to civilization, and the only access road was on the other side of the river.

Bracing himself as best he could with his paddle, with one hand he quickly unfastened the bungee cords securing the dry well at the front of the kayak, opened it and grabbed out the single wet suit. He wrapped it around his neck like a big scarf, then rummaged for the roll of duct tape he knew must be there. Finding it, he shoved it on his arm above his wrist. It was good for patching kayak cracks, but also for immobilizing sprained or broken bones. Being careful not to tip the kayak, he loosed the spray skirt and was surprised he was sitting in water. The cockpit was partly flooded, but he'd been so intent—and so much colder from the waist up—he hadn't even noticed. His sweatshirt over his T-shirt was soaked and heavy.

He half dragged, half hoisted himself onto the tree about four feet from Lisa. Holding on to protruding broken limbs, he crawled toward her. Her wet blond hair looked like a curtain covering her face. Though his instinct was to lift her into his arms, he reached down to feel for her carotid artery with two fingers. Her skin was so cold it shocked him, but he felt frigid, too, his fingers numb and fumbling.

Yes! She had a pulse—faint, maybe fluttering, or else he was shaking too hard to tell. She was breathing, steady but sure, so he wouldn't have to do mouth-to-mouth. Gently, he pushed her sopping hair back from her face. She looked pasty and bruised.

"Lisa. Lisa, it's Mitch. You're going to be okay. I'm here to take care of you and get you home—at least to my home, the lodge."

Nothing. No movement, but a pulse and breath was enough for now. He'd seen his uncle revive one of his homesteader friends who fell in years ago, though that had been near lodge property where they could get help, as slow as it was in coming from Bear Bones.

Praying their combined weight would not shift the tree trunk and send them barreling down the river with it, Mitch put his hands under her armpits. Slowly he lifted and laid her out on her back. Her legs flopped on either side of the trunk. Dragging her crawling backward, he inched along the log toward the low ledge where the roots of the tree had caught. Sunlight poured onto them. Sunlight! But it would not last long in this narrow gorge, even with the nights still filled with light.

It seemed an eternity before he had her laid out on the ledge. He curled her up, hoping to preserve whatever core body heat she had left.

"Land ho, sweetheart. You're going to be all right," he said as if to convince himself, but his voice broke.

He ventured out onto the tree trunk again, still on all fours. Sprawled on his belly, he carefully reached down to unrig the trapped kayak's other dry-storage well. Besides the extra PFD he'd shoved in there, he wasn't sure what was stowed, but it was the first break he'd had all day. He pulled out a four-pound butane camp stove and a one-person tent, though he saw no sleeping bag. There were no provisions but a small, plastic, zipper-locked sack of what Christine called squaw candy—dried salmon. He tossed the PFD and food up on the ledge and, pulling his backpack up over his shoulder by one strap, carefully hauled the tent and stove along the trunk to safety.

At least he had four ginger ales. Otherwise he'd be pouring boiled river water into Lisa. He could carry the tiny tent and stove with them if they could get off this ledge to hike out. But first things first.

Huddled over her to make a windbreak against the breeze, Mitch removed her PFD and stripped her down to her black bra and panties—stunningly sexy even out here where they seemed so fragile and fancy. Despite her tan lines, she looked fish-belly white. Her beautiful body now seemed a cold, marble statue. He moved fast to cover her with the neoprene suit, not putting it on her yet because it felt cold. Rafters and kayakers often wore a layer of fleece under it to maintain body warmth, but she had been depleted of that.

He unzipped the tent from its pack and formed it into a windbreak, making sure it didn't shade her from the sun on the wall and floor of the small ledge that made—he hoped—a lifesaving pocket of warmth. He needed her conscious to be sure she didn't drift away, so he kept talking to her as he moved her arms and legs to check for broken bones. She looked battered and bruised, but he was amazed she seemed to have escaped without any serious injuries, not even signs of frostbite.

He tossed her clothes farther down the ledge to dry, then rubbed her all over with the neoprene wet suit, the only dry garment he had, since he was thoroughly soaked, too. He chaffed her fingers and toes in his hands, then wrapped her in the small canvas tent. She'd need his body heat—what there was of it—to come back, to survive, but he could put the wet suit on her later. He had to get hot liquids into her first. It was just as important to be warmed from the inside as out.

With its burner protected by its little windscreen,

the butane-fed, self-igniting cooker heated rapidly. He had a small pan, but, shivering, he ignored that for now. Somehow his stiff fingers got two of the cans of ginger ale open. He put them directly on the burner. When he realized the bag that had held the tent was still dry, he put it over Lisa's head like a too-big bonnet. So much body heat was lost through the head. He'd kidded Jonas about that, but the big guy never seemed to get too hot or too cold. Damn, what he wouldn't give for a hairdryer out here, and the lodge's hot tub.

While the cans of ginger ale heated, he huddled close to the stove's burner to get feeling back in his fingers. Shaking in his haste, he stripped off his PFD and his own wet clothes. With one can of ginger ale in his hand, he managed to wrap himself and Lisa in the small tent as if it were a double sleeping bag. He pressed his hip to hers and threw one leg over her to warm her thighs. The sudden, sweeping impact of mingled protectiveness and possessiveness astounded him.

A memory leaped at him of the day he'd really looked at her for the first time as a beautiful woman and not just as an associate at the firm. She had not been wearing much that day, either. In a way he'd wanted Lisa the moment he'd seen her on the beach, when he was coming in from windsurfing. What a shock to see Ms. Wet Behind The Ears Lawyer out of a business suit and wet all over.

At work and especially in court, as if she'd wanted

to hide from something, she'd often worn dark-rimmed glasses and her hair pulled back. Yet that day on the beach he saw classic features with a naughty tilt to her green eyes even sunglasses couldn't conceal. Her lithe body in that black bikini was so graceful, even when she spiked a volleyball with her long blond hair flying. Yet there was always something vulnerable about her.

"That's Lisa Vaughn?" he'd said to himself that day. He'd decided right there he'd do what he shouldn't—date a colleague and hope she wouldn't only agree to see him socially because he was Graham Bonner's heir apparent at the firm. There was nothing on the books about not dating coworkers, though he knew it was a bad idea, and one Graham would frown upon.

He soon learned Lisa was so much more than a beach babe or an ambitious attorney. She was bright and funny, though she had a problematic past she hadn't mentioned for the first few months they dated. She'd finally shared that she'd seen a shrink for years when she was a child and in her teens. The doctor had told her that her history, what she called her Darth Vader secret—her dark side—was a combination of shock fatigue and survivor's guilt from witnessing the drowning of her mother and little sister.

Now, come hell or high water, he was not going to let her be a victim either of the Wild River or the wilds of Alaska. He had to get some of this warm liquid into her, so he lifted her head into the crook of his arm and pressed the heated can to her lips.

"Lisa, drink this. It will warm you."

He got some in her mouth. It dribbled back out, so he tried again. His chest pressed to her breasts and his cheek to hers, he spoke close to her ear. "Lisa, it's Mitch. You're going to be all right. You have to drink this to get warm."

"M-M-itch."

Thank God! He was so thrilled she was still in that stone-cold body he could have flown.

"Drink this. You have to drink this."

Her teeth began to chatter, and she quivered all over, actually a better sign than nothing moving. She was hopefully coming out of hypothcrmia, and he was shaking as if he was plunging into it.

"Mitch." It was a mere whisper. She still didn't open her eyes and had barely moved her swollen, bluish lips.

"Yes, it's Mitch," he repeated. "I'm here and I'll take care of you. Drink this."

She sipped some. Praying he had enough warmth to give, he held her closer. The slant of sun helped so much. If you could find the right spot in July or August, get out of the wind, the sun could get the temperature up to the high eighties.

She drank. He positioned himself ever closer, trying to get in contact with every inch of her. Hating that he had to let cold air into their cocoon, he reached for the second can of soda, then thought to shove the first warm, empty can down at her feet like a heated brick.

He took a quick swig from the second can, then

poured more into her. When that was gone, she broke his heart by cuddling close, though she still seemed limp and cold. With her upturned face tucked under his chin, he held her tight again. He knew she wanted to sleep, but he had to keep her awake and talking. Hypothermic people often felt warmer, even stripped off their clothes before they went comatose and fell asleep forever.

"Lisa, talk to me. Keep talking. How did you fall in the river?"

Her eyes still closed, she frowned. "Dunno."

"Did you stumble or trip?" he asked.

A tiny shake of her head, but no answer. Of course, it wasn't unusual for someone in trauma to lose their memory of the horror of it. But since her memories of the ultimate horror of her life—the shock of witnessing the terrible loss of her mother and sister—were so vivid and, he knew, sometimes haunted her yet, surely she'd be able to recall how she'd fallen in.

Suddenly, strangely, she went stiff in his arms. "I'm here," he said. "It's all right."

Her eyes opened wide for one moment as if she was seeing something again. She shook her shoulders slightly. At least she was moving, but was she trying to shake off his arms from holding her?

Then she frowned, squeezing her eyes tightly closed. "Pushed," she whispered. "Pushed in."

"Someone pushed you in the river?" he demanded, much too loudly, because she flinched as if she'd been struck.

"Yes. Pushed."

"Pushed by whom?"

"Didn't see."

"Did you hear anyone?"

"Heard the river—rush of river."

She was talking, but she must also be hallucinating, he thought. The shock of it had made her—hopefully temporarily—delusional. He knew his staff and his guests. No way had someone pushed her in the river.

"The sun..." she whispered, suddenly opening her eyes and blinking into its brightness, her mind evidently wandering again. She looked slit-eyed at him before she seemed to almost swoon in his arms. Her pupils were huge. Could she have a concussion? That would explain her thinking she was pushed.

He gave her a tiny shake to keep her conscious, happy to change the subject from what would be, in a court of law, attempted murder. "Yes, summer Alaska sun. Our own northern light," he said.

Even so, he knew it would be shifting away soon, and it would be a cold night on the ledge. When would Christine or Spike or someone else realize they were gone? What would they think? Even if someone figured out they needed rescuing, no way could they be spotted by an airplane here or be helped if someone didn't tackle that damned dangerous river. Even if the sheriff came from Talkeetna or Spike and Christine summoned a search party from nearby little Bear Bones, the two of them were on their own.

* * *

"So, do you need any help?" came the melodious female voice.

Hearing the tap-tap of heeled boots on the pine floor, Christine turned from setting the table to see another of the guests, Vanessa Guerena, come in from the wooden deck overlooking the lake. She'd been out there, pacing like a caged cat, as if waiting for someone to arrive or something to happen.

From their first introduction, Christine had admired Vanessa's appearance—sleek figure, shiny, shoulder-length ebony hair, bronzed skin and flashing, dark eyes. In another world, they could have passed for Yup'ik cousins with the same height and build. Christine guessed the woman must be about her age, thirty-five or so. But Vanessa reeked self-confidence and charisma, the words Spike had used to describe her. He'd probably had to pick his jaw up off the ground when he first saw Vanessa.

But size, skin and hair was about where it ended for her and Vanessa's similarities. With her suede boots and her butterscotch-colored leather knee-length pants and jacket—in this warm weather, no less—she looked so dressed up next to Christine's running shoes, jeans and layered T-shirt top. For everyone else, including the obviously wealthy Bonners, denim was the name of the fashion game around here. Maybe Vanessa hadn't gotten the message about how to pack for the land of remote fly-in lodges and cabins in America's "last frontier."

Vanessa's pent-up energy and jumpiness made her stand out. The woman's Cuban heritage and temper, which Christine had noted when she'd seen her arguing with Jonas from a distance earlier, was a far cry from a Yup'ik personality. Yet Christine saw Vanessa had a good side, what the Yup'ik called *catngu,* the gift of friendliness and helpfulness. Had she been hanging around the back of the lodge just waiting to help out? Maybe she thought being prompt would impress the Bonners, when they hadn't even come downstairs yet. Or was she lurking around, maybe trying to keep an eye on her competition for Mitch's old job?

"I'm just fine, but thanks for the offer," she told Vanessa. "You just make yourself at home. Go ahead and enjoy some of these appetizers. I'm sure the others will be here soon, and you don't have to wait for them."

"Thanks," she said, shoving her hands in the pockets of her jacket. "So, have you seen Mitch?"

"Not for a while."

"Lisa?"

"Briefly."

"Were they together? Oh, sorry, too used to interrogating potential witnesses, I guess," Vanessa said with a little shrug and smile.

Christine nodded and went back out in the kitchen for more food. She glanced out the window down the path toward the lake landing. No Mitch, when she was expecting—wanting—him back.

She carried the last plate of appetizers to the table. Now Vanessa was pacing inside, pretending to look out the big bubble window. When she saw Christine was back, she said, "I didn't want to miss anything, but I've got to get my exercise in, since my appetite's gone as wild as the woods up here."

When Christine put the last plate of food down, the woman came over and pounced on it. "I hope I burn off these calories with everything Mitch has planned," she said, pouring herself a glass of Chardonnay to accompany her full plate. "Jonas said he's ready for more of your delicious deep-forest fare, too."

Christine was willing to bet both of them—Lisa Vaughn, too—had been just plain hungry for Mitch's old position since he left the law firm. But, yes, where in all creation was Mitch? And, as Vanessa had asked, where was Lisa?

All Lisa wanted to do was sleep, to get lost in the arms of warm, lazy sleep. She must be on the beach because a canvas cabana covered her head and wrapped around her. She loved the sun but knew too much of it on her skin could be dangerous, even deadly. Dangerous...deadly...just get warm. So sore and exhausted... Just stay warm and go to sleep...sleep...

Someone shook her, held her. A lifeguard? Was a lifeguard here because a big wave had hit her?

A man with a deep, raspy voice said, "Lisa, I said you have to keep moving your arms and legs. Wiggle your fingers and toes."

She dragged her heavy eyelids open. Mitch. Mitch on the beach with her. No, there were tall stone walls, and she could hear the roaring surf. But this wasn't Florida. "I guess we're not in Kansas anymore," Dorothy said to Toto after the tornado had picked her up and spun her silly. Lisa tried to do what Mitch said, what the good witch told Dorothy to do to get home. She tried to click the heels of her sparkly shoes together and make a wish but she had no shoes, and her feet were so cold....

Someone shook her again. Mitch. Mitch was here.

"Lisa, listen to me. I wish we were back at the lodge but we're not." He shook her shoulders and squeezed her tighter to him. "You fell in the river. You are hypothermic and you have to get warm. Drink more of this and move your arms and legs."

It took great effort, but she obeyed. Sore, so sore. But shc swallowed a warm, fizzy drink. Champagne? No bottles or glasses were allowed on the beach.

Then she really remembered. Back at the lodge, outside on the lake landing path, she'd been waiting for Mitch. Looking at the roiling water and almost seeing Mother and Jani there, Mother's face staring up at her through the river foam. And then—

She jolted alert in his arms. Someone had pushed her in! Hadn't they? No way she had fallen or jumped just because she was thinking about Mother and Jani. Surely Mitch had not pushed her, then rescued her, so he could be a hero, so he could win her back. No, wishful thinking, wishing upon a star. *There's no place like home, there's no place like home.* Home was where your loved ones were. But her loved ones had been swallowed by all that raging white water.

A second jolt shot through her, cosmic compared to anything else except the initial impact of that freezing water. She was in Mitch's arms, in some sort of bed, and they were both naked.

She tried to sit up. He pulled her back down. Where were they? What had they done? No, no, Mitch was right. She fell in the river, and he must have come after her, saved her. But she fell because she was pushed. But by whom and why?

She went rigid against him. "I'm better, warmer. You can let me go." She didn't sound like herself. Her lips were swollen and bruised. She was almost mumbling, stuttering.

"I'd like to believe that, but you were close to comatose. You've only been out of the river for about two hours."

"I—th-thank you. You came in a b-boat?"

"I chased you in the kayak that we were going to take across the lake."

"Oh." She tried to process that. Yes, they'd agreed to have a talk, but now this.

"M-Mitch, someone pushed me in the river. I fell down the bank and rolled, but someone pushed me first."

"You said that."

"Don't you believe me?" It came out as *Don't you leave me.*

"When we get back, we'll look into it. I did see the stuff Christine packed for us strewn down the bank toward the river. Why didn't you go down to the lake landing to wait for me? Didn't you see or hear anyone?"

"Hear them, with the roar of the river? I—I was just looking at the salmon in the water. My mind is working all right now. I'm better," she said, shifting away again. She wanted to remember what had happened, but not feel the hopeless panic, the fear of riding the river. Was her memory messed up like her mind?

And Mitch—he felt more solid than she recalled, so good, warm and strong with rock-hard muscles like the ledge under her. Had Alaska done that to him? Yes, he'd looked more bulked up when she'd seen him yesterday after an entire year apart. If it wasn't a crazy idea, she'd almost think his new life had made him taller, too.

"I'll see if your clothes are dry, and we'll get the wet suit on you for warmth, too," he said. "The little cookstove may warm your hands, but don't be in too much of a rush to get up. The shock of it—you'll come back slowly and may have some scrambled thoughts."

That's for sure, she told herself, but demanded, "You don't believe I was pushed in?"

"It's good you're getting angry at me. That will get your blood and temp up—and besides, that's more like picking up where we left off, isn't it?"

"That's all past now. I can't thank you enough for risking the river to come after me. Can't I just get d-dressed, curl up and sleep for a while? I'm so exhausted. It's a trauma for both of us."

"Sure has been, and not just this river ride. But no, you can't just go to sleep yet. I'm not the doctor in my family, but I know a hypothermic victim shouldn't do that—too dangerous for a while. I think it's like having a concussion. My clothes were soaked, too, and you needed core body heat badly, so if you're wondering why we're both undressed in here—"

"I knew that. See, I'm *compos mentis* again." She had to fight very hard to form thoughts and words. It was like groping for something in the dark. "Thank you, but I'm all r-right now. And if you're thinking I did really fall in, or just trip—or if you're thinking what you know about my mother, it isn't that. Someone pushed me, and I can think of at least two people with motives, maybe more. I wasn't halluc... hallucinating...."

Her voice trailed off as her thoughts swirled again. Or had she been? Had she actually been pushed in, or had that river lured her, seduced her because, after all was said and done, little Lisa had actually wanted to be with Mommy and Jani? Was little Lisa still terrified that she had sent them right over the edge?

Even though she hadn't seen her psychiatrist, Dr. Sloan, for years, she heard his voice. "You have to get over the idea you should have died with them or that you caused their fall. I know you blame yourself for not realizing your mother was so sick, but you were just a child. It wasn't your fault. None of it was your fault."

Mitch's voice broke into the memory. "Lisa, can you hear me? Your eyelids fluttered, and you looked as if you were going to pass out again."

"Only to sleep. I need to sleep."

"Me, too, but no. We're miles overland from the lodge and help—from any civilization—so we're going to have to hike out of here. Just rest here a few more minutes. I'll get dressed first, if my stuff's dry. But keep your eyes open and keep talking."

"I—I don't have shoes to hike. The river took them."

"I know. I'll make you some from our extra PFD, tape pieces of it around your feet."

"Wow, a guy who understands how girls love shoes."

He actually chuckled as he moved out of their warm little cocoon. She caught a glimpse of skin and curly, black chest hair. The cold air slammed in on her, and she fumbled to pull the canvas cover closed. But his laugh had warmed her. That and the fact he told her to keep her eyes open while he crawled out naked on the ledge to get dressed. But she didn't want to give him the idea she cared about him that way, so she pulled the canvas bag closer around her and turned away.

Just business—and survival—between them now. She had to be strong to help get them out of here and so that he could give a good report on her to the

Bonners. At the very least they would think she was a klutz for falling in the river. Would they all think she was crazy if she claimed someone had pushed her? Maybe she should tell Mitch she had just imagined it, not tell people what had really happened. Then she could investigate who could have pushed her, set someone up for a confession—or, God forbid, another attempt to eliminate her. But who would be that desperate to get rid of her?

But then another thought drifted in. Maybe the person didn't think she'd really fall in the river, just wanted to warn her or shake her up. But why? Maybe it wasn't just Jonas or Vanessa who had motive, means and opportunity to shove her down a clearing toward the river.

On Spike Jackson's plane, flying in from Anchorage to the lodge yesterday, she remembered a strange exchange between him and the Bonners. "So this is some kind of a marathon or endurance test for your candidates?" Spike had asked Graham. Strapped in next to Lisa, Vanessa had strained forward to hear what Graham said over the loud hum of the plane's single engine.

"Sure, a test of sorts, both with the activities Mitch has on tap for us and some others we have planned," Graham had said. "We'll have some group endeavors, some individual efforts."

Jonas had joked from the single jump seat in the back, next to the pile of luggage, "Like pitting us against an Alaskan bear or wolf in a deep-woods arena?"

"Nonsense," Ellie Bonner had piped up. From her place next to Spike in the copilot's seat, she'd twisted around to face the rest of them. "This is not some face-your-worst-fears, *Survivor*-like game show. Graham and I want you to enjoy yourselves and focus on what are essentially bonding, not competitive experiences."

"Just so long as she didn't say 'bondage,'" Jonas had whispered from the backseat so only Vanessa and Lisa could hear.

But *could* the Bonners have planned some sort of face-your-worst-fear survival test, and hers just got out of hand? Several years ago, after she came to know and trust both of them, she'd confided in them about her childhood tragedy and trauma over dinner at their home.

No. No, she scolded herself. She had to fight being paranoid, had to fight to show everyone she deserved the senior partner position and that she didn't want Mitch anymore. Maybe bringing her to face Mitch was *really* her endurance test, and now, here she was, alone with him and dependent on him. Surely the Bonners—or Mitch—could not have planned or wanted that.

Her head snapped down, then jerked up. She'd almost nodded off, but he hadn't seen. He was her rescuer, the one who knew the wilds, so for now she would try hard to do what Mitch said. She chatted, even chattered, tried to answer his questions about how she felt. She was bruised and battered all over but grateful no bones were broken. She was absolutely aching for sleep. But she had to cooperate so he could get them back to civilization, back to safety at the lodge. But, since—if—someone had pushed her, was it really civilized or safe there?

4

Mitch knew they had to get off the ledge. He had planned to spend the night here, but if he made Lisa get up and walk, she'd have to stay awake. He was also exhausted and feared he'd fall asleep. The worst scenario was that he'd have to hike out for help alone, but no way could he leave her near the river that could have killed her.

Besides, when he explored, edging along a narrow curve of cliff face, he was excited to discover a cleft in the gorge rocks, one he could even glimpse sky through. On one side of the cleft was a ledge where they could make their way out. From flying over the area with Spike, he knew that beyond these rocks lay not only muskeg, a shallow bog, but dry tundra. And he knew that, because of the contour of the land near the lodge, it would take them days to hike directly back to the west.

So if they could get beyond this gorge, they would go east, then ford the river below the falls where it was divided into braided streams that were much more shallow. The salmon had easier going there, and they would, too. On the other side of the Wild River was a dirt access road, which might have some traffic from fishermen or hunters who could give them a ride back home. But he wouldn't tell Lisa all that right now. Finally, he was making decisions for her as he had for so many others.

But, unfortunately, like a few other clients Mitch had defended, he questioned if she was a trustworthy witness of what had actually happened to her. He just couldn't accept Lisa's claim she'd been pushed into the river. Who at the lodge would be that desperate and dangerous? Opportunity for that must have been pure chance, and what would be a motive? Surely not just this competition among colleagues the Bonners had set up.

If Lisa had hit her head in a tumble down the slope near the lodge, she could have just thought she was pushed—or be lying about it so she didn't look careless or reckless to him and the Bonners. No, she wouldn't be that devious to gain sympathy, even if she'd always been ambitious.

Granted, she had been haunted by the drowning deaths of her mother and baby sister for years. He was sure, though she'd denied it, she'd been suicidal years ago, survivor's guilt and all that. But to think of her jumping in of her own accord was as crazy as the idea she'd been pushed.

Whatever had happened to get her in the Wild River, they had to risk the ledge over the chasm to get away from it right now. Even if rescuers rafted or kayaked down the river after them, their attempting to land on the ledge where they were hemmed in could be deadly, or they might shoot right on by toward the falls.

"Lisa!" He hurried back to her. She sat slumped on the ledge with her back to the rock face. Upset she'd fallen asleep even sitting up, he shook her shoulders. "I see a way we can walk out. I think we should go now, since we've lost the sun on the ledge. And if the river rises even more, we'd get more than wet here. I'm going to fill our empty cans with water and get things together. Can you get dressed by yourself?"

"Yes. Yes, of course," she insisted, sounding and looking annoyed right back at him. "I'm just f—"

"Don't you dare say you're fine!"

"And don't try to read my mind! I'm just feeling a bit funny but more alert—that's what I was going to say."

"Sorry I jumped to conclusions."

"Since you only saved my life today, you're for-given—for that," she grumbled.

That warmed him, not only because her spirited response sounded more like her but that she was grateful. She'd thanked him already, but he'd felt so guilty for so long about throwing a fire bomb into her life and then leaving Florida, that maybe, just maybe, what he'd done here could begin to make up for it. Not that he wanted her back—for sure not that—but it might make him feel less of a heel. On the other hand, he thought, hardening his heart when he realized he wanted to hold her, if she'd really loved him in the first place, she'd have understood and maybe even come with him to Alaska, taken a leave of absence, or visited the lodge on her own—at least given it a shot. He sure wasn't the only one to blame for their breakup.

The moment stretched out between them as, both frowning, they looked deep into each other's eyes while the river roared.

"We're partners at least for getting out of here safely," he said, then cleared his throat when his voice caught. "And when we get back, we'll look into what really happened to you."

She started to say something, then just nodded.

"I'll pack our stuff," he added, taking his Swiss Army knife out of his jeans pocket so he had something to do with his hands rather than touch her again. He rose and moved a few feet away on the ledge. "I'll cut up our extra PFD for your feet."

"I'm hungry enough that I could eat a piece of a PFD!"

He tried to grin but he knew it was more a grimace. She was not the only one who felt stiff all over. "We'll have to stick with some of Christine's dried salmon. Not sure what we'll find on the other side of the chasm through the gorge, but there should be some berries to eat and fish to catch, if we get out of here."

"If?"

"I can only see so far down the ledge. We'll have to watch our footing, that's all. As a matter of fact, maybe you should go out barefoot, and we'll put these fancy, schmancy Manual designer shoes on you after."

"Do you mean Manolos?" she asked with a little laugh.

"Yeah. Just testing your memory."

He turned away to let her get her clothes on over the body-hugging wet suit she already wore for warmth. He glanced at his waterproof watch and noted it was way past pre-dinner time back at the lodge. Surely they would realize that he and Lisa had not just decided to run away together.

Spike and Christine were overseeing the search effort. Of course, Spike was trying to order her around, but she wasn't taking any guff from him. Whatever she'd done in the past, she wasn't going to be a doormat for any man.

Iah, but Spike Jackson was an imposing man. Nearly six and a half feet tall, red-haired and big-shouldered, he seemed larger than life—certainly larger than any Yup'ik man she'd ever known. Yet he had a lanky grace and a boyish manner at times. But when cornered, or upset as he and all of them were now, he turned into a real macho man.

"Okay, listen up here," he told the guests assembled in the great room of the lodge. "I radioed my sister, Ginger, and she checked the area across the lake where Mitch said they were going. No sign of them. The red two-seat kayak's missing, but sure as hell someone as skilled as Mitch didn't capsize in the lake."

"I repeat," Graham Bonner put in, "I'll gladly pay for an air search and rescue."

Christine figured Mr. Bonner was used to being in charge. Still, the Bonners had pitched in to help scour the immediate area of the lodge for Mitch and Lisa. The Bonners were such a handsome couple—trim, silver-haired and blue-eyed. Although they were fish out of water in the Alaskan wilds, she could tell they were used to being in control of all they surveyed.

"Yes," Ellie Bonner added. "Spike, if we take your plane up, we'll pay for the gas, and I'll go with you to copilot while you use binoculars or vice versa."

Christine guessed Mrs. Bonner was in her late fifties, a natural beauty aging gracefully, petite and pretty with a cap of hair that contrasted with her sharp, sparkling eyes.

"Thanks," Spike said, "but thick tree cover around here and the river gorge and mountains make that not a good option for spotting them. Besides, they couldn't have hiked out this fast to the flatter tundra and valley areas where we could see them. Both of his vehicles are still here. They've gotta be around somewhere—maybe took a walk in the woods, skidded into a hole, someone turned an ankle, then 'cause of predators, they thought they had to stick together, something like that. The locals we got coming from Bear Bones know the area and can fan out around the lake. Mitch and Ms. Vaughn must have decided on a different place than where he told Christine he'd beach the kayak so they could talk things out."

"On a private little picnic?" Christine heard Vanessa whisper to Jonas behind her. "Talk things out, my foot!"

"Just don't put your foot in your mouth," he muttered back. "You'd better cooperate with all this and look like you mean it."

Christine didn't let on that she'd heard them. Spike was saying, "Mitch must of just pulled the kayak up on a stretch of beach where we haven't spotted it yet, that's all."

The sound of vehicle engines and the blast of horns drew them all outside. At least forty people, nearly half the population of the nearby town of Bear Bones, piled out of pickup trucks or SUVs. Some wore backpacks; some carried rifles.

Christine went back inside quickly. She didn't need their stares right now and even the sight of guns made her uneasy. Her stomach was tied in knots already. Lisa lost was one thing, but she couldn't lose Mitch.

"Okay," she heard Spike tell everyone in a booming voice from outside, "you all know what Mitch looks like, but the woman he's with—Lisa Vaughn—is about five feet five, blond hair to her shoulders, slender, but athletic-looking, green eyes, real pretty face…."

Oh yes, Christine thought, a real pretty face all right. Obviously Mitch's ideal, maybe Spike's, too. She saw out the opposite set of lodge windows that Ginger had come back across the lake. She was not putting in at her usual spot but ran the prow of her old motorboat up on the shore farther down. Christine went out to fill her in. The two of them were going to hold the fort in case Mitch or Lisa came back or the sheriff or medical help needed to be summoned from Talkeetna.

Christine strode the path to the lake landing and hurried down to it.

"Any news yet?" Ginger asked as she tossed her little anchor on the pebbled shore. Like Spike, she was lanky and redheaded, but with gray eyes and a distant gaze that could really unsettle you. Sometimes she seemed to look past or through you. Even for backcountry Alaska, Ginger Jackson was as eccentric as they came, dressed in a combination of gypsy and frontier-woman clothes.

Ginger lived mostly hand to mouth. Besides baking for the lodge, she picked up random short-term jobs in Bear Bones and always helped Mitch with ziplining for his guests. Ginger's brother, Spike, loved flying, but Ginger's high-flying thrills came from zipping along on a steel cable through tall Sitka spruce. Christine admired Ginger's independence. She'd turned down an offer of marriage from a guy because he insisted she move into town. Ginger wouldn't accept anything from her big brother but the firewood he cut for her baking and heating stoves for the cold months. She was even scrimping to save money to pay Spike for that, since the price of jet fuel was, literally, sky-high. Yet since Ginger's mail came to the lodge, Christine knew that she received lots of high-end catalogs with all kinds of exotic luxury goods—her "dream mags," she called them.

"We still don't know anything," Christine called to her, hurrying closer. "It's like they vanished into thin air."

"Maybe they just had things to settle and said the heck with everyone else. That's what I'd of done. Did Mitch talk about her? I mean, we knew somebody threw somebody over, but I've learned never to hold people's pasts against them."

Christine wondered if she meant her own past. "No, he didn't talk about her until just before they arrived," she admitted, wishing Mitch had confided more to her. That was another thing she liked about Ginger—live and let live. But she didn't like the way the woman was staring at her, still standing in her boat, hands on her hips, head tilted, almost as if she were accusing her of something. Christine had gone through enough of that.

"What?" she challenged Ginger.

"There!" Ginger pointed past her. So she wasn't staring at her after all. "Maybe Mitch didn't put the red kayak I saw here earlier into the lake. See? Someone shoved a kayak up or down here and to or from where? That ridge path above the lake and river?"

Christine turned and looked, then had to shade her eyes and stand back a bit to see what Ginger was pointing at. She gasped and scrambled up the bank toward the path with Ginger right behind her.

They looked at the path, then down it to the other side. Strewn there was the food and cooler Lisa had carried as well as the path of what could well be the kayak sliding down toward the river. A wolverine hunched there, too stubborn to move, bolting down the food, but that wasn't what upset them.

"Mitch decided to take her white-water kayaking?" Ginger screeched. "Is he nuts? We gotta make folks search the river!"

"But this food strewn here…" Christine began, then stopped in midsentence. "Or maybe she just set the cooler down here and that wily wolverine opened it after they took off. But I can't believe Mitch would do that."

The wolverine hustled away as Ginger skidded off the path and looked downriver, shading her eyes with both hands. "No one. Nothing!" she shouted up over the river's roar, but Christine was already running to tell Spike before the searchers set out on a wild-goose chase.

"Feel your way with your feet, one slow step at a time," Mitch told Lisa as they edged into the cleft in the gorge, both facing the rock. "Don't look down!"

"I won't!" she vowed, but she already had. About twelve feet below, she had heard and seen white water surging into the bottom of the cleft, then being sucked back out. She could almost feel it washing over her, like when she was in the river, or in her worst nightmares. But Mitch was just behind, talking to her, urging her on.

Because she could feel the firm rock under her, she was glad she was barefoot, even though she ached all over, including the soles of her feet. Words from her grandma Colleen's favorite Psalm came to her: *Yea, though I walk through the valley of the shadow of death...*

Mitch had said she should lead the way out because he needed not only to watch where they were going, but watch her. They'd abandoned the kayak. All their other goods were strapped to his back, but he wouldn't let her carry one thing.

"You're doing great," he said. "We're making good progress."

"I'm shaking. It makes me feel as if the wall is," she admitted as she tried to find handholds, yet not push away from the rock face so she tipped back. Their yellow brick road out of here was only about two feet wide in places. She knew she had to do this just right, because if he had to make a grab for her, they'd both bounce down into oblivion.

Finally, finally, the ledge widened, but then it came to nothing.

"Mitch, dead end."

"So I see. But we're almost out of the gorge. Just stay very still."

"I feel like we've already climbed Mount Mc-Kinley—Denali, you called it."

"Don't talk."

He came very close to her, even putting one foot between hers where she was standing with her legs apart for better balance. He pressed her closer to the rock face. It almost felt as if she were sitting on his lap. She could feel his breath on her temple, stirring her hair. Her heartbeat kicked up even more than it had from fear. In the worst of extremities, why did she let this man who had deserted her and hurt her get to her like this?

"I see a place just a ways down where we can get onto another ledge to make it out," he said. "I'm going to take this weight off my back and drop our stuff down to the ledge below. Stand very still. I may have to press into you harder."

She closed her eyes and held her breath. Why a certain memory came to her then, she wasn't sure, but she saw—and felt—Mitch standing behind her on his boat, *Sea Dancer,* to help her handle her fishing pole when a big fish had hit off Key Biscayne in that warm, sparkling water. It had been a very calm day, no waves, no white water, no turbulence. They had just started dating, and she'd thought he was so perfect then. A combination of *GQ* magazine handsome and *Pro Football Today* rugged. Whether in a tuxedo or cutoff jeans, the man reeked of masculinity with his dark hair, square jaw and thick eyebrows over deep-set, coffee-colored eyes. His voice, somehow both refined but rough, sent shivers down her spine. Then they'd landed that big fish together and—

She felt him drop his pack and heard it hit below.

"How far down?" she asked, not daring to turn to look.

"Not too bad. I'm going to lie on my stomach, help you down to our stuff, then scoot down to join you. Here, turn carefully and sit on the ledge. You'll have to look down, just for a sec, so you know what I mean."

As he held her, she turned and sat. Pressing her back to the rock, she looked down and gasped. The ledge was at least five feet below and only about four feet wide! Although no water churned beneath them now, their escape route had narrowed so much that if they slipped, they'd be wedged in jagged rocks.

But looking left, she could see that from the lower level, they could work their way down to the valley that spread out below. And the most glorious sunset stretched across the sky, streaks of pink and orange and fuchsia. In blinding colors, it looked almost neon, like in *The Wizard of Oz* she'd been somehow thinking about—hallucinating—the part where Dorothy lands in Oz. This was the part where the movie went from being black and white to amazing hues.

"Lisa, you ready?"

"I better be. I don't see we have a choice. And, at least this time, I'm ready to ride off with you into the sunset."

The minute that was out of her mouth, she regretted the choice of words, but he only said, "That's one of the treasures of living in Alaska. This time of year, though you can't see the aurora borealis clearly, that kind of sunset will last all night."

All night. It must be night now, she thought as she somehow found the courage—or sheer desperation— to turn on her stomach and inch her legs and lower torso over the edge while he held on to her. She scraped her thighs, belly, breasts and chin while he slowly dangled her lower. After what seemed an eternity, she stood alone on the ledge, praying silently for his safety, while he scooted closer on his stomach.

"I said, don't touch me in case I fall," he gritted out, but she pressed her hands to the backs of his thighs, then to his hard buttocks as he came over.

"On second thought," he said when he finally stood beside her, "that felt great. Maybe you can boost me up there again and—"

"We're just hiking and camping buddies, remember."

"And we're going to have the time to talk we've needed."

"I'd like to say 'water over the dam,' but it isn't, is it? Not with either of us."

Pressing his lips tight together, he just shook his head, then bent to pick up their gear again. He slung the makeshift pack over one shoulder. "Let's find a good place to rest, and we'll get these shoes taped on you," he said, sounding all business now, just the way he always had in the office or in court when she used to study how controlled he was, how self-assured. Even that had moved her deeply, because she knew the other, passionate side of him, when they were alone—as they were now.

5

When Spike told the search party what Christine had said about the kayak trail from the ridge to the water, many of them rushed to the river. A few went down to look at the exact spot, but most stood on the lawn of the lodge, gazing in the direction Mitch and Lisa must have gone in the two-seat kayak. Some whispered and shook their heads, then turned away, heading back to their trucks.

"But why?" Mrs. Bonner asked her husband. "Has Mitchell become such a daredevil in extreme sports here? He seemed all about safety rules and regulations yesterday."

"Life in Alaska can be an extreme sport," Spike said just loudly enough for Christine and Ginger to hear from his position between the two of them. The Bonners stood directly behind. "But something's weird—really wrong," he added.

"And I can't believe," Mrs. Bonner went on to her husband, "Lisa would agree to such a thing, not after losing her family that way."

Despite the fact Christine never would have let on she could overhear, Spike turned to the Bonners and said, "You mean her family drowned in a river?"

"An accident in the Atlantic—or maybe it was the Caribbean," Mr. Bonner said, frowning at the churning foam.

"What kind of accident?" Spike pursued, though Christine elbowed him as subtly as she could.

"Boating, not swimming," Mrs. Bonner said, sounding brusque. "Her mother and her sister drowned. It was a long time ago, but I'm sure it's something one never gets over."

That was sad about her family, Christine thought, but she couldn't help resenting Lisa Vaughn's continued sway over Mitch, her power to still hurt him. Christine had seen it in his eyes and heard it in his voice.

"I'm going to phone the state troopers," Spike told them. "I'm not sure what they can do if Mitch and Ms. Vaughn are kayaking the rapids, heading for the gorge, but they gotta be informed."

"Wait!" Mrs. Bonner cried, grabbing for Spike's arm. "I—I was reading online about Alaska before our trip and learned that law enforcement officials are really scarce and have to cover hundreds of miles. Maybe my husband can pull some strings to get some here."

"Here wouldn't help," Spike told her. "In that river they're long gone—from this area, I mean. But the local police may be able to get the Denali Park Rangers to help with the search way downriver. I'll call the locals and the feds."

He strode away briskly, with the Bonners following. Christine went, too, leaving Ginger with just a few stragglers to gaze out over the river. Spike muttered, talking aloud to himself as he often did, "They'll have to look for them below the series of falls in case they got around or over them."

"Falls?" Mr. Bonner said, his voice stern and clear, compared to his wife's sweeter tones. Christine had seen lawyers up close and personal. That's why the guests made her uneasy. She could just imagine Graham Bonner cross-examining someone on the witness stand. "Waterfalls?" he repeated in his clarion voice. "How many, how large?"

"Four fairly small ones, but any one could put you in that cold, rough river," Spike said, still walking. "Mrs. Bonner, as soon as I contact the police and park rangers, I'll take you up on that offer to fly with me for an air search."

"But with these rapids—and the falls—you think they can survive all that?" she asked, tears in her eyes and her hand clutched at her throat. "They are both very dear to us."

"Gotta try."

"Mitchell should have known better," Christine heard Mrs. Bonner mutter as the couple fell behind and she and Spike hurried into the lodge to make the calls. "Graham, it just shows you they are both a bit foolhardy yet, just when you think they'd learned to stay apart and away from all that past pain."

Christine stood next to Spike while he used the

kitchen phone. She wrapped her arms around herself tight, as if to hold herself up. She shook all over and blinked back tears. If she lost Mitch, she lost her future. Mrs. Bonner was right. Mitch knew better than to risk the river, no matter what the reason. But she kept hearing Mrs. Bonner's last words: *You think they'd stay apart and away from all that past pain…*

She and Clay should have stayed apart. She should have left him—fled—but Yup'ik women were loyal and tenacious. She bit her lower lip hard, trying to stop the jagged memories of the lawyers picking apart her testimony about being beaten black and blue…all that pain…but she stayed with him too long….

But now—far worse—she knew Mitch had been gone on that devil of a river far too long.

Lisa hurt all over, as if she'd been beaten by someone's fists. Her skin, what she had seen of it before donning the wet suit earlier, was turning black and blue, even greenish in spots. A new fashion statement in an eco-conscious world—green blotches to complement her green eyes. She was so exhausted she thought she could fall flat on her face and drown in this shallow, spongy-bottom muskeg they traversed. But she went on, step after painful step, behind Mitch as he made a wobbly path for them around thickets and through grass and sedge in about one foot of water.

"How are those Mitchell Andrew Braxton designer shoes holding up?" he asked. He sounded and looked exhausted, too, plodding under the burden of that pack like some old, worn-out Santa Claus.

"They're a bit buoyant so I'm almost walking on this water."

"When we were first dating, I used to think you could walk on water."

"I know you keep talking just to keep me going, but I can't even concentrate—can't go on."

"You can because I see tundra instead of this muskeg ahead of us, and, I think, some berry bushes. It's about time for blueberries but that might be lingonberries, something like cranberries."

"I just want to lie down."

"We will, soon as we hit dry ground. By the way, in case an airplane should fly over, looking for us or not, raising two hands means we need help. Raising one means we're okay."

"I don't have the strength to raise one, let alone two."

"You know what? It looks like a patch of blueberries, so I hope the bears have left us some."

"Bears?"

"They love them. Come on, Lisa Marie!"

"I told you a long time ago not to call me that, even if it is my name. I hate my middle name. It reminds me of Elvis's daughter, who married Michael Jackson, no less. Married Michael Jackson!"

"Yeah, but they didn't last long. You know, it sounds like you're awake enough to be mad at me and at Michael Jackson, Lisa Marie."

"You're just trying to get me riled so I keep going to spite you."

"Riled? Now, isn't that a good frontier word? As it says on the state's license plates—The Last Frontier."

"Yeah, I'm starting to get that picture. And you're starting to sound like a travel brochure."

But she had to admit, as he'd said earlier, the sunset never ended. It was still glorious, a rainbow of hues that didn't just hang in the west but covered the entire sky. Mitch turned back to help her up to higher, dry ground. She didn't care what he said, if he insulted her or praised her. She sank down where she was, surrounded by some sort of spiky pink flowers. He dropped his pack beside her with a thud.

"I'll be right back," he said, jolting her alert again.

"Right back from where?" she blurted, getting to her knees to rise until she realized he might have to relieve himself. They'd both managed some privacy for that, on and off the ledge, but she seemed to have sweated all her hydration out now.

"I see a birch tree, and I'm going to use my knife to cut you some of the inner bark to chew. It's what the Inuit use for aspirin. I know you've got to be hurting."

Got to be hurting. When had she not? Actually, as sore as she was, as many aches and pains that plagued her right now, she knew from experience that this physical agony was nothing next to that of the heart and spirit.

She closed her eyes. Did she doze off?

"Chew this," Mitch said, already chomping on a piece of bark when he came back and offered her a short, white strip. "Honestly, it will help. Then, take my knife and cut some of these fireweed greens for us. They make good salad greens, even though I don't have a variety of salad dressings to offer. I'm going to get the backpack full of berries, and we're going to have a feast before we go to sleep."

"Sleep right here? Will it be safe?"

"You said you couldn't go on and neither can I."

They ate the last of their smoked salmon, gorged themselves on plump blueberries—the best she had ever tasted—and chewed fireweed washed down by river water. Mitch had made stoppers for the soda cans with plugs of neoprene so it wouldn't spill out. Neither of them said much, until she watched him spread out their tent, lie down and gesture for her to come into his arms.

"We can't sleep the way we did before," she protested. "Both in there, I mean."

Looking exasperated, he shrugged. "Suit yourself, but after being hypothermic, I'd think you'd want to keep warm. This cover is fine for two and, once again, we'll need the body heat. Nothing personal, Ms. Vaughn. Besides, I'm expecting some voracious females tonight, if I'm not covered up."

"What?"

"Mosquitoes. The females of the breed are vampires, you know, but I think we'll be safe from everything else."

"I've got this wet suit on under my clothes, and I'll put your backpack over my head. I'll be fine."

He snuggled into the canvas tent, and his voice came to her, muffled. "I thought you were exhausted. Say your prayers but quit talking."

She lay down about four feet from him. At least he could have let her use the tent he made a big deal of wrapping tighter about himself like a cuddly cocoon. Facing him, she curled up on her side and pulled her knees up nearly to her chest. What if a bear came by after those blueberries? She heard the high-pitched whine of a mosquito, and she swatted at it. But she was so tired, nothing would make a difference now, nothing....

She drifted away—away on the foam where her mother beckoned to her through the whirling white water.

"Well?" Christine said to Spike when he hung up after the second call to the authorities. "Can they help?"

"Yeah, but they wanted to know why he'd be crazy enough to kayak that part of the river. They said he had permission only to put rafts or kayaks in six miles to the west of here which is a good mile before all the rapids get dangerous."

"He knew that. I—I can't understand it either. Unless—"

"Unless what?" he said, turning to her. He looked into her teary face—he had never seen her cry—and put his hands on her shoulders. Big, warm hands when she was shaking all over. She lifted her hands to clasp his wrists.

"I don't know. Unless he was showing her something about the kayak, and it just took off with them in it."

"Not like him. Too crazy," he said, then leaned against the counter. He pulled her into his arms and held her tight.

For once she didn't flinch when a man so much as touched her. Her head found a perfect fit under his chin. Mitch always smelled of pine and fresh air, while Spike emanated Lava soap, gasoline, motor oil and his precious sled dogs. But she didn't care. She needed his strength right now, maybe more than that. She sniffed hard, then, instead of just standing stiffly in the circle of his arms, hugged him back hard, her arms around his waist.

"I don't think of you this way—crying and needy," he murmured, his lips moving in her hair atop her head. "You're always so strong, even…with everything. Hell, honey, got to get going," he said, setting her back and avoiding her eyes now as if he'd seen something there that scared him.

"You and Ginger stay near the two-way. I'm gonna go get the plane and fill it up, then take Mrs. Bonner up with me. Hard to believe it, but that little lady knows cockpits, loves to fly. Keep the home fires burning now," he added as he made for the door, nearly running into his sister as she came into the kitchen.

"Spike!" Christine called to him, and he turned back. "If you go right now, you'll have the sun in your eyes over Denali and the top of the gorge. You may have trouble seeing anyone. Just be careful...."

Had she called him back for that? He knew this area better than she did. Or was it that she just couldn't bear to let him out of her sight right now?

"I'll be in touch," he said, and hurried out.

In touch. She still felt his touch as she turned away from Ginger's probing gaze.

Lisa heard herself crying in her grief, howling inside her head like an animal in pain. She felt so alone since Daddy ran off with some woman, with Mommy and Jani dead. Grandma Colleen took her in and loved her, but it wasn't the same, wasn't right. Nothing was right until she made friends she clung to and then Mitch... Mitch, let her down, down onto the next ledge.

She dragged herself from the depths of sleep. Where was she? She saw strange colors overhead, more muted now.

She jerked fully awake. She was sleeping in the Alaskan wilderness with the man who had ruined her life but then saved it.

She saw he had moved a bit closer to her in the twilight. Yes, he'd said it never got dark this time of year. The sunset had faded to pale hues with cirrus clouds roped across the heavens. Mitch had been right—she was cold. But nothing compared to being in the river. Yet a chill snaked up her spine when she remembered that someone had shoved her in that river. Hadn't they? Jonas or Vanessa? Christine Tanaka knew where she was going and maybe knew that Mitch was running a bit late. Surely not the Bonners? Or could she have just stumbled and hit her head? No way had she been so drawn by that white water, felt so strange and guilty and then leaped toward it of her own accord.

The howling, long, low and lonely, came again. What was it? How close? Surely that was not a bear.

"Mitch. Mitch!"

He stirred, then lifted his head. "What?"

That horrible howling again. The hair prickled on the back of her neck, and her stomach cartwheeled.

"Just wolves," he said.

"Just? Then what are we doing here near them? They hunt in packs to eat big game, don't they?"

"My guess is they have plenty to eat out here besides humans. That's probably their version of a love song to a mate. I think they avoid people."

"You *think* they avoid people?"

"Yeah. Bears do, too, if you make enough noise—unless they're protecting cubs. Are you warm enough?"

"Not really."

"Since you won't sleep with me—you know what I mean—you could take my knife and cut some more fireweed and make a kind of extra blanket for yourself."

"I changed my mind. I want in the tent."

He said nothing, but unwrapped and lifted the edge of it for her. She scooted close, put her back to him and rolled inside the warmth and safety of his arms. Her cheek was on his bicep, as hard as the ground had been, but so comforting. She felt his hot breath on the nape of her neck, and her bottom pressed against his thighs. What would it have been like to have a lifetime of closeness like this with him, not forced but chosen? A relationship not damaged and broken but healthy and whole?

"When are we heading out?" she asked.

"Let's give it a couple of hours unless those howls get closer. Blueberries and water for breakfast, then we'll head for the river below the falls. The Wild River's not so wild there, divides into four or five more shallow braided streams where we can walk across. There's a road on the other side. We can hike out on it or maybe even hitch a ride."

"How long a trek?"

"Never walked it before, only seen it from the air."

He yawned, stretching a bit, flexing his muscles, then relaxing. She was panicked to realize she could feel his merest movement in the pit of her belly. Even in this tight wet suit, her breasts tingled. She had to get him talking, maybe really wake him up so they could push on now.

"I'm sorry I ruined everything," she told him. "I mean at the lodge, where you had those bonding activities planned for everyone."

"Yeah. The Bonners' bonding experiment."

"It's not fair if this disqualifies me."

"Maybe they'll see you as a survivor who can handle anything after this."

"I'd like to pretend so—that this is all some sort of test, and they'll jump out of the berry bushes and say, 'Surprise! You were just on *Candid Camera*,' or something like that. Then the emcee will say, 'Here in the Alaska twilight, we have seen how a wimpy South Florida native was saved from the raging river and taught to survive in the wilderness by—'"

"Shh!"

"Sorry. I'll shut up and try to sl—"

"Lisa, shut up! I think I hear a plane!"

He yanked their canvas cover open and jumped up. She heard it now, too, a much better sound than wolves howling. She staggered to her feet as he ran back toward the bog, into more of a clearing than where they were with bushes and birch trees.

"Damn!" he shouted, pointing back toward the river. "I think it might be Spike's plane, though there are lots of red ones. But it's over the gorge, heading west!"

"Can we wave something? If we only had something for a signal!"

"It may circle back if they're searching. If they've found evidence we put a kayak in the river, maybe they'll look below the falls, and that's where we're heading—right now. Come on. We'll sleep when we get back to the lodge. Let's pick some more blueberries and head out."

She helped him gather their goods and stuff them

in the tent that made his pack. The drone of the plane faded, but at least it wasn't dark, and Mitch's shouting seemed to have made the wolves move on. Now they had to move on, too.

6

"It will take us an hour to hike around that lake up ahead!" Lisa cried after they'd walked about two hours. "How did the stream we've been following turn into a big body of water?"

"Beavers dammed it up," Mitch said. "See them over there?"

He pointed to a group of them. Each sleek, brown animal looked busy as a— Yes, an apt old adage, she thought. Every beaver she could see in or out of the water was either moving wood or gnawing at it, and their half-submerged, haphazardly piled homes were visible from here, a village of them.

As they got closer, Lisa saw the mud-and-stick dams were also embedded with rocks and tree trunks. "Amazing," she said. "And look at their little humped houses."

"They're called lodges. I own one Alaskan lodge, but they own a whole chain of them."

The sleek furry heads made little waves through the water as the beavers ferried logs, propelling themselves with their large flat tails. Several of the animals were quite close by, gnawing at trees along the bank of the lake.

"They're smooth in the water but clumsy on land," Lisa whispered, "but then we all have our own habitats." She thought of herself, a South Floridian, a fish—no, a beaver—out of water here in Alaska. And had she ever actually seen a beaver, even at a zoo? To be so close up, so intimate, was awe-inspiring. She could even see what appeared to be baby beavers, playing atop the dam, chewing leaves and twigs.

"Do they actually eat wood?" she asked. "It looks like they're chewing on the sticks for food."

"They eat the inner bark layer, something like the way we've been chewing on the inner birch bark."

Fascinated despite her predicament, Lisa moved a bit closer to the fringe of the pond, until a big beaver, glaring at her, swam closer and smacked its tail, spraying water. The splash resounded, echoed. She expected to see the other beavers scatter, but they didn't. The defender flaunted his big square front teeth and smacked the water again.

"Why don't the others hide if we're a danger to them?" she asked, despite the fact she could tell Mitch wanted to move on.

"He wants to scare you away, not warn them. Come on. We're rocking their boat, so to speak, and we have a long way to go."

"This place is starting to remind me of the Animal

Planet cable channel, but close up and personal," she said as she turned reluctantly away.

"You must watch one hell of a lot of TV these days—this last year," he said, flexing his back muscles. "You've mentioned a couple of shows since we've been walking, including that *Survivor* show—though I could see why—and something about that old movie, *The Wizard of Oz*. Staying home a lot lately?"

That annoyed her. He was goading her, implying that since he'd left, she had no social life. Even out here, even if it was true, she wasn't going to let him get away with that.

"Of course, now that you're helping others bond and build great relationships," she said, her voice dripping sarcasm, "you're too busy and fulfilled to waste your time on such plebian pastimes as television. You've probably been using sad illustrations of your own family and former fiancée to contrast how great you are at personal relationships. Everyone in your past has been shallow and selfish—except you, of course."

He spun back to face her. "I came to a crisis in my life and thought I could count on the woman who said she loved me." He blocked the path and dropped his pack. "We've tiptoed around the big discussion we were supposed to have yesterday, but your sudden attack indicates the time and place is now." He crossed his arms over his chest. He looked big and forbidding, but so much had been building inside of her that she had to let it out.

She thrust her fists to her hips to counterattack his body language. "I loved the Mitch I knew," she insisted, "the one I thought was being honest with me about his and our future when we got engaged!"

"Yeah, well, people change and need help sometimes, and if you, of all people, haven't figured that out by now, I'll have to tell Graham you'll make a lousy lawyer in general, let alone a senior partner— or marital partner. You've had crisis points yourself and gotten help along the way, but evidently you can't accept the same for someone else."

"Oh, now we're to the nitty-gritty, aren't we? Back in your element, the man of clever words—talk about an attack!" She found herself flinging gestures despite how her arms ached. That was a nervous habit she'd worked hard to conquer, yet he was making her regress—in so many ways. She spit out the wad of birch bark she'd been babying, because it did help the pain, but it was keeping her from enunciating clearly. Most lawyers knew better than to tangle verbally with Mitchell Braxton, but she was determined to finally tell him off.

"You have no right," she rushed on, "to blame my childhood trauma for making me sound like someone who was so devastated that she can't give love or understand someone else's problems. Your childhood wasn't as hard as mine, but you've never gotten over being overshadowed by an older brother you thought your parents loved more! Well, that's nothing compared to what I've been through, but I've risen above it, so—"

"So, *did* someone really push you in the river?" he interrupted. He leaned back slightly on his heels, gazing down at her from his height as if he were about to pass sentence on her. "Or was that just a crazy whim of yours to get attention, sympathy from the Bonners maybe, or to make me feel bad—then, of course, it went awry, and you really did slip in. You told me once that foaming water fascinates as well as scares you. You underestimated the power of the current, didn't you? You could have killed us both. I rest my case."

"Your case is flimsy—worse than ridiculous! You think I'd so much as get near that raging river after what happened to my family? You're the one who's crazy, not me!"

"Evidently true, since I risked my life to come after you and am still stupid enough to care about y—Oh, hell, forget it. But you'd better be damn sure you don't get back to the lodge and start accusing someone of shoving you in or start playing detective when this could easily be all your own fault!"

He cut himself off, yanked the pack back into his arms, turned and started away, taking huge strides. She stood there for a moment, stunned. Her own fault...her own fault. Those words, that fear—maybe that truth—swam through her brain. What he'd said was true, partly. She had felt guilt over her childhood losses—not just survivor's guilt, but the guilt that maybe pulling away from her mother, instead of trying to hold her on the railing, on the deck, might have been the jolt that sent her loved ones overboard to their deaths.

So could she be punishing herself again by intentionally falling in, maybe even by throwing herself in the river? No, surely not, surely not.

Mitch had stopped and was looking back at her. "We're wasting time and strength, attorney Vaughn," he threw back over his shoulder as he started away again. "I suggest you follow in my footsteps here, though. If the Bonners ask me, I'll have to tell them you're too unstable to follow in my footsteps at the firm."

So maybe the Bonners were relying on him to help choose the next senior partner. Maybe she was unstable, but what about his picking up stakes and leaving all he'd ever worked for in Fort Lauderdale?

She wanted to scream that at him, but she was out of breath and had to hustle to keep up. That other Mitch, she had to admit, was not this Mitch who lived in Alaska. And she was indeed crazy to turn him against her, at least until she could get back to the Bonners and explain what had happened. But what *had* happened? They would all think she was demented if she accused someone of a premeditated, attempted homicide on the Wild River, with her as the intended victim.

They didn't speak for a long time, not until they finally arrived at the spot Mitch knew they'd find the braided river. He was still fuming. He supposed she was, too, and he was trying to convince himself that he didn't care.

"Damn." He summed it up when he saw their fording place.

"Oh, no," she agreed.

All along where the narrow riverbed finally widened to four shallow, snaking streams surrounded by gravel banks, huge brown bears, both in and out of the water, fished for salmon. Fourteen of the beasts ranged up and down the best crossing spots.

"I've never seen so many at once," he told her.

"It's a far cry from the serene, calm lake with the beavers. Violent but still awesome. So—real."

"Some of those are unusually massive, up to twelve hundred pounds, I'd guess. They're taking on fat to survive during the winter hibernation. It's an absolute feeding frenzy."

"They're beautiful in a scary way, so bulky with that huge muscle mass over their shoulders, and they're not just brown. Some look almost blond and some black, at least where they're wet. That icy water doesn't seem to bother them a bit," Lisa said.

Mitch saw she edged closer to him as they watched two bears rear up on their back legs to argue over fishing territory. She shuddered, yet her gaze on the fighting bears didn't waver. He was tempted to put his arm around her, but he just pressed his shoulder into hers to steady her.

"The bear version of fast food," she said, her voice not trembling when he'd expected that. "Takeout but not eat-at-home."

He almost smiled at her clever comments and the

fact she seemed to look to him for protection, even at this distance from the big beasts. They watched in silence as razor-sharp claws speared the egg-laden fish heading upstream to spawn. Sharp teeth tore them apart, flaying the rich, red meat on the spot. The bears immediately devoured them, except for the big sow who was feeding two cubs.

Mitch finally said in a normal voice, "At least they don't seem to hear or smell us. With cubs present, you just never know how touchy and aggressive they can be."

"Like people," she said. "We really don't know some people like we think we do."

He thought about Jonas and Vanessa again, then his mind skipped to Ellie and Graham. He still couldn't get his mind around the fact that any of them would have pushed her, and no one else had opportunity but Christine and maybe Ginger. But there was no motive.

They both gaped at the bloody mess littering the banks where the bears heaved the fish remains before snatching their next prey. Occasionally, when one got too close to the other's territory, there was growling, shoving and swatting before they lumbered back to their task of gorging themselves.

"So much for trying to cross here," she whispered as they stayed hunkered down behind a rock. "Could we try it a bit upstream, even if it's deeper?"

"You're sounding brave all of a sudden. No, we can't take that chance. When you get back home to peaceful Fort Lauderdale, you can regale your friends with the fact that brown bears are called grizzlies outside Alaska, and that any bear anywhere always has the absolute right of way."

"Maybe that airplane will come back—or others."

"Bears or not, if the plane returns, it would be tough to land here even with pontoons. They'd need to send a chopper with a basket." He heaved a huge sigh. He saw her reach out to touch him, maybe even to try to comfort him, but then draw back. He cleared his throat, willing himself not to just pull her into his arms. "We're going to have to go downriver a bit farther where there's another way to get across," he said.

"But I can see beyond where the valley narrows, and it turns to one river again. Deeper with more rapids. Get across how?"

He turned to look in her eyes for the first time in hours. The mark of a good lawyer was to be inquisitive, to leave no stone unturned, plan ahead, no surprises. But he dare not tell her the truth until they got there and it was too late for her to turn back, or she'd balk for sure.

Why did this stubborn woman exert such a pull on him? Again, as at other points on this journey, he felt a surge of desire for her. He was impressed with her resilience after all she'd been through. But there was no one worse for him in this life he'd chosen and desired, so why did he still want her? He might as well propose to Christine Tanaka, take a chance on her despite her past. At least she loved this life and place the way he did, and was tough enough to flourish here. Yet soft city-girl Lisa, as banged up and scared as she still must be, managed to look back at him unflinchingly.

"I got us this far," he said, "so I'm asking you to trust me. Take it or leave it."

She bit her lower lip, then said, "I have to, of course."

"I don't want to hear 'I have to.' I want to hear 'I do.' You know what I mean—that you really do trust me to get us out of this."

"All right, to get us back to civilization, I do trust you. But you know what this scene reminds me of? And it's not some TV show. In a way it reminds me of what we call civilization."

"Wall Street devouring people's lives? Lawyers or businesspeople?" he asked.

"That's scary if we're starting to think alike. Yes, people doing anything to protect their profits and desires at any cost to others. Frankly, the bears remind me of some of Carlisle, Bonner and Associates' clients."

"Or fellow lawyers desperate enough to push a rival into a roaring river?"

Before she could answer, he said, "Come on, partner, we've got to push on." He patted her shoulder, hefted his pack and turned away from this dead end where he'd hoped to cross the river.

The moment Spike's plane landed, Christine and Ginger, followed by their guests, ran out on the floating boat dock to meet it. Christine had gripped her hands together so hard that her fingers had gone numb.

"Any sign of them?" Mr. Bonner called out before she could ask.

"Nothing!" Spike answered as he helped Mrs. Bonner climb down from the cockpit to the dock. He usually tied the plane at the other end of the lake, closer to Ginger's place.

"But then," Christine said, "that could be a good sign."

"Right," Spike agreed and threw his arm around her shoulders. No one said what they must all be thinking—no bodies or wrecked kayak, at least. She leaned into Spike. If any good came out of this, it was that she and Spike seemed to be more of a team. He'd always been wary of her, almost tiptoed around her, and she knew why.

Like most people in these parts, he knew her past. She prayed that wouldn't come back to haunt her if there was some sort of investigation here. After all, she'd probably been the last person to see both Lisa and Mitch alive. *Iah!* No, she would not think that way. Even if Lisa was a greenhorn around here, Mitch wasn't. But if Lisa's loss ended up harming Mitch, Christine would never get over it.

Her chin quivered and she almost burst into tears, when she'd vowed never to cry again after she'd been acquitted. That old, heavy weight of guilt sat hard on her heart again.

"What are we going to do?" Vanessa asked. "Should we fly home, or just wait around for—"

"No one should go anywhere yet," Jonas piped up. "We'll find them—local law enforcement or the national park guys will, at least."

"No, of course, we stay right here," Mr. Bonner said. "We have four full days left in our stay anyway. We've left capable staff behind. We do what we can and hope and pray for the best. Mitch was a great attorney. I just hope he's as good at what he does now. And Lisa's resilient and determined, however much she'd be out of out her element in these wilds."

Spike said, "We'll go back up again as soon as I refuel and get someone to feed my dogs. They're all out on lead lines without enough water to tide them over this long."

"I'll do it," Christine offered, surprising herself as she'd blurted that out.

"Better let Ginger, so you can still host the lodge guests," Spike said, giving her shoulders a little squeeze before he let her go. "But thanks for saying so when I know a dozen big hungry huskies aren't your thing."

"But they are yours so that's okay," she said, looking up at him. She felt a blush starting, though her tawny skin probably wouldn't give her away. Even with everyone looking on, even in these dire straights, she and Spike Jackson seemed to have a common cause that went beyond the lodge, even beyond finding Mitch and Lisa Vaughn. That bond certainly wasn't the dogs. Her husband, Clay, had kept snarling, half-hungry dogs, and any group of huskies still set her teeth on edge. No, their other common cause in this potential tragedy was taking care of each other.

Lisa could not get the sight of the bear-eating-fish carnage out of her mind. The river was both life and death to those determined salmon. And it could have been death to her, but—with Mitch's help—she had survived.

And those bears! At first the voracious bloodlust had horrified her, but she had swiftly accepted it as—if not beautiful—part of this beautiful, raw land. Survival. The basic elements of life. And yet in the midst of all that potential violence, there was a mother feeding her cubs, teaching them what they needed to know to flourish here in this land of stark contrasts and stunning sights.

Now she and Mitch sat on boulders at the edge of the beaver-made lake about a half mile from the river, but distant from the beavers themselves.

"It looks pretty deep here," she said, gazing into the lovely lake the beaver village had created. She was eager to keep the conversation on anything but their past. She shouldn't have argued with Mitch since she had to rely on him to get out of this wilderness.

"Yeah. Lots of pond vegetation down there makes that green, wavy look."

"I think I'm going to wash my face and hands here. The water's not as cold as—well, nothing I've ever been near was that cold."

She took off her denim jacket and rolled up her wet suit sleeves, then rinsed her face and hands in the sun-warmed water. She blinked beads of it off her lashes, then stared down into the green water at her own face, slightly distorted in the wavering reflection. Something shifted beneath the surface. It reminded her of her childhood nightmare, one her psychiatrist had helped her to handle. Her mother's face, more and more like her own as she grew up, was staring at her through a watery barrier, calling her, beckoning....

A burst of bubbles pulled her from her reverie. Bubbles from fish? Had a beaver come over? The silvery beads were in the shape of a question mark. She dangled her hands in the water, swishing the bubbles and nightmares into oblivion, staring into the swirls she made.

If she was sure she'd been pushed in the river, the question was by whom and why? A few motives were obvious—Jonas and Vanessa wanted the same fat fish she did from the river of ambition, but would they go so far as to push her in? The idea of the Bonners testing her was too far-fetched. She didn't dare to ask Mitch about his relationship to Christine, so her thoughts kept swirling, fading in and out.

Besides, she needed Mitch's help out here, despite the fact the so-called Alaskan frontier didn't scare her half as much as she'd expected. Once she was out of the river, that is. Even those bears flaying and gobbling down live fish—she accepted it. The howling of the wolves had a certain lonely, austere loveliness—at least that's the way she recalled it now. The beaver village was fascinating and the sunset stunning. Despite her agonizing over what she faced back at the lodge, she could almost—almost—have enjoyed at least parts of this adventure.

Perhaps this vast, awesome land helped to put things in perspective. Out here, her troubles back in so-called civilization didn't seem so all-consuming. The chance for her to be granted the senior partnership at Carlisle, Bonner & Associates might now be, sadly, gone with the wind, at least endangered, she admitted silently. But, if she had to, surely she could find another law firm at home and make her new colleagues a sort of family as the Bonners had been to her. Yes, she'd get busy as a beaver once again and make a new life, she tried to assure herself. She was learning to be a strong, independent woman, whether in the fun-in-the-sun southeast or here in the northwest Land of the Midnight Sun.

Maybe she should tell Mitch just that, since he'd said he was going to tell Graham she shouldn't be the one chosen—

Huge and horrible, the monster rose from the lake. It emerged just four feet from her with massive, bloody horns and the face of a furry ogre, snorting—

Screaming, she vaulted backward, flinging water

as the thing came closer, looming larger. She threw herself into Mitch's arms and held tight with her heart slamming against her ribs.

"Moose, Lisa!" he said, picking her up. "It's a bull moose just coming up from where he's been eating those underwater veggies I mentioned. He's not dangerous unless you're another bull moose. He's just—magnificent."

"Oh! Yes. Of course. But his red horns—"

"Antlers. That stuff is the velvet he's shedding off his rack this time of year. Man, almost five feet across. That big boy's almost nine feet tall at the shoulders—wow! His antlers will be all bone so he can fight other bulls for the choice mates in the rutting season coming up," he said and bounced her once in his arms, as if to convey some secret, extra message.

"It—it just startled me. I don't know what I thought," she admitted as he put her down.

After staring at them, still chewing his cud, the big bull sauntered sideways in the lake, snorted and submerged again in a circle of bubbles.

"We're not getting much of a rest," Mitch said. She wasn't sure, but he looked as if he was trying not to laugh. Thank heavens, she hadn't been preaching to him what she'd been thinking about her independence and growing self-confidence here.

"I'm sorry I jumped on you," she said as she dried her hands on the outside of her jacket before slipping back into it.

"Just now or earlier?"

"You know what I mean."

"I think we could use some solid food, and those bears back there gave me an idea. I could probably catch a salmon with the corkscrew on my Swiss Army knife. Sorry we don't have a bottle of Pouilly-Fuissé to go with it. We've got to use this four-pound stove I've been carting around for something."

And so, by quickly moving on in topic and place, he seemed to give her at least the remnants of her dignity back, Lisa realized. He wasn't such a barbarian after all. And now that she'd been back with him a while, she was starting to remember even more things about him. His instincts had always been to protect her, to coddle and spoil her even—that is, before his big, out-of-the-blue bombshell to move her to Alaska.

Anyhow, she sensed there was something he wasn't telling her right now, maybe about how they were really going to cross the river to get to that access road. If he thought she was going to walk across a big tree trunk over the rapids or cross in a boat someone had stashed, he was crazy. She'd stay behind, and he could send that chopper with the basket for her. No more white water, not even on a raft farther upstream from the ledge, where he'd assured them all that the river wasn't as rough as when it rampaged past his property. Again, she thought that maybe the plum position of senior partner at the firm was not worth some things. Not only almost dying but the vast beauty of Alaska made you think about what life was really worth.

7

Mitch was proud of the meal they'd just had, and prouder yet that Lisa seemed to appreciate it. For the first time since he'd left the lodge, he felt full. He'd caught a large salmon with a corkscrew, much like the bears speared their fish, and he'd cooked it on their small stove.

"Just like I've never had better blueberries," she told him, "I've never had better salmon."

"I don't want to sound like your idea of a travel brochure again," he told her, "but water tastes the best and food even better in Alaska."

"Yes, but there's something to be said for Florida lobster, stone crab and citrus salads—not to mention key lime pie."

"True. And I miss those things, but that doesn't mean I can't go back—to visit, I mean."

"You could become a snowbird."

"Maybe. For a month or two. If things go well here financially and Spike and Christine could keep an eye on things when I'm gone."

"I can tell she thinks a lot of you. I take it she's single."

"She is now. Her husband abused her."

"So she left him. Separated or divorced?"

He frowned out over the water. Everyone around Bear Bones knew, but he'd promised Christine he would never tell any of the guests, and he felt he should get her permission first before telling anyone, even Lisa.

"Separated," he told her. "Permanently because he died."

"Oh. She seems to have a mixture of sadness but pride about her. But I guess the Eskimo people have to be strong."

"Most people in the lower forty-eight don't know it, but the term Eskimo is about on par with calling Native Americans just Indians these days. We say Inuit or use tribal names. Like a lot of people in these parts, Christine's Yup'ik."

"I certainly don't want to offend anyone. I'm glad you told me. I didn't know."

There was a lot that she didn't know, Mitch thought, because he'd told her a couple of half truths—but with good reason.

They sat close together on the bank of the river. Though it roared past them again, it wasn't quite as fierce as it was near the lodge. But Mitch knew it was deeper, since it had picked up several other streams that fed it. Sometimes he could hear granite boulders, grinding, rolling along in its depths like distant thunder. He figured they were just around the bend from where their only shot at a crossing for miles would be, so he had set up their last stopping point here. They both needed strength from a meal. And, he feared, once she saw what he intended, he'd have trouble on his hands. He might have to overpower her and tape her hands and feet to get her across. He wouldn't even know about the way to the other side if he hadn't remembered what one of his uncle's hunting buddies had said about the crossing below the braided rivers. He prayed really hard that it was still there.

It bothered Christine that Spike had taken Mitch's chair at the head of the table for this very late meal, but everyone was famished. Ginger was the only one not there, because she had gone to feed Spike's dogs about a mile away.

Though they all desperately needed sleep and it was getting lighter outside again, no one had gone to bed, though she noted that Vanessa had gone up to take a shower, wash her hair and put on fresh makeup. Compared to everyone else, she looked rested and calm. Jonas had taken over the pacing Vanessa had done earlier, but it was actually Mrs. Bonner who had insisted on helping Christine get this food on the table. The woman was rock solid—going up with Spike, being such a support and pitching right in when she and her husband could have lorded it over everyone.

"I regret that the salmon's cold, but it would be dry

if I rebaked it," Christine told everyone. Spike had insisted she eat with them, just as Mitch always did. If Mitch never came back…

"It's delicious—all of it," Mrs. Bonner said. "Salmon is excellent hot and cold."

"Christine's a great cook," Spike said. "And thanks for saying you'd stay and for buying the airplane fuel, sir," he told Mr. Bonner.

"Mitch was—and I only use the past tense because he chose to leave us for a different life last year—like a son to me, to us. Since I don't have an heir—"

"He means a son," Mrs. Bonner interrupted. "We have an heiress, a wonderful, bright daughter in law school who will join the firm next year."

"Exactly," Mr. Bonner said with a nod. "Just like Ellie's father, Cameron Carlisle, who mentored me and took me into the firm when I married his daughter, I had similar hopes for Mitch."

"That he would marry your girl?" Spike asked, a sourdough biscuit halfway to his mouth. *Iah!* If Christine could have reached him under the table, she would have kicked him.

"At least," Mr. Bonner said, "we had hopes that our Claire would marry someone who would take an interest in the firm—keep the majority of the control all in the family. When Lisa and Mitch announced their engagement, of course—and then Mitch left— the other was out of the question."

"That they were even dating," Vanessa said, "came as a huge surprise to everyone, because they kept it

very sub rosa—secretive," she added as if Christine
and Spike needed a translator.

"I certainly don't mean to rush anyone," Christine
told them, pushing back her chair and starting to
clear dishes, "but we won't be any good for the search
if we don't get a little rest."

"Will the sheriff be coming out here, Spike?"
Jonas asked. "Or the state patrol you mentioned? If
they start asking questions, will you need some counsel around? If I can help you with any of that, just say
so. I owe Mitch a lot."

"I'm going up in the plane again and I've got two
other guys who fly to search, too. Christine's in
charge here if there's any questions from the sheriff
or troopers."

She almost dropped the plates she held. No way
did she want to be answering any law enforcement
questions.

Spike continued. "Still, the law better be looking
for them and not wasting time here. See all of you in
a few hours. Keep your spirits up. Just like Mitch was
a good lawyer, he's a smart Alaskan, even though he's
not lived here that long."

Taking a couple of his sister's homemade sourdough biscuits with him, Spike left to get the plane
refueled. When Christine came back in to clear more
plates, everyone else was still sitting there until Mrs.
Bonner, then Vanessa, jumped up to help her. Though
she would have protested that just yesterday, she

nodded her thanks, because once she got everyone in their rooms, she needed to search Mitch's.

"I can't believe it!" Lisa cried when she figured out where Mitch intended to cross the river. "Another gorge starts here. This surely isn't where you said we could get to the other side. Do you have a boat here somewhere? The water's just as violent here as by the lodge."

"Not quite. We're not going through the water, but above it. See?" he added, pointing.

"What? No, I don't see— Oh. A cable goes from side to side. But we can't just hang on that."

"Come on. I'll show you," he said, setting out ahead of her again, climbing uphill on a rocky path as they had for the last half hour. "Up ahead, where that cable is tethered, is called a gauging station, a spot where scientists—hydrologists, specifically—used to drop a weighted plumb bob to measure the water's depth. I heard it was built by a geological survey team but was abandoned for lack of funds. Hunters use it now."

He kept talking. She could tell he was nervous, too. "It's like a little ski lift, I guess, with a cable car. At least that's what I heard from a friend of my uncle's. I'm just glad I recalled what he said."

"But that cable—"

"It's made of braided steel."

"I don't care. It sags. It's old."

He didn't answer as they neared the spot where the cable was connected to the gorge, bolted into solid rock on this side and attached to what looked to be about a ten-foot tower so it would be fairly level. But the so-called cable car was actually a big, aluminum bucket, a bit smaller, but shaped like the gondola baskets that hung under hot-air balloons. It measured maybe two feet by four feet, and its height might come to Lisa's chest.

"No way!" she told Mitch, and sat down right where she was.

"It's the only way across for miles. We'll be over the river in minutes, onto the access road and home quickly."

"My home is thousands of miles away. I'll stay here while you go and send help. But I don't think you should trust it either. I haven't looked down, but, honestly, I just can't do it, and it looks like we'd have to cross one at a time. Alone. The weight of one person in there would be scary enough, but two?"

"I'll test it first with a trial crossing. We can't send it over empty because it looks like the pulley system will have to be worked by hand to haul it up the last little distance on both sides."

"Even more than the worry about its condition, I just cannot go in or over this river. It almost killed me—that and whoever pushed me," she protested.

He came back, dropped the pack and sat down beside her with his knees bent up almost to his chin and his arms linked around his long legs. She thought he would berate her, but his voice was calm and steady, almost seductive.

"So how are you going to handle that when you

get back? Call the sheriff in from Talkeetna and ask him to arrest whom? Pretend to go back to normal, trying to get the senior partner position as if you just fell in? Or do you plan to carefully investigate—try to discover or set up whoever shoved you?"

"You believe me now?"

"I'm just strategizing like I would with a client preparing a defense. Whichever of those paths you take, unless you're just going to run—and back to where, to the law firm where someone might have tried to kill you? Those are your choices. You and I made a good legal team a couple of times—the Dailey case, then the big casino money-laundering investigation. You cross that river, after I've checked out the steel cable and aluminum tram first," he went on, pointing down at it, "and I'm your sidekick private detective and co-counsel on this attempted homicide investigation. Even if someone ends up claiming they didn't mean for you to fall in that foaming, freezing river, we'll know who did it and can find out why. Or maybe we'll figure out the why first and that will lead us to the perp. It's possible that the why involves me, too."

"I'm remembering why you have such a great reputation as a persuasive attorney. But what do you mean it could involve you?"

"Two reasons. One, maybe someone didn't want us back together to talk things out."

"About our breaking up? Who cares about that but us?"

"We're just in the realm of 'what ifs' right now."

"Do you mean someone could be afraid we know about something they did?"

"Or didn't do. I don't know. I'm just fishing here again and not even with a corkscrew."

"Maybe Jonas or Vanessa thought I could sway you to tell the Bonners I'd be their best bet for senior partner. But is that enough motive to try to kill me?"

"I've been trying to reason it out, but I'm too exhausted to think straight right now," he said.

"But you have thought straight. I've been agonizing over the *who* and *why*, too, and if I just say I slipped on that ridge above the river it would give us at least a couple of days to investigate what really happened."

"One drawback here is that the perp would know you're lying about falling in."

"We could say I hit my head and couldn't really recall what happened. We could intimate my memory might come back, then set a trap. But we can't let him or her get wind that we're investigating. Once we get back, he or she will be nervous enough we've had some time to talk, to reason things out. Mitch," she said, turning more toward him, "you really do believe that someone pushed me?"

"Despite your love-hate relationship with churning water, I believe you would not jump in. And, even under duress and in pain, you've been surefooted and brave on this trek, so I don't think you fell."

"Thank you. Even though we're not going to be

life partners, I appreciate your advice and your offer," she said, putting her hand on his arm.

"So do we have a deal? After I test our tram, you will let me send you over to the other side before I join you there?"

She stared into his dark eyes, sharp and steady—stern but sweet. Yes, Mitchell Andrew Braxton had always shown a tenderness, a gentleness beneath his go-for-the-jugular instincts. But that foaming water would be under her, and she was terrified of falling in just like—

"Yes," she said. "I thought I'd never trust you again after we broke up, but yes. That much is a deal, and I am grateful for your help when we get back."

She stuck out her trembling hand to shake his. He took it, pulled her close and kissed her cheek. His beard stubble burned her sore skin, and his words and touch seared deep into her heart.

8

Christine knew she didn't need a key to get into
Mitch's suite, because, so far at least, he'd never
locked it. She ducked inside and quietly closed the
door. It was a long shot, but perhaps she'd find something here that hinted at what had happened, such as
a note from Lisa Vaughn. She was getting desperate.
She could not lose Mitch.

She scanned his small sitting area—ever neat and
tidy—and moved quickly to the big rolltop desk that
had been his uncle's. She saw stacks of bills to pay,
future reservations, some from Tokyo. Those guests
would start arriving late next month. Though darkest
winter was the best time for viewing the aurora
borealis, it was possible to catch pale, wispy glimpses
of its grandeur anytime soon.

Without going through his entire in and out baskets and desk drawers, she didn't see anything unusual, such as a personal note. If she had time for a
more thorough search, she'd go through all that later.

But there was a wadded up, printed e-mail in the

otherwise empty wastebasket. She picked it up, unwrinkled its violently twisted form and scanned it. She was sure it must be from Lisa and whatever it said had angered him.

But it was from his brother saying he was too busy to come this summer, and the kids would be in school in the fall, but he wished him the best in his "frontier adventure." Then a final line that revealed so much. "After all, Uncle John left that place to you, not me."

Christine sighed. Another family with damaged relationships as sad and bad as her marriage had been, as icy as the whiteout fogs in Fairbanks.

Mitch hardly ever talked about his brother, but he had his family's photograph prominently displayed on the desktop. She saw it was now lying on its face as if he'd knocked it over, but she'd looked at it several times. An eight-by-ten in color of his surgeon brother, Brad, his pretty wife—another blonde, so maybe both Braxton boys liked blondes—and their two kids, a boy about ten and a girl about six. No doubt, Mitch, too, longed for a family. Well, Christine was never going to have that and maybe Mitch wouldn't either.

She tiptoed into his bedroom, moving like a leaf on the forest floor. His bed was covered by a quilt in browns, muted blues and greens. The bed was carefully made, though she'd volunteered when she first came to make it every day. He'd told her she wasn't a hotel maid but the lodge manager and chef, and that had given her an early glimpse into the heart of the man.

She scanned the top of his bureau, his book-shelves, the compartments built into the headboard of his bed. Why he slept in a king-size bed, she hadn't asked, but maybe it was because he was restless at night, thrashed around a lot. Maybe like her, he had bad dreams.

The folklore of her people taught that each human being had a *joncha,* a secret identity linked to an animal the person could contact through dreams. When you discovered which *joncha* was yours, the old belief was that you could change into that animal at will, but were also plagued by its weaknesses.

Her *joncha* was the silent, stoic and observant wolverine. Though Spike and Mitch weren't Yup'ik, she pictured Spike as the powerful but sometimes bumbling bear. Mitch Braxton was an eagle, wise and daring, but one who could be snared by wanting too much. She'd seen an eagle try to snatch a too-big salmon from the river and get pulled under, his talons caught in the flesh of the fish, the river pulling him down to destruction, just like Lisa Vaughn might have ruined his life—again.

She collapsed on the edge of the bed, put her face in her hands and sobbed. But did she hear footsteps? Could Mitch be back?

She bolted off the bed, nearly slamming into Spike as he came around the corner and looked in.

"What the hell are you doing in here!" he demanded, striding in and grabbing her hard by her shoulders, then pressing her between the wall and his big body. She hit hard at his hands and kicked at his shin, though he barely budged. Memories of brutality, of beatings, roared at her.

"Don't grab me like that!" she cried.

He released her immediately, but shouted, "You told me you weren't sleeping with him!"

"Don't shout. I'm the lodge manager, and I came in to see if he'd left any clues behind, that's all."

"You haven't answered my question."

"It wasn't a question but an accusation. You think that of us, you ask him when he gets back! *Iah!*"

At first he seemed angry, but she saw realization dawn on his frowning face. "I—I didn't mean to hurt you—or remind you of...him, your husband. It's just—I lost my head. My temper. I won't grab you like that again, I promise."

Linking his fingers and putting both hands on top of his head, he leaned back against the door frame and stared up at the ceiling. "Sorry. I blurt things out. And I didn't mean to frighten you."

"It's all right—this time. We're all on edge."

"Truth is, I just checked Lisa Vaughn's room."

"Anything there?" she said, glad for the shift of subjects as she subtly smoothed the sleeves of her blouse he'd wrinkled.

"Her room's a lot messier than here. Christine, I really am sorry," he said, finally looking at her and folding his arms over his chest.

"I'm flattered you were upset and happy you can humble yourself to apologize."

"It wasn't personal—just…I gotta go. I'm taking the plane up again."

"With Mrs. Bonner?"

"She's like that bunny in the battery ads. Yeah, she insists on going, and they're paying for the fuel again. They're probably used to buying anything they want, but I still like both of them." He lifted one hand and started for the door before turning back.

"I think," he said, "after she fed my mushers, Ginger went to look for Mitch and Lisa over near her place again, even though the kayak obviously went into the river. She—when she gets something in her head, there's no stopping her. Gotta go," he repeated and hurried out.

Lisa told herself to breathe. In, out. Calm, steady. Just breathe.

But she could hardly stem her terror as she watched Mitch unhook the basket—thank God, it was on this side of the river—and climb into it. This was to be the test run, but she suddenly didn't even want him to do that. What if it dumped him into the raging torrent? She couldn't bear to lose him, her rescuer and ally. And her partner for what might turn out to be an attempted-murder investigation.

"Help me hold it steady until I let it go," he told her. "Then stand way back. Don't look down at the river. You do not have to look down." Then, he added, so quietly she could hardly hear over the roar of the water, "How about a kiss for luck?"

He quickly kissed her cheek but then he molded his lips to hers with one hand behind her head to hold her to him. His mouth opened slightly, exciting, enticing. A jolt of power shot through her, nose to toes. The kiss made her feel she was in the basket with him, flying, looking down over a whirling vortex.

"Okay, get back now," he said, freeing her. "And when I return, you may have to help me get the tram back up here, because it looks like the cable dips on this side a bit more than on the other. Watch how I use the pulleys to give a hand-over-hand pull up at the end of each side. Let go, get back! Here we go!"

We, he said. As if they were indeed a team. She stood back, her hands pressed over her mouth and her spine pressed against the solid rock into which the cable had been grounded. Still, her legs trembled. She watched wide-eyed as he hunkered down a bit in the basket, edging it out over the void—and then let go of the pulley and flew, down, away, the hook screeching over the steel cable until the river devoured the sound.

He slowed in the sag of his steel lifeline, dipping to maybe twenty feet above the river. It seemed an eternity to her before the aluminum tram slowed as it started up the other side of the cable, where he had to use the pulleys.

Instead of going clear to the tower, he let go again and came flying back. On this side, he didn't even have to pull himself up very far. When he was over solid ground, she held the basket to stop its rocking. She smiled through her tears, and he gave a little cheer.

"Not much different from a roller-coaster ride at Disney World!" He exulted, looking like a boy who would love such a ride. "Your turn."

The time had come to face her worst fears. She'd promised him, but she hadn't looked down yet and now she would have to. No way could she make this trip with her eyes tightly shut.

Mitch clambered out.

"What's downriver from here?" she blurted.

"Don't start thinking too much. If you must know, miles away, massive Denali Park—eventually, the Bering Sea and Russia—okay? Just concentrate on the here and now. You'll be fine."

He lifted her up to swing her into the basket, but she held hard to him, her arms around his neck. She pressed her cheek to his despite the stubble of his beard.

"Mitch, if anything happens, I'm sorry about what I said about your family and your brother. I'm sorry I couldn't change enough to move here with you."

Holding her, he kissed her again, hard, a rotating, grinding kiss that she felt in her bruised lips and deep in her belly. "We'll work everything out back at the lodge," he told her, breathing hard in unison with her.

He put her down in the basket that reminded her of a big tin can.

"Kneel down and hang on," he ordered as he shoved the basket away. "See you on the other side of this big river."

"Mitch, I can't—"

She wasn't sure what she was going to say, but he gave a last little shove and the basket fell free of solid ground. She closed her eyes and let out a little scream as it careened away, faster, over the river that had almost killed her. Someone had wanted that, someone had tried that.

In the central sag of the cable, she imagined herself crashing into the current. She fought hard to keep from seeing Mommy and Jani disappearing into the depths again. Terrified she'd fall into the roaring foam, she gripped the sides of her little basket so hard her fingers went numb.

Then the basket slowed. What if it stopped, dangling her over the water so Mitch had to come across it hand over hand to save her?

She opened her eyes and saw she was almost at the tower on the far side. *Don't look down,* she told herself in a frenzied little mantra. *Don't look down into that screaming white water.*

Looking up at the cable line, she feared it would snap, but it held. Shaking hard in the swaying basket, she reached up and worked the pulley the way she'd seen him do it. Yes! Yes, she was over land, but what if this thing took off before she was out? What if it didn't get back to bring Mitch over and she had to walk out of here alone? He'd said there was an access road if you just walked south, but she was terrible at directions and she'd be so alone in all this vastness. And with the roar of the river, they wouldn't even be able to shout back and forth across it.

But as she got out and felt dry, firm rock under her feet again, feet still covered with the shoes Mitch had made for her, she heard an inner voice clearly say, *You can do whatever you have to.*

Shivers shot through her. It wasn't her mother's voice that she so often tried to remember. It wasn't her psychiatrist's from long ago. It wasn't even Mitch's, though it almost could have been. Perhaps not even the Lord God's or some kind of guardian angel's. It was almost as if this vast, powerful land had spoken to her, taught her that she could survive despite her fear of the raging torrent of troubles or the unknown side of some deep, dark chasm.

As she waved across to Mitch and shoved the basket out so it would return for him, she made a vow. No matter what, with his help, she was going to find out who had tried to take her life and why.

PART II

Walking the Wave

The frontier is the outer edge of
the wave—the meeting point
between savagery and civilization.
—Frederick Jackson Turner

9

"Thanks for your help!" Mitch told Gus Majors as he drove them onto the lodge property in his rattle-trap pickup. Gus was a big bear of a man, and Lisa was squeezed in between them. The pickup was old enough that it didn't have seat belts, or else Gus had ripped them out.

Gus ran the hunting supply and hardware store called Whatever in Bear Bones, and did taxidermy work on the side. Like Spike, he ran a team of sled dogs. Many Alaskans held numerous jobs to survive. Like some other local guys, Gus had never married— literally not enough women to go around. He'd tried to court Ginger for a while, which Mitch figured took nerves of steel, but nothing had come of it. As a matter of fact, Mitch had heard the two former lovebirds had had a shouting match in town at the Wolfin' Café a few days ago.

"We really owe you, Gus," Mitch added.

"Naw, glad me and old Betsy was comin' down the road. Bad huntin' for moose, but good for lost neighbors, eh?" Gus said with a slap at his steering wheel and a hearty guffaw. "You'd a done the same for me, Mitch."

With a honk-honk of Betsy's horn, Gus hit the brakes in front of the lodge, and the three of them piled out.

"Glad to meet you, too, Missy," Gus added, snatching off his Yukon Quest ball cap when Mitch helped Lisa down.

Mitch waited for her to correct Gus. Though he called most women Missy, she'd probably think he'd forgotten or screwed up her name. She'd had a habit of correcting people's pronunciation in practice sessions before they went on the witness stand, when Mitch had always thought they should just be themselves. But now, to his surprise, she gave Gus a hug.

"Mitch saved my life," she told him, "but you saved us from a long trek back, Gus. I'm glad to meet you, too, and you're invited to the lodge, for dinner on me, before we leave."

"Just better not have Ginger there, too, then," he said, "because—"

He stopped mid-sentence as Christine tore out of the lodge.

"Thank God, thank God!" she cried, and hugged Mitch hard before holding him at arm's length. "*Iah! What happened?*" she asked, staring over his shoulder at Lisa before looking back to him.

"*Cu'paq,* thanks for holding down the fort."

"We were worried to death. We've even got Denali

park rangers looking for you way downriver. Spike's been up a couple of times with Mrs. Bonner, and they just got back. I'll go tell them...."

She turned and ran for the lake.

"Best be goin'," Gus said, shaking Mitch's hand and patting Lisa on the shoulder. "Now don't you think nothin' of it—all in a day's work 'round here. Right, Mitch?"

They waved to him as his truck chugged away. Jonas and Vanessa barreled out of the lodge with a beaming Graham Bonner right behind. Spike and Ellie came running from the lake, with the little woman in tears but managing to keep up with Spike's long strides. Spike slapped Mitch on the back, and Ellie hugged Lisa, then him. Mitch noted Ginger kind of edging around the corner of the lodge, hanging back, watching rather than joining the party. Either she'd seen Gus here or just didn't want to get in the middle of all the hoopla. She seemed a sort of split personality at times—sometimes private, other times almost pushy.

Everyone spoke at once, asked a hundred questions, but always the big one. "What happened?"

"Lisa?" Mitch said, turning to her.

"Things are really fuzzy," she told them, as everyone hushed. "Besides the shock of the icy river, I must have hit my head at some point, because I can't recall exactly what happened. It may come back to me. Some things have. Right now I only know that Mitch got in a kayak and rescued me at this end of

the gorge. I had hypothermia but he saved my life by getting me warm again."

Mitch noted the toss of Vanessa's head and the roll of her eyes. She glared at Lisa before she managed a merely concerned expression. Why did that woman always suspect the worst? Could she still be fuming that he and Lisa had managed a secret relationship? Just a couple of months before he had started dating Lisa, Vanessa had aggressively propositioned him at a New Year's Eve party, and he'd turned her down. Jealousy was always a powerful motive for revenge. Maybe, in this case, exacerbated by the fact the Bonners had forgiven him and Lisa. Maybe Vanessa could not stand for Lisa to best her again if she got senior partner.

Lisa was winding down her succinct explanation. "We had to hike out through the swampy muskeg to dry tundra and then to a spot we could cross the river to the access road where Gus Majors picked us up."

"Right." Mitch backed up the story they'd decided on. "I first spotted her clinging to a rock near here— I'll point out which one later. I moved the kayak from the lake to the river and went after her, even when she got swept farther away. We've had a real adventure hiking out, but we're both exhausted, aching and starved—"

"But if she hit her head and can't recall, she'll need a doctor," Ellie said, wringing her hands. "Being battered in that river, a thorough checkup is in order. She's all black and blue—as if she's been beaten."

Mitch and Christine exchanged a quick look as Lisa insisted, "I'm fine now, really. Mitch made sure I didn't have a concussion. I think it might just be the shock of that cold water that's jumbled my memory for now. I'm even getting used to walking off my aches and pains."

"Walking all that way in those shoes?" Vanessa asked, pointing. Everyone looked down at the beat-up, makeshift padded cloth and duct tape shoes Mitch had made for her.

"Yes," Lisa said, tossing her head so her already wild hair flew up in the breeze behind her, making it look as if she was in an electromagnetic field. "Ironically, Mitch made them for me from a life preserver. Alaskan wilderness chic, I think."

"My shoes were too big for her, so we had no choice," he explained as he took her elbow, and they started toward the lodge.

"All she's been through," Graham said, keeping up, "makes me think she has the stamina and courage to fill your shoes at the firm. Lisa, if you can't take part in the other activities we have planned, I won't hold it against you."

She turned back to face him and Ellie. "Despite what's happened, I'm blessed to be alive and well. But I want to be a part of things here. Unless I have to get back in that rough river—"

"No one does," Mitch cut in, "because when we get to our river day, we're going way upstream where it's a lot calmer, and we're going in a big multiperson raft—and not until the very last event."

Mitch heard Jonas mutter something to Vanessa but he couldn't catch it.

"Graham," Mitch told his former mentor, "we've got a few days left before you leave, so how about full steam ahead with our plans? That is, after a hot meal, a good soak in the hot tub and some sleep?"

"We never gave up on either of you," Graham said as he walked between Mitch and Lisa with his hands on their shoulders and the others scurrying to keep up. "And it looks like you've worked together as a team again, just as you did at the firm."

Mitch saw Vanessa's frown deepen, and she elbowed Jonas, who just shook his head. Christine ran past them, hopefully to get some food out. And so, Mitch thought, unless Lisa really did hit her head and hallucinate being pushed into that violent river, building their case against someone here had begun.

As she stood under a pounding, hot shower, Lisa tried to calculate the time they'd been gone. It seemed to have both stood still and flown while she and Mitch had been in the wilds. Besides, she needed to think of something else besides this water sluicing over her, however good it felt. She had to establish a timeline, so she could track everyone's moves back here and eventually test their alibis. Hopefully with Mitch's help.

The Bonner party had arrived at the lodge on Tuesday and she'd been pushed into the river the next day, late afternoon. The fact that the sun never really set had made it seem as if they'd been gone for only one long day, despite the fact she and Mitch had huddled together in that little tent twice.

The first night had passed while they had edged away from the river and seen that glorious sunset and hiked to the blueberry bush and gotten some rest. Then only one more long, light-filled day had passed before they finally crossed the river at the gauging station. It was now the second night. She was so tired and full of Christine's good food, her body was aching for bed. Yet her mind was still alert. Coffee and chocolate always got to her like that, but her anger over what had happened—and the panic someone might try to harm her again—beat any other stimulant, however exhausted her body was.

Could Vanessa and Jonas be somehow working together? They had seemed to be sticking tight when everyone had greeted them. But they, too, were rivals, so why would they be in collusion? Besides, surely they were smart enough to know that once a criminal told someone of the crime, or had someone abetting it, secrets would get out. *Two can keep a secret if one of them is dead,* as the old saying went.

Besides, she couldn't just suspect the two obvious people. Christine seemed possessive of Mitch and moved on deer's feet. If anyone could have sneaked up behind her on the ridge path, it could have been her, because the woman knew she was there then. Spike could also resent her. He might be afraid she'd hurt someone he obviously looked up to. Perhaps he was afraid that if she and Mitch reconciled, she'd get him to move back to Florida. She had to learn more about his staff from Mitch, if he wouldn't just defend them.

She finally climbed out of the shower and toweled off. She'd shampooed her hair so she blasted it with the blow-dryer, still thinking, agonizing. Yes, this twilight—she couldn't think of it as night—must be the end of Thursday, and they weren't supposed to leave until next Tuesday morning, so she and Mitch had four full days. Graham had called the time left a "few days." She had to move quickly, not waste even one day recovering. It was high time to find a killer who now might want to correct the problem of her surviving the river.

Though the bed beckoned, Lisa pulled on her bathing suit—she'd looked like one big bruise in the steamy bathroom mirror—because she knew Mitch was going to soak in the lodge's large outdoor hot tub and she needed to talk to him. She didn't want anyone—including him—to see her knocking on his bedroom door. If others were in the spa, it would just have to wait. Taking a fresh towel and donning the thick, white terry-cloth robe the lodge provided, she went out and down the hall.

Through the next room's closed door, Lisa could hear Vanessa talking, but to whom? Cell phones didn't work here, and no room had phones, though, ironically, since the great room downstairs was equipped with Direct TV, the guest rooms offered

Internet service. Could Jonas be in there with Vanessa?

If she had to pick one or the other as her number-one suspect, she'd choose Vanessa, but Jonas was desperate for the promotion because of his financial obligations with his sick son. He didn't know it, but she'd seen him playing online poker on his laptop one time when she went into his office to ask him a question. And she'd accidentally taken a call for him once from a collection agency. So how desperate was he to make senior partner? Did he see her and not Vanessa as the front-runner?

She stopped in the hall, tempted to put her ear to Vanessa's door, but then realized she was not talking to someone, but chanting some hip-hop song in Spanish. The woman who had clawed her way up from a Miami *barrio* was proud of being fluent in her native language—such a help in a South Florida law firm—but not proud of the tough past she tried to hide. Her father was in prison, and she was twice divorced before she was thirty. Talk about ambitious men having starter and trophy marriages on their way to the top—don't mess with Vanessa Guerena and, unless you're a useful or wealthy man, get out of her way!

Lisa went downstairs and out onto the stone-flagged patio that overlooked the lake. It was under the wooden deck above, which was really on the first floor, for the land sloped down to the dock. She could see Spike's bright red plane tied up there now instead of at the far end of the lake. With her flip-flops making a gentle slap-slap sound, she walked past the sauna. It looked like a small log cabin, off a ways by itself, with its wood burner standing outside it. She knew how good a sauna would feel, but Mitch was in the spa, so that's where she was going. She passed the stone barbecue and a bonfire pit on the way to the big hot tub Mitch was soaking in. Though he had not turned on the overhead light, she could see he was alone.

Like an emerald set in azure mist, the water, lit from below, bubbled and steamed around him. She hesitated. The roiling water produced roiling foam. For one moment, her waking nightmare leaped at her—her mother's face staring upward from fierce water, haunting her head and heart. Lisa blinked to clear the vision.

Eyes closed, Mitch was leaning back against the side but looked back to reach for a plastic glass and saw her. He seemed surprised, but he'd mentioned it before and repeated to her quietly after dinner that he'd be here.

"One of the perks of civilization," he said and stood to lift a hand to help her down the steps. Water slicked over his muscular shoulders and chest. Surely he wore a swimsuit in there. She shed her towel on the bench where he'd put his and gave him her hand to step down into the warm water. The black bikini she wore seemed out of place here in the Alaskan wilds. She saw—and felt—his eyes on her, riveted.

"Did you think I'd stay out of anything larger than a bathtub?" she tried to kid him, but her voice sounded shaky.

"No, I just knew you were exhausted out of your mind."

"I am, and you must be, too, but that doesn't mean I can sleep. But you don't think I'm out of my mind, or you wouldn't have agreed to help me," she said, settling into the warm foam, clear up to her shoulders. They had things to decide and do, so she had to keep on track.

It was a big hot tub, but she sat close so they could talk. She hoped the others wouldn't be showing up. From her bedroom window, she'd seen Vanessa, Jonas and Graham use it the night they arrived. So, she encouraged herself, since she was remembering all sorts of details, surely she was correctly recalling being pushed into the river.

They had to raise their voices slightly to be heard over the spa motor and gurgling water, so she looked around—even straight up at the veranda over them—to be sure they were alone, then moved closer to him on the curved tiled bench.

They discussed Jonas and Vanessa. She told him she remembered that Jonas might be in debt not only from medical bills but from gambling. He told her Vanessa had not composed her face fast enough upon realizing that they were safe. "You don't think the two of them could be in cahoots, do you?" she asked.

"Probably not," he said, sinking down a bit so his

chin nearly rested on the water. He hadn't shaved yet after their ordeal; the stubble shadowed his face. His eyes were deep in darkness. Although he had eaten enough for two men at dinner, he had a sort of gaunt-faced, hungry look. He didn't seem to be moving or even listening, but his hand touched her thigh, then took her hand and held it. Their fingers intertwined. That simple, strong but gentle gesture hit her harder than if he'd grabbed her and kissed her again.

"Working on this, together, we've got to remember that the walls—even the trees—have ears and eyes," he said. "We're looking for someone, but someone may be watching us."

"I know. I feel it, too. Like that time we were both being tailed when we were on that money launder-ing case—the one Graham took away from us be-cause he was afraid we were going to get hurt, even that organized crime might be involved. I wanted him to keep us on that, but he said our safety came first."

"Yeah. Or second at least, after the firm's good name."

"I can't believe you said that."

"Graham's a great guy, just like Ellie's father was, but they didn't get where they are, with all those powerful clients, just playing patty-cake. Hardball, more like."

She sighed. "I know." She was surprised at his criticism of Graham because the older man had seemed to fill the void in Mitch's life left by his yearning for his parents' and his older brother's approval. "But," she went on, trying to stay on track, "when the Bonners were raising money for Ellie's brother to run for state senate, they did everything aboveboard—no big lobbyists or other donors who would want a favor later—and look how well he's done. I suppose Graham's told you that Merritt's on the short list to get a cabinet position if the Democrats take back the White House."

"Ellie told me. You think I don't read papers or see the news up here?"

"You pooh-poohed my watching TV, but let's not get into that again."

"What should we get into again, sweetheart? Other than a hot tub?"

"When you rub your thumb on my palm like that, I can't think. At least it's better than our yelling at each other."

"Yeah, and I don't think a bull moose is going to rear up out of here, but you never know about a bull of a man. As I recall, you once called me a bull in the china shop of your life."

She laughed, but her voice sounded rough, low. She wasn't sure if he was trying to tease her or seduce her, but she had to get out of here, and now, because she was getting crazy—crazed—enough for him that she didn't care who saw them do what. "Your memory is too good," she said. "But I need to ask you one quick thing. How are we going to set things up for tomorrow so we can keep an eye on everyone? I could say more memories are starting to come back to me, then see who reacts how or tries to corner me."

"I'm going to tell everyone at breakfast that we're going to see Spike's sled dogs, even ride behind the teams, see how everyone does learning something really different."

"Without snow—the sleds have wheels?"

"It's how they work the dogs in the warm weather. Yeah, you go ahead and say something like that, but then don't get out of my sight in case someone does try to corner you."

"There are risks involved, Mitch, and we—I—may have to take them. Whoever shoved me in the river is hardly going to take out a gun and shoot me. I'm going to have to get alone with them individually, give them a chance to make a wrong move. And that reminds me, even though the site where I was pushed has surely been compromised by now, we should look at the scene of the crime, but I'm not going back there alone."

"I'll give it a quick early-morning search, but I probably obliterated footprints or anything else when I shoved that kayak up and over the ridge. I'll watch you walk to your door and you try to get some sleep," he said. "I'm hitting the rack really soon."

They stood, and he gave her a hand as she climbed out. She wrapped her robe around herself, then bent down to whisper, "I'm glad the lodge is online even if cell phones don't work here. I'm going to do background checks on our possibilities."

"Fine by me."

"Mitch, I—I think that should include your staff bec—"

"Whoa—"

"—because they might have been panicked I'd try to take you away or angry because I hurt you before. They're very loyal, at least Spike and Christine, especially Christine—"

"They wouldn't shove a guest in that raging river," he said, forgetting to keep his voice down. "Christine and I are just friends and coworkers who admire each other."

She opened her mouth to tell him he was blind if he thought Christine only admired him. Another woman could tell she adored him at the very least. Besides, he was so protective of the woman, just as he had been of her. But she just nodded and said, "Good night," and walked away before they could argue more.

From her room upstairs, Lisa looked down to see if she could tell if the underwater hot tub lights were still on. They weren't, so Mitch must have quickly followed her inside.

The sunset was smeared across the sky again, but not quite as colorful as the one she'd never forget. The twilight it cast was about that of a full moon. But then she saw a form move in the dusk, coming from the corner of the lodge, the same spot where Ginger had hovered when they'd returned. She couldn't tell if it was Ginger or not. Wouldn't she have gone back to her cabin at the other end of the lake by now? Her boat wasn't in sight.

It was just dim enough outside and the deck slanted at such an angle that she could not make out who it was. Probably not Spike or Mitch—too short, though the figure was slumped over and her perspective from this height distorted things. Wouldn't Graham's or Ellie's white hair show up, though the person could have on a hoodie or hat. He or she seemed to retrieve something from near the hot tub, then moved slowly back inside. Perhaps someone had been down to use the spa earlier and had left a watch or something, at least on one of the other benches she hadn't used.

Still in her bathing suit and robe, barefoot, Lisa tore into the hall and went partway down the stairs, stooping to see who had or would come in from the stone patio. No one. No one, at least, she could see.

Then Christine passed from somewhere below and went down the short hall into the kitchen with something in her hands. Such strong hands. She moved so silently.

As exhausted as she was, Lisa went upstairs, locked her bedroom door, looked in her closet and under the bed—even behind the shower curtain. Then she wedged a chair under her doorknob and took out her laptop to search the Internet for "Christine Tanaka" + "Yup'ik" + "Bear Bones, Alaska."

10

Lisa found nothing about a Christine Tanaka in her search, but then newspapers seemed scarce here on the Alaska frontier. Of course she hadn't seen the nearby little town of Bear Bones yet, and they were not going into larger Talkeetna until Saturday for something called—of all things—the Mountain Mother Contest, but she had seen no newspapers around the lodge. Small Alaska towns might have weekly papers or even monthly ones, she thought. She could try accessing the extensive personal information banks the law firm paid for, but then her search would be recorded for her coworkers to see.

Frowning, her bloodshot eyes almost crossing from exhaustion, she skimmed down through later pages of search entries. One had hit on Christine and Yup'ik. A Yup'ik woman, Christine Kagak, had been tried for the murder of her husband in a trial where she claimed to be an abused woman.

Lisa clicked on the article and watched wide-eyed as it filled the screen. Could it be the same woman?

Yes—a photo of her, leaving the courtroom in Fairbanks four years ago. Damn! Mitch said her husband died, not that he'd been murdered by Christine! Acquitted. She'd been acquitted! Her heart thudded as she forced herself to read slowly.

YUP'IK WOMAN ACQUITTED
OF SHOOTING HUSBAND
By Sara Whitehead

Fairbanks Daily News
September 4, 2004

Fairbanks—Cu'paq (Christine) Kagak, 27, was acquitted Tuesday of a charge of aggravated murder for shooting her husband, Clay Kagak, 34, with his own rifle. Had Mrs. Kagak been convicted, she would have served fifteen years to life. The defense claimed that Mrs. Kagak had been abused by her husband during their two-year marriage and produced photos to prove it. Her lawyer, Michael Vincent, said his client feared for her life.

Mrs. Kagak claimed that her husband had been drinking and was beating her again, so she shoved him down the stairs outside their home and tried to run back inside. When he pursued her, claiming he'd "kill her this time," she grabbed the rifle he'd used hunting caribou that morning and fired twice. He died later in the hospital.

Mr. Kagak was a plumber and the eldest son of a Yup'ik elder. Mrs. Kagak makes Inuit dolls for sale in local gift shops. The couple have no children. Yup'ik leaders who attended the trial told this reporter that Mrs. Kagak was no longer welcome among their people, but they and the exonerated woman refused further comment.

Lisa realized she wasn't breathing. She exhaled slowly to steady herself. Now she knew what Mitch had called Christine when she greeted them today—*Cu'paq,* her Yup'ik name. And she knew who made the exquisitely detailed dolls in the little library off the great room.

But beyond all that, she now knew what Mitch wasn't telling her. Could she trust him to help her, or was he withholding other things she should know? At least she'd found the truth about Christine's past. Lisa's heart went out to her for being a battered woman rejected by her people. But she had killed a man to protect herself. Would she try to kill a woman to protect the possibility of losing Mitch or the safe haven she'd evidently found here?

Lisa kept going back to one line of print, one thought. When Christine's first attempt to stop her husband didn't work—shoving him down the stairs—she had found another foolproof way.

Mitch came late to breakfast as everyone—including Lisa—ate heartily. She knew she'd need her strength today. Despite being upset about Mitch's covering for Christine, Lisa had eventually fallen asleep last night, but had plodded from nightmare to nightmare, not about her mother this time, but of herself tumbling down stairs into the river.

"Sorry to join you late," Mitch said as he seated himself at the head of the table, facing Graham at the other end, and reached for one of Ginger's huge blueberry muffins. Christine immediately appeared from the kitchen to pour him coffee, leaning close over his shoulder from behind. That move seemed so intimate to Lisa. And strangely nostalgic, too, for her grandmother had been a wonderful baker of muffins, pies, cookies and breads. She'd taught the art to Lisa and handed down her recipes, but Lisa hadn't had the time to bake those favorite old pastries for years.

"At least," Mitch went on with a nod Lisa's way, "I finally got everything settled with the Talkeetna sheriff and the state troopers. The *Talkeetna Good Times* wants to do an article, but I told them no interviews now—though they may show up anyway. I'll talk to them later. The article won't be out until Lisa's long gone—back in Florida, that is."

Graham, halfway through a stack of sourdough hotcakes, said, "I knew you could patch things over, handle it all without a ripple. You always were good at that."

Lisa saw Mitch's face light up. The two men had always had a mutual-admiration society going. She knew Graham and Ellie had once hoped Mitch might link up with their daughter. But surely, the fact he'd chosen Lisa instead was not motive enough for murder. No, that was too far-fetched.

She wondered how was she going to get Mitch alone with everyone around and a full day planned. She had to confront him with his skirting the truth about Christine. Or should she not bring that up and just see how far he went with half truths when he had vowed to help find her would-be murderer? Lisa had seen how he'd protected her in the river and on their trek back, but now that they were here, maybe he was protecting someone else.

"I was able to smooth things over with the authorities because it was an accident," Mitch said, ladling strawberry jam on his muffin while Christine put a plate of eggs and venison sausage in front of him. "Of course, if there were any hint of foul play, the Talkeetna sheriff—and I—would be all over things."

"Foul play?" Jonas said, with a sharp clink of his fork against his plate. "You've got to be kidding. Who would push or throw Lis—"

"No one here would," Mitch cut in. "That's why it's back to normal today."

Mitch's mere mention of foul play had taken Lisa,

as well as everyone else, by surprise. But she'd looked carefully, quickly at each face, exactly as she had last night when they'd told everyone the details of their ordeal. Mitch's ploy was a tactic she'd seen him use in court more than once. An apparently off-the-wall question, a bolt from the blue, the sudden reversal of direction. She should be used to it by now, especially since it was exactly the way he'd handled telling her he wanted to move to Alaska.

She noted that Graham had merely frowned. Spike looked so shocked he still held a big piece of his sourdough hotcake on a fork halfway to his mouth. And she'd seen that Jonas and Vanessa had exchanged swift looks.

"Lisa's falling in the river's a sad and bad enough event as is." Spike broke the silence. "So, thank God, it was just an accident and not deliberate. No one here would hurt any of our guests."

Lisa noted Christine said nothing but went back into the kitchen. Ellie, ever the upbeat, complimentary hostess, even when it wasn't her party, said, "Let's put that potential tragedy behind us, as Lisa has been brave enough to do, and treasure this day and this lovely place. I always like to look at the bright side of things. We are in a beautiful place with a fun day ahead. Breakfast has been hearty and delicious. Why, these pastries and breads are fabulous. I'd like to have a chat with Ginger about some of the recipes, though I'm sure it's the local ingredients that make the difference. Lingonberry tarts—it's a whole new world here. My, but she's a clever one to turn all this out each day, because I saw she has a hurt hand."

"Yes, ma'am," Spike said, obviously relieved at the change in topic. "An injury when our dad cut a tree down years ago. She uses a wood-fired cook-stove and oven, too, pretty much one-handed."

That probably eliminated Ginger as her assailant, Lisa thought. Whoever had pushed her had used two strong hands.

"Ah, her kitchen would give a glimpse into the pioneer past," Ellie said with a sigh. "I'd love to see Ginger's cabin, if she wouldn't mind a visit. I believe she is rather a private person. Perhaps you can tell me more about her later, Spike."

Lisa downed her coffee and peered over her cup rim. You'd think that Ellie, instead of Mitch, had been enlisted to investigate suspects. Though Ginger hadn't pushed her, she might inadvertently provide more background on Christine or Spike. "I'd love to see her place, too," Lisa said, "if you want someone to go with you later, Ellie."

Evidently not to be outdone, Vanessa chimed in, "Me, too, but I'd be even more excited about seeing how Christine makes those gorgeously detailed little Eskimo dolls in the other room. I'd love to buy one or two."

The conversation segued to their walk to Spike's place about a mile away. When he described it as being in the woods, Graham excused himself and went upstairs. He quickly returned with a wooden-framed picture he'd obviously taken off a wall—no, Lisa saw it was a framed quotation.

"Mitch," Graham said, "I hope you don't mind if I share these lines with the others. Mitch has this hanging in his suite upstairs."

Lisa put her cup down with a too-loud clink. Graham had not only been in Mitch's quarters, but had felt he could go back up without permission and take something out. Maybe they'd planned more than just sporting activities. Maybe Mitch *was* helping with the Bonners' selection process and this was somehow a setup.

"Sure," Mitch said, "but I'll bet some of you know this already. It's my favorite quote."

"Thoreau, from his *Walden Pond,*" Graham said, turning it toward himself to read, "'I went to the woods because I wished to live deliberately, to front only the essential facts of life, and see if I could not learn what it had to teach, and not, when I came to die, discover that I had not lived.' No doubt," he said, "Lisa and Mitch learned a lot about themselves these last difficult days, facing life and death."

Though Lisa was strangely touched, she noted Vanessa narrowed her eyes—an almost feral expression flitted across her face.

"I believe," Graham went on in his deep, oratorical tones, "we'll all learn a lot—and Ellie and I will learn what we need to know to decide."

"Alaska does that," Lisa said, almost before she realized she would speak. "It teaches you about yourself—but a lot about others, too." She leveled a look at Vanessa, then Jonas, then Christine, who was refilling Jonas's coffee cup, but looking up for once. Lisa looked at Mitch last. No one blinked; they all seemed frozen in a tableau as if waiting for her to add something else. Finally, Vanessa looked down at her empty plate. Mitch dared a nod and a smile at her, but it was Jonas who finally spoke.

"Anything that's a challenge does that—my son's illness has made me do things I never thought I'd do."

"Emerson's a brave kid," Graham said, somehow managing to break the tension as he reached over to squeeze Jonas's shoulder. "Let's make sure we get some pictures of you with Spike's huskies, because your boy will love that. Maybe we can even send some to him online before you get home. Okay, everyone, see you on the front porch in about fifteen minutes, then off we go into a part of that other world Ellie mentioned."

It's another world all right, Lisa thought, recalling her hallucinations about being in the land of Oz when Mitch rescued her from the river. No one was in Kansas—or South Florida—anymore.

Christine had no intention of going along with the guests to Spike's place, but both he and Mitch invited her. At least with so many other people around to see the huskies, it would be an opportunity to try to get over her nervousness. Clay had often abused his dogs, and they'd been snarly and nasty. She could understand why, but they'd been frightening to feed. If animals reflected their master's personalities and the treatment they'd been given, surely Spike's dogs would be happy and well-behaved. Still, she had a big knot in her stomach.

"I'm glad you came along, Christine," Lisa told her, dropping back to walk with her. Vanessa looked at them, but stayed next to Jonas. "I hear you made those beautiful Inuit dolls on display in the library and wanted to tell you how amazing they are."

"Did Mitch tell you that? Most visitors don't know to say Inuit instead of Eskimo."

"He told me about saying Inuit or Yup'ik, but not about the dolls. Vanessa mentioned it. So, you seem very content here at the lodge. Are you from this area?"

Mitch had told this woman she was Yup'ik, so what else had he told her? Christine wondered. "From Fairbanks," she said, "but I like looking forward, not back. And yes, I'm more than content here. I've finally found a good job—a home."

She glanced ahead at Mitch, leading the group with Mr. Bonner beside him. They were strung out on their walk to Spike's place along the forest path lined with thick birch and alder, overshadowed by the occasional tall Sitka spruce. This was one of the hiking trails groomed for cross-country skiing in the winter. It was at least ten degrees colder here, and she shivered. Ahead, Mrs. Bonner was now walking between Vanessa and Jonas. Other than snatches of conversations, Christine heard only birdcalls and the crunch of last year's leaves underfoot and the bear bells Vanessa carried, though bears would never bother a group of people. And she heard her own heartbeat and too-rapid breathing, not from the walk but from this talk.

"I hope," Lisa said, "you can give me a little advice about Ginger. She seems to like her solitude, so do you think she'd mind if some of us visit her, or should we ask her first—maybe have you do it for us?"

"Most Alaskans value their privacy and independence. But I'm sure she'd like the extra money, too, if you'd want to buy some of her baked goods to take home. She's saving money to pay Spike back for all the wood he cuts for her, though I don't think he'll take a dime, even with the cost of airplane fuel. I'll ask her when she brings tonight's things—late this afternoon."

"Late afternoon? Oh, yes, I saw her boat just before I fell in the river. I remember that much. But I'd appreciate it if you ask her. I'll try to head Ellie and Vanessa off at the pass if they plan to visit her earlier. Please tell her we'd like to place an order for some items—which reminds me again, as Vanessa mentioned, do you sell your dolls?"

"I made those several years ago, but I'm pretty busy here. I used to make them not just for money, but to preserve Yup'ik ways, but now I just have other interests. Mitch wanted them on display there, not me..."

Her voice trailed off. She hoped that didn't sound lame or rude. In a way it was the truth. This woman Mitch had almost married was watching her very closely, out of the corners of her eyes. *Iah,* that was the look of a lawyer, all right.

"Sorry," Christine blurted, "but I need to talk to Mitch about something for later. The hand-cranked aurora borealis ice cream, our special surprise for all our guests."

Though Christine had no question about that or anything else for Mitch right now, she forced a little smile and hurried faster before Lisa Vaughn could ask her more questions.

Jonas came back to walk with Lisa shortly after Christine left. "I just wanted to tell you something I hope helps," he said. "I was in a real bad car wreck when I was eighteen—I wasn't driving. Anyway, I got banged around pretty good, even with a seat belt on—concussion, brief coma. But what I wanted to tell you is that, even though I recovered—no residual problems—I never could recall the wreck itself, or what led up to it, the few minutes before the car rolled. Hopefully, your memories of that tumble in that monster river will be just like that."

"Hopefully?"

"Yeah, you don't want to be reliving that over and over in your mind. Just let it be blanked out—the things surrounding it. Is that the way it is for you, just a blank right before and during your fall?"

A chill snaked up her spine. Jonas was trying to find out how much she could recall? But why? Just sympathy and support? Or was he desperate to know if she'd seen or heard something—someone? Maybe him.

"That's the way it was at first," she told him, keeping her eyes on the forest path, hoping he wouldn't see the lie on her face—lawyers were skilled at psyching such things out. "But I really feel some of it's coming back to me, bit by bit. I really think I will recall everything."

"Well, sometimes it's best to just let tough times stay buried. You know—considering where we're headed—to let sleeping dogs lie. Can't wait to see these huskies. In photos they seem to have the bluest eyes. Never had a job interview, so to speak, where the criteria had to do with racing dogs and zip lines and river rafting. What a résumé we're going to have when we get out of here. I was really nervous about all this at first, but what could possibly happen on a dog sled, especially one on wheels on grass in warm weather?"

He sounded nervous. Very nervous. Either from what lay ahead or what she'd said. "I would have agreed with you a few days ago," she told him, "but what could happen just standing on an elevated path between a lovely lake and a white-water river, right?"

"Famous last words, you mean?" Jonas said with a forced laugh that showed his white teeth.

Sharp teeth, Lisa thought, as they came into the

clearing where Spike's property began. Teeth like the beavers cutting down trees or bears ripping apart river salmon. However much Mitch had not told her about Christine, she had to at least find a way to get him alone to tell him about Jonas.

11

Lisa thought Spike's Siberian huskies were beautiful. As Mitch had said about the moose that had terrified her at first, they were also majestic—their thick, silvery coat hairs tipped with gray or black, their deep-throated, eager barks. They sounded like howlers, but her feelings toward them were a far cry from hearing the wolves that night in the wilderness. The dogs had perky ears and curled, wagging tails and alert, sky-blue eyes. She could tell how much they wanted to please their master, especially when they saw him pull the three-wheeled sleds out of the storage shed.

"Okay, here's some info before I hitch four dogs to each of your sleds," Spike announced as everyone gathered around him at the gate to the dog yard.

Lisa eyed the metal and wooden sleds, mounted on sturdy-looking wheels for the dogs' summer exercise. "I'll give some background on mushing and how to handle the teams, because you'll each—Lisa, Vanessa and Jonas—be getting a chance to control one of these sleds on a short run thataway," he said, pointing.

All around them, grass about a half-foot high and white wildflowers blanketed the clearing, blowing like green waves with whitecaps, like river foam. Lisa could picture the dogs rushing into it, pulling her deeper into a whirling current of green and white... She jerked alert. That memory, that vision, had sneaked up on her like it used to. A flashback of being in the river, or of losing Mother and Jani again. Or was she still so exhausted she'd dozed off for a microsecond, falling into the dream that had haunted her for years? Mother's face through the blurry barrier, her voice calling, calling, "Come with me— come on." Her mouth open, her eyes wide from behind the glass or water or—

Lisa shook her head to clear it and forced herself to look around at the here and now, to recognize reality. Spike's log cabin and his dog yard were in a large, oval-shaped clearing on the edge of the forest they had walked through from the lodge. The huskies lived in a miniature fenced-in village, where each dog had one of the small wooden houses set in two neat rows.

Spike had said the dogs slept, ate and played with their neighbors, stealing bones or nipping at ears or tails, but they were always ready to run. *Ready to run.* She could recall Graham saying, "So, are we ready to run?" more than once before a team of Carlisle, Bonner & Associates attorneys went into court on some huge corporate lawsuit or defamation trial. Not "are we ready to go" or even "ready to rumble," like Vanessa sometimes said, but *ready to run.*

"Here's the main thing," Spike told them, stepping up on the back of one of the sets of runners elevated on temporary wheels, as if he were on the witness stand, testifying in court. "It's easy to feel out of control on a dog sled, but you have to control yourself and the dogs. If you don't display leadership to them, they won't bother to obey you. They're intelligent pack animals, but they need to be led. To their way of thinking, I'm the alpha dog here. Likewise, you need to keep control while you're each in charge of four of them."

So, Lisa thought, this activity did make some sense in a race to see who could assume the leadership role of a senior partner. She tried to focus on Spike's advice. He seemed totally in his element here.

Vanessa asked, "Are their doghouses really warm enough in the brutal winters? You know, animal rights and all that."

"Sure," Spike told her. "Just take a look at their coats, even thicker than that in the winter. The breed can withstand temps as low as seventy-six degrees below Fahrenheit. Their cold months are like how Florida feels to you in the winter. Still, I keep lots of straw in the houses, the same houses that give them needed shade in these warm months. Like Mitch and me, these dogs thrive in Alaska.

"The word *musher* can mean the drivers or the

dogs," Spike went on. "When it's the dogs, there's two kinds of mushers, the long-distance ones or the sprint mushers, like mine. They run shorter courses at faster speeds than those in the Iditarod or Yukon Quest races, but these are my kind of dogs."

"Fast dogs and fast airplanes for Spike Jackson," Ellie said.

"You got that right, Mrs. Bonner. Okay, just a few instructions, then we'll try it, maybe get us a little race going, since you're all here for a race for the senior partner position."

So, even Spike knew Graham and Mitch's game plan, Lisa thought. Not as much bonding as competition, at least in this activity.

"You stand back on the runners, see?" he went on, demonstrating. "And you hold on to the handlebow, this piece here. And I do mean hold on for dear life, 'cause the dogs will yank and lunge at first, though it's a smooth ride—'specially in snow—once they get going. Their towline's attached here to the front of the sled, see? There's a foot brake here for slowing or stopping," he said, demonstrating it, "but you really got to lay into it. The dogs will be harnessed, but there's no reins."

"Then how do you steer?" Jonas asked.

"Fortunately, on this run, you don't have to worry about a lot of commands to your lead dog and team. All you've got to know is my dogs follow the command 'mush!' to get going and 'halt!' to stop. Lots of folks these days use 'hike!' for the start, but that sounds like football to me. I like the old ways. I still use leather towlines 'stead of that new, fancy polyethylene rope, too."

"But on grass like this," Vanessa said, "we won't go too fast, right? I'm as raring to go as these dogs and love the speed of water sports, but a group of dogs pulling all this weight—on wheels—can't go too fast."

"Just remember," Spike told her, "these dogs are bred to run, so once you're on and moving, don't try to get off. And, like I said, don't let go, or you could get throwed."

Don't let go and *keep control.* Lisa clung to Spike's words of advice. That was the key to sprint racing behind sled dog teams, but it was also the story of her life right now.

Christine hated to admit it, but she was forming a grudging admiration for Lisa Vaughn. First of all, for someone to survive the Wild River was awesome, as if the woman had a supernatural protector way beyond Mitch. While Spike was hitching four dogs to each of the three sleds, Christine poured coffee into cups Spike had set out and just watched the others.

She noted that only Lisa was showing any interest in the dogs themselves right now, and they were the engine that made everything run in a race like this. Vanessa, who looked like she could have stepped out of one of those luxury-goods catalogs Ginger was obsessed with, stayed clear of the excited animals and sipped her coffee at a distance. Now that was body language to show what she really felt about this opportunity. Jonas had Mr. Bonner taking photos of him with the dogs in the background. Mrs. Bonner and Mitch were talking off to the side as Christine moved closer to Spike.

"They're great-looking mushers," she told him. "You take good care of them."

"Glad you came along. Yeah, they're tough and feisty, real special. It's my honor to care for them. I swear, some of them are smarter than I am. I control them only to the extent that we make a good team."

She had to smile at that. And the warm—even hot—look he gave her was a revelation. His eyes burned into hers, went down her body, then up like a caress before he turned away to bring up the next dog to its place on the towline. *Iah,* but she felt like he'd really touched her. Little butterflies beat in the pit of her belly. It was the closest she had ever felt to him, and yet there was a big dog between them.

"I just had a bad experience with them before," she tried to explain. "With some huskies that weren't loved but abused. Since yours are raring to go, I guess I'd better not pet one of them."

"I'd say pat, instead of pet, but sure you can," he told her. "You gotta be a bit strong with them or they won't even feel it. Even in these warm months, their thick coats are like armor."

His eyes devoured her again. Was he talking about being strong with the dogs or with him? Christine gave the one he'd just harnessed a good, strong pat on the back.

Clay's dogs had been howlers and growlers, as if he'd left them behind in the yard to keep her in the house. But this husky wagged his tail and gave her almost a grateful look. She blinked back tears at how good that felt, like she'd connected with this powerful animal. She sucked in a deep breath, held it and let it out. Something sharp and hurtful inside her uncoiled. It was like the armor that had kept her from Spike and Spike from her had a chink in it. But she was still scared of the feeling of trusting him, so she blurted out, "Lisa said the ladies would like to visit Ginger's place, but I don't know. I'll ask her."

"I know. Suggest to them that they go one at a time," he said as he brought the next eager dog over to be harnessed. "If they want to place bakery orders to take home when they see her kitchen, she'll probably say it's okay. I could stop by her place if she'd rather have me there."

"Wait till they see it," Christine said, patting this dog, too. *"Little House on the Prairie* with Neiman Marcus, Gucci and Tiffany catalogs all over. Yeah, for the extra money, I bet she'll agree."

"Okay, listen up, you mushers!" Spike called out. "I'm almost done here, then a few more instructions. You'll be taking your teams in a straight line to the edge of the clearing, so just let them run. See that barrier of straw bales down there by the trees? You should try to stop them with the brake and yelling,

'Halt! Halt!' But if they don't, they'll stop at the bales. There's only one little dip in the course, a pretty straight shot, but if you want to walk it first, go ahead, then get back here for 'on your marks, get set—go!'"

He lowered his voice and looked at Christine again. "You want to try this sometime, just let me know. Or I can put you in the sled and off we go. Well, darn—a poet and I didn't know it."

He grinned as he went to get the first dog for the last sled. Christine gave the nearest husky another strong pat, and, smiling, went over to clean up the coffee cups.

Lisa surprised herself. Her insides were doing flip-flops when she didn't think driving a husky team on a sled—with wheels, no less—would bother her at all. Besides, after being in that *monster river,* as Jonas had called it, she didn't think anything would scare her again.

Just as when she was assigned to a new case, she'd done her best to assess this situation. She'd examined a sled close up, talked to the dogs, patted them, observed how eager they were to please. She had skipped the coffee, even though Spike had said anyone who wanted to could use the facilities in his log home. Anytime she got keyed up, she felt she had to run to the bathroom, and coffee wouldn't help.

She had only examined the course to the dip in the blowing grass, though the others were walking the entire distance. Looking at Jonas and Vanessa ahead of her, she realized she should have gone with them instead of continuing to study the dogs and the sleds, because she wanted to see how comfortable her rivals were together and around her.

It was still a long shot that they were working together against her, but they could have made a pact to reduce the senior partner candidates by one. After all, how many coworkers had tried to sabotage another's career? She'd had several defamation and discrimination cases based on that sad reality and had won good settlements for her clients, too.

She saw Mitch was finally alone, coming out of Spike's cabin, and she strode straight toward him. "Mitch, I need to talk to you privately and that's obviously easier said than done. I don't mean here—no time."

"I know. Rather than sneaking off the lodge grounds or whispering in a corner—or sneaking into each other's rooms—let's just make the lodge wine cellar our meeting place."

"I didn't see a wine cellar on our tour."

"I never show it, my ultimate sanctuary. The small door in the reading room goes down to it. There's a light switch at the top of the stairs. An underground room in Alaska is really rare with the permafrost and rock barriers under almost everything, but Uncle John dug it out bit by bit over the years. Close the door behind you and watch the steps going down, but once we're there, it's soundproof. Midafternoon, about three, okay? If someone's in the reading room so you can't come down then, we'll get a Plan B. Here comes Graham, so if you found out anything, save it until then—unless it's life-and-death."

You might know he'd put it that way, she thought, annoyed at him again for what he hadn't told her about Christine's past.

"One quick thing," he added, and she turned back. "Before breakfast, I went out and checked the site where you fell in. No telltale footprints since you and I, then Christine and Ginger, were all over the area and my shoving the kayak through obliterated a lot."

"Ginger was there?"

"She's the one who spotted the kayak trail from the water and told Christine. She said Ginger picked up the cooler you dropped and gave it back to her. They saw the food being eaten by a wolverine they surprised at his feast. So—site of the crime—nothing helpful."

"Hey, you two," Graham greeted them. "With all the time you had wandering in the wilderness, I'm glad you still have things to say to each other. I know there were hard feelings on both sides for a while, and I was hoping this visit would allow you to settle things before you both go back to your own worlds."

He stood between them, holding one of each of their upper arms so they were facing each other. Lisa had been planning to ask Graham to give her away at their wedding. Their positioning reminded her of that, as if Graham were ready to hand her over to Mitch at the front of the church.

"No, really," Graham went on, "did you get the past settled while you were gone? You used to be quite a legal team for us."

"Yes, we did reminisce a bit," Mitch told him. "Cleared the air, which is clear enough in Alaska anyway."

"I must apologize again for taking you two off the casino money-laundering case right after you told me you'd been seriously—secretly—dating, but, as I said then, I didn't mean it as any sort of censure or punishment. You know I was starting to have a concern that some of our clients or their competition were playing too rough, trying to find out how much we'd dug up."

Lisa said, "Being tailed and having my condo and car bugged with a listening device was a pretty good hint someone meant business. But it was a key case, Graham, with important repercussions to expose people in high places. We would have both stuck with it—"

"Except then," he interrupted, "when you didn't stick together personally, everything changed. Then, with Mitch leaving, I just couldn't have you alone on that case, Lisa."

"I'm glad you took her off it," Mitch admitted, "but Jonas could have come on board. I was surprised you got permission from the court to withdraw from the case, yet didn't report the harassment we were getting. Frankly, I was afraid someone had gotten to you—threatened you—to make you back off."

For a moment Graham looked furious. His nostrils flared and his eyes narrowed, but he quickly got control of himself. "No, nothing like that," he insisted, shaking his head and finally letting go of their arms.

"Yeah, but I could smell a distant rat behind our client's maneuverings," Mitch argued. "I just wonder how far the stench would have gone up the trail if we'd pursued it."

"*Up* the trail?" Graham challenged. "I'd say more like *down* to the dregs of society. Some sort of mobster or even foreign scum. So, did you two ever find—"

"Okay, mushers, let's go!" Spike's voice resounded. "And remember the key term for when you want your dogs to start running. I'm not gonna say it yet, or you'll be chasing your sleds. You'll shout the word. And don't use it unless you're set for a big jerk into action."

Lisa, Mitch and Graham went over to the starting line. "Just remember, hang on," Spike repeated. "Lisa, your sled is over there on that far side, Jonas in the middle, Vanessa here."

As she'd seen Spike do, Lisa climbed up on the back runners. They were plenty wide for her feet but were off the ground the height of the eight-inch wheels. She gripped the bar as he'd showed them and pressed the brake hard, to see how much it gave. "All right, boys and girls," she said to her team of four jumpy dogs, in the calmest but sternest voice she could manage, "we're going to win this race."

"Lisa," Jonas said beside her. "Graham's going to take pictures of me for Emerson, so could you and I switch sleds? That way I'd be on the outside where he can get better shots."

"I guess so," she said. "The sleds all look the same."

She jumped down and switched with him, talking now to these four eager dogs. Had Spike put Jonas between her and Vanessa's sleds because the middle team needed stronger handling, or had it been random? Whatever. She could handle the middle position.

Spike had his back to them as he talked to Vanessa. Did she need extra instructions or courage? Lisa heard her say, "These pets of yours are way bigger than my chihuahua, that's all!"

"These are working dogs!" Spike said, evidently not getting the humor. Then he bellowed, "Okay, everybody. Three, two, one—let's go!"

Lisa managed to shout "Mush!" to her team before the others did. The dogs jerked and strained in their harnesses; the towline pulled taut. She shot out in front, but the other two teams were soon nearly even with hers. The lunging huskies got the sleds going fast, faster.

It was exhilarating. As fast as on the river, but, thank heavens over solid ground and green grass. She felt she was flying, like riding the outer edge of a huge cresting wave. A sense of power, her own and the dogs', filled her. She held on for dear life, as Spike had said. Hang on—keep control. She had to control her investigation into who pushed her, but keep Mitch on her side, too. The wind whipped her hair. Was that just from her speed, or was a storm coming up? Beyond the forest, the cumulous clouds looked like snow-topped trees, and the lofty Talkeetnas speared the endless azure sky.

The dip in the ground came closer, closer. The dogs took it at full speed, down—up. She bounced hard at the bottom, almost off the runners, but held on. Vanessa was way behind, and Jonas...

He gave a shout, almost a shriek. Lisa turned her head only to see him fly backward off the sled while his team rushed on, dragging their towline while his empty sled slowed and stopped. She stepped hard on the brake, shouting, "Halt! Halt!"

Vanessa's dogs, then her sled, whizzed past as Lisa's team slowed. She stood on tiptoe on her sled and windmilled her arm for help from the others, then jumped off and ran to Jonas. He lay flat on his back in the grassy swale, staring straight up at the sky, not moving. Was he in shock? Paralyzed?

"Jonas?" she cried, kneeling next to him. "Jonas, are you hurt?"

Nothing at first. No response. It brought back to her the way she felt when Mitch pulled her out of the river. Dazed. Scared.

Mitch and Spike, both out of breath, got to them first, just as Jonas blinked, then shut his eyes tight before opening them again. Groaning, he looked up into Lisa's face, then, blessedly, moved his arms and legs.

"Not quite like the car wreck," he said, "but damn near."

"Thank God, you're all right," Mitch said, kneeling on his other side. "That's never happened before. Let's check for broken bones."

Graham, Ellie and Christine arrived, pressing in, and Vanessa came running back from the finish line where her team had stopped at the straw bales.

"Is he all right?" Graham demanded as Mitch and Spike helped him sit up slowly. "Jonas, that's going to be one hell of a picture for your boy to see."

"Yeah. I think I'm fine—just surprised," Jonas told them, moving his arms and legs again.

"Stand back and let him have a moment," Mitch said.

Lisa walked to Jonas's sled, where Spike was examining the towline. It was broken, but had it been chewed through, or even sawed apart? The end Spike held looked ragged. And no one had said so yet, but this sled was the one Spike had assigned to her.

When they all gathered in Spike's living room over more coffee and a tray of Ginger's cookies, Mitch was surprised that his old lawyer self rose to the surface. He knew Jonas could sue Spike or even him. Some attorneys were even more litigious than their clients.

"Are you sure you're all right?" Mitch asked Jonas again. "We can call for a doctor to check you out."

"No, I'm fine," Jonas told him. "If Lisa was fine

after her much worse ordeal, I'm more than fine." They'd insisted he tilt back in Spike's leather recliner; the other chairs were all straight-backed Sitka spruce. "My pride's the only thing that's hurt, but my boy's going to get a good laugh out of it, and that's worth something. Those dogs must have almost chewed through that old, traditional leather towline you like, and you didn't spot it," he said, turning to Spike. "But we learn a lot from our mistakes. No, just like Lisa who walked miles with her bruises and pain, I'm raring to go. And I think we've had enough so-called accidents for one trip."

Spike looked like he wanted to defend his dogs, but he just nodded and mumbled that he was sorry. Actually, he was seething, because he thought he'd been set up, but Mitch had told him not to say anything about it, other than that he had no idea how the accident happened. Mitch's eyes met Lisa's across the pine-walled living room lined with aerial photos of Alaska. He wondered if she was thinking what he was—that Jonas might be using this accident to get attention, to draw it away from her harrowing river run. She'd been brave; now Jonas was making a comparison.

But could his former protégé have set himself up for this? Mitch agonized. Jonas had traded sleds with Lisa at the last minute, changing what Spike had arranged, so rigging the potential accident—for Lisa—could also fall on Spike's shoulders. Or could Jonas have sawed through his own towline after the dogs started out? Spike had whispered he was positive that sabotaged piece of leather was intact before the race. And it was really worrying him that Jonas had just called what happened to him as well as to Lisa a "so-called" accident.

Mitch told Jonas, "I can walk back and get the truck so you can ride to the lodge."

"Hey, my man, I'm cool—really."

"Then we'll head back in about ten minutes," Mitch announced, forcing a smile. "Now, don't eat too many of Ginger's great sugar cookies, because we'll have a light lunch and then get some downtime this afternoon."

Mitch went into the kitchen and slipped out the back door to get a minute to himself. He loved his new life and trusted his staff, but something bad was going on here. Two potentially injurious, possibly fatal events with his old friends and associates—both maybe aimed at Lisa. He needed to clear his head.

Taking slow, deep breaths, he looked up at the vast sky. As usual, it seemed to offer several scenarios—clear blue to the east, gray clouds coming in, and to the north he could almost imagine the early wisps of the aurora borealis they'd enjoy this winter. But would he really enjoy it anymore during those long nights after Lisa had come here, walked here, slept here—then gone. Though the day was still warm, he hunched his shoulders as the wind ruffled at his shirt and hair. It would really ruin his and Graham's outdoor plans for these final days if the wind brought rain.

He turned to go back inside, but Graham stepped out, as if his thinking of the man had summoned him.

"Jonas is right," Graham said, blocking his way and stepping out to push him back a bit. He talked fast and low. "We all learn from our mistakes. As desperate as he is for money, it may have been his mistake—or even setup—but don't let on I said that. Anyway, I won't let Jonas sue, so stop worrying."

"You read me pretty well."

"So, Jonas's accident aside, how do you assess the way our three candidates reacted here today?"

Mitch cleared his throat, stalling to decide how forthright to be, then decided to just go with the truth, even though someone else here must be living a lie. Graham's support had meant a lot to him over the years, and he had been honored when the Bonners decided to bring the firm's business to him, especially after he'd deserted them. Besides betraying Lisa, letting Graham down then had also been hell.

"Lisa realized that understanding the dogs—maybe even bonding with them—was what mattered," he told Graham. "Jonas and Vanessa walked the entire course to check out the lay of the land, which was good, but Spike had suggested that. Lisa went down partway, but she was doing more homework and independent thinking in what was a new situation."

"True," Graham agreed. "Points on all sides, but advantage Lisa—and I won't call you prejudiced for her on that. Plus, she was willing to forfeit winning the race to stop and help Jonas. Sympathy, empathy, whatever you want to call it, has always been one of her strengths, probably because of her own tragedy."

Yeah, Mitch thought, unless it meant understanding and forgiving the man she'd promised to marry. But he said only, "Vanessa claimed she didn't see Jonas was down."

"Do you believe her?"

"No. I saw her turn back and look, but she must have either decided Lisa could handle it or that she wanted to win the race at any cost. And I think she was scared of the dogs, despite how two other women—Lisa and Christine—were making friends with them. But this outdoor life stuff is hardly Vanessa's thing. She can come off as bold, almost brazen, but strange situations can scare her. I think she knows things aren't black and white, but always sees potential problems in between."

"As a lawyer, she's got to learn to deal with the grays, then present them to a jury or judge as black and white, if need be. So the question is, if Vanessa lied to protect herself, is that a weakness or strength for being senior partner? Let's face it, having a savvy Latina as senior partner's a good move for the firm— a woman, and one who's the right ethnic mix for South Florida," Graham said.

"I'd like to think you'll make your final decision on who will tell you the truth in any sort of a race or struggle—or when the pressure's on in a case, black, white or gray."

Graham's steely eyes met Mitch's steady stare.

"Mitch, a word to the wise." Graham tapped his index finger on Mitch's chest as he spoke. "Whether or not Jonas is milking this accident for all it's worth to get attention today, if you take other bonding groups to Spike for sledding on grass or snow, make sure he examines his equipment. He's not the sharpest knife in the drawer, and you are, so watch him. And I don't want Ellie going up alone in that plane with him again," he concluded and went back inside.

Mitch was glad he'd left, because his first instinct was to defend Spike. And he would defend him—and himself—if anything came of a potential lawsuit later, no matter what Graham had just promised. At least he'd jumped through the proper hoops to be able to practice law in this state. Sure, he needed to keep an eye on Spike, but on everyone else, including—as much as it hurt him to think it—Graham. And, evidently, he was just blowing it off that Jonas might have sabotaged his own towline so that he could milk the situation for his own benefit, despite the risk of injury. Jonas was a good athlete, a former college football player who no doubt knew how to take falls. If Graham knew all that, he wasn't letting on. So, how truthful was his former mentor and boss in general?

Hell, Mitch groused silently as he headed back inside, once a suspicious lawyer, always a suspicious lawyer. But was someone after Lisa and/or Jonas? Was Vanessa to blame, or was she next in someone's vendetta? Or was all of this part of some sort of test he hadn't been clued in on, a secretive trial by the clever Graham Bonner?

What was that crazy quote from Shakespeare he'd thought of in the middle of the night when he was agonizing over keeping Lisa safe if someone really was out to hurt her? *The first thing we do, let's kill all the lawyers.*

12

Lisa was really ready to talk to Mitch as she entered the library just before three that afternoon. She needed to have it out with him about Christine, Jonas—even something she'd noticed about Graham. So she was really disappointed to find Christine in the little room, dusting her dolls.

"Your dolls," Lisa said, eyeing the door to the wine cellar. "I'll bet they bring back memories."

"I try to live in the here and now."

"Well, I think they're lovely, and I'm sure each tells a tale, or preserves some precious piece of the past."

"You should have been a writer, not a lawyer."

"Lawyers do a lot of writing."

Lisa approached the four-foot-long shelf of dolls, none over one foot high. Most were of single adults, but there was a group of children with one child on a blanket four others were holding.

"What are the children doing with that blanket?" she asked, then realized she should just sit down and pretend to read a book and not engage this woman in conversation. Maybe then Christine would leave. The woman reminded Lisa of the sort of elementary school teacher who had eyes in the back of her head. Mitch had said not to get upset if someone here kept her from coming down, but she was feeling so uptight about seeing him, frustrated but so eager.

"Blanket toss game," Christine replied, blowing on the white fur parka of a female figure.

"I've heard of that. It must be fun and a little scary."

"It is. I made it from a real piece of my own baby blanket."

"I had one of those. I tried to give it to my baby sister once, but it had been washed so much it was pretty ratty at that point, and my mother said not to. It looks like all these clothes are so authentic—not that I've seen Yup'ik clothes."

Christine nodded but Lisa saw her eyes fill with tears. "These are all made from coiled grass I picked, cured and dried," she said. "Sewn with caribou sinew, seal skin *mukluks* on all their feet, just like full-sized ones. I carved their wooden faces with my knife. And these decorations," she added, pointing to a dry, whitish material, "are scraped-out dried seal gut."

Christine turned to look at her as she said that. Their faces were only a foot apart. "I'm really impressed," Lisa said, not budging.

"You're the first white person who didn't say *ick* or *yuk* when I said that."

"Cultures are different. I still think these are beautif—"

"Yup'iks believe in modesty. Cooperation, not competition, like what the Bonners have set up for all of you. That would be frowned on among my people, so I must not boast of my own work."

"I agree that humility and cooperation are admirable, but my culture is losing that with its emphasis on self-esteem, getting ahead and besting the next guy." As she said that, Lisa realized that she, too, had been caught up in that race, maybe a rat race. Where was the line between civilization and wilderness? And were things really different here?

"Since you understand, I will tell you more. This doll here," Christine said, picking up one of a pretty girl in a beige parka with a black-and-white design, "is my 'putting away doll,' the one each girl stores when she has her first menstruation." She put that back almost reverently and selected another one of a young girl who held a half-woven basket in one hand. It looked more worn that the others. "And this is a doll my mother was given as a child to replace a lost sister, just to play with, to hold in the night because of the death—

"What?" she asked as Lisa's eyes brimmed with tears which, when she blinked, speckled her cheeks. "What did I say to—"

"I lost a sister, just a baby. Lost my mother at the same time in an accident—a drowning. I don't tell many people. I just— That's a lovely custom," she said, pointing at the doll again, then fumbling for a tissue in her jacket pocket.

To Lisa's surprise, Christine turned to her and rested her big, strong hands on her shoulders. Lisa stiffened. Were they hands that had pushed her down the ridge into the river? Here, Lisa thought, she'd meant to draw this woman out to find out more about her past and she'd blurted out the defining moment— besides Mitch deserting her—of her own. She had to pull herself together and get down to see him.

"I'm sure you have things to get ready in the kitchen," she told Christine, swiping her tears from under her eyes as the woman pulled her hands back. "I— If you don't mind, I'll just stay in here a few minutes."

"Having some time to yourself can help," Christine said with a solemn nod. "But being alone too much does not work in the long run. Here in Alaska, with so few folks for so many wide-open spaces, people need each other."

"Yes, I see that, and not just because I would never have survived without Mitch in the river and the wilds. People here seem to have time for each other, back to the basics of living and friendship somehow. They seem open, honest and trustworthy."

She studied the striking woman to see if there would be a flicker of uneasiness, guilt, even shame over what she'd just heard. But Lisa saw none of that in her face, body language or demeanor. And in trying to trap Christine, Lisa realized she'd been deceptive herself and that she truly believed what she'd said about the Alaskans she'd met so far.

Christine's gaze remained steady; she even nodded in understanding that made Lisa not mistrust this woman so much as her own past. Had she been superficial with others, too busy or afraid of loss to build deep relationships, maybe even with Mitch? And then, had she shut herself off even more when, like her mother and sister, he'd left her? Now she was suspicious of almost everyone here, when she wanted to be able to trust people more.

"I've gotta admit," Christine said in a soft, steady voice, "despite some problems I've had, this lodge and this wilderness is right where I want to be and stay."

Was that an inadvertent admission Christine had decided not to be alone and to protect her place here with Mitch at any cost? Was it a carefully, softly delivered threat, or was it more Alaskan straight talk, real life?

Here Lisa had been planning to accuse this woman to Mitch and she was coming to trust and like her. But then, she'd once felt the same way about the other suspects, too.

After Christine left her alone with only the dolls watching her, Lisa dried her eyes and blew her nose. She hoped Mitch was still waiting below for her, if he was down there at all. He had responsibilities and needed to keep all his guests happy—even the one he was trying to expose.

She opened the narrow wooden door a crack. A breath of chill air and wan light emanated from below. "Mitch?"

"Be careful on the steps." His voice floated to her.

She saw the steps were actually large notches cut from a big, debarked tree trunk that slanted downward in a narrow passageway of hewn stone. The more she saw and learned about Duck Lake Lodge, the more she wished she'd known Mitch's uncle John, the man who had left him this precious heritage.

She closed the door behind her and descended, keeping her hand on the cool, rough stone wall since there was no banister. Mitch appeared at the bottom of the steps and gave her a hand.

"I used to love this hideaway when I was a kid," he told her. "I don't share it with many people."

She wondered if Christine had been down here, but of course, the chef and housekeeper could well have been. She saw the three walls of shelves were lit from behind. They were not tight to the stone walls but had space for a person to squeeze in behind, either to access wine bottles from both sides or to keep them dry if the walls were damp or cold. He gestured for her to follow him around a shelf, and she was in awe. It was like being in a dim cave with huge, backlit sparkling gems studding the stone. Or as if they were being watched by glowing ogre eyes of green and amber.

A vision flashed at her quick as lightning—her

mother's eyes, green as the sea, staring at her through glassy water. She forced it away.

"Quite a collection," she said, looking around. The room itself was only about five feet square, with one chair and an overturned crate for a table. They stood facing each other on the rough-hewn floor.

"A hobby of my uncle's, but I've added to it," he explained. "So, what did you think of the Jonas-fall-from-grace fiasco today? Spike says he's positive all those leather towlines were in excellent working order and that the dogs had no chance to gnaw through one."

"But he can't prove it."

"Did you see anything to make you think Jonas took the risk of cutting his towline?"

"I can't be positive, but if I had to testify, I'd say it was intact when I was briefly on that sled before him. I was looking out at the dogs, talking to them, so I didn't think to check on that. He's the one who suggested we switch sleds, so Graham could get better pictures of him—which means we could ask to see those photos, try to tell if Jonas was bending forward to cut the line. Still, if they're in his possession, he could have edited all that out by now. Like all three of us, he brought his laptop." She heaved a heavy sigh.

"If he risked tampering with the sled, he's desperate."

"Someone's desperate. But is that someone only after me? That was to be my sled, but only Spike could have known that at first. But the point is, Jonas needs watching, not to mention Vanessa."

"Graham warned me Spike does, too, but I know the guy. He wouldn't screw up like that. I've worked with him ever since I've lived here, and knew him from before when he worked for my uncle."

"Besides, Spike emphasized we mushers were to hold on to the handlebow at all costs, and Jonas didn't do that. Even if the towline broke, he wouldn't have toppled off if he'd held on, so he had to have let go."

"You're right. Whether he let go intentionally or not, one way or the other, he caused his own accident."

"Speaking of Spike, you told me not to suspect your staff, but I looked up Christine and am glad I did. Mitch, I found out about the Kagak trial. And the fact you more or less lied to me about her past so—"

"I did not."

"Oh, yeah, fine. Good, brief answer without offering anything else."

She could see Mitch grit his teeth, then unclench his jaw muscles. He crossed his arms over his chest, jamming his fists under his armpits. "She asked me never to tell any of our guests, so I kept that promise. I was going to ask her permiss—"

"Well, I won't tell anyone else, but I should have been told. Of course, I can see why you didn't want me to know. Not only—yes, I know it was in self-defense—did she kill someone, but she pushed him down the stairs first. And she's the only one who knew when and where we were meeting on the ridge. Mitch, listen to the facts. She *pushed* him."

But even as she said that, Lisa knew she was the one who felt guilty and torn. Hadn't she and Christine just started to build some sort of woman-to-woman understanding upstairs, and now she was trying to accuse her of murder—another murder?

"I get your point," Mitch said, "but too circumstantial, not enough connect-the-dots. Someone else could have seen you—anyone. Vanessa or Jonas, even the Bonners, looking out a window from the second floor when you walked away from the lodge alone."

"But how much does Christine—or Spike—think I need to be punished for hurting you? Or want to scare me off or even eliminate me to be certain I don't try to take you away from all this? Christine's a quiet person, but smart and determined." Again, she felt a stab of guilt, betraying her better judgment about Christine, but she had to pursue all possibilities.

"Forget the idea she thinks you could take me away from here. As for Spike, he's not devious, not clever that way. Graham's lectured me about Spike, and I don't need you siding with the firm's managing partner, who is too damn good already at managing people's lives."

Their voices kept rising, but the deep walls seemed to swallow up the sound. Lisa realized they were getting angry with each other again, going into their argument mode, the one that could accelerate to accusations and rampaging emotion.

"So let's look at Graham," she insisted, desperate for answers at any cost. "If he has a vendetta against anyone, it would be you, not me or Jonas."

"Yeah."

"I'm just grasping at straws with Graham. But with Christine, Spike—even his sister, Ginger—who are obviously loyal to you for keeping the lodge going… they know I hurt you and rejected this life they love so much. Christine especially cares for y—"

"And I care for her, but not the way you're implying."

Hands on hips, she stepped closer to him, however forbidding he looked. "What am I implying?"

"Oh, hell, listen to us when we're supposed to be on the same side. Two bickering lawyers. And certainly, Christine, as perceptive and protective of me as she is, knows there's nothing between you and me anymore that way. Right? *Right?* There isn't, is there?" he goaded, stepping closer also.

Their gazes held in the reflected light of the wine bottles. It was like a distorted rainbow down there… the reverse of somewhere over the rainbow. Lisa stood mesmerized, frozen with her hands on her hips. His arms were still crossed over his chest. The air between them in the little space seemed to vibrate. She wanted to hit him. She hated him.

They came together before she knew either of them would move, her arms tight around his neck, his hands hard on her waist and bottom, caressing her, molding her flesh to his touch while their lips held, moved, demanded. Pressed to him breasts to chest, her hip bones to his hard thighs, the madness went on and on.

He backed her up as if he'd pin her against the wall, until the bottles behind them shifted and rattled. It was like being in the wilderness again without the rules of civilization, like riding a wild river wave. She ran her fingers through his hair as he clutched her to him so she could hardly breathe.

Yet they did breathe in unison, slanting their lips, missing noses, to get closer, closer. Tasting each other, devouring the painful past. She tingled all over, and a shiver wacked her.

"Mitch!" was all she could manage when they finally came up for air.

She needed him, but not this life he had chosen. She trusted him to help her through this, and yet he'd deserted and hurt her before.

To her utter dismay, he set her back at arm's length, still holding on to her upper arms as if to prop them both up.

"I'll have to plead," he said, breathing raggedly with a determined expression hardening his rugged features, "temporary insanity. We can't—this isn't going to help. I want more, and there's not going to be more."

She stared dazedly at him.

"I've got to be sure you're safe and we discover who might want to harm you. You trust me to help, don't you?"

"I'm afraid I'll commit professional suicide with the Bonners by accusing Jonas or Vanessa." Her voice was still shaky and breathy—not her own. The old, ambitious lawyer Lisa talking.

"I want to hear you say you don't think *I* was the one who tried to harm you."

Hair prickled on the back of her neck and a shiver snaked down her spine again. "And then risk your life to save me? No. I'm so sorry we didn't—it didn't work out for us, but I do trust you in this. Mitch, I brought the bracelet you bought for me—a pre-engagement gift, you said, the seagulls flying. I know it was expensive, and I want to give it back, a pledge that I do trust you—forgive you."

"I'm glad for that, but you keep the bracelet. I gave it to you in happy times. You gave me the ring back, so that's enough. Wear it if you want—if you trust me still."

He loosed his grip on her upper arms and nervously wiped his palms together, a move so uncharacteristic of him, since he always seemed to be in control. He looked as shaken as she felt. And he wanted her to keep the bracelet he'd bought her when they first knew they were in love; it was such a pretty piece, two seagulls with wings outspread, flying high together. Now he wanted her trust more than kisses.

She took a small step away, back into the center of the cellar. "About Graham," she said, trying to get back on track so she didn't throw herself at him again. Her voice was shaky. "When you mentioned you were afraid someone had gotten to him on the casino case, he looked like he was going to explode until you added that you thought someone might be threatening him. So that means it upset him that you thought someone could be bribing him—his fault. But when you explained that someone might be threatening him—their fault—he calmed down."

"And right after that, he took offense when I said we needed to trace someone up the trail of suspicion. He quickly insisted it was some lowlife who must have been behind it. So what if he wasn't trying to protect us but himself or some of his wealthy, powerful cronies from something he didn't want us to know in that case?"

"The Bonners and their crowd are definitely on the high end of the social and political feeding chain in the sunny south. But I still think our number-one candidates are Vanessa or Jonas. I'm going into Bear Bones with Vanessa before dinner so I'll see if I can rattle her cage a little more."

"I'll drive the two of you in. Maybe we can work on her together, and I don't want you alone with her."

"Mitch, whoever shoved me in the river was sneaky, when she's more blatant. I can handle Vanessa face-to-face."

"I'm still going along. I have a few errands to do while the others have their downtime."

"Vanessa's across the lake visiting Ginger Jackson right now, then Ellie's going over. I'm going over tomorrow. We didn't want to inundate Ginger with chattering, gushing females asking for recipes and gawking at her. If she's anything like Christine, she's very humble about her accomplishments."

"Glad to hear you say something good about Christine," he said as he followed her to the steps. Without his even discussing it, she knew they needed to go upstairs one at a time.

"You called her *Cu'paq,*" she said as she started up.

"You pronounce it better than I do. Duck Lake is really Lake *Dukoe,* you know, and it doesn't mean duck. That's just another distortion by the whites who came in and renamed everything, including turning *Denali,* 'The Great One,' into Mount McKinley."

Lisa turned back on the third step, putting her hand on the sharply slanted tree trunk above her. "So what does *Dukoe* mean then?"

"Christine said the lake was named for its shape. A *dukoe* is a large war club made from the leg of a moose."

She shuddered. Again, that moose rose up before her from the depths of the lake after she imagined her mother's face there. Again, she recalled running to Mitch's arms, just as she had today—but should never do again.

It shouldn't have surprised her that a *dukoe* was a war club. Someone was at war here—against her.

13

"So," Vanessa said to Lisa and Mitch as he drove them into Bear Bones in his black four-wheel-drive SUV, "did the early settlers or whoever named this place realize they were making a pun? Talk about a town being pared down to the bare bones—it's really tiny."

"Anything looks tiny compared to Fort Lauderdale," Lisa said, feeling a strange urge to defend this town she'd never seen. But everything about Vanessa made her want to argue with her lately. Should she pay attention to her woman's intuition that Vanessa was the one she should suspect of much worse than big-city snobbery?

Granted, Bear Bones wasn't much to look at. About one block long, facing both sides of a narrow two-lane road, it didn't even have a streetlight or stoplight. There was a gas station with a big sign that read Bulk Fuel and Propane. The Wolfin' Café seemed to hold center stage. A sawmill, the "Homesteaders Cemetery," a Methodist chapel, and a couple of houses straggled beyond the cluster of commercial establishments. The American flag and Alaska state flag flew from more poles than there were stores.

Lisa saw one sign that read Lucy's Deli/Pizza. So did the Duck Lake Lodge denizens ever go out or send out for pizza? There was the Kleen-It Laundromat, the Gold Rush Saloon with swinging doors painted on its real wooden doors, and a place called Trader Dan's with a weather-beaten sign that advertised Groceries And Drugs For Sale. Not a pharmacy, not a drugstore, just drugs. South Floridians would get a laugh out of that—and it looked as if Vanessa was.

"It's not as bare-bones as it looks," Mitch told them. "The post office and lending library are in the back of the Community Hall, down there, the same place they have poker and bingo nights. Bear Bones serves its purpose and has a definite charm," he added as he pulled up in front of Gus Majors' store, where the large sign read:

WHATEVER: HUNTING SUPPLIES,
TAXIDERMY, CHAINSAW REPAIR, ECT.

"I guess that last part is supposed to be ETC.," Vanessa said. "Actually, the town reminds me of a set from one of those old Clint Eastwood spaghetti westerns."

"I'm impressed at the breadth of your knowledge and honored you're comparing Bear Bones to Italy," Mitch countered.

Lisa could tell that Vanessa's attitude was getting to him.

"Eastwood was big with someone I dated briefly," Vanessa said as they got out. "A cardiac surgeon who tried to operate on my heart, if you know what I mean. So—those little gift shops you mentioned are in the fronts of houses down that way? I hope they have postcards, because I know a lot of people who knew *the* Mitchell Braxton who won't believe this is your closest town."

"Talkeetna, where we're heading this weekend, is 'the big city,' so save your real shopping and comments for that," Mitch said. "Besides, can you get out of your car in Lauderdale or Miami and leave it unlocked like this? Lisa, what do you think?"

"I think it's the most real place I've been in a long time. No pretense, no false fronts, no hype—unlike a lot of places and people I know from what we like to call civilization."

Her eyes met Mitch's and held. He nodded. Vanessa gave a little snort. "Meaning something deep and dark, like a slap at me?" she challenged.

"Of course not," Lisa told her. "Why are you so thin-skinned lately when—"

Lisa's urge to tell Vanessa off was waylaid by Gus Majors barreling out the front door of his shop, shouting, "Glad to see you two river rats!"

He slapped Mitch's shoulder and give Lisa a quick, one-armed hug. Vanessa looked as if the largest animal in the zoo had just gotten loose from its cage.

"Gus," Mitch said, "how's this evening for dinner at the lodge? About six-thirty? Christine's getting all the fixings together for aurora borealis ice cream for dessert."

"On one condition—same one I mentioned before. If Ginger's there, I'll take a rain check, 'cause after seeing you two yesterday, I got to thinkin' about that showdown her and I had at the Wolfin' Café. So just a while ago I drove way round the lake to make it up to her. Then we got ourselves into another fuss, and I said the hell with her. You sure she won't be there?"

"She drops her bakery goods off late afternoon— like right about now," Mitch said, frowning at his watch, "but doesn't stay for dinner when we have guests. And I'd like you to meet one of them. Vanessa Guerena, this is Gus Majors, jack-of-all-trades, master of only one—big talk."

"Pleased to meet you, ma'am," Gus said as Vanessa nodded but didn't extend her hand. "Well, I'm working on a moose head, so got to get back to it, but I'll be there tonight. Thanks for the invite!" he said over his big shoulder as he went back inside.

After Mitch went off to do his errands, Vanessa turned to Lisa. "So, before the moose-head man came out and was invited to dinner at the lodge, were you going to get into a fuss with me—to say the hell with me, to use your friend's patois?"

Lisa turned to face her on the sidewalk. "My grandmother used to quote the Bible a lot, and I can remember her saying, 'I have learned in whatever state I am to be content.' You should work on that, Vanessa. Just appreciate being someplace different while you're here—see the good side of th—"

"'In whatever state'? Well I don't like the state of Alaska I'm in, and—Mitch Braxton or not—I'm shocked you do, especially after you could have drowned and frozen solid in that river! The senior partnership is worth a lot, but this place is not only laughable," she said, flinging her arm at the town, "but deadly. You could have been killed in that river, probably more than once."

They glared at each other before Vanessa stalked away toward a house that had a swinging sign that said Alaska Gifts. The last few words of Vanessa's tirade still hung between them as if it echoed off the sign, the buildings and mountains. She hadn't said that Lisa could have died in the river, but could have been *killed*. Lisa realized Vanessa had said nothing to really implicate herself, yet it seemed she had made not only a subtle confession, but a possible threat.

"I hope Gus leaves right after the dessert," Christine whispered to Mitch as she stood back to watch Gus cranking the homemade ice-cream maker on the dining room table. After taking brief stints turning the dasher, their guests had relocated to two facing leather couches and a couple of chairs in front of the low-burning fire.

She kept her voice low. "Ginger sent a note back

to me with Vanessa after her visit. She wrote she's been so busy with her guests today—Mrs. Bonner, Gus and Vanessa—that she's bringing the breakfast goodies here later. She didn't get them all done. And she's been baking and stockpiling things to sell at her booth at the Mountain Mother Festival this weekend. I'm not to tell Spike, but she wants to pay him for all the wood he cuts for her stoves."

"I'll try to keep an eye out and ear cocked for Ginger's boat, then give Gus a heads-up if it comes to that. We do not need an episode of that soap opera of yours played out here—what's it called?"

"One Life to Live."

"Yeah, well, we've got enough of a soap opera going on here right now. You all set to back me up on these aurora borealis stories for everyone?"

Although Christine never liked to be center stage, each time Mitch had a group here, they served this vanilla ice cream with blueberries and cranberries swirled through it and gave a brief talk about the aurora borealis.

"Sure," she said. "You start while I stir in the fruit and dish it up, and I'll chime in later."

"While you're all enjoying the aurora borealis ice cream Christine is dishing up," Mitch said, raising his voice so everyone could hear and walking over to sit in a chair facing the hearth, "we'd like to tell you some things about our famed northern lights. Needless to say, as attractive as the ice cream is, the swirl of colors in it doesn't do the real thing justice. You're here about the time we might begin to glimpse them, and it's nice to see them in the milder temps of autumn, because it's down-to-the-bone cold when they are usually seen dancing across the sky. Viewing is best between midnight and three a.m. and can go until late March. Since I used to visit my uncle here during my summer vacations, I was totally blown away the first time I saw them in the cold—just this past winter."

"I've seen pictures of them, even moving ones," Mrs. Bonner said, "but I'm sure those don't do them justice either."

"Nothing but the naked eye does," Mitch said. "Even though the lights are associated with Alaska, they are a northern hemisphere phenomenon. The Scandanavians used to associate the light with the Valkyries riding down to do battle from the skies. Some biblical scholars think the heavenly wheel Ezekial saw in the Old Testament was the northern lights, which do dip down to the south once in a rare while. The name aurora borealis comes from two Latin words. Aurora was the Roman goddess of the dawn and Borealis was the god of the north wind."

"That's some Latin I never learned in law school," Jonas said as Christine stirred the fruit into the ice cream and Gus joined the group, standing behind Jonas's chair.

Christine had noticed Jonas was walking with a slight limp since his sledding accident, but only sometimes. Spike was still worried Jonas might sue, and she knew how that fear felt. Clay's father had not only banished her from the Kagak family, but had threatened to bring a civil suit against her since she'd escaped punishment for the criminal charge. But that had just been talk. He didn't want the names Kagak or Yup'ik "shamed in the papers" anymore, as he put it. She should assure Spike that it would come to nothing. Maybe she'd even open up to him about her own situation some.

"So what really makes the northern lights?" Jonas was asking.

"Scientists say it's like a solar wind, carrying protons and electrons streaming out from the sun—bands of energy," Mitch explained, gesturing. "The earth's atmospheric gasses collide with the particles, and they explode and glow in different colors. The northern lights are actually there all the time, but much of the year, the sun blocks them out. As a former lawyer, I first thought of it as someone who is guilty of something—hiding something—who manages to keep his or her true intentions invisible, but they remain, and will eventually be found out."

Christine looked up from serving their guests as Vanessa and Lisa took dishes of ice cream from her tray. Mitch had never said that before to a group. Gus and Mitch took the last two bowls from the tray. Funny, but almost everyone was frowning and looking intently down at their ice cream, except for Lisa and Mitch, who were staring at everyone. So what was going on here? She had to ask Mitch. *Iah,* had he meant more by "a soap opera" than she suspected?

On the way back to the kitchen with the empty tray, Christine strode past the bubble window and looked down the length of the lake. No Ginger yet. "Christine," Mitch said, "can you share some of the local folklore about Alaska's version of sky lights?"

She walked back toward the group. Lisa made space for her on one sofa by moving closer to Gus, so Christine sat there, smoothing her long denim skirt over her knees. "In the old days," she began, "people in these parts believed you must respect the spirits of the sky so they wouldn't be harmful. They believed the lights are departed souls, playing up there, happy people."

"Kind of like heaven," Gus put in.

"Right," she said. "Alaskan native people associate the aurora with death. One belief of the Athabascans—they were the language group my people descended from—was that through the lights in the sky, the spirits of the dead watch over us and send us messages. And that chosen ones could see the faces of the dead through their dreams."

"See their faces of the dead through dreams?" Lisa asked.

Christine nodded. Lisa looked pale, her hand halfway to her dish, her spoon suspended in midair.

"And one group believes when the aurora borealis falls," Christine went on, "when it runs too close to man, the human brain goes mad and man is seized by the heart and killed. So, yes, to some the aurora used to mean happy heaven unless it got too close, then murder to others."

Christine saw Lisa shudder. She almost put her hand out to the woman's arm to comfort her. It was silent in the room, but for the ever-present distant rumble of the river. She still didn't hear the *put-put* of Ginger's motorboat.

"Well, I wish we could see the lights." Mrs. Bonner broke the silence. "We'll just have to come back another time, Graham. It will give me a good excuse to buy a fur-lined parka."

"It's something to see, all right," Gus said.

Christine had learned a lot more about their guests from the way they had treated Gus tonight. The Bonners were kind and courteous, Jonas off base by suggesting to Gus he go online to find a mail-order bride, Vanessa obviously annoyed he was here, but trying not to let the Bonners see that side of her, and Lisa attempting to make him feel at ease.

When Lisa helped collect the dishes and brought them to the table, Christine asked, "Are you feeling all right?"

"Yes, I'm fine. The ice cream was great and the folklore, too. Why do you keep looking out the window?"

"Since Gus is here, I'm glad Ginger's late, but it's not like her."

"I was going to go see her tomorrow morning. I could take the rowboat and go now. It's still plenty light. Wish I'd catch a glimpse of the aurora."

"I'd go with you, but I've got to clean up here. See what Mitch says. He won't let you go alone."

"I'll just see if Vanessa will go with me. We have some unfinished conversation, and she knows the way since she was just there. But yes, if Vanessa will go, too, I'll tell Mitch where we're going."

Christine liked Lisa's attitude. Never let a man really rule the roost, but listen to his advice—if it wasn't shouted at you in a drunken rage, that is. But she didn't intend to let her softer feelings for this woman keep her from doing whatever she must to protect Mitch and this haven he had made for her.

"So," Lisa said to Vanessa as she rowed them across the lake, "wasn't that interesting about the aurora?" Vanessa had been willing to come with her, once Lisa had promised she'd handle the oars. Mitch thought it was fine since he and Jonas were sitting on the patio and he had binoculars to keep an eye on them clear across the lake. Lisa figured she'd have to ask Ginger a couple of questions if she could get her away from Vanessa for a minute. As they crossed the water, a fitful breeze started up to ruffle the lake.

"Primitive beliefs are always interesting," Vanessa said, trailing a hand in the water, "but both Christine and Mitch kind of overdid it with the dramatics—him comparing the lights to guilty people hiding something and her with that death-in-the-sky stuff. You'd think we were all sitting around some campfire telling chainsaw-murder or ghost stories. By the way, good old Gus sharpens chainsaws for a living—did you know that? Keep an eye on him if there's some massacre up here."

Lisa narrowed her eyes and pulled harder on the oars. Once again, was Vanessa just mouthing off because of her disdain for this backwoods place, or was there something hidden in her language? Subtle threats? Freudian slips? Lisa hoped she wasn't back to being just plain paranoid, slipping back into her old fears where her nightmares used to merge with reality.

She was rowing into small waves now, but at least it would be easier going home—back to the lodge, that is. They would volunteer to take Ginger's breakfast goods back for her, if that would help. If she could get Vanessa to carry some things to this boat, she'd have a moment alone with Ginger.

"So," Lisa said to try another topic, "what did you find interesting about Ginger when you visited her earlier?"

"Ellie came back all enamored of how quaint her place was, but it's a log cabin, for heaven's sake. Young Abe Lincoln would have been happy there."

"And you've never seen someone living in such primitive conditions?"

"Is that a comment about my past?"

"Vanessa, get over it. I am not attacking you, just defending Ginger."

"These people are all eccentrics here. It wouldn't hurt them to be a little more...more..."

"Modern?"

"Mainstream. Talk about Clint Eastwood's old westerns. Ginger and probably others are living it. Sourdough bread starter rising in big bowls, not only a Ben Franklin potbellied stove, but a wood-burning cookstove. See that smoke coming out of the chimney there?"

Lisa turned around and looked in the direction they were going. Yes, a plume of smoke rose from a line of tall Sitka spruce where Vanessa pointed. And aloft, far above that, where she'd love to see the aurora lights, at least three huge raptors soared on the thermals. She turned around and pulled harder against the rising wind and waves now showing wisps of white-caps.

They could see Ginger's motorboat bobbing, tied to the short dock, one that could be rolled out of the water when the lake iced up. Spike's plane was tied up at the very end of that dock. Ginger wasn't in sight unless the plane hid her. Lisa put their boat in on the other side of the dock, across from the empty motorboat. Vanessa finally did something helpful by getting out and tying the rope from the prow around a metal post.

Lisa climbed out, and they both looked down into Ginger's boat. They must have caught her in the middle of loading. Two plastic-covered trays of baked goods were in the bottom of the boat, with probably more to come.

"She's obviously just running late," Vanessa said,

starting up the dock, with Lisa behind her, "but what does it matter since it's light so late? She could bring that breakfast stuff over in a couple of hours with no problem. Oh, yeah, you asked what I found most interesting about Ginger Jackson? She's living in the past except for one thing. She's got mail-order catalogs all over the place, I kid you not."

"I doubt if she shops online, unless she uses the Internet at the lodge, but maybe she shops by mail."

"The point is they are luxe catalogs, Lisa. Neiman Marcus, Saks, Nordstrom, Dean and Deluca—I don't know what else, but there's not one thing in sight to say she ever buys from them." She cupped her hands around her mouth and called, "Hey, Ginger! Ginger! Christine sent us over to see if you need any help with the bakery things for breakfast."

Lisa saw the cabin was shaped similar to Spike's but was a bit smaller. Spike had all the modern conveniences, but this definitely seemed more primitive. A small shed, also of logs, was just beyond the back corner. "She doesn't use an outhouse, does she?" Lisa whispered as they went up onto the porch.

"Thank heavens, it's not that bad. Ellie said she has a composting toilet just like the ones at the lodge. Leave it to Ellie to have to use the ladies' room while she was here. I'm pretty sure she ordered a lot of stuff from Ginger. I saw she took a couple of hundred dollars with her, no less, but maybe some of it was charity. You know bleeding-heart Ellie—excuse me, I mean philanthropist and humanitarian."

"Ginger!" Lisa called out, choosing to ignore Vanessa's subtle dig at Ellie. Vanessa sounded bitter about everything lately. So was that a mere step away from actually doing something rash?

They peeked in the two windows fronting the lake. The cabin itself couldn't be seen from the lodge, but it wasn't set too far back in the trees. Lisa realized she'd feel a whole lot better knowing Mitch could see them, even at a distance.

No sound. No Ginger. This would alarm everyone at the lodge. They'd have to go back, then send Spike or Mitch over. A winding road made a long drive from the lodge, but at least it was accessible. Vanessa had said Ginger didn't drive and relied on Spike's plane to land on the river or ice to keep her supplied in the winter. Lisa shuddered as if a cold breeze had hit her. The trees were shifting.

The door wasn't locked so they went in. "Ginger?" Lisa called. The main room smelled wonderfully of baked goods, yeasty and rich. Lisa recalled coming home from school, when Grandma always had milk and some treat waiting for her. They saw many items—even loaves of bread—laid out on the table, nicely wrapped in colored cellophane and labeled.

"This can't all be for the lodge breakfast," Vanessa said.

"Mitch told me she's been baking for that Mountain Mother Festival we're going to in Talkeetna—to sell things there."

"See what I mean about the catalogs?" Vanessa

asked, pointing to one open on the end of the table as if Ginger had just left the room for a moment. "Look, she's even circled some things in red pen—luxury linen sheets and down pillows at...two hundred bucks a crack, no less. Talk about fantasy island!"

They looked in the bedroom, even under the bed and in the closet, then in the bathroom. "So, where's the phone?" Lisa asked. "Maybe we should call the lodge."

"No phone. I'm telling you, we're back to pioneer days here. She has what she calls a root garden in a clearing she insisted on showing me. I'll just look to be sure she's not there. You check the shed, and I'll meet you at the boat, pronto. Actually, with this wind kicking up, I'm not sure I tied our boat that tight and we don't need Ginger's pulling away from the dock."

"All right," Lisa said, then realized she'd broken her promise to Mitch not to be alone. She hurried to the shed, fully expecting it to be unlocked. It was. Holding her breath, standing back a ways, she pulled the door open. She saw a snowmobile that must get Ginger around in the winter. Also rakes, hoes, spades—and in plastic bins, stacks and stacks of more catalogs. Those reminded Lisa of the legal briefs piled up on her desk when she was a lowly associate.

Shaking her head, she closed the door and hurried down to the lake to check the boat lines and turn their prow outward. Yes, it was going to be much easier rowing back with the wind. They had to hurry, get help to search for Ginger. Was this the way people had panicked when they realized she and Mitch were missing? So much for her big question for Ginger. She'd wanted to ask if she'd seen anything strange the day she was pushed, someone other than her or Mitch walking the ridge path.

Lisa knelt on the shifting dock to turn their rowboat prow out, then refastened its rope and moved across the dock to be sure Ginger's motorboat was fastened securely. It had pulled away a bit. Should she take the baked goods out, in case it rained or water from the waves splashed in?

The motorboat bumped the dock, then shifted away from it. Lisa heaved a sigh of relief when she saw Vanessa come running toward the dock, yelling, "Didn't see her!"

Lisa looked down to try to hold Ginger's boat steady while she tightened its tie to the dock. She saw the anchor chain was over the side, so at least it wasn't going to drift away even if the rope loosened.

And then, below the surface, she glimpsed what at first she thought was her own reflection, broken by the waves.

A scream shredded the air—her scream. Through the shifting, swirling water etched by foam, her mother's face stared up at her, hair waving, hand bobbing and beckoning, green eyes wide, mouth moving to say, "Come to me, Lisa, come to me…"

14

Lisa's long scream seemed to release her terror. This was not a nightmare, not her mother. *Dear God, help us, it's Ginger!*

"What is it?" Vanessa shouted as she ran down the dock. Wordlessly, Lisa pointed into the water. Vanessa bent down to look and gasped. "Should we pull her up?" she choked out as she fell to her knees beside Lisa.

"Accident? Crime scene? We can't tamper..." Lisa muttered.

"Right. Maybe the authorities can glean something from this, but to leave her in the lake... I can't believe I just saw her earlier today. Poor Spike. We have to get help. One of us has to stay here and the other get help even if Mitch said we should stick together."

"I—I only screamed because it was such a shock."

"Lisa, you were screaming for your mother!"

"I was not!" she insisted, but it was no time to argue. She dragged her gaze from Ginger's face. "I think I know a way we don't have to leave her and can get them here." At least she was thinking clearly now. Yes, she had a plan.

"Like what? Smoke signals from the chimney? We can't just gesture from the end of the dock, because their view of us is blocked by the plane," Vanessa pointed out.

"When we were in the wilds, Mitch told me the sign for getting help. I just need to get up on the plane."

"On it? You might fall in, too. Ginger must have slipped and hit her head while she was loading her boat. But the way she's still moving—eyes open— it's horrible."

Determined to make up for her initial reaction— had she screamed for her mother, because how could Vanessa have made that up?—Lisa stood on shaking legs and walked to the end of the dock. The plane was bobbing more than ever, but if she was careful, she could step onto a pontoon and get a handhold near the door and climb. Besides, she had to prove to herself she was not afraid of falling into water. After her nearly fatal river ride, it was like getting back on a horse. She'd swum in the ocean after her family died. She had to do this now.

She leaped onto the nearest pontoon of Spike's plane and grabbed a door handle. It was already a rocky ride. She couldn't believe this so-called bonding experience the Bonners had planned. First, someone pushed her in the river, then Jonas fell off the sled, but this—this muted all that by comparison, though she herself could very well have been the corpse floating faceup in the water.

She began to tremble, but she started to climb. The wing was supported by a metal strut. She stepped onto that and grasped the edge of the wing. She shifted her weight and clung to the body of the plane. With one foot on the strut, she belly-crawled up onto the nose near the outside of the windshield, holding on by grabbing the ridge that held the recessed wipers. The plane's metallic finish was sleek and cold. She slipped, hitting her chin so hard she bit her tongue and tasted bitter blood.

Blood, bruises, death by drowning. It would have been enough to make her flee this rugged land, but now something inside her had changed. The challenge of it spurred her on.

She felt almost nauseous—from the rocking or from her grim discovery in the lake—but she'd have to stand to be sure she was seen. What if they weren't watching right now? She had to hold the position with both arms raised in a *V,* as Mitch had said. Two arms up means: need help. Like a baby raising its arms to its mother— pick me up and hold me. Mother, holding little Lani in her arms... No, don't think of that again. One arm up meant no help needed, like a wave goodbye.

"Lisa, be careful!" Vanessa shouted, still kneeling on the dock above where Ginger had gone in. Fallen in? Pushed in? By whom? Maybe the same person who tried to kill her.

Lisa tried not to look down at the whitecapped waves. The water kept rolling under the plane as if it were going to take off. This was like walking the edge of a wave, as if the width of the shiny wing was a surfboard to ride the water. She could not fall, not go in again. No Mitch to save her this time. It wasn't the Wild River, but she didn't want to hit her head and become a second body in the lake.

Balancing, bending her knees to take the rocking, glad she wore her old pair of rubber-soled shoes, she held up both arms in a *V,* at first shakily, then strongly. *V* for victory, if they saw her. If not, should they move Ginger, haul her up?

Picturing one of those old wing walkers from the pioneering days of aviation, she held her stance as long as she could, then dropped to her knees and grabbed the edge of the wing again. But from here it might be worse to get down than it was to get up.

"Could you see anything from there?" Vanessa shouted. "Maybe we should row out in our boat a ways and do it from there. I think this anchor chain's wrapped around her somehow. It seems taut, but when I try to move it, she floats up."

With a shudder at that description, Lisa squinted down the lake to see if a boat was coming. Nothing. Nothing moving but the marching waves. Should she try to stand and make the *V* again?

As she pulled herself into a kneeling position to try once more, Vanessa shouted, "I just wish her eyes weren't open, like she's watching me!"

Lisa tried to shut out those words as she got up from her sore knees and signaled for help again.

Blessedly, within ten minutes after Lisa made it back to the dock, they heard the hum of a motor. Vanessa ran along the shore, waving her white jacket.

"They must have seen you!" she cried to Lisa, who refused to leave Ginger alone and sat on the dock with her hand steadying the anchor chain. "A boat with at least three people in it! I'm pretty sure one of them's Spike—he's tall! I think it's Christine with Spike and Mitch!"

Lisa fought to stay calm though thoughts bombarded her. How she wished she'd had the chance to question Ginger about what she'd seen the day someone shoved her in the river. Poor Ginger with her rough life and posh dreams—all those magazines she, no doubt, could not afford one thing from, especially since she was saving to pay her brother back for the wood he'd cut for her over the years. All those baked goods sitting in the kitchen, as if she'd prepared them not for the lodge or the Mountain Woman Festival but for her own funeral.

The motorboat wheeled around the plane and came to the side of the dock where they'd put their rowboat. The two men had brought Christine with them. Poor Spike, poor Ginger. All hell was about to break loose.

Lisa glanced down one more time at Ginger in the water, rocked by the lake she must have loved, her face partly obscured by darkening water and waves. *Now we see through a glass darkly, but then face-to-face,* their minister had read at Grandma's funeral service. Now Lisa had to see through the facade someone had built to find and face down who had pushed her in the river—and, if this wasn't an accident—who had done this.

As another Alaska twilight set in, Christine comforted Spike on the dock while Vanessa and Lisa sat on rocks on the shore. Mitch had taken the boat back to the lodge to call the sheriff in Talkeetna. Christine didn't like Sheriff Moran coming, but she was heartbroken for Spike and would stick tight to do what she could. Ginger's death would leave a big hole in his heart she would try to fill.

Spike was crying unashamedly, and she was scared he was going to haul Ginger's body up despite Mitch telling him not to. The three lawyers had agreed they shouldn't even go back into Ginger's house. To determine if there had been foul play, they would need to give evidence, the cabin would have to be fingerprinted and, since Ginger had several visitors today, a lot of prints eliminated. Remembering the police investigation that had swallowed her up, Christine frowned as she rubbed her right hand hard against her denim skirt.

With her other, she held Spike's. He stared down at his sister in the water. But, she thought, what if some of those prints in Ginger's cabin shouldn't be eliminated? What if Gus had gone back to talk to her yet again, after the visit he'd mentioned to Mitch in Bear Bones, after Mrs. Bonner and Vanessa had been there? Ginger and Gus were like oil and water together, and Christine knew where that could lead.

"I can't believe it," Spike said, swiping at his face with his jacket sleeve. "I tried to take care of her, special care because of her bad hand. I'll get whoever did this."

"Spike, she was loading things in the boat. Maybe she fell—"

"Loading things like she'd done five hundred times before with no problems—in all sorts of weather? I don't care if she was handicapped and the wind picked up, she was sure-footed. I promised my mother on her deathbed I'd take care of her."

"You did. All that firewood, the supplies, the visits. She really appreciated it, loved you."

"Ycah, well, there's no one left who loves me anymore."

"I know the feeling."

He sniffed and nodded. He wasn't staring down into the water now, but still had a hard hold of the anchor chain. Christine knew that Vanessa and Lisa had been holding it, too, so would all their fingerprints be on that, if it was a kind of murder weapon? Would Ginger's be there, too, as she grabbed at it to stop herself from going in, or would the water have washed all that away? It had been raining the day she shot Clay. She'd thrown the gun out the back door into the mud, but it still had both their prints on it.

She had terrible memories of returning home after the trial and finding smears and smudges of that black graphite fingerprinting powder the police had used. For months after, she felt smeared and smudged with guilt, as if everyone could tell what she'd done.

But now, she only wanted to help Spike, so she told him, "Ginger was saving up money to help you buy fuel from whatever she made at the Mountain Mother Festival this weekend. See, she really appreciated you."

He sniffed hard. "Saving money for me? She had so little, just dreams. She wouldn't take more from me. She secretly lived on those fantasies about what she'd buy from those catalogs someday." He shook his head and glanced up toward the cabin. "No one will want this remote place she loved. I'll probably have to get a second loan on the plane or borrow from Mitch to even bury her."

When they let you have the body back, Christine thought, but didn't say so. Autopsies could take a while and death rulings even longer, at least in Fairbanks. "I've got some money squirreled away I'll give you," she said.

Spike turned his ravaged face to her and looked deep into her eyes for the first time since he was hitching his dogs to the sleds. "I need your strength," he said. "I know you've been through bad times, Christine. I need your strength."

She nodded. She would have put her arms around him, but Vanessa shouted from the shore, "Mitch and the sheriff are coming!"

* * *

The sheriff had insisted Mitch bring him over by boat. The coroner and two police officers were driving the long way around with an ambulance. Though Mitch had had few dealings with Sheriff Mace Moran, he liked the man, a Gulf War army veteran and native Alaskan. He was a sturdy, compactly built man, still in excellent shape at around age fifty, with silvering hair and a wind-weathered face that made him look older. He was a no-nonsense kind of guy. He wore his uniform, his utility belt and sidearm, but never seemed to flaunt his power.

The small police force of Talkeetna worked their tails off in the summer when the place was filled with tourists—and the town was the jumping-off point for those planning to climb Denali—but in the winter, they dealt mostly with drunks and domestic disturbances. With the Mountain Mother Festival hoopla starting tomorrow, Mitch knew this was not a good time for the sheriff to have to investigate a backwoods drowning.

"So, could she swim?" Moran had been peppering him with questions clear across the lake.

"Never saw her do it. You'll have to ask Spike. She had one bad hand, but handled her boat really well."

"You say she had a lot of visitors today—one at a time—some of your people. I'll need to speak with them, maybe even tonight. Got to get a handle on this fast and be in Talkeetna tomorrow with the crowds. You know what they say about death and taxes, only you know when taxes are going to hit, but with death…"

Mitch cut the motor to swing around the dock. He was going to just run the prow up on shore this time to keep the dock free for the authorities. He saw Christine and Spike still huddled by Ginger's boat. At least she'd managed to keep Spike from pulling Ginger out.

"You've sure had a lot going on with Lisa Vaughn falling in the river," the sheriff was saying. "She's one of the women who found the body, you said. No offense, Mitch, but I'm not real thrilled about having to deal with a pack of lawyers."

"I'm sure they'll be savvy and helpful," Mitch assured him, but he hardly assured himself. He wouldn't complicate things right now—yet—by telling the sheriff that he and Lisa were covertly investigating her near drowning and hypothermia as attempted murder. If the sheriff knew, he could blow things wide open, and whoever had pushed her would go to ground, even more than he or she already had. If Ginger's death wasn't an accident, the person they were looking for could have succeeded with a drowning this time.

15

Lisa, Mitch, Vanessa, Spike and Christine stood on the shore while the coroner—a Talkeetna general practitioner, Dr. Sam Collister—the sheriff and two deputies retrieved Ginger's body from the water. Mitch and Christine kept Spike between them; Lisa stood between Mitch and Vanessa. Despite the fact it wasn't really dark, the authorities had two high-powered lights trained into the water, then on the body when they laid it on the dock. Their words floated over the water.

"One leg was wrapped in the anchor chain," they heard the sheriff say. "It musta pulled her in or at least held her down somehow, or maybe her boat bumped in above her next to the dock and she couldn't resurface for air. She had only one useful hand, so it's possible. Doc, can you tell right away if she's got a head wound that might have knocked her out on the boat or dock? With the waves, the boat could have been shifting in and out, so she put the anchor in. Maybe she missed stepping in the boat."

Lisa saw Mitch had to hold Spike back from racing down the dock. "Give them some time," he told his friend. "I'm sure they'll let you have a minute with her."

"I don't want them cutting her up later, and I'm going to tell them that right now."

"Spike, listen to me," Mitch said, grabbing his friend's arms and facing him. "They have legal authority to order an autopsy. It's standard for something like this. And you want to know what happened."

"She's dead, that's what happened!"

Sheriff Moran stood and turned away from where the men knelt around Ginger's body on the tarp that Mitch realized was probably a body bag. "You just hold on there now, Mr. Jackson," the sheriff called out. He turned back to the huddled men. Like the others, Lisa strained to hear.

"Yes, concave trauma of the back of the skull," the doctor said. "But no clotted blood means she probably went in quickly after the injury. But that's all I can tell you without more time. Drowning deaths are complicated to assess. It's hard to tell whether the victim was dead or alive at the time of water entry. The lungs are going to fill with water even if drowning wasn't the cause, and with her floating faceup like that…" Finally, mercifully, his voice trailed off.

"If you can make it quick for the family and friends and for me, I'll owe you, Doc," the sheriff said. "I'll be watchdogging the festival this weekend, but this will have to take priority if it's suspicious in any way. Okay, Mr. Jackson," he called to Spike. "If you want to come out here a minute—but not touch the victim—that will be fine, an official ID by next of kin. Then I need to have a few words individually with you ladies who discovered the body while we tape off the cabin and check things out there."

Spike walked out onto the dock, quickly at first, then slowed. Mitch stood on the shore, watching. Lisa's heart went out to Spike. She knew how this felt, though she'd never had a body—bodies—to grieve over in her family tragedy. Sometimes that fact, even after all the years, made her think that somewhere, in her wildest dreams, her mother and sister were still alive.

The sheriff spoke to Lisa first, since she'd actually found the body. He sat on a rock facing her while Vanessa paced the shoreline waiting her turn for interrogation.

"Quite a vacation, huh, Ms. Vaughn?"

"It's been challenging."

"I like your attitude after all you been through. Things are tougher in Alaska, like that TV show title says, but that makes people tougher, too. Seems you're holding up well."

"Yes and no, Sheriff. I saw my mother and sister drown when I was a child, so that makes this—and my river ride—even worse for me." She had decided to explain that up front, because she figured Vanessa might tell him she'd screamed for her mother—if she actually had. But if she hadn't, that meant Vanessa was working on her somehow and had researched her past—that is, unless the Bonners or Mitch had told Vanessa about her childhood tragedy when she'd trusted them not to.

Worse, Lisa was starting to wonder if Vanessa could have somehow known Ginger's body was in the water and had set her up to discover the drowning. Vanessa was probably the last person to visit, so maybe she had seen Ginger was dead and realized seeing her drowned would freak Lisa out, and she could use that against her in the senior partner competition. No, that was too farfetched. She was getting paranoid again. Yet Vanessa had told her to check if Ginger's boat had pulled away from the dock. And if she suspected Vanessa of setting her up to find the body, did that mean she also thought Vanessa could have actually harmed Ginger?

"I said, you sure you're okay?" the sheriff asked, touching her arm. "Real sorry to hear about your own tragedy, Ms. Vaughn."

"Lisa. Lisa is fine."

"Are you fine? That is, considering you just discovered a drowned woman, which obviously reminded you of your own tragedy?"

"My lawyer training kicks in when necessary. At least, I hope so. Go ahead with your questions. I can be objective."

"Real interesting, dealing with a lot of lawyers. Not my cup of tea."

"I can understand that. Dealing with some officers of the law isn't a lawyer's favorite cup of tea either."

"I think we understand each other, so let's get down to brass tacks."

She recounted why she and Vanessa had come across the lake and said Christine would back all that up. She led him step by step through their search for Ginger, giving him time to take notes on a pad he'd pulled from his shirt pocket. When he asked, she told him who had visited Ginger earlier in the day and why. She included her firsthand information about Ginger and Gus Majors because that had to come out anyway.

"Big guy, isn't he? I know who he is," he said, frowning, and underlined something back and forth on his notepad.

"I found him to be very congenial and honest. He clearly told Mitch, Vanessa and me that he'd seen Ginger and had words with her earlier today. I could tell he was expecting her to show up at the lodge this evening. Those aren't the sort of words or actions of a man who had hurt her earlier."

"Gotcha on that, attorney Vaughn, but I'll draw my own conclusions. Passions can flare just as hot in Alaska as anywhere else. So, the other lodge visitor besides you and Ms. Guerena was Mrs. Ellen—called Ellie—Bonner, and she's back at the lodge. I'll need to talk to her there."

"Look, I've been here for a couple of hours, and I'm exhausted. Do you mind if I ask Mitch to take me back to the lodge now?" She had to talk to Mitch, had to tell him how Vanessa might have staged some of this.

"Sure. Both of you can go, and I'll drop Ms. Guerena back there after I talk to her and come to interview Mrs. Bonner. Needless to say, I might have to ask Mitch's guests to extend their vacation if there's any need."

"I understand. By the way, in the cabin are a lot of freshly baked goods Ginger was evidently going to sell at the festival tomorrow. Rather than just let them go to waste—if it's all right with Spike—could some of us sell them in town tomorrow for her estate? We were going in anyway, and Christine said Spike will need the money to bury Ginger."

"I'll go take a look-see at them, and if Spike says so, fine by me. You want to go ask him?"

She went to Christine first and explained her idea. Christine wiped her eyes and nodded. "It would be a way to help Spike and honor Ginger's wishes," she said with a decisive nod. "Baking and helping with the ziplining—Ginger loved to do both. Does he— Does the sheriff, the coroner, too, think she slipped?"

"That would be their first assumption, but they have to look at all the possibilities."

"And that means murder?"

"Other than suicide—and that's a real long shot here—that's the last option. If they find someone caused this, depending on what they can prove about intent, the authorities could bring charges."

"If they can figure out who did it," Christine interrupted with a visible shudder and a stifled sob. "Don't I know how all that goes? Mitch says you looked up my past, but you've been kind anyway."

Lisa wasn't sure what to say. She had expected Christine to be more upset.

"Well," Christine went on, "after you were rescued, he told me about yours, too, your family loss, even before you shared that with me. So we understand each other on grief and regret at least."

"Yes," Lisa whispered as tears blurred her vision so that this woman's face, like Ginger's in the water, her mother's in her dreams, seemed to waver and shimmer. They embraced quickly, then stepped back. In years of closing remarks and court summation, Lisa had never heard something so terrible and complicated put so concisely and so right.

Lisa sat facing Mitch as he took her back to the lodge in the motorboat. The wind raked his hair with invisible fingers and ballooned his unzipped jacket. The bottom of the boat pounded from wave to wave. The roar of the motor made them shout at each other as she told him her new suspicions about Vanessa.

He listened carefully, nodding. "Are you sure you didn't actually cry out something about your mother?" he finally asked.

"I had a flashback to my nightmare and screamed, but I swear she made that up. Mitch, she's been looking into my past to see how she can psychologically rattle me and might have let me find Ginger to set me off."

"I'm sorry that had to be you. I guess Vanessa could have set that up, but we can't prove anything from what you said."

"I never really exchanged one word with Ginger, but I intended to. She could well have been in the area when someone shoved me in."

"Yeah. I saw her boat but not her when I ran down to the lake to get the kayak to come after you. Move here on this seat with me, so we don't have to shout. We're both getting hoarse."

He gave her a hand, and she moved beside him. Just behind them, water from the outboard motor plumed in a white rooster tail, just like water bursting over rocks in the river. She shuddered and put her arms around herself for warmth, then Mitch put an arm around her and steered one-handed, probably the way Ginger had always steered her boat. When they'd left, one of the policemen was going over the boat with a flashlight and tweezers, no less.

"Lisa, it's a leap to think Ginger's death and your possible drowning are related. The two of you never really met and seem to have nothing in common."

"So we're back to the big possibility that my would-be killer thought—or knew—Ginger had seen something. But with all the visitors she had today, how could someone else have sneaked over there and hurt her? As we agreed before, someone's desperate and devious."

"Yeah. We have met the enemy and he is us."

"Mitch, it *has* to be someone at the lodge, some-one from the firm. We need to re-examine every-thing, everyone, even Graham and Ellie."

"I know. I have been. Meet me about an hour before breakfast in the wine cellar tomorrow morn-ing. The sheriff will be at the lodge soon to talk to Ellie, and there's going to be a lot of unrest tonight, when both of us—all of us—need some sleep. I swear, I've never caught up with sleep since our river run. I'm like a zombie, not sure if I'm thinking straight. Almost there, sweetheart. I see Graham waiting on the shore."

She moved back to the other seat so Mitch could maneuver the boat in. *Sweetheart?* He'd called her sweetheart. Graham would have seen his arm around her, but so what? It had been one horrible, long day, and it was not even nearly over yet.

"Was it an accident?" Graham shouted as Mitch edged the boat up to the dock.

Now, that was the question, Lisa thought, looking down into the roiling water.

Before the sheriff questioned Ellie, Graham in-sisted that a lawyer sit in with her, one that was not her husband. Lisa was touched and Vanessa annoyed when Graham asked Lisa to be that person. With cocoa Christine had fixed for everyone, the three of them sat before the cold hearth. It was nearly midnight. The sheriff had Ellie explain her visit to

Ginger's—she had driven the spare car from the lodge around the lake—and listened patiently to her tell how impressed she was with Ginger's baking skills and quaint cabin.

"So you ordered some baked goods to take back with you?" he asked, obviously surprising Ellie.

"Why, yes, I did. I suppose Vanessa or Lisa told you that. She was to bake them later. The items she'd been working on for a couple of days were to sell at the Talkeetna festival."

"Lisa," he said, turning to her, "I forgot to tell you, I got the baked goods in the trunk of the car. It's okay by Spike, it's okay by me, a nice way to honor Ginger's memory. But if word gets out you're selling a dead woman's items tomorrow, don't you or anyone else be telling your theories about what happened. Got that?"

"Got that, Sheriff. And thanks for permission."

"Now, you ladies recall if anyone paid her up front for the goods she was gonna bake for you?" he asked.

"Actually, I did," Ellie said, her index finger hooked over her gold necklace, sliding back and forth. If Lisa had had any prep time with her, she'd have told her there was nothing to be nervous about. But she could understand. Ellen Carlisle Bonner was hardly used to being interrogated by the police.

"I gave her fifty dollars," Ellie said.

"Nice price for bakery items," the sheriff said, writing in his notebook again. "But then we're gonna have to figure out where she got this—whose handwriting's on it, too, though we can sure lift prints." He turned around to pull a ziplocked plastic bag from a paper sack he'd placed behind his chair. "There's not fifty but two hundred dollars in cash in the envelope inside here, with the printed return address of The Duck Lake Lodge, Bear Bones, Alaska," he told them. "Besides Ginger's name, the envelope bears the words *more to come.*" Lisa leaned forward far enough to see that was exactly what it said.

"Found in a drawer in her bedroom," the sheriff added. "Of course, we'll fingerprint the envelope and money—we're kinda low-tech around here, since fancy DNA forensic work goes to Fairbanks or Anchorage. But we can also trace the handwriting on the envelope." When Ellie sat back farther in her chair as if it was beneath her to squint at the envelope, the sheriff dropped it back in his sack.

Then, as Lisa's clients had done to her many a time, Ellie blurted, "You won't have to look far, Sheriff. I did order only fifty dollars of baked goods, but I put the other one hundred and fifty in there as a gift. That's my writing. But I promised Ginger I wouldn't tell anyone, and now I have."

Thank heavens, Lisa thought, the explanation was perfectly in line with the way Ellie and the Bonners operated—gifts for the needy, generosity on a grand scale. She wouldn't embarrass Ellie by extolling the Bonners' various kindnesses in front of her, but she'd make sure the sheriff realized that there was nothing suspicious or unusual in that gesture. To the Bonners, that sort of donation was like her leaving a dollar tip on the counter at a Starbucks.

"And the more to come?" he prompted Ellie. "Why that?"

"The woman was good-hearted, and I liked her. I have discretionary money for when I see someone in need."

The sheriff nodded and said no more. He didn't seem upset, but Ellie was. After all, Ellie had been coddled and protected by strong men all her life. But after being around so many attorneys and her father's and husband's precious law firm, didn't Ellie know when she'd said enough? Lisa's lawyer sixth sense made her feel more was coming.

"Sheriff," Ellie said, "I just thought she needed encouragement for standing up to Gus Majors when he tried to bully her. I wondered why he didn't want to be around her when he brought Lisa and Mitch back from their river adventure, so I asked Ginger why. It seems she was quite afraid of the man."

"That right, Mrs. Bonner?"

"That's right, Sheriff."

Damn, Lisa thought, as he scribbled something, then flipped his small, spiral notebook closed. She hoped Mitch would take on Gus as a pro bono client if serious charges were filed against him, because she couldn't practice law in this state. And despite that Gus seemed an obvious suspect, she just didn't believe he would hurt Ginger. But then, in her deepest being, she still couldn't fathom that anyone had tried to kill her, either.

16

Lisa tiptoed downstairs before anyone else was up and headed for the library and the wine cellar. She was hoping no one would be in her way as Christine had been last time. Noises from the kitchen and a half-set breakfast table told her Christine was up and busy. The more she got to know the woman, the more she became convinced that, despite Christine's past, she would not have pushed her into the river. Lisa's original theory about Christine protecting Mitch or even wanting him for herself could be valid, but the fact she'd reached out so emotionally to Spike made Lisa think Christine was just as close to both men who were part of her little family here.

As Lisa opened the door to the cellar, she saw that the light was on. She closed the door behind her and started down the steps.

"Mitch?"

He didn't respond. Maybe he'd turned the light on for her, then gone for something he'd forgotten. Pulling her sweater tighter around her shoulders, she went down and sat in the single chair. The lighting behind the bottles bathed the area in a warm, greenish glow, but it was cool down here. She'd never forget how cold the river was. The slightest breath of chilly air made her remember the numbing feel of it. The hot tub that first night back had helped, but she'd try the sauna soon, maybe tonight. She'd loved the sauna at the club where she used to work out. At least Mother and Jani hadn't died in cold water. They were lost in the Gulf Stream that the cruise ship's captain said might carry them far away.

She hadn't slept well last night, but that was to be expected. No doubt, the others hadn't either. Her mind drifted, pulled away by the current...down, around rocks, trying to catch hold...hold of herself in the green shifting, rushing waters...tried to get hold of Mitch...

Lisa jerked alert. Had she dozed off?

Feeling groggy, she opened her eyes and saw her mother's face again, staring at her through green water, her eyes huge, wide, like Ginger's death stare. She leaped to her feet, knocking the chair and crate table over, slamming backward into the bottles behind her. They rattled and shuddered, making reflections jump and sway. She was in the dark depths of the sea with Mother watching her....

Her heart nearly pounded out of her chest. No, this was reality, not even a dream. Wake up, wake up! The staring eyes were just strange lights through the bottom of two big bottles. She'd imagined she'd seen human eyes there, magnified, huge. Nothing there. Nothing. She was going crazy.

This was all too much, delayed reaction from her river ride, childhood flashbacks again. Paranoia that someone had tried to kill her. Exhaustion, physical and mental. Survivor's guilt. Compassion fatigue. She knew all the terms, the psychobabble buzzwords, diagnoses and verdicts. She was what an attorney would call an unreliable witness. Had she been pushed into the river? Should she tell Mitch she was wavering on that and just back off on Vanessa and Jonas?

She heard the door open above and quickly righted the crate and chair. Her pulse still pounding, she moved toward the stairs as Mitch came down.

"I was hoping to get a good night's sleep, but I guess none of us did," he greeted her. He looked as if he'd tossed and turned all night. His hair was mussed like a boy's and little wrinkle marks where he'd slept against a pillow or blanket marred his left cheek.

"I know I look like a wreck," she admitted, wanting to stroke those lines from his cheek and brow, "but Ginger's face haunted me."

He pulled her to him in a strong hug. She held on to him hard, her chin clamping his shoulder to her throat, her arms tight around his waist. He felt so strong, so stable in her sliding, shifting world.

"So," he whispered, his warm breath moving the hair by her ear, "I heard Graham and Ellie arguing last night."

She raised her head to look at him as he set her back, then pushed her gently down into the single chair. He sat with one hip on the edge of the crate, leaning toward her. "I don't think I've ever heard them raise their voices to each other before."

"Me neither. Could you tell over what?"

"Her giving money to Ginger and promising more. Since I'm playing Sherlock Holmes lately, I actually listened at their door."

"I didn't think he ever objected to her charity projects, large or small. I used to think it was because the firm's financial base—and his wealth—was really from her father, and that gave her a certain unspoken power over Graham."

"Agreed, but he may be worried Ginger's death will turn out to be more than an accident, and he doesn't want his wife—or any of his lawyers—to be even slightly involved or tainted."

"Why would he assume her death might be more than an accident? He should be thinking just the opposite."

"Because he's been a lawyer for years, and he's seen the worst in humanity. He's dealt with some really devious people who could swear up and down they were innocent when they weren't and then—I'm sorry to say—he'd defend some of them anyway."

She heaved a huge sigh. "I know you've always admired him."

"Haven't you?"

"Of course. But, if someone's clever, apparent accidents can actually be murder, which is what we could be up against here. On the other hand, I'm wondering if I should stop suspecting anyone of attempted murder for pushing me in the river."

"Second thoughts on if that really happened?"

She looked up at him. Maybe she should stop suspecting people she thought she knew and respected and just go on. Be very careful and aware, but just go on. No one had murdered her mother and Jani— no one but life's hardships and her mother's sick soul. But the denial of her being deliberately shoved into the river wouldn't come to her lips.

"I still think I was pushed," she whispered.

"Then we go with that. So have you thought any more about Vanessa setting you up to find Ginger's body?"

"As you said yesterday, it's all circumstantial. It's like, maybe Jonas cut his own towline on the sled, maybe Vanessa is out to cut me off from the competition...or from life...maybe, maybe... Mitch, it's driving me nuts."

"Though I don't want you to go, I'd send you home, but no one's going anywhere until the sheriff says so."

"Except to the Mountain Mother Festival. I think we'd all agree to cancel that, but we can't just sit around here and stare at each other while waiting for the coroner's report. And it is a good idea to sell the baked goods Ginger left to help Spike out."

"Ordinarily, he'd be taking festival visitors flightseeing on short jaunts today, but he's not up for that. The sheriff told him he could have access to Ginger's cabin, so he wants to spend the day there. I told him I'd go with him, but he wanted to be alone, and I had to honor that."

"I'll bet Christine would like to be with him, but she's going with us, too. She said Ginger had a booth rented, so setup won't be too hard."

"I thought maybe you were learning more about what Christine's really like, one strong woman to another, who has risen above a personal tragedy."

"But it's still pulling me under," she muttered as she turned away. She started up the steps, careful not to look at the array of bottles lighted from behind again.

"What did you say?" he called after her.

"Onward and upward. See you at breakfast." She hurried up out of the green-gray depths of the little room.

Maybe, Lisa thought, as they carried Ginger's baked items into the Mountain Mother Festival grounds in Talkeetna, this would be good for all of them. She saw normal people everywhere—families, activities, laughter, noise. Reality that didn't threaten and endanger or drown one's rational thoughts.

As they set up their money box and neatly arranged the variety of muffins, breads, cookies and cakes with their price labels, Lisa looked around. In the next booth, a woman hung small, quilted wall hangings, now and then shouting at her two young boys to stop hitting each other. Across the way two women who looked like sisters put out painted tole wear in their booth; both had babies in carriers on their backs. Two men helped to tack up a sign reading Talkeetna Tole Wear Tells A Tale. What would it be like to live here, to raise a family here?

"Talkeetna certainly is the big city compared to Bear Bones," Vanessa said, interrupting Lisa's musings. Vanessa had been really cold to her on the way in, but everyone was uptight, so she'd tried to ignore that. No way was she going to let herself get all tied in knots every time Vanessa said something bitter or nasty. She had to accept that, once out of the office where camaraderie was expected, the woman's snippy self came out. But mostly, Lisa was trying to cut Vanessa some slack because she'd scared herself lately, wavering on whether she'd really been pushed. One minute she was certain of it, the next, she realized her flashbacks could have made her memory untrustworthy, no matter what she'd vowed to Mitch in the cellar earlier this morning.

Also, Vanessa seemed to really be sucking up to Ellie today, much more so than usual. Perhaps she sensed or had been told how shaken Ellie was from her interview with the sheriff.

"You think this place is packed now," Christine told them, "wait till you see it later. People around here go on what they call 'Talkeetna time'—always running late—but they'll all be here in time for the Moose Dropping part of the festivities."

"The what?" Ellie asked. "Vanessa, you've done several cases concerning animal rights. Christine, exactly who is dropping a moose from where around here?"

Christine smiled—a rarity, Lisa thought. "No, Mrs. Bonner," Christine told Ellie. "It's the moose that make the droppings, and people find plenty of them each year when the snow melts. While they're frozen, they get shellacked—the, you know, the droppings, not the moose—and made into either jewelry or something to throw at a target today. See here, these earrings I'm wearing today," she said, pulling back her black hair and shaking her head so her dangling earrings bounced. "You haven't been to Talkeetna if you don't have some of this jewelry!"

"Oh, my word!" Ellie muttered with a roll of her eyes as Christine displayed her shiny gems.

Vanessa grinned, too. "I thought those were polished or shellacked Sitka spruce," she said. "Mitch said it's used to make Steinway pianos and other wooden instruments, because of its tight spiral grain, so I just thought…"

Despite their dire circumstances and Ginger's lovely baked goods laid out before them like a memorial to her, they all had to laugh. It felt good, so good, Lisa thought. Poor Ginger had evidently loved life. In honor of that, suddenly, Lisa was determined to have a good time today. Maybe nothing else terrible would happen on this entire trip—that is, until she had to say goodbye to Mitch again.

* * *

When Lisa took her turn to walk around the festival for a while, Mitch quickly appeared at her side. "So what do you think?" he asked, with a sweep of his hand around the bustling, noisy scene.

"I think it's great. A far cry from the Broward or Dade County Fairs."

"Come on over here so you can see what a Mountain Mother is supposed to be able to do."

"Swim a rushing river and come out alive?" she asked, as he took her hand and pulled her into a cheering crowd.

"Not even some of them could handle that—unless they had Mitchell Andrew Braxton at their beck and call, of course."

She laughed for the second time today and punched his shoulder with her fist.

They wove their way through the thickening crowd to a central area with a lake and a culvert filled with water. With baby dolls in their backpacks, ten women took turns walking a log in hip waders while toting two buckets of water. Their audience whooped and hollered encouragement. One woman had a sign on her back under her doll baby: Attila the Mom!

Other parts of the round robin of tasks included chopping firewood, carrying bags of groceries, and running an obstacle course which included a simulated river crossing, using logs and stepping stones.

"That's nothing!" Lisa told Mitch with an elbow to his ribs. "Where are the live bears and the cable car?"

Lisa was especially touched by the children cheering on their mothers, while the fathers clapped and hooted encouragement. She wondered again what it would be like to be a mountain mother here, not in this fun festival but in daily life.

She and Mitch wandered past stores with sidewalk sales, art galleries, museums and restaurants.

"The cultural side of the town reminds me some of Taos, New Mexico," she told him. "I had no idea about the art galleries and museums. I just expected gift shops."

"Some great restaurants, too, not just greasy spoons if that's what you were thinking. By the way, the prize for winning that Mountain Mother contest is a trip to Europe. See, we're not all heathens and savages here."

She turned to smile at him. Again, despite the whirl of noise and movement, their gazes met and held.

"Except in bed," he added with a grin and turned away before she could comment.

They wandered over to the Moose Dropping Festival near the VFW building. "Even this has a veneer of civility," Mitch told her. "It's a fundraiser for the Talkeetna Historical Society, and it brings in a bundle. There's a raffle, and people buy numbered, shellacked moose droppings that are let go from that big net up there," he said, pointing. "See that moose-shaped board on the ground? Whoever has the number that hits closest to the bull's-eye on it wins big prizes."

"Most unique," she said with another little laugh. "But, still, I preferred the way I played my own moose game. Of course, I just pretended that bull moose coming out of the lake scared me so I could jump into your arms."

"Hah! Wish that were true!"

Lisa knew they were flirting just the way they had when they first knew each other. Here she was with a man she'd thought she never wanted to see again. Being with Mitch might be a dead-end street, but she loved it—maybe still loved him.

As the two of them headed back toward the rows of rented booths, they saw Jonas, Graham and Ellie in the distance, heads bent together in earnest conversation. Then nodding at something and somehow looking relieved, Jonas went off by himself, talking into and snapping pictures with his cell phone.

"That reminds me," Mitch said. "Graham wants to have one-on-one interviews with his three candidates this evening. More of a debriefing, if you ask me. Then tomorrow, I thought we'd have a memorial service for Ginger, and Spike really liked that idea. He asked that we have it at the ziplining site, since she liked that so much, but I'm wary of actually doing the ziplining. Too many so-called accidents lately."

"But if it means something to Spike..."

"Yeah, I know. Maybe we can just have the service out under the platform and make the ziplining completely voluntary. I can picture Ginger now, zinging along, red hair flying, whooping and hollering. She never liked flying like Spike does but she loved zooming along on my zipline."

"You know, when Spike was flying us in to the lodge, Jonas was kidding about our challenges here being like that *Survivor* show, but Ellie vehemently said this was as much for bonding as competition. At that moment, it almost made me think this might be her idea as much as Graham's. I think she's always been the power behind the throne, but she sure was shaken last night."

"Alaskan sheriffs aren't supposed to step behind the throne or even near it," Mitch muttered so darkly that Lisa turned to look at him. He'd seemed so even-tempered and strong through the chaos of this week, but she saw that he, too, was deeply bothered by the betrayal of someone he knew and trusted.

As they turned the corner toward the bakery booth, where Vanessa and Christine were taking their turns, Gus appeared, putting himself in their path. Lisa thought he must have been waiting for them. As far as she could tell, the cranberry muffin he was just finishing had been baked by Ginger, so he must have been over to the booth. Wasn't the fact he wasn't shunning any of them a sign he wasn't guilty of anything? The guy didn't seem to have a duplicitous bone in his big body.

"Hey, Gus," Mitch greeted him.

Gus motioned them off to the side, and they walked over to a quiet spot where they could hear

each other better. Gus kept looking around, rather fur-
tively, and Lisa's lawyer antennae went up. She could
tell the big man was distraught, so he'd probably not
only been told about Ginger's bizarre death, but interrogated about it. Lisa had known the sheriff would
question Gus immediately.

"Sheriff Moran came to Bear Bones to talk to me,"
Gus said, "then drove me here to get fingerprinted. He
was asking all kinds of stuff about me and Ginger.
Mitch, you know I'd never hurt her. Fighting—arguing, I mean—that's how we got along half the time.
She wouldn't move into town, said I'd have to live in
the boonies if we got married, but I said no way."

Mitch put his hand on the big man's shoulder.
"We've all been questioned and several of the
women, including Lisa, were fingerprinted, too. The
sheriff has to look at all angles."

"Never thought I'd say this, but I might need a
lawyer. Heard tell you got your license for here."

"I did and I'm willing," Mitch assured him. "Listen, Lisa, could you give us a minute in private so I
can talk to my new client?"

Mitch knew Lisa would understand attorney-client
privilege. She nodded, patted Gus on the shoulder and
moved away from them, strolling past the craft booths.

"So, Gus, let's just get to it," Mitch said as they
walked farther away from the crowd. "When you left
Ginger, you swear she was all right?"

"If you call spitting mad at me all right. Cussed

me out, said she had a ship coming in, whatever that meant. Said she didn't need a man in her life who tried to tell her how and where she had to live. Except for the ship coming in, same stuff she yelled at me at the café in town—which lots of people saw and will prob'ly tell the sheriff about."

Mitch realized the ship coming in could be the money from Ellie that both Ellie and Graham had mentioned to him. He told Gus, "Mrs. Bonner gave Ginger some cash but she can't have thought that would add up to much or be a long-term thing."

"And Ginger said she was selling some of her baked stuff to your guests, but I didn't figure that was much of a ship coming in."

"I take it the sheriff didn't charge you with anything," Mitch said, looking the big man straight in the eye.

"Naw, but he told me not to leave the area. I just didn't like the way things were going when he questioned me."

"Then until something else happens, lie low, and don't tell anyone you've hired a lawyer."

"You need payment up front? I always pay my bills."

"How about free chain-saw sharpening for life?" Mitch told him. "But there's something else I would like to know. Did Ginger say anything at any time about enemies or someone else she was angry with besides you?"

"Naw. Angry with not having money for what she wanted sometimes, that's all."

"Did she ever say anything about the day Lisa fell in the river?" Mitch asked. "We think Ginger was in the area that day and might have seen or heard someone or something."

"You mean like a scream when she fell in? Someone like who?"

"Gus," Mitch said, "Lisa and I will keep your secret that you're lawyered-up, so we'd like you to keep one of ours. She didn't just fall in the river. She was pushed."

"Who by?" he demanded, frowning, then shook his head. "Not by Ginger."

"I didn't say that. We're trying to find out who. So did Ginger ever breathe a word about seeing or hearing anything that day? You did talk about driving us back to the lodge, didn't you?"

"Yeah, she was glad I found you. But she said nothing about the day Lisa went in the river. Did you tell the sheriff she was pushed? What if there's like— I mean, a mass-murderer type who drowns women or tries to, anyway?"

Whoever thought Gus Majors didn't have much upstairs was wrong, Mitch thought. Dead wrong.

PART III

Meeting the Monster

It was a monstrous big river down there.
—Mark Twain

17

"Lisa, please come in and sit down," Graham said as she entered the lodge library that evening for what the Bonners were calling an informal interview and Mitch had called a debriefing.

He'd rearranged the furniture and was sitting in a chair under Christine's shelf of dolls. At a glance, Lisa could tell the dolls had been moved around, but by Graham or Christine? Did he hope to manipulate his three candidates the same way in these private sessions?

She sat in the leather chair facing him, one that was lower and smaller than his, much the way he had things set up in his office back home. A table next to him displayed neat piles of magazines on Alaska. Graham's chair had arms so he could rest his elbows; hers did not, so she clasped her hands lightly in her lap. He had no notes, not even a pen out, but she saw a small tape recorder on the table. He was going to tape these sessions? Perhaps another ploy to keep his candidates off guard to see how they would react.

"I hope you don't mind if I record our conversation," he said. "I borrowed Ellie's recorder."

"She's always been like a silent partner, a home-based senior partner, too," Lisa said, forcing a smile. Despite all they'd been through together, even after how supportive Graham had been over the years, she suddenly felt uneasy with him. She had a feeling if she blew this interview, she could kiss the senior partnership goodbye. Strange how her passion for that had faded after the events of the past few days.

"So, first of all, Ellie and I want you to know again how sorry we are that you had the accident with the river, but, thank God, Mitch realized what had happened and had the skills to save you. But that brings me to my first inquiry. No doubt, facing Mitch here in Alaska—being civil to him, after how he let you down—was one thing you had to overcome that the other two candidates for this position did not. Yet you seem to be getting on well with him, to have buried the hatchet, so to speak."

"I was angry and hurt by his decision to move here, and we both reacted emotionally. I couldn't understand why he'd throw everything away—until I came here."

"An appreciation of the place or a real reconciliation of sorts?" he probed. She could read nothing in his expression.

"A peace treaty at least," she said, choosing not to elaborate. Just answer the questions, she told herself, at least until the closing argument. Besides, she wasn't exactly sure what the terms were between her and Mitch, because they'd talked of everything else—survival in the wilds, who tried to kill her, Ginger's death, their past, but not their future. Because, of course, there was no future for them, not together.

"Did being with him under extreme circumstances remind you at all of when you were both under surveillance during the casino case—the stress, threats and danger?"

In a way, she thought, she was under surveillance now. By the Bonners and her two rivals—as well as Mitch for a different reason, and the ever-watchful Christine. And now she was being recorded. Could the unidentified person she saw from the window the night she and Mitch talked in the hot tub have come down to retrieve a voice recorder that had been left there? That possibility would never have crossed her mind, but mention of the casino case reminded her that her condo and car—Mitch's, too—had been bugged.

"Quite honestly, Graham, nearly drowning in the river and then our struggle to get back here reminded me not of the casino case but of the terrible time when I lost my mother and sister."

"Yes, of course. Again, I'm so sorry, and I do understand," he said, tapping his clasped fingers against his lips. "Still, you've worked your way out of that trauma and instability before, and you evidently have again, but a senior partner position adds a lot of stress. And then for you to be the one to find poor Ginger drowned like that—what was your immediate reaction?"

"Shock and horror, of course. Disbelief at first. I screamed for Vanessa to come out on the dock and look."

"Just screamed her name?"

Her eyes bored into his steady stare. Vanessa must have told Graham that she'd screamed her mother's name. But had she really done that or had Vanessa made that up?

"Just screamed—no one's name," she insisted. "But I also recovered myself quickly enough to tell Vanessa we should not pull the body up as she'd asked at first. Whether it was an accident, suicide or murder, we needed to preserve the scene. And I recalled what Mitch had said about the sign for summoning help from a distance, so I managed to climb onto Spike's plane to get their attention."

"So I heard. Ellie and I were in the sauna and missed all that. Spike and Mitch didn't even tell us they were leaving, but jumped in the boat and took off. You do realize I'm not questioning your judgment or ability to be calm in tough situations? You've proved that both in Lauderdale and here. I just wanted to hear things in your words, just as I've interviewed Vanessa and Jonas a bit ago about their experiences here so far. His back's hurting from his fall off the sled, but he's a trooper. Vanessa, of course, is always tough as those acrylic nails of hers. Is there anything you'd like to say about either of them in this competition?"

"I won't presume to judge them, since that's your business—yours and Ellie's. I would not have wanted this position so badly if it wasn't for you, Graham, your kindness over the years, your eye for talent and opportunity, your example, and, of course, your amazing rainmaker talent for attracting influential clients. I certainly trust you to make the right decision for who can best help Carlisle, Bonner and Associates to be even stronger and better, not only for your attorneys or yourself, but for your daughter, when she joins us."

He nodded and reached over to switch off the recorder. "You always had a way with words and with people, Lisa. I regret the hard times in your life, but I believe they have made you stronger. What's that Nietzsche quote about that?"

Again she looked straight at his deep-set blue eyes, and a shiver snaked up her spine. He knew that quote, so why did he want her to recite it? What else was he setting her up for? Was this some sort of message to her—even a threat—or was she making too much of things again?

"I know the one," she said. "'That which does not kill us makes us stronger.'"

The moment Mitch came downstairs from his office to wait for Lisa's interview to end, Jonas waylaid him and motioned him toward the windows overlooking the river. Mitch and Lisa had decided to meet at the spot where she'd been pushed in so she could perhaps recall more about what had happened. She hadn't wanted to go near the place before, but she was obviously desperate enough to do it now. Mitch knew he'd have to make this quick with Jonas, because he didn't want her going alone.

Jonas waited in the corner of the great room where Mitch had left a few of his uncle's many hunting trophies hanging, a pursuit he did not choose to follow. Mounted heads, most done in Gus's taxidermy shop, used to dominate the walls all over the lodge. When Mitch was a kid, the ones that hung in his bedroom used to give him the creeps at night. A moose head with a huge rack of antlers and a caribou gazed down on them now as they huddled together.

"I just want to assure you again," Jonas said, "that, despite back and neck pain, I won't be bringing any sort of action for the sledding accident against you or Spike, the poor guy."

Mitch chose not to ask him why he'd brought it up then. He nodded. "We appreciate that," he said and started to turn away, but Jonas grabbed his arm.

"I was going to ask Graham if I could have my interview in the spa or sauna because that helps my pain, but figured I didn't want to push my luck with him—that he'd think I was trying to play on his sympathies. But if anyone can do that, it's Lisa with all she's been through."

"Are you accusing her of that for some reason?"

Mitch countered. "Spit it out, man. I told you more than once when you were new at the firm that, between colleagues, straight talk is the way to go."

"Okay, okay," he said, holding up both hands. "I know Graham thinks a lot of you and vice versa, just like I always looked up to you, and you helped me get grounded in the firm, taught me a lot. Now I'm asking for your continued help and support. If the Bonners ask you for a recommendation for the senior partner position, I'm hoping, since I was your protégé, you'll put in a good word for me. Vanessa's volatile, and Lisa shaky at times. You know that."

"Shaky?"

"Yeah, about her past, about her life's disappointments."

"And your quest to help Emerson, the fear of possibly losing him, the stress of all that care and money hasn't shaken you up at times?"

Jonas suddenly looked frustrated and furious, but Mitch could tell he fought showing it. And he'd called Vanessa volatile? Suddenly, Mitch was certain Jonas had rigged that fall from the sled, but he'd probably never prove it. Could that mean this man he'd liked, trusted and groomed could have been desperate enough to push Lisa in the river?

"So, what do you think of these trophies?" Mitch continued with a nod toward the mounted heads. "My uncle was proud of them, but my trophies in life are a different kind. Not head-hunting, but I share with him his goal of helping people to find a beautiful place and find themselves. Jonas, your real trophies in life are your family and the career you've worked hard to build—helping people that way. It's admirable, and whatever happens, you've got a lot going for you. I'm not a senior partner for the firm anymore, and the decision about the new one is up to Graham, so let's leave it at that."

"Yeah, yeah, I hear you," Jonas said, his voice cold and hard as he frowned up at the mounted heads, wiping his big, strong hands on his jeans, repeatedly. It was as if he wanted to wipe away something he'd said. Or done.

Lisa wanted to wait for Mitch, meant to wait for him, but he wasn't in sight yet. She didn't want someone to see her standing on the patio and join her. Besides, she had to prove to herself she was not afraid of the river, however much she'd been avoiding it, even when its continual rumble reminded her of its power. Mitch had checked the area where she'd been pushed for clues, so she'd told herself she didn't have to go there. But now, she felt she did.

She slowly left the lodge behind and strolled the ridge path between the lake and the river, sure he'd soon catch up. She looked behind and ahead constantly, even glancing down both slopes below the path. Bird sounds were muted; the breeze through the branches became muffled; only the roar of the river filled her ears and her head.

Lake Dukhoe, now looking fairly placid, had

probably taken Ginger's life, whether she was the victim of an accident or of a murderer. Lisa felt certain she had not committed suicide. But was it coincidence that Ginger drowned, or was it a second and intentional attempt at murder by water, this time a success for someone?

She went a bit farther on the path and glanced back to where she knew Ginger docked her boat near the lodge. Either from the lake or on her way into the lodge after she put in, Ginger could have seen someone on this path, maybe saw someone push her, or at least later learned Lisa had fallen in and had drawn her own conclusions. Lisa squatted and checked the sight angles again. Yes, that was possible.

She looked back toward the kitchen windows to see if Christine might have noted anything from there. No, she could have seen Ginger but not the spot where Lisa had stopped to spray herself with mosquito repellent and where someone shoved her.

Though she'd avoided doing so before, Lisa glanced down at the white water beneath her. It still frightened her, like some monster in a fairy tale. She leaned against a young tree and clamped her arms around it to anchor herself. Ginger's anchor chain— did it just snag her, or did someone wrap it around her leg to hold her down?

Again she looked back down the path and then ahead. Still holding the tree, she glanced down toward the spot on the lake where Mitch had left the red, two-person kayak for their trip that day—could it be only four days ago? Mitch had been forced to abandon the kayak back in the river canyon. She hadn't offered to pay him for it, but she should. She owed him so much—so much....

The roar of the river riveted her. Just ahead, she saw the general area she'd been shoved in. Maybe if she stood there again, tried to reconstruct, to recall... But she wanted Mitch here first, someone with her.

She had to admit that water was mesmerizing. It made the Wild River look not only wild, but wider, deeper than it must actually be. Over the years, it would probably grow in her imagination, in her nightmares. The rush of the white-water current, the swirling eddies were compelling, like a huge, living creature beckoning her to come into its arms, to come along....

She let go of the tree and took a step along the path. This was the very place she'd tumbled in—she recognized the sapling she'd tried to seize, but it had only bent under her weight. Bent but not broken, bent but not broken...

"Lisa! You said you'd wait!"

Mitch hurried toward her. Then came the flurry of something nearby, a sharp scream, a shrill cry. She saw a blur between them with white wings vibrating, a neck and head of shining copper in the slant of sun.

The scream, Lisa realized, had been hers. She fought hard to push away the memory of herself tumbling in the river, of Ginger beneath the water. Worse, her mother in her mind's eye.

A bird! Mitch had startled a bird, that's all. The

roar and rush of the water—the monster river would not devour her this time.

"Sweetheart, I said to wait for me!" Mitch said, taking her shoulders in his hands before he pulled her to him.

They held on to each other. "It just happened, step by step," she said, her voice shaky, her mouth near his ear before they stepped apart. "But what was that bird?"

"A ptarmigan."

"Never heard of it."

"It's Alaska's state bird, and they're proud of it. Special—unique."

"I guess so! It—it actually sounded like a really loud frog."

"They have feathered feet and don't migrate. If Alaskans say a person has feathered feet, they mean they'll stay, not go back to the lower forty-eight. A special bird, special people who stay. You sure you're all right?"

"Absolutely. At least I did better than when that moose rose from the lake. Mitch, I'm sure this is the place, right here, where I went in."

"Yeah. I can tell from the smashed vegetation and scraped lichens where I shoved the kayak up and down. Did anything come to you?"

"Just the magnetism of the river. I really think, if someone stared into it long enough, it makes you feel you're moving with it—or want to be."

"Yes, I can see that. You can get almost dizzy. But

are you certain that's not what happened to you? Stand right there a moment and remember once and for all," he said, stepping behind her.

Reluctantly, she turned to look at the fabulous but fearsome river again. Although Mitch stood behind her, just like whoever had pushed her, with him here, she was not afraid.

"I couldn't hear anyone because of the roar, because I was fascinated," she said over her shoulder, raising her voice to be heard. "I was remembering when I lost Mother and Jani, but I did not leap toward it. If I wanted to jump in, I would have gone down this bank, gotten closer first. Mitch," she said, turning to face him, "I have wavered on this, I know I have. You have, too, wondering what really happened. Like Ginger, I hit my head—the shock of the water... But I *was* pushed, and I'm going to find out who did it."

"I'm with you. I always have been on this."

"I need your help. Even if the sheriff says we have to stay here a few days longer until the autopsy results are finalized, we don't have much time. I've got to do something to make someone come to the surface."

"What are you thinking?"

"Maybe I could tell Vanessa I think Jonas pushed me in—divide and conquer, swear her to secrecy. Maybe tell him just the opposite. But then Vanessa and Jonas might both tell Graham I'm trying to play one against the other—which would be true. Let's see what the coroner and sheriff say about Ginger. If it's murder, we'll tell him what happened to me and let him take over, though that would be the end of me at the law firm. But this has become more important, when I never thought anything could be. Alaska and your love for it have helped me to put things in perspective."

"It means everything to hear you say that. I'd like to think you could forgive me for leaving you the way I did. And remember about feathered feet—just don't let them get wet."

18

"I finally got some sleep," Lisa told Christine the next morning. She poured herself a glass of orange juice as Christine set the breakfast table. "I guess I was too wound up before, because I've been exhausted ever since I—I fell in the river."

"*Iah,* emotional exhaustion's awful. You're so tired, but your mind keeps going. So, if you need a jolt of carbs, I bought some muffins and rolls while we were in Talkeetna," she said, arranging some on a plate. "Still, nothing's going to replace Ginger. One of a kind."

"For sure. When my grandmother, who also made great baked goods, died, I couldn't bear to bake for the longest time, though she'd taught me everything I know about that, and I loved to do it. As for Ginger being unique, it seems most things and people in Alaska are one of a kind."

Christine nodded at that, her eyes sparkling with approval. "You're still black and blue," she observed. "You ought to use the sauna like Jonas has since he got hurt. Good for what ails you."

"I've been meaning to. I'm sure it would help, but I've just been so busy and distracted. I will later today. I guess after the memorial service for Ginger, we're all going ziplining. Have you done it? I never have."

"Sure. Good for clearing out the cobwebs and lifting the soul. In Ginger's honor, I'll do it today if it's okay with Mitch."

"You two are a good team here at the lodge," Lisa said.

"With Spike, a trio. Look, I got something to tell you, 'cause Mitch said I should."

Lisa put her glass down. With her empty tray in front of her, Christine sat across the table, so Lisa sat, too. What was coming next? A confession about something? She sensed some sort of warning in the air.

"Don't think I believe all this old lore," Christine said, keeping her voice low, "but I got to tell you about a legend, the kind of story my people call *suktus*. A lot of the old tales have the same hero, but he's really evil, a trickster, the raven, called *chulyen*."

"An evil hero?"

Christine nodded. "Raven gets away with everything in the stories—lying, conning people, stealing, even murder. And the stories, to teach our children to beware of two-faced people, all end with something like, 'the raven was very wise but very crooked.'"

"But I don't see—"

"You and Mitch watch all the others. If I note it, someone else might, too. You're studying their faces, how they act. You are both trying to see who did something very crooked, but remember, raven is also wise, so you must be careful."

Lisa glanced around the room. No one else in sight yet. This woman was in earnest. She was warning her because she cared, maybe only for Mitch, but she cared. Christine wanted to help not harm; Lisa felt that to the very marrow of her bones. Mitch knew and trusted Christine, and he knew her much better than Lisa ever would.

Before she even realized just how much she'd come to trust Christine, she told her in a low, urgent voice, "I was pushed in the river. I didn't just fall in."

Christine's eyes widened, and she nodded. "And maybe Ginger was pushed, too?" she whispered. "Spike still doesn't believe she fell."

"About Ginger—I don't know. But I'm asking you to tell no one what I said right now—even Spike— but to keep your eyes open. I see you do that, too."

"I can tell you one thing. I overheard Vanessa tell Mr. Bonner you screamed and screamed your dead mother's name when you found Ginger's body."

"I knew it! I did not, but she—"

"Sorry to interrupt." A man's voice came from the kitchen as the door opened. Spike walked in. "Thought I'd find you in here, Christine. Hi, Lisa. Is everyone going with us for the memorial today?"

Christine stood, went over to Spike and took his

hand to tug him over to the table. "Yes, to the ziplining platform, like you suggested. They may all be gone when we have the funeral service in Bear Bones, and they want to pay their respects before they leave."

"Good morning, everyone." Ellie's voice resounded as she came downstairs. "Oh, Spike, I didn't know you were here yet. We are all so deeply sorry for your loss," she added, looking as if she would cry.

"I know you understand, Mrs. Bonner," Spike said as Christine put a cup of coffee into his hands and poured one for Ellie. "I remember on our flightseeing tour to Wasilla, you told me how proud you are of your brother, how you'd hate bad press like what happened to our governor. Christine, Mrs. Bonner's younger brother's big in Florida politics and is probably going to be a secretary of something or other in the new administration in Washington."

"Yes, I'm so proud of Merritt," Ellie said. "Who knows how high he can climb, and he began as a lawyer in our firm. And you are so right, Spike. My closeness to my 'little' brother, my only sibling, makes me sympathize with the loss of your sister. I think a memorial service she would have liked is a lovely idea, and Graham and I are honored to be a part of it."

The others filtered downstairs: Jonas, still limping slightly; Vanessa, dressed all in black, even to her jewelry, as if she were in formal mourning; then

Graham and Mitch, who came downstairs together talking about something. Everyone took their places at the table.

Christine had just carried family-style plates of eggs benedict, sausage and bacon from the kitchen when there was a knock at the front door. Before anyone could answer, it opened, and silence fell in the room. As if he were a harbinger of doom, in full uniform with a paper in his hand, Sheriff Mace Moran walked in the doorway.

Mitch jumped up and went to greet the sheriff.

"Sorry my timing's so lousy," he told Mitch, shaking his hand and glancing over his shoulder in the expectant hush. "I asked Sam Collister to expedite the findings on Ginger Jackson, and he did. Got the results right here."

"Would you like to go upstairs to use my office, just tell Spike first?" Mitch asked. Not a murmur or a clink of dishes came from the table behind them as everyone obviously strained to listen.

"It will soon be public knowledge anyway. The local paper's already been asking, and a Fairbanks reporter in town to cover the festival wants the story. Mitch, when I hauled Gus Majors in again—"

"A second time? After yesterday?"

"Yeah, early this morning. Thought maybe he'd crack, but he didn't. I swear he only told me you represented him after I had another go at him."

Spike rose from the table and came over. "Is this

about my sister?" he asked the sheriff, pointing to the paper in his hand.

"Yes, Mr. Jackson, it is. The coroner's report is inconclusive about whether or not it might have been foul play."

"Foul play—a stupid way to put it," Spike insisted, balling up his fists at his sides. "It sounds like a mistake in baseball, not a cold-blooded murder."

At that, Graham and Jonas came over with Ellie and Lisa right behind, followed by Vanessa and Christine.

"Those are the findings, Mr. Jackson. It wasn't a cold-blooded murder or any murder."

"You want me or Spike to read the ruling, Sheriff? Or will you?" Mitch asked.

The sheriff cleared his throat, glanced down at the paper and said, "According to Dr. Samuel Collister, coroner, Gingcr Jackson died of asphyxiation—lack of oxygen—not drowning per se."

"But she was in the water!" Spike protested. "You don't mean she was strangled?"

"No, not at all," the sheriff said. "Actually, Doc Collister said it's called a dry drowning. Her lungs were dry because she'd had a—" he glanced down at the paper again "—a laryngeal spasm, which kept water from entering. The doc says about fifteen percent of drownings are like that. It's no doubt why she stayed so buoyant in the water—air in her lungs."

Mitch shook his head, remembering how Ginger had looked below the surface, moving, shifting. No wonder Lisa had nightmares about her own mother and sister's deaths, because Ginger's haunted him.

"She did have a head injury to the back of the skull," the sheriff said, "but that's consistent with her hitting her head on the dock or boat when she fell in. No doubt, it disoriented her, may have almost knocked her out."

"But," Lisa said, "no one saw any blood on the dock or boat, right? I didn't, and I sat there a while."

"Right," the sheriff said, sounding annoyed and frowning at her. "But I figure, if she fell right in, she may not have bled right away, then the water washed away whatever there was on her skull. Obviously, the heart stops pumping at death, so bleeding stops, too. But hemorrhaging was found in the sinuses and airways," the sheriff went on, then paused. "You sure you want this read aloud, Mr. Jackson?"

"Go ahead. Dry drownings don't make sense to me, but we're loaded with lawyers here."

"The hemorrhaging means she was conscious when she entered the water and struggled to breathe," the sheriff said, looking more nervous after the reference to a lot of lawyers. He spoke more deliberately and slowly, as if that would clarify his explanation. "She sucked in water and her larynx spasmed, so indirectly the water still caused her death. The blow to her head could have incapacitated her from getting back up for air. She had tiny plants and lake-bottom debris under her fingernails but nothing else—nothing to show she'd struggled with a person, that is."

"But depending how long she was in the water, that trace evidence, like the blood, could have been washed away," Lisa argued, despite the fact Ellie put a restraining hand on her arm. "Did the coroner calculate a time of death?"

"Only within a big time frame that takes in the hours she had all those visitors. He recorded the time he pronounced her as the time of death—perfectly legal. Lastly, I surmise that, as she tried to kick to get herself back up to the surface, she snagged her leg in the anchor chain, and that was the last—the last straw. I'm very sorry, Mr. Jackson, Mitch, everyone, but at least we can now close this inquiry as a freak accident and not something else that needs to be pursued. End of story."

End of story for Ginger, Mitch thought, but what about for Lisa? If they had proof she had been pushed, they would lobby for Ginger's case to be reopened. But now that everyone could still leave in forty-eight hours, was it end of story once again for him and Lisa? Worse, if someone had meant to kill her here in the Alaska wilds, away from the Fort Lauderdale police and gung ho Broward County prosecutors and D.A.s, the murderer's time was also running out.

The mourners for Ginger's memorial service walked along a cross-country ski path through a pine-scented forest, with Spike leading and Mitch bringing up the rear. Mitch had explained to everyone that the steel cable zipline began at a high point from a tree platform, built in a sturdy Sitka spruce, and ended over a thousand feet away. It crossed through a treetop canopy, above a small, subalpine meadow and a white-water stream that fed the river before bringing the rider back down to earth about fifty feet from the river itself. He had promised it would be exhilarating but not exhausting, and assured them that they could control their own speed using thick gloves that would protect their hands from burns and slow them when necessary.

"You feel really free when riding it," Spike had said before they'd set out. "Anyone who wants to do it in Ginger's honor today, that's fine. If not—no problem."

No problem—that was a good one, Lisa thought. She'd had nothing but problems since she'd arrived at the lodge, yet she understood that Spike was trying to be certain no one would be accident-prone today.

Christine walked at Spike's side, silent but supportive. Ellie and Graham came next, as the path was only wide enough for two, then Vanessa and Jonas—who forgot to limp at times, Lisa noted. She walked next to Mitch.

"I see the steel cable overhead," she told him, looking up. "The last one of those I rode didn't just cross a stream but the river."

"And you handled that really well. But, as Spike said, don't zipline if you don't want to. I came over early today to check it out—rode it myself—but don't do it if you have the slightest qualm. And Jonas, with your strained back and neck, don't you dare try it."

Lisa saw Mitch's firm mouth quirk up in the corner. He was subtly goading Jonas. So did Mitch believe his former protégé wasn't really hurt either? And if Jonas had lied about that, what else was he covering up?

They stood in a circle under the elevated platform for a moment of silence, then the usually reticent Spike spoke about his sister's life and loves—her home, her baking, ziplining, her dreams about buying "pretty things." He also spoke about how sure-footed she was, though he admitted, with a glance at Christine, that everyone, sooner or later, slipped up in life one way or another.

Christine talked about Ginger's strength. "To be maimed for life as a child, but to still remain one of the most independent women I ever knew."

Mitch explained how he had to practically force Ginger to accept a salary for tending the zipline and for helping him with guests riding it, because "she considered the fun and freedom of riding it payment enough."

Vanessa recounted how proud Ginger was of her cabin and kitchen.

Lisa, with tears in her eyes and a catch in her voice, took her turn. "As terrible as it was to find her in the water, she seemed at peace. She was calmly rocking in the lake she must have loved, somehow at one with nature."

"Exactly," Ellie added. "Although I did not see her in the water, from all of your descriptions, that's the way I pictured her—eternally at peace, rocked to sleep in the beautiful setting she loved."

"I'm real grateful to you," Spike said, turning to Ellie. "For giving her the extra money and saying there would even be more. I don't mind telling everyone what the Bonners suggested I keep secret. They asked to pay for her funeral and burial, now that her body's being released. I'm going to pick out a real nice wood coffin for her."

That generosity hardly surprised those who worked for the Bonners. Graham nodded, and Ellie, with tears in her eyes, went on. "I must share with everyone that I have a favorite painting, but I hesitated to bring the copy of it I ran off yesterday on Mitch's printer. The original is hanging at the Tate Museum in London, a serene, lovely painting called *Ophelia.* In case you don't know, she was a character who drowned in Shakespeare's tragedy *Hamlet,* but let me describe the painting. She lies so calmly, cradled by the water, looking up, surrounded by tree limbs and boughs hanging over her. Flowers float in the water. I think it would be lovely if we cast some flowers in the lake in Ginger's honor. Well, I didn't mean to get carried away, but I will think of her that way, at rest, in peace."

Lisa had never seen that painting, but she could grasp how it could be both lovely and horrible with a compelling yet monstrous beauty, death almost defied. She'd seen such visions in her head for years.

* * *

"You sure you're all right with this?" Mitch said to Lisa after he sent Spike down the gravity-driven zipline to await everyone's arrival at the other end.

"You said it's safe, and it obviously is. Yes, let the others go first, but I'd like to do it, too. I could use a dose of Ginger's gumption to really enjoy it."

One by one, everyone took a turn on the steel cable challenge course except for Jonas, who had no choice but to walk to the zipline terminal. Finally, only Mitch and Lisa stood on the platform, high in the big tree, with blowing limbs and leaves around them.

"Have you thought any more about pitting Vanessa and Jonas against each other?" he asked as he helped her into one of the harnesses.

"I think one or both would run to Graham, but I've been considering something else. I still say that Ginger could have been hit on the head and held down under the water. But what I've really been agonizing over is Graham. Mitch, speaking of *Hamlet*—"

"Were we?"

"Ellie was—that painting. Graham doth protest too much, methinks."

"What are you talking about?"

"About the casino case. His pulling us off the case because it got so dangerous, then our breakup and your leaving kept us from talking about that again, but he keeps trying to find out if we've reminisced about it since we've been back together. He recorded my interview today and told me he'd done that with the others, but I heard Jonas tell Vanessa that Graham took notes during his. So I'll bet he wasn't recording them. Does any of that make sense?"

"The fact we had our phones bugged and got some threatening phone calls to cease and desist—it's not enough to make the link, but let's consider that. I had the strangest feeling from the first that an attack on you here could be an attack on me somehow, only you were more vulnerable. Look, we can't take all day, or they'll think we're making love in the treetops—which does seem like a good idea," he added with a quick caress of her cheek followed by a pat on her bottom.

Even in the cool breeze, he saw her face flame. He wanted to seize her, make love to her right there on the hard wood of the platform.

"But, no, it doesn't make sense," he went on, his voice husky. It was difficult to reason right now, but she was probably on to something he'd subconsciously tried to ignore, because of all he owed Graham. "Graham does seem hung up on that case," he admitted. "Maybe he feels guilty he copped out in the face of opposition, reined us in too fast. The leads should have been followed to expose whoever was behind all that money laundering and why. Maybe we'd better get our heads together fast about what we do recall besides being threatened during that trial preparation. Meet me in the wine cellar before predinner-drink time, if you can manage it," he said, snapping her harness onto the pulley and helping her pull on the pair of thick gloves. "You set to go, sweetheart?"

"So have you ever made love in the treetops?" she asked with a smile that tilted up the edges of her green eyes.

"There's always a first time, but not with everyone waiting for us."

With both hands under her bottom, he lifted her so her legs straddled his waist. The front of the helmet she wore clunked him in the forehead but he kissed her anyway, while she wrapped her legs tight around his waist and linked her gloved hands behind his neck to kiss him back. He felt a surge of desire for her that almost shot him off the platform. His tongue invaded, and hers danced with his. The harness she was in came across her breasts and between her legs like a barrier.

When they came up for air, he whispered, "You ready?"

"Getting closer every day," she said so breathily he almost had to read her lips.

Reluctantly, but with another pat on her bottom, he turned her outward and let her go.

It was almost like flying, as if she were a bird, maybe a ptarmigan with feathered feet as well as wings. Ellie and Vanessa had let out thrilled screams at the beginning of their flights, but Lisa took it all in silently. After what she'd been through these last few days—and after all that from Mitch just now—

this seemed wonderful but tame, sensational but not scary.

Trusting her harness, she spun and swayed, descending from the trees and sailing over the blowing meadow splashed with many-hued wildflowers. She had no desire to slow her speed, which Mitch had said would be around thirty miles per hour. Down, faster, past the silver ribbon of water threading from the Talkeetnas to feed the Wild River. Wind, wild wind in her hair, caressing her cheeks still burnished from Mitch's touch.

But then, ahead, the river itself loomed, like a huge, writhing white snake, magnificent but monstrous. Even when she saw the others at the bottom of the cable waiting for her, the river seemed a threat, as if it could suck her into churning, white-out oblivion again. But she'd come a long way in determination and courage since she'd ridden a cable car over the river that had almost devoured her.

The slope of the cable leveled out, and she slowed her descent before Spike stopped her. "Took you a little while to decide to do it, right?" he asked, making her wonder just how long she and Mitch had been kissing. With him, kisses and caresses seemed to fly by and yet be in her brain and blood forever.

"I'm fine," she said. "I wanted to do it in honor of Ginger. I see now why she loved it. If I were going to be here longer, I'd take over this job for her—and baking, too, though I'd never come up to her standards."

As soon as Spike unhooked her from the line, Graham took her elbow and pulled her out of the way while they waited for Mitch to come careening after her. Looking around, Graham said in a loud voice, "Lisa, Vanessa and Jonas, too—you just worry about staying up with Carlisle, Bonner's standards. Soon we'll be heading home, and I'll make the senior partner decision just before we leave. I've told Mitch we'll go river rafting this afternoon—upriver, where its relatively calm—and then for the competition, you're finished."

You're finished, Lisa thought. Why did everything Graham said lately sound so ominous?

19

Just to be near the river, let alone on it, made Lisa's heart pound. But the rapids were lower and the roar less upriver where they'd driven a gravel road in Mitch's SUV. Spike and Christine weren't along, so it was just Mitch and his Carlisle and Bonner guests.

This is a safe part of the Wild River for multiperson rafting, Lisa told herself, repeating over and over silently what Mitch had said. The local authorities deemed it safe; Mitch had a license. And she had a PFD on again, the same kind that had kept her afloat downriver. Everyone was going in the same big raft, and Mitch would be there from the first. She could call it quits—no matter what Graham thought—at any time, and they would put her off on the bank where she could walk back on the road to the SUV. They were not in any sort of canyon, thank God, and Mitch said there were numerous landing spots in this area.

"Everybody, strap your helmets on," Mitch ordered. "Jonas, are you sure you want to do th—"

"I said I did," Jonas interrupted with a sideways glance at Graham. "I have a high tolerance for pain and fatigue. Learned that playing college football and from the demands of law school and working hard at the firm. I can take it."

Lisa thought he might as well be wearing a placard around his neck with huge print: Pick me, Graham. I can take it—the promotion, the river, anything life throws at me!

She saw Vanessa roll her eyes, so maybe the two of them really weren't in cahoots. *The raven is very wise but very crooked.* She seemed to hear Christine's low voice echo in her head.

Really, she tried to buck herself up as Mitch demonstrated the correct paddling movements, this was a lovely spot. Two thin waterfalls spilled down a rock face like a crystal necklace across a line of Sitka spruce. Everyone had laughed at four bright Harlequin Ducks slurping down clams. She studied the Inuit fishing wheel Mitch had pointed out as it revolved in a mesmerizing motion, plucking the occasional reddish king salmon out of its watery home. Maybe those were some of the same fish she'd seen in the rougher water downriver, fighting their way back to their breeding grounds. She told herself, if they could make it through the brutal current, she could fight through her struggles. Yes, this area of the river was an inspiration, not a lurking boogeyman.

"Okay, so you get the idea," Mitch said as everyone copied his movements with their own paddles.

"Dig into the water, don't just take a swipe at it. Listen to my commands about paddling fore or aft or holding up, and, most of all, be a team. If you hit each other's paddles or get off rhythm, we're going to have the river controlling us instead of the other way around."

"Bingo!" Vanessa whispered to Lisa. "Not much of a hidden lesson for Graham's agenda. Take your orders and do your best despite circumstances. And be sure to say, 'Sir, yes, sir!'"

"A question or comment, Vanessa?" Mitch asked.

"Just anxious to get going. I suppose for best effect, it matters who you put in front or in back."

"Graham and I will have the tiller. Ellie's next to Lisa in the middle of the raft, and Jonas is across from Vanessa in front. After we put in and get to a rest spot, we may switch positions. And lastly, enjoy yourselves. The ups and downs are a lot of fun, a combination of low-grade roller coaster and a water flume ride."

"Lisa," Ellie said, turning to her, "are you sure you want to do this? You do not have to prove you can get back on this river to get the position, I promise you don't!"

Lisa's eyes teared up behind her sunglasses. "Thanks, Ellie. It's really not the same river. Teamwork's a lot better than riding raftless and solo. I'll be fine."

Once again, Lisa thought, as they clambered into their assigned spots in the raft and Mitch and Graham prepared to push them off, there was proof that Ellen Carlisle Bonner helped to steer decisions that seemed to be only Graham's.

"Thanks for coming with me to help feed the dogs," Spike told Christine as they left the sled dog compound and walked back toward his house.

"It means a lot to me to get to know well-kept ones. I guess it's been one of my secrets that my husband abused his team something awful, and I hated them, was really scared of them."

"And he abused you, too. And that's why…" Spike opened the front door for her, but she hesitated to go in until they had this talk that had been coming for months. Had the death of someone close to Spike made him want to know about her husband's death? He'd avoided the subject and her like a curse until recently, but she needed to unburden herself to him. She sometimes wondered if it wasn't the fact that Mitch trusted her that had helped to win Spike over.

"Let's sit out here a little," she suggested, perching on the end of the wooden bench on the porch. He nodded, closed the door and sidled over to sit down beside her. She took a deep breath, then began. "Yes, Clay beat me. He drank a lot. I should not have stayed. But he was a tribal elder's son, a good match, everyone said. My parents were dead, and my older brother was honored by our links to Clay's family. I had some money from making my dolls, but not enough to go out on my own, so I stayed. In that way, what happened was my fault, too."

"Not really," Spike said, turning toward her. "You didn't deserve that, no matter if you would have been a bad wife, and I know you weren't."

"No. But I—I lost a baby—in the womb, a boy, and Clay hated me for that, too. He blamed me."

"But you didn't do anything to cause that, did you?"

She shrugged her shoulders and stifled a sob. "Fell out of bed, trying to sleep so far away from Clay he couldn't grab me when he was drunk."

"The guy was an idiot!"

"You're the first person outside of Clay and my brother—we saw the little mite was buried proper— I told about losing the baby. Not even my lawyer, though it might have helped get me off. My boy's death, it is like a sacred secret to me, but now—now I'm glad I told you, even though you have your own grief, rawer than mine."

"I'm glad, too. Honored you told me, not even Mitch."

"You know," she said, gripping her hands together hard in her lap, "I did hate Clay, especially after he called me a murderer of my own unborn baby. So maybe, deep down, I thought about killing him, like premeditated murder. I don't know. But I never would have just—just killed him in cold blood if he hadn't threatened to kill me that day. He probably wouldn't have done it, but he would have beaten me bad, and

I was angry. I said in court I wasn't angry but scared for my life, but I was angry and hated him when I shot him! So, however much it turned me into a Yup'ik outcast, God forgive me, I got some justice out of his name being smeared when the jury ruled for me."

She almost choked on a sob she'd been holding back, holding back for years. She hadn't shed a tear over Clay's death, not after the big river she'd cried over her lost son.

Spike put one large hand over hers. She shook her head. Why, she wasn't sure. Still regretful of what she'd done or that she'd finally come clean with someone? Or was she trying to tell him not to take the next step with her she felt coming, especially when his emotions were so raw over Ginger.

She sat stunned that she'd told someone her true feelings—that she shot Clay in anger and hate, not just fear. That could have sent her to prison for fifteen years to life. Motive. Premeditation. Her lawyer had harped on all that. She'd never even told Mitch. Fifteen years to life! Years away from this life here, this place, her job, her blessed boss—and this man.

"Sorry," she said as tears plopped on his hand clasping hers. "It's not like me to cry. I didn't mean to dump all that on you, with Ginger's loss."

"It's all right," Spike said, lifting his arm from her hands to put it around her shoulders and hug her sideways to him. "Somehow, we've got to make things right." She wasn't sure what he meant, but she was amazed to feel the big, strong man was shaking, too.

* * *

Mitch kept a close eye on Lisa, but she was doing great. Everyone whooped and hollered at each pitch over a small rapid or spin in a whirlpool they got snagged in. More than once, on one side or the other, they had to use their paddles like braces to get the raft around a rock.

Despite the fact Christine had warned both him and Lisa not to be too obvious watching others, he, like Graham, was taking mental notes. Jonas was powering his oar as if he were trying out for an NFL team; Vanessa obviously hated getting her hair and clothes splashed; and Ellie, as petite as she was compared to the other two women, was really pulling her own weight, but then she was in great shape for her age and had worked out for years with a personal trainer who came to their house.

Although both he and Graham had their hands on the tiller that controlled the rudder, Mitch was doing most of the steering while Graham intently observed. He'd said earlier he'd be watching for teamwork and wanted no slackers. Mitch had tried to read him for days, trying to figure out which person he favored for senior partner, but he had to admit Graham had a good poker face.

And once he'd made his selection, would he invite "the chosen one" to the Bonner weekend estate in West Palm Beach, and would their precious daughter be home from college for it? Or had that been a setup only for him, Ellie's matchmaking at its finest? He knew how upset Ellie had been when he and Lisa told them they had been dating and were going to get married, as if she had him picked out for Claire despite the difference in their ages.

At first he'd thought that might be why Graham had pulled them off the casino case—punishment to have that potentially high-profile case taken away— but he'd obviously had other motives. Lisa was right. They had to get their heads together on that. So why was it he kept thinking of getting their bodies together? He was going to set up some private time with her tonight. If he had his way, private, passionate time. Business first in the wine cellar, then later, if he could manage it, in his room.

They were almost to the landing spot from which they could walk back to the lodge, but, as the water was pushed between narrowing banks, a series of rapids got stronger. A salmon, leaping over a rock, flopped right into the boat between Lisa and Vanessa.

Vanessa screamed and stopped paddling, which spun the raft a bit, but Mitch was pretty sure Graham wouldn't hold it against her. How much could being senior partner in a Southern, urban law firm relate to liking Alaskan outdoor life? And Graham had said Vanessa had two things going for her: her gender and her ethnicity.

Jonas looked like he was going to either bash the fish or flip it back into the water with his paddle, but Lisa was faster. Just as she'd run to Jonas earlier when he'd fallen off his sled, her instinct was to help.

"Oh, look," she cried as she managed to pick up the struggling fish, "his sunset colors are fading already, out of his element."

"Good observation," Graham said. "If you'd ever been fishing, you'd know that's what happens as they die."

"I knew that," Jonas said. "Lisa, leave him in the bottom of the boat for Christine to cook and get your paddle back in."

"No," she said, "this salmon's almost home and deserves to live." She hefted the heavy fish back into the current and began to paddle again. "And that fish is a female," she said, "full of eggs. I hope she names some of her offspring after me for giving her a second chance."

Mitch had to grin at that; Graham didn't change expressions or blink an eye. Vanessa snorted, Ellie shook her head and Jonas frowned at being put down a bit.

"Yeah," Vanessa said, "but they are just hustling into this area to die, and that's not fair, not after all that hard work."

They shot over a thick plume of water and got thoroughly soaked as foam sloshed into the raft.

"So who said life's fair?" Ellie's voice rang out as they all shivered from the chill wash of water.

Mitch was waiting for Lisa later as she managed to avoid Jonas and Vanessa and hurry down the steps into the wine cellar. She saw he had a large piece of paper spread out on top of the crate and two glasses of white wine balanced there precariously. And he'd brought an extra chair down.

"The light's not great in here," he said, "but I thought this might help us to get down to business about the casino case."

She noted he had drawn some sort of diagram on the paper. Picking up her wine, she started to lift the glass to her mouth, but he said, "To us—remembering." He clinked his goblet to hers.

She stared at her hand on the stem, remembering the night he'd told her he was leaving Florida, leaving the practice of law, and asking if she would go with him. She'd snapped the stem in her anger and cut herself—but not as deeply as he'd cut her. She realized how strongly she felt for him now that she'd been here and they'd gone through so much together. They had less than twenty-four hours left. Not much time to straighten out so many things.

"I thought I'd mention business," he said, leaning over the diagram, "because my mind keeps wandering to other things when we're together, especially alone like this. Oh, hell, all the time." He cleared his throat, still not looking at her. "I've sketched a sort of combination flow chart and Venn diagram here, so we can try to track who was who, who knew whom, all of that."

Though she wanted to touch him, she stared down at the intersecting circles he'd labeled with people's names—the client and his corroborating witnesses,

informants they'd been working with, potential character witnesses. She was amazed at how much he
recalled after he'd been living in a completely different world for over a year. How brilliant Mitch had
been at what he did hit her with stunning impact. And
he'd left all that—not that he wasn't good at what he
was doing here. But for him to be brave enough to
step out into the relative unknown made him seem
even stronger in her eyes.

She helped him fill in names and connections she
remembered. "You know," she said, taking a big gulp
of wine as if to fortify herself, "this guy here—the
Miami Herald reporter Manuel Markus went to jail
for contempt of court shortly after you left town. He
refused to answer a federal judge's questions about
interviewing Frank Cummings."

"Ah, Cummings, the money man who was funnel-
ing big cash into something—but, we thought, not
terrorist activities. So Markus is still rotting in jail?
He had a large family to provide for."

"And I never read him to be the kind of guy who
would go to jail to protect someone. I'll bet he was
threatened to shut his mouth—maybe by the same
people who threatened us—and/or his family is
being taken care of in style by someone while he's
locked away."

"Doesn't this kind of remind you of Nixon's
Watergate mess?" Mitch said as he drew in extra
arrows and wrote *in prison* by the reporter's name.
"I mean, this reeks of a big cover-up from the top

down by whoever was really getting this money laundered through the South Florida casinos."

"Like you said before, it's a spiderweb. But who's the spider?"

20

Dinner, though it was their last one at the lodge and the food was delicious, seemed to drag for Lisa. She and Mitch had agreed to meet on the patio in the midnight twilight to take a walk and talk about the casino case, and about their future. She wondered if he'd agree to visit Florida now and then and if they could try to establish a real relationship again. She knew he was hoping she might visit him for a while in the autumn or winter, so that—without the pressure of everyone else around—they could backtrack and then, just maybe, go forward, not at zipline or river-rafting speed, but step by step. Still, someone was going to have to compromise on location and career if they were to be together permanently, and she still couldn't quite fathom that.

Everyone scattered after dinner: Jonas to his room, Vanessa to walk off their meal. The Bonners and Mitch were huddled in quiet conversation by the hearth, unfortunately, because Lisa wanted to whisper to him about another casino case connection she'd remembered.

During dinner conversation, she'd suddenly recalled she'd heard that Manuel Markus had once
written political speeches for several state congress-
men, which meant he might have known the Bonners
through their political fundraising for Ellie's brother,
Merritt Carlisle. Maybe he'd even written speeches
for him. If the coast was clear, Lisa decided she
would pop down into the wine cellar and write that
on their chart, then see if any of Mitch's lines and
arrows connected to anyone else high up. Absolute
power corrupted absolutely, and the spider in the web
must be someone powerful.

She peeked in the deserted library and opened the
cellar door. Utter blackness below. She switched on
the light, closed the door behind her and hurried
down the steps. The chart was where they'd left it,
rolled up in one of the wine cradles, wedged in above
a bottle of Chardonnay. In their haste to leave, they'd
left their wine goblets on the crate. She unrolled the
chart and, sitting in one of the chairs, smoothed it
across her knees. Hunched over it, she took the pencil
he'd left and, squinting to see in the watery, greenish
light, she wrote her information in the correct place.

But then, a slight shadow shifted and she looked
up.

She jumped to her feet and backed into the wall
of bottles behind her. Two huge eyes blinked, shifted
away. She refused to believe she was going crazy. She
had not screamed for her mother when she found
Ginger, and she had not imagined eyes staring at her.

She grabbed a bottle and, holding it by its neck, she hefted it like a club. She edged toward the stairs and, bottle raised, peeked behind the opposite wall-to-wall rack of bottles.

Vanessa was wedged in the narrow space between the back of the rack and the stone wall with an unlit flashlight raised like a weapon.

"What the hell are you doing?" Lisa shouted, hoping Mitch would hear and come down.

"What the hell are *you* doing?" Vanessa echoed. "I thought you might be planning another lover's tryst, sneaking down here to meet Mitch again to convince him to put in a good word for you, convince him with wine and kisses and the rest of you!"

"I have not. You're a spy, Vanessa! You were here before. We've just been trying to work things out so—"

"Oh, I'll bet. I'm telling Graham about this little love nest."

That was the last thing in the world Lisa needed, but she knew better than to show Vanessa any weakness, so she counterattacked. "You just do that. He'll love to hear how you've been eavesdropping on us— probably on him and Ellie, too."

"You mean like Mitch told you he was listening at the Bonners' bedroom door? I know what I'm up against with you! I was only down here once before, but I'll bet you've been meeting Mitch day and night. I'm surprised there isn't a bed down here, but I guess the floor will do."

"You don't know what you're talking about, or you're projecting your own M.O. on me."

"Yeah?" she challenged, shaking the flashlight as if she'd hit her with it, however trapped she looked in that little space. "I heard Mitch say he was playing detective for you, but I'll bet you just want the attention from him. 'Someone pushed me in the river, Mitch, I'm sure of it,'" she mocked. "Or you hallucinated you were pushed. You're unstable, Lisa. I'm sorry about your tragic past, but you're imagining things, and I can't think of a worse quality for senior partner."

"And I can't imagine Graham entrusting the position to someone who spies and lies."

"Oh, really?" she said, folding her arms over her chest with the unlit flashlight held straight up between her breasts. "You think a few high-tech, underhanded things are beyond Graham, think again!"

"Like what?"

"Never mind changing the subject. I'm talking to him, and you're not stopping me."

"Then I'll go with you. It will give me the opportunity to tell him you're not only lying about my screaming my mother's name when I found Ginger's body, but that you're the one who set me up to find her."

"I heard you pull that one on Mitch down here before, but you're crazy! How could I do that? She was alive and well when I left! So what if I asked you to go tie up the boat on the dock in all those waves?

You pull that one on Graham, and I'll sue for defamation of character. If you and Mitch kept that insane theory to yourselves, I was going to let it pass, but I'm sure you knocked your head on a rock in the river!"

"Don't you wish. Actually—and we'll tell this to Graham, too, if you haven't already—someone did shove me in, and the lead candidate for that is my female rival for the senior partner position!"

"Ridiculous slander! Jonas says you're whacked out from seeing your mother and sister drown, that's all."

"That's *all?*"

"Look, Lisa, I didn't mean it like that, like it was nothing. My point is no one shoved you in, just like that wasn't your mother in the water but Ginger. I'm sorry, really. Let's just back off, okay? I apologize for checking on you and Mitch, but it looks like you're trying to sway him and, through him, the Bonners. It's like tampering with the jury. It looks bad, you've got to admit that. Let's just put our dueling weapons away and swear we'll keep each other's secrets, let things play out, see who Graham names tomorrow."

Lisa's mind raced. Let things play out. Vanessa had known for days that Lisa had been pushed in the river but evidently hadn't tried to use it against her—yet. Was that because she was the culprit and she was hoping it would remain a secret, maybe until she could finish the job? And if they went to Graham, it might spook him before she and Mitch could get their thoughts together on the casino case he seemed so concerned about.

"A truce then," Lisa agreed, glaring at Vanessa. "All this will be over tomorrow anyway, one way or the other."

"Yeah, one way or the other," Vanessa said bitterly, putting her flashlight down at her side and edging closer, sideways out of her narrow space.

Still unwilling to trust her, Lisa darted back into the room, grabbed the chart and hurried up the stairs before Vanessa got out from behind the rack. She had to tell Mitch all this when she saw him later tonight, because she feared her forced truce with Vanessa was hardly a cease-fire.

Lisa went directly to her room, locked the door behind her and leaned against it. She panted as if she'd run miles. Yes, Vanessa was the one she suspected of pushing her in the river, but what if things did just play out and she and Mitch could never prove the woman's guilt?

She shook her head to clear it. She ached all over from being so tensed up confronting Vanessa. Or was it the ziplining and the rafting that had brought back all the aches and pains from her battering in the river, even after she'd felt she was healing a bit? She still had to pack to leave the next day, when she could not bear to leave at all. Restless, she decided she'd take advantage of the sauna as Christine had suggested. She wanted to be calm when she met Mitch later.

As she walked away from the door she stepped on a piece of paper someone had evidently slipped under it, as if it were a bill for a hotel stay. Maybe a note from Mitch? In the room's dim light, with the muted roar of the river outside, she picked it up and walked to a window. She gasped.

It was the printed copy of the painting of the drowned Ophelia that Ellie had mentioned earlier. Someone had written on it. *Since you showed interest in this at the memorial service today, I thought you'd like to see it, death beautified.—Ellie*

It was both stunning and haunting. Painter, John Everett Millais, 1851–1852, Tate Gallery, London, England, was printed under it.

Lisa looked away from the picture, but too late. Like Ginger floating in the lake, like her mother floating in the depths of her soul, the drowned woman stared up with her hands open, beseeching....

She threw it in the wastebasket, then dug it out again, but left it facedown on the dresser as she darted into the bathroom and donned her bathing suit.

Ellie should not have shared this with her, but she evidently thought it was comforting or helpful. Yes, that was Ellie, always wanting to help others.

Feeling suddenly chilled, Lisa wrapped the thick terry-cloth robe around her trembling body. That sauna would feel great. Water, water everywhere, but in comforting, warm, relaxing steam.

Locking her room, she hurried downstairs and out onto the patio. It was either her confrontation with

Vanessa or that picture that had made her feel chilled, because the evening was mild enough.

She glanced up into the gray twilight sky, wishing she could see the dancing colors of the aurora borealis Mitch said were always there, but could not be seen unless the sky was dark. That's how it was for her attempts to discover who had hurt her, she thought. The danger, that person's evil was there, but hidden in the light of pretense and lies. If events got even darker, would that reveal the murderer, the crooked, clever monster?

She forced her fears away and checked to see if the sauna was empty. She was relieved to see it was. The sauna fit the patio and lodge, for it looked like a small rustic cabin. It had an external wood-burning heater. She walked around to the side where Mitch had pointed out the timer and temperature-setting dials. She set the timer for six minutes and the temperature to a hundred and thirty, although both dials could go much higher.

She hit the button to start the firebox next to the eight-gallon stainless-steel water tank that vented into the sauna. That first day, Mitch had also demonstrated for them how you could pour extra water on the heated river rocks inside for a moister, thicker steam.

She couldn't wait to get inside, to just let all the tension drift away.

Mitch took the phone call at his desk as the Bonners left his office. They'd not only paid him the rest of what they'd negotiated but included a hefty bonus. They'd agreed on another local pilot to fly them to the airport in Anchorage, since Spike was going into Talkeetna to pick out a coffin for Ginger.

"Mitch Braxton," he answered the phone.

"Hey, Mitch, it's me—Lucky, at the saloon in Bear Bones. Gus is in here, drunk as a skunk, shooting off his mouth and getting kinda rough. Says you're his lawyer, but he doesn't need you 'cause he didn't do nothing wrong—cryin' in his beer about Ginger. Nobody seems to be able to talk him down and, if he starts breaking the place up, I'm gonna have to call the sheriff. Considering things, that would be bad news."

Mitch looked at his watch. Nine-thirty. He had time to drive in, get Gus home and get back before meeting Lisa.

"Thanks, Lucky. Tell him to cool it, and I'll be right there."

He scribbled notes to Graham and Lisa. For something like this, he would ordinarily have sent Spike into town, but no way was he mixing Spike with a drunk Gus right now.

He shoved the note under the Bonners' door, because talking with them again would take too long, then hurried to Lisa's. He listened for a minute but heard nothing, so she might be lying down. She needed her rest, so he pushed the note under her door and rushed downstairs to tell Christine he was leaving.

* * *

Lisa went into the sauna and closed the door. The cedar interior smelled good. It was about eight-by-six feet with an built-in L-shaped bench she gratefully sank onto, then remembered she should leave her robe outside so it wouldn't be a sodden mess. She got up again, opened the door and put it over the bar outside. That was one way, she supposed, people would know the sauna was being used and could knock before coming in. A lot of people she knew saunaed in the buff, but she never had. Still, if she took a sauna with Mitch here someday…

Already she heard the steam hissing through the vents as they circulated heat and humidity into the small room. She'd wait to see how thick it got before she poured a wooden ladleful of water onto the heated river rocks from the very river she'd conquered—with Mitch's help. Nothing like bodysurfing the Wild River in the heart of Alaska, she told herself, still trying to shut out the image of that painting, of Ginger, of—

No. From now on, it was going to be mind over matter. Although her psychiatrist had told her that repression was worse than letting terrible memories surface, she was just going to shut out nightmare images from her past. She would go on, face the future, maybe with Mitch back in her life.

The increasing steam and temperature felt great. She warmed up, then began to perspire. Yes, sweat it all out, all the poisons, physical and mental, she thought. Pour it out through those pores. Get those endorphins released from the pituitary gland to get a natural high—not that she needed that around Mitch—as well as relieve aches and pains. Tension and stress should melt away. Besides, she knew taking a sauna increased the heart rate, so it had the benefit of mild exercise without moving, the perfect prescription for her. For a moment, sitting there, leaning back against the fragrant cedar wood, she almost nodded off to sleep.

She jerked alert. Had she slept? Obviously, the six minutes she'd set weren't up yet, but the steam was so thick, the heat still rising. She had selected a heat she could tolerate, hadn't she? If it got any warmer, she'd end her session early, go out into the evening air, then hurry up to her room to take a cold shower.

Mitch had told them he'd had people use the sauna who had then gone outside to roll in the snow. Maybe that was the Japanese couples who came here to see the aurora borealis and conceive a child.

What would this area look like all covered with snow with the shifting, wavering lights of the aurora overhead? The river, beneath a thick coat of ice, would be silent. Or would it still murmur its depths and dangers? She'd never cross-country skied, but the groomed trails in the forests were lovely and, of course, they could go dogsledding, flying along through the white depths...and then cuddle up before a roaring fire.

The temperature and hissing of steam hadn't seemed to level off. No way she'd pour water on those river stones. She was so thirsty she could drink a river.

Feeling groggy, she got to her feet. She dare not lie down for a nap in her room before she packed her bag and then met Mitch at midnight, or she'd never get up. At least she felt relaxed now. Too relaxed, wobbly legged.

She had to find the door by feel. She pulled at the handle, but nothing moved. Surely, she hadn't found a closet in here, disoriented about where the door to the outside was. Could it be stuck? She hadn't noticed a lock, but could one have somehow slipped into place?

She tried again, then pushed at it with all her might. Nothing moved.

Lisa pounded on it, shouting, sucking in what seemed now to be searing breaths of steam. "I'm in here! Help me! Let me out! The door's stuck! It's Lisa! Help me!"

Panicked, she braced her foot against the wall and pulled up on the door handle with all her might. The wooden handle cracked, flew off to throw her back onto the floor, where she hit her head against the base of the bench.

She shook her head, trying to clear it. She felt so dizzy. The room was fogged with thick steam, but she found the crack that was the door. She tried to push it open again from the floor, then clawed at it, gasping, panting.

She lay on the floor, looking up through the white water around and above her. Drowning in the heat and steam, in the river. Where was Mitch? Beside her in the water, she saw Ginger in a painting Ellie gave her. And then, staring from the whiteout mist, her mother's green eyes. "Lisa, come with me, honey. Take my hand. I have Jani, here, come on now…"

Lisa's heart beat so hard, so fast, pounding like the engines of the monster ship. "No! No!" she screamed as the cruise ship's powerful wake sucked her under.

No, no, she had to fight that memory, stay with what was real, she told herself. There was no cruise ship, no pounding, rushing river.

She knew where she was trapped, entombed in a wooden coffin, just like Ginger, not drowning but already dead.

21

Mitch had Gus talked down, back home and snoring in bed in record time. No way was this guy—client or not, and he'd been through hell for clients—going to keep him from spending time with Lisa on her last night here. He drove too fast, roaring out of Bear Bones and heading back to the lodge.

He wanted to convince Lisa not to leave tomorrow. Commitments or not, she would have to admit it would soon be safer here than in Florida, since one of her colleagues had evidently tried to kill her, and that's where they were all heading. If Vanessa or Jonas had pushed her into the river, they could try something again on their home turf.

Or—the worst scenario that plagued him—what if Graham was somehow involved in the casino money-laundering scheme? Could Lisa be endangered from that? But what was the missing link? What was it that Graham was afraid would come out if the two attorneys who'd worked on that case put their heads together? Despite the fact Mitch longed for tonight to be about him and Lisa, it had to be about Graham and the casino case, too.

He jumped out of the SUV and hurried toward the lodge. As he went in, he saw he'd have to get past his guests to be alone with Lisa tonight. Graham, Ellie, Vanessa and Jonas were huddled around a card table before the hearth, playing a board game. Christine was serving them beer and a stack of sandwiches. At least Lisa wasn't in sight. She'd managed to get away from the crowd and was no doubt either in her room waiting for him or maybe even out on the patio where they planned to meet. He didn't like the idea of her waiting out there alone.

Graham looked up from the game. "Hey, Mitch, glad you're back. How's Gus?"

"Sleeping it off—the booze and his loss of Ginger."

"Mitchell," Ellie said, "that man's obviously very volatile. I still think he could have hurt Ginger, even if it was in a moment of passion."

A moment of passion, Mitch thought. That's what he was feeling for Lisa—a long moment of passion. He had to keep moving.

"He's a guy who wears his feelings on his sleeve," Mitch said, "therefore he's a guy who doesn't hide things."

All four of the game players looked up at him as he strode toward the stairs. Which of them, he wondered in a moment of silence with the fire crackling as if they all sat with an inferno threatening, was intent on hurting Lisa?

Christine cleared her throat. "You hungry, Mitch? I've got three kinds of sandwiches here."

"No, I'm fine. I've got something I need to do. I'll see everyone in the morning for our farewell breakfast."

"Which is where I'll make the senior partner announcement," Graham said. "I need one more night to sleep on it. I think Lisa's exhaustion finally got to her because she hasn't come out of her room since dinner."

Mitch nodded and started up the stairs.

"Don't you want to know who's winning?" Jonas called after him. "We're playing State of Alaska Monopoly, and I just bought a hotel in the Talkeetnas."

"That's the place I always like to land," Mitch said, but didn't stop. Since Lisa was in her room waiting, he'd take her down the back stairs so no one knew they were going out together. Maybe he'd bring her back up to his suite that way, too, if she was willing.

If she was willing... She had to be willing, he chanted to himself as he raced down the hall and rapped on her door.

"Lisa? Lisa."

He knocked louder, hoping nosy Vanessa didn't come upstairs to see what was happening. Could Lisa be sleeping that soundly? He felt hurt. He was so revved up to have this time with her, so how could she just fall asleep? He was exhausted, too, but running on pure adrenaline—or libido long denied.

Mitch hesitated, then used his master key to enter Lisa's room. His note for her still lay folded on the floor. He picked it up and opened it to be sure it wasn't one she'd left for him in return. No, it was his note.

He rushed into the room, looking around. The bathroom door was open, no water running. The bed was neatly made, with slacks, sweater, panties and a bra tossed on it. He recalled undressing her along the river when she was so cold, then warming her with his own body. Damn, if he didn't start to sweat at that mere memory—or with foreboding.

He glanced around the rest of the room. A piece of paper lay on the dresser, maybe a note for him.

He flipped it over. A color reproduction of the *Ophelia* painting Ellie had mentioned, with a note from Ellie. His stomach knotted. This Ophelia did remind him of Ginger drowned, but had it set Lisa off to nightmares of her mother and baby sister again? And, if so, where was she?

Gut instinct, tinged by fear, racked him. The river? The lake?

He closed her door behind him and went downstairs by the narrow back steps. Out on the patio, he called out quietly, "Lisa? Lisa, you out here?" There was no sound but the wind through the trees mingled with the eternal rumble of the river. Spike's plane was tethered at this dock now, rather than down by Ginger's cabin, and he'd brought Ginger's boat here, shoved up on the shore.

"Lisa," he shouted. "Lisa!"

The stone-flagged patio stood empty, the hot tub quiet. He dashed inside by the same back entrance and went to find Christine, just as she was heading toward her room, which overlooked the patio. He hurried toward her and grabbed her elbow. "Have you seen Lisa? She's not upstairs or outside."

"No. I was just going to bed. Mrs. Bonner's going to turn off the lights. What's wrong? Want me to help look for her?"

"No—go ahead. We were going to take a walk. See you in the morning."

He turned away and made for the back door again. "Mitch," Christine called after him, "I just remembered. I think she was going to use the sauna."

He exhaled hard. That was it. That's why her clothes were on the bed. He should have checked to see if her robe was on the back of the bathroom door.

He went back out without going through the large patio doors where everyone could see him. He could hear the sauna's motor now and her robe—stark white in the twilight—was hanging on the far side.

He heaved another sigh of relief. He was tempted to join her, just strip down and go in to surprise her. His desire for her kicked up again. He assumed she'd be wearing a bathing suit since someone else could join her, but what if she wasn't? What if—

He checked the temperature control and timer. The temperature was well within the comfort zone and the time had five minutes left. As tired as she was, he hoped she hadn't nodded off in there.

He put his hand to the door and pulled. Steam swept out, making it impossible to see. "Lisa!" he called inside. "Hey, sweetheart, time's up, except with me."

No reply. The steam began to clear. The first thing he saw inside was a limp arm and an open hand on the floor.

Lisa heard a voice, a man's voice, calling her name. It echoed through the darkness until it found her. Someone was touching her, feeling her neck and wrist.

"Lisa! Lisa, wake up! Lisa!"

Time to get up. Was she late for school? Did she have a court case today? Yes, some kind of test, but she could not recall what it was for.

She tried to open her eyes, but they were so heavy. Mitch! It was Mitch. He had pulled her from the river, and she was cold. No, that couldn't be. She was so thirsty, hot all over, so hot, but funny... floaty.

Now she remembered. She was staring up at him through white water, too much water, drowned and dead, and she was dreaming this.

He slapped her cheeks and kept saying her name, but she was swimming farther away, pulled under by the monster current. And then he left her, so she closed her eyes and floated farther away, downriver.

* * *

Mitch ran toward the lodge, to the bedroom window that was Christine's, and pounded on it. She swept the curtains aside and cranked the window out.

"Call the Talkeetna rescue squad and get them out here now!" he told her. "Lisa's unconscious in the sauna, and I don't know how long she's been there. I think she's burning up with fever, but her skin's dry, so she's dehydrated—tell them that. If I can do anything with her besides trying to lower her body temperature in the lake, send someone out to tell me. Get someone on the phone who knows what I should do."

No hysterics or even wasted words from his *Cu'paq.* That was his girl. She simply nodded and turned away, letting the curtains swing closed. He ran back to the sauna and lifted Lisa into his arms. How could anyone survive this— nearly frozen in the river and steamed in the sauna. His insides lurched. Had she just fallen asleep inside and done this to herself, or had someone possibly set this up, attempted murder—again?

Holding her close, he jogged to the lake. It was the fastest way to lower her temperature. She had dry, doughy skin. She looked like a ghost when she should have been sweating. He had to get her to drink some water. The lake was crystal clear, and this was no time to worry about water purity when she could die.

He strode knee-deep into the lake. The bottom dropped off quickly, so he didn't go far out. This would do. The water was always chilly, but nothing like the snowmelt river. He knelt, lowering her carefully into the water, keeping only her head above the surface.

She stirred in his arms. Maybe this could bring her back. To his amazement, she began to struggle feebly against him.

"It's all right, sweetheart. I've got you. We have to lower your temperature. Here," he said, loosing her a bit to ladle a handful of water to her mouth. "Drink. Drink." He got some water in her and she tried to swallow, but most of it spilled back out.

"I can't believe it!" Vanessa's voice echoed as she rushed to the edge of the water. "This is terrible. Listen, Christine says the medics are on their way but the 9-1-1 receptionist put her through to an E.R. doctor. The big scare is that Lisa's heart can go into atrial fib or something, and if she becomes unconscious her prognosis is not good. How is she?"

"Go get me some water in a glass," Mitch ordered.

"However did she manage to stay in that long so that—"

"Vanessa, go!"

She brought the water, even waded out with it, and he got Lisa to take some. The nightmare of the river rescue again, Mitch thought. Did she have some sort of death wish? No, he could not accept that. He knew better. It meant someone here had tried to kill her again in a way that made it look as if she could have caused it herself.

Everyone, except Christine, who stayed on the

phone and sent Vanessa back and forth, was gathered by the lake now. "Would someone go wait for the squad and someone bring her robe that's hanging outside the spa?" Mitch asked.

When he glanced away from Lisa at his guests, he saw the moon had risen over the canopy of spruce trees. That and the twilight bathed Lisa and the rippling water in a golden glow. Suddenly, he wished his lodge was in the desert with no river, no lake, no need for a sauna. If he lost Lisa again, nothing would ever be the same.

Jonas came hustling around the side of the lodge, shouting, "The EMR's here. They're here!"

It had seemed to take forever. Graham escorted them to the lake, the two men jogging, one of them pulling a gurney on wheels. Graham was telling them what had happened. Mitch lifted Lisa out of the water, and they helped him lay her on the dock. Images of Ginger's soaked, drowned body on her own dock jumped at Mitch. As the two medics bent over Lisa, he dragged his eyes away from her to look at the faces of his gathered guests. All looked genuinely concerned and scared. Christine ran out and stood behind the others, wringing her hands.

"Tympanic thermometer," one of the medics said. The younger man took an instrument and put it in Lisa's ear while the other took her pulse while pressing a stethoscope to her chest. "Tachycardia," he said. "IV fluids and transport. Let's go."

Mitch knew that "cardia" meant something with

the heart. "Can I go, too?" he asked. "Are you taking her to Talkeetna?"

"No, sir," the younger man said. "We'll have to take her to Columbia Regional in Anchorage."

"That's seventy miles."

"Why don't you follow us in your vehicle if you're next of kin?"

He wasn't next of kin, but he had almost been her husband. He helped them lift Lisa onto the gurney and they quickly moved it across the stone patio. The wheels rattled. Mitch dug his car keys out of his pocket and hurried behind them.

"Mitchell, you're soaking wet," Ellie protested.

He only nodded and kept walking.

"I'll go with you," Graham said, keeping up. "She's my responsibility, too."

"I may have to stay with her, and you're heading out tomorrow," Mitch argued, not breaking stride.

"We'll postpone. I'll help with the payment, insurance she's covered with. You need someone there you can trust."

Mitch didn't argue. But he wondered, considering what he and Lisa had deduced about the casino case so far, if Graham wasn't the last person on earth he could trust. And like so much else lately, that broke his heart.

Mitch gripped the steering wheel and kept up with the ambulance. Its siren pierced his ears, and its pulsating lights burned deep into his brain. Surely Lisa had not just nodded off in the sauna, however exhausted she'd been. She would have woken when she got too hot. People could only take so much of that, and she was way past sweating. The temperature control had been set in a safe range—unless it had been adjusted. He should have looked to see if the door could have been jammed closed somehow.

But, damn, what if she'd turned suicidal with all the pressure here—seeing him again, wanting the senior partnership, reliving her mother and sister's drowning by staring at the white-water river? Maybe all that had sent her over the edge. Her mother had killed herself. He'd read that tendency ran in families.

On the other hand, he believed she'd been pushed into the river, didn't he? And Spike was adamant that Ginger had not slipped. Now this. But nothing fit. What motive called for murder?

"Mitch, I said your teeth are chattering." Graham interrupted his agonizing. "I'm turning up your heat, and when we get to Anchorage I'm going to hire someone to go out and buy you dry clothes."

"I didn't want to waste time. Faster to hang with the ambulance. Besides, I need to be with her in the emergency room whatever happens."

"I understand. I also understand she's unstable at times."

"That's what Jonas wants me to emphasize to you."

"I figured he'd try to get you to stand up for him. And Vanessa—never met a man she didn't like when it came to getting what she wants."

"Including you?"

"She knew better, since Ellie was around and now sits on the advisory board."

"I didn't know that."

"I guess it slipped my mind. This trip has been one thing after the other, a tragedy of errors, in a way."

"Errors?"

"Accidents, people slipping and slipping up. You don't think something else, do you? The sheriff said events have been accidental."

Mitch stopped talking as they made the switch from Route 3 to Route 1, which would take them into the city. *Please, Lord,* he prayed, in fragmented, frantic thoughts, *don't let her die. Even if she did something to harm herself, please don't let her die.*

At the hospital, he pulled up right behind the squad. "I'll park for you," Graham told him. "Go ahead. And tell them I'll be in with all the insurance info ASAP."

"Thanks, Graham. For everything."

For everything? His own words echoed in his head. This man had been the older brother, almost the father figure he'd missed growing up, and he'd been suspecting him of murder over some old case? What a screwed-up world, especially with Lisa in danger again.

He followed the medics pushing her gurney through doors that whooshed open for them. They had Lisa on an IV. The bag of fluids dangled from a metal pole. What else had they done for her during the ride in? Vanessa had said the prognosis could be bad if she was unconscious, but she looked groggy now, not out. His hopes soared. When they paused at the triage desk, he leaned over her and took her hand.

"Lisa, I'm here with you at the hospital in Anchorage. You're going to have to fight to stay awake again, do everything they tell you."

"The door..." she whispered, and he bent even closer.

"It's all right. We're in the E.R., and the door just closed behind us."

"To the sauna. Stuck."

"No, I opened it to find you, but you'd fallen on the floor."

"The door—locked."

"It doesn't lock, just to be sure that you can't get caught inside—" he said before he realized she must be delirious. But then, he'd thought that when she told him she'd been pushed into the river. So had someone jammed the door shut? He had to call Christine. See if there was any sign of tampering with the door or the controls. Everyone's fingerprints would be on the dials, so that wouldn't help. But first he had to take care of Lisa.

Graham rushed in and patted Lisa's shoulder. "You'll be all right, Lisa. Mitch and I will take care of everything."

"Hit my head—just like Ginger."

A primal fear made Mitch shudder. Graham pulled him a step away and whispered, "That explains this accident. Just like with the river, she slipped—hit her head and stayed in there too damn long. Insist they do a brain scan on her. She might be having fainting spells. Low blood sugar, stress, who knows?"

A woman appeared to lead Graham to a cubicle to register Lisa and take care of the insurance paperwork. Before Mitch could say more to Lisa, two nurses wheeled her gurney away. He stood alone and bereft, shivering and scared to the bone, but damned if he wasn't going to get to the bottom of this.

22

"Christine, it's Mitch."

"How is she?"

"They've just taken her away for treatment. I don't know yet. I'll talk to a doctor soon, I hope. She says she—"

"She's conscious? She's talking?"

"Yes, but not really making sense—I think. She says she hit her head and that the door wouldn't open."

"*Iah,* that does make sense. Inside the sauna, it looks like she broke the handle, maybe trying to get out. Mitch, there are even scratch marks inside the door at the bottom, like she tried to claw it open."

He was stunned, and yet he shouldn't be, he told himself. He had to face it—someone really did want her dead.

"Mitch?"

"Yeah, I'm here. But someone who wanted to harm her wouldn't risk standing out there to hold the door shut."

"I can go back out and see if there are any marks from a stick being put through the outside handle or something being wedged against the door. What if the person turned the temperature and time way up?"

"Yeah. Exactly," he said, holding himself up with one arm stiff against the wall by the pay phone and staring at the floor.

"I'll get a flashlight and go out to look more carefully, so just hang on a sec."

"Wait! Christine, no. If someone did that, you could be in danger if they see you checking."

"I'm not afraid."

"No, I want you to do it, but call Spike and have him come over to be with you. I think it helps him to keep busy right now. Besides, this could throw some light on what happened to Ginger, too."

"But who would do such a thing—things—to either of them?"

"That's the big question. As soon as I make sure Lisa will be all right, I'm going to find out. I've got to turn into a bodyguard for her right now—maybe get the sheriff's help, I'm not sure. One more thing. Our four guests who were playing Monopoly tonight—did you see any of them go out back for a while, go anywhere about the time Lisa could have been in the sauna?"

"Who knows when she went to the sauna? I was in and out of the kitchen. But yes, I'm afraid at one time or another, each of them went to the john or somewhere. I'm not sure, but I think only Vanessa went out twice for any length of time."

"So maybe once to jam the door closed, once to remove the jam so it would look as if Lisa was to blame for her own demise. Promise me you'll get Spike there. Don't tell anyone but Spike about any of this right now."

"When it does come out—especially if we bring in the sheriff and he questions the Bonners again—we'll lose their support and business. Mrs. Bonner was talking tonight about how they want to come back, bring their daughter here for her graduation from law school gift and send others they know. Oh, and she called and cancelled their departure tomorrow. It's a good thing we don't have other guests scheduled until next week."

"I know, but first things first, and that's Lisa's health. Gotta go. I see Graham looking for me. I'll call if I get news of how Lisa's doing. Thanks, *Cu'paq,* for everything."

"You saved my sanity, Mitch, and I'm gonna help you save yours."

The doctor's name tag on his white coat read Dr. Jason Kurtz. He was probably mid to late thirties, with dark hair and piercing blue eyes. Mitch, wearing pale green scrubs they had given him since his clothes were still damp, realized he was trembling as he shook the doctor's hand. Graham stood with him shoulder to shoulder. Once that would have encouraged him, but now it only made him more upset.

"Friends of Ms. Vaughn, not family, is that correct?" the doctor asked as he shook hands with Graham, too.

"That's right," Mitch said. "I'm her friend Mitch Braxton and this is Graham Bonner, her employer at a Florida law firm."

He nodded at Graham, but seemed to address Mitch. Was it so obvious how much Lisa meant to him?

"We have her stabilized," the doctor informed them. "Her core body temperature is dropping with the help of a cooling blanket and some icing, but she's having heart palpitations—atrial fibrillation— which we will deal with. She's also lost some trace body minerals with her profuse sweating, but we hope to replace those after we run more tests."

"Thank heavens," Graham said. "It sounds like she'll not only pull through but fully recover."

"It's early to promise all that yet. After an EKG, she'll be on a heart monitor all night, then we'll reassess in the morning. She has a large contusion on the left temple above her hairline. No blood but edema. She also has a few black and blue marks on her body. I'm theorizing she fell and hit her head. Do either of you know if she's prone to fainting or black-outs?"

Graham cleared his throat, but before he could speak, Mitch said, "Not that we're aware of, and she's quite athletic. As for most of her bruises—not the head injury—last week, she fell in a snowmelt river, and suffered from hypothermia, just the opposite of this."

"Ah. But the shock to the body was no doubt considerable. Was she admitted for the hypothermia?"

"No. I pulled her out of the river, and we had to hike back to the lodge, and, other than bruises and exhaustion, she recovered well."

The doctor frowned. Was he just upset that she hadn't been hospitalized previously, or did he know something worse he wasn't saying?

"It may be a long night," he said, indicating the waiting room with a wave of his clipboard. "There are inherent dangers with this besides the cardiac fluctuations—circulatory collapse, possible renal failure. We'll keep you apprised of her status and consult when we have her test results. She tells me she was alone in the sauna and hit her head, but the head blow and the excessive body temp could have caused her to be confused and disoriented."

But not, Mitch thought, so disoriented that she had shared with this doctor that someone had shut her in and tampered with the door. She was still thinking that they had better not spook whoever was behind this—and maybe behind Ginger's death—until they could flush the killer out. Lisa might have cheated a second murder attempt. She was still one sharp lawyer.

Although Christine had been tempted to disobey Mitch's order and just check the sauna door on her own, it did give her an excuse to phone Spike and see him again. As they played the flashlight beam over the faint scratch marks at the bottom of the sauna door, she said, "I should tell Mitch to look under her fingernails for splinters. She was desperate, all right, and that had to mean the door wouldn't open—at least for a while."

"And it means much more," Spike said as he examined the wooden door handle. "If someone tried to kill Lisa—twice—it means that same person killed Ginger."

"Spike, that's a pretty big leap."

"I don't care what you or anyone says. I know it! She must have struggled, too. Remember how the coroner's report said she had lake mud and stuff under her nails from fighting to get free? Ginger might have died because she knew too much about what happened to Lisa. If it wasn't for Lisa, Ginger might still be alive."

Christine faced him squarely in the sauna. Unfortunately, they'd found no evidence to show something had been jammed through the handle or in the door. "You sound like you're blaming Lisa when she's a victim. Next, you'll be blaming Mitch or me."

"You're siding with Mitch. No, I'm not blaming him. He's been great. If the Bonners wouldn't have helped me out with the funeral costs, he wanted to, but just don't jump on me for bringing this back to Ginger. And Lisa is to blame in a way, breaking her engagement to Mitch in the first place, not wanting to set foot here. Then here she comes to screw up his mind again. He wants her here, but I'll bet she wants him there—Florida. She's been nothing but trouble, and she's pulled Ginger and all of us in."

"I know you're upset and have every right to be but—"

"Hey," a woman's voice said from outside. "What's going on out here?"

Vanessa peered at them through the door of the sauna. Something really stunk about Vanessa, Christine thought, and it wasn't the pricey perfume she always wore.

"I was just taking a little walk on the patio and heard your voices," Vanessa said. "So, have you heard how Lisa's doing?"

"They're running tests. Not sure yet," Christine told her.

"Are you going to close the sauna until it gets fixed?" Vanessa asked. "Wow, how did that handle get broken?"

"It's been loose for a long time," Spike lied before Christine could think what to say next. "When Mitch shoved the door aside to rescue Lisa, he probably knocked it off."

"Well, let me know if you hear anything about her. All of us are starting to think this place is cursed—you know what I mean. Besides, all of us, Lisa included, have clients scheduled and have to get back to reality—our reality—on the other side of the country. And with this new accident, I'll bet Graham postpones naming the new senior partner again. At least, with all Lisa's been through and her sad past,

I think we're down to two candidates, but Graham Bonner has always been full of surprises. See you in the morning, but let me know if there's any news before."

Spike and Christine stood silently as Vanessa's footsteps faded, then the patio door opened and closed. Finally, Spike said, "She didn't believe me about how the handle broke. But was that because I'm a bad liar when I'm so upset, or because she knew damn well Lisa was trapped in here? And she was the last one we are sure saw Ginger alive."

It had been one hell of a long night. Not only was Mitch mourning all that had gone wrong this past week, but he was afraid Graham had betrayed him. Again, over breakfast in the hospital cafeteria, he didn't respond to Mitch's probing of whether anything else had come of the casino case. As a matter of fact, he changed the subject, except to reveal something pretty interesting about Vanessa.

"After I pulled you and Lisa off the case to be certain you weren't endangered, Vanessa insisted I let her get in on it," he finally admitted. "I knew she wanted the publicity if it started to hit the papers, but I told her the managing partner controls assignments, and I didn't want any of my lawyers to be harassed or hurt—still don't."

"You've always been protective of your attorneys, as if we were family."

"But you were always special, and I—we—hated

to lose you. Of course, that's why I'm so distraught about Lisa, as we've brought her along, too. I need to get her back in her own environment, where horrible things won't happen to her—no offense, Mitch."

"None taken. It's been a crazy week. I know you all have key clients scheduled, and it was tough to block out this much time."

"As a matter of fact, I want to fly Lisa home and get her some psychiatric counseling. I know she saw a psychiatrist years ago, but she may need help now."

That was exactly what Mitch had thought at first, but not now. Someone was definitely out to eliminate Lisa from more than the senior partnership, and he might be chatting with that very bastard over pancakes and sausage right now.

"So," Mitch said, trying to keep his voice in check, "I'm assuming Lisa's out of the competition for senior partner."

"Remains to be seen." Graham leaned closer across their small Formica table as if someone could overhear. "I had planned to name her to the position this morning, before all this happened. The adversity she's been through past and present have made her stronger, more empathetic, maybe even more driven, all qualities that would help her in the position. There are drawbacks with all three candidates, ones you could no doubt list for me. So, the truth is, I'm still considering Lisa."

Mitch was speechless. If Lisa accepted such an offer, that would keep her away from him. She had wanted that position, argued with him about it, but how did she feel now, after all she'd been through? Or, if Graham was hiding something—namely, that he himself might be the spider behind all the money machinations in the casino case—was this a way to buy Lisa off, to assure her silence when destructive tactics hadn't panned out? Or would the fact that, as senior partner, she would have insider information and access to more people and past records endanger her even more, an entire continent away from where he could help to protect her?

"Nothing to say?" Graham asked as they got up from the table to go check in with the nurses' desk on Lisa's floor again. "You thought I'd take Jonas? Ellie and I both admire Lisa, you know that."

Mitch nodded, trying to process everything, including Lisa's insisting that Graham "doth protest too much" about the casino case. Now, it seemed he was doing the same thing about how much Lisa meant to him.

"Listen," Graham said, "I know it was hard for you to give up what you left in Lauderdale. Ever think of coming back to the firm and using the lodge for an investment you can visit? The best of both worlds? Spike and Christine could run it for you, you could work part-time for us, mostly consulting, which would give you time to visit Alaska often."

Mitch had no trouble looking surprised. He had not and would not consider such an offer, but he didn't say so now. He was being played here, gamed by a master. And maybe so was Lisa. He had to find a way to keep Graham away from her for a while so he could talk to her privately. Would she be doped up or asleep now so that would be useless?

The familiar nurse at the reception desk on Lisa's floor saw them coming. "This time," she told them before they could ask, "one of you can see her. The doctor said one at a time—no excitement."

Mitch almost laughed out loud. No excitement? Lisa's life—his, too—had been nothing but that since she'd set foot in Alaska. But he could have kissed the doctor, because now he had an excuse to see her alone before Graham tried to control everything and everyone again.

"I should see her first," Graham told him, "assure her we're not heading home without her, tell her she's still in the running and try to convince her she needs some counseling."

"This is my bailiwick, so I'm going to pull rank on you," Mitch told him. "I'm the one responsible for her well-being here, maybe her problem in the sauna if the controls were defective. Didn't you ever hear the Chinese belief that, once you save a person's life, you're responsible for them?"

"Mitch, I just—"

"I might have saved her life twice," he interrupted. "After I see her, I'll let you know if she's strong enough for a visit from you, too." Before Graham could say another word, he turned away and strode down the hall.

* * *

Lisa felt really strange, in a different way from when she'd survived the river. She was still floaty, though they had her practically anchored to the hospital bed with wires to monitors, IV tubes and a cooling blanket tucked in over her to lower her core body temperature. She was on a blood thinner. She'd had tests for blood count, electrolytes, liver and kidney function and a urinalysis and was awaiting those lab results. A catheter had been inserted to be sure she kept in more liquid than she lost, but the only true violation she felt was from someone she knew and trusted trying to kill her again.

Despite all the poking and prodding, she liked Dr. Kurtz and her nurses very much, because they explained each step they were taking and why—unless all that was just to make her stay awake and occasionally respond to them. Everyone here had been kind and helpful. She felt protected, sheltered. And they had said that she could have a visitor before she would be allowed to finally sleep.

Thank God, it was Mitch and not Graham. Before she saw him, she heard his distinctive step. Despite the fact he looked like hell with dark circles under his eyes and beard stubble and wore wrinkled hospital scrubs, he'd never looked better to her.

"Hey, sweetheart," he said, looking immensely relieved.

"On the staff here now?"

"Feels like I've been here long enough to qualify,"

he said with a tight smile, though his eyes were luminous with unshed tears. "They said I get some scrubs for bringing in Wonder Woman."

With a glance at the monitors behind her, he pulled up a chair and leaned closer, grasping her shoulder because her hand on his side had needles for the IV tubes. "When this is all over," he whispered, "you and I are going to fall into the same bed and sleep forever."

"Just sleep? Mitch," she whispered, lowering her voice even more, "it was another murder attempt, I swear it. Here I was expecting someone to make a move during ziplining or river rafting, but he or she is a murderer of opportunity. The sauna door might not have been locked, but it was held shut somehow. And to think, if Christine hadn't encouraged me to use it, this never would have happened."

"I know. She told me on the phone you broke the inside handle and left fingernail marks trying to get out."

"I've got broken fingernails to prove it, but not a broken spirit! Mitch, you saved my life again."

"Grateful gestures will be readily accepted later. The thing is, when I found you, the sauna temperature was in a reasonable range, there were five minutes left, and the door was unobstructed. But you did slip and hit your head? Did someone hit you?"

"No. I fell asleep for a moment and woke up really confused before I fell. But I'm still betting someone hit Ginger before dumping her in the lake. Mitch, even if we get the sheriff in on this now, it could still be construed that it was all my fault, just like with the river, that I was at best an unreliable witness, at worst a hysterical, traumatized woman."

He glanced at the door to the hall and went over to peek out in both directions, then partially closed it, leaving it barely ajar. "I suppose you don't like closed doors right now, but you've almost convinced me Graham could be our traitor. You do recall he's here with me?" he asked, returning to her bedside.

"Yes, so was that just nice of him, or is he making sure he gets another crack at me somehow?"

"Hardly here. Never again!" He frowned and sat down, leaning close, caressing her cheek with the backs of his curled fingers.

"Christine says the evil raven is not only crooked but wise," she protested.

"I've been trying to rank our suspects and still think Vanessa's mug should be on our 'Most Wanted' poster. Jonas needs the money and wants the prestige, but she's hell-bent on the promotion...."

"I know you can't bear to think it's Graham," she said when his voice trailed off, which reminded her that her throat was still dry. He helped her take a drink of water from her bedside tray. "But," she went on, "what if the firm was hired for the casino case because Graham himself was involved in the money laundering? Whoever hired him might have figured he could keep certain names out of it or manipulate things in their favor or else he'd go down with them. Pressure was obviously put on the newspaper reporter who went to jail rather than talk, but could pressure have been put on Graham—or maybe Graham *is* the spider?"

"I don't know, but I'm going to tell him you're too exhausted to see him until you've slept. Then I'm going to call Christine to drive in here and stay with you while I take Graham back to the lodge and maybe consult with the sheriff about this."

"Not yet!" she insisted. "Once we get Sheriff Moran involved, there's no going back. Everyone will be questioned, maybe accused, and just lie or clam up and we can't prove anything yet. You saw how Gus reacted to the sheriff's interrogation."

"Yeah, up close and personal. I had to go into Bear Bones last night before he broke up a bar. So, can you sleep? I'm going to call Christine from your room phone, then sit right here until she arrives. When I can get you out of here, Spike, Christine or I will be with you 24/7 until we get to the bottom of this. And I'll hold off on the sheriff—for a little while longer."

"Mitch, thank you. As awful as some of this has been, at least we patched up our past differences a bit."

"Enough to manage the present, but what about a future?" Again, he lifted his hand from her shoulder to stroke her face with the backs of his fingers. "Sweetheart, Graham says you're still in the running for senior partner, and he wants to fly you back to Lauderdale so he can really take care of you."

"Past time for Lisa to get some sleep now," a nurse said as she bustled into the room. "I told your friend out in the hall one visitor was enough right now."

"Out in the hall, maybe trying to listen?" Lisa whispered. "Mitch, I—"

He put two fingers over her lips. "Thanks for coming back into my life, to remind me what I've missed, what I've screwed up. Despite how I handled things last year, I still love you, Lisa," he whispered.

She sucked in a breath. Her sight blurred with tears, making two Mitches bending closer, two nurses hovering. It was the first time in days—years—that, looking through any sort of wavering water, she had been blessed and not cursed.

He kissed her cheek, then her lips, and stood. "Her skin feels almost normal again," he told the nurse, who was pretending not to look.

"Then," she said with a little smile, "that's a better test she'll be fine than all the other ones we've run. If her heartbeat's a bit erratic, I'll tell the doctor I know why."

Lisa swam up, up from heavy sleep. Before she even opened her eyes, she remembered where she was. Really remembered, without slipping back into the nightmares of fighting the rushing current, of drowning...or of losing her mother and sister...of losing Mitch. Above her head she saw not roiling white water, but a calm white ceiling with pock-marked patterns in it. Yes, she knew where she was and what she had to do. Get better. Return to the lodge. And drag some monster she once thought she could trust out of his or her hiding place into the light.

She started when Christine's face popped up over her.

"Good, you are awake," she said and patted her arm. "Mitch will be back soon and tomorrow, they say, maybe you can go home from the hospital. But where is home now, right?"

"Thanks for staying with me. How's Spike?"

"More than ever convinced that someone meant to hurt Ginger."

"I'm just hoping she wasn't murdered because of what she saw the day I was pushed in the river."

"If she saw something that evil and didn't come forward with it right away, then she had her own reasons, her own part in what happened to her. Lisa," Christine said, sitting in a chair where she must have been waiting at her bedside, "I have something for you. It is something more than belief you did not harm yourself, something more than good wishes for you and Mitch, because I see how much he needs you—like I know now I need Spike."

Lisa nodded. She had come to admire this strong woman she had at first mistrusted. It was just the opposite of how she'd shifted her feelings toward her law firm colleagues.

Christine reached for something on the floor. Paper rustled, then she held up one of the Yup'ik dolls from the shelf in the lodge library. It was the worn one, the young girl with a half-woven basket in her hand, the one Christine had confided had been given to her mother to replace a lost sister.

"For you," Christine said, putting the doll with its fur parka and carved wooden face into her hand on the bed. "To help you have only good memories of those you lost, not nightmares."

"I will treasure it forever," Lisa choked out, lifting her hand to see the doll better and finding she was no longer tied to IVs. Her first impulse had been to say she could never accept such a precious, personal heirloom, but she sensed that would have saddened, maybe even insulted Christine. "I see her basket is only half-done, which means a lot to me, too, that I have much life to live, to weave together strands to see how it comes out."

"*Iah,* for sure, putting pieces together to find out who hurt you and Ginger. And then the other things like where is home and who to share it with."

Christine stood and bent over to press her cheek to Lisa's before straightening. "But, I got to tell you," Christine added with a taut smile, "that doll's happiest if her owner lives in Alaska."

23

Lisa was especially grateful to be alive the day they buried Ginger in the Homesteaders Cemetery in Bear Bones. It was late morning of the day after she'd been released from the hospital. The beautiful day had blue skies and soft winds. It was also the day after they should have been back to work at Carlisle, Bonner & Associates in Florida. But here they all stood, surrounded by the townspeople, circling the open grave of a woman whose life had been cut far too short—and because of Lisa?

The polished oak coffin Spike had selected for his sister, paid for by Bonner bounty, gleamed in the sun as it rested on its cradle, waiting to be lowered later. Several sprays of confetti-colored wildflowers lay atop its sleek veneer as the Methodist minister finished his final prayer and led everyone in the familiar hymn, *Amazing Grace.*

"Amazing grace, how sweet the sound that saved a wretch like me..."

Lisa felt she was so blessed to have been saved

from a wretched death like Ginger's, like her mother's and sister's. But that wasn't enough. Only justice for Ginger and herself was enough. And she wanted to know why. *Why?* It had to be more than the senior partnership.

As she stood between Mitch and the Bonners, her gaze drifted to Spike, standing tall at the head of the coffin with Christine at his side. Spike was the only one she knew who had seemed unhappy to see her back from the hospital. He'd glared at her, and she'd noticed Christine shaking her head and whispering as if to calm him. She would have to ask her new friend to help intercede with Spike, especially if he was blaming her for somehow causing Ginger's death.

"I once was lost but now am found...."

She had found that she still loved Mitch and wanted a life with him, but she felt confused and lost about her old life. She couldn't leave it as cleanly and decisively as Mitch had. She couldn't come to stay in Alaska, to become a ptarmigan with feathered feet, however much she felt the camaraderie and support of all these people she hardly knew.

But it was the present that was as confusing as the future. She and Mitch had thought they'd be able to find her enemy, but, as Christine said, the evildoer was not only crooked but clever. Graham? Vanessa? Jonas? And now, did she have to worry Spike might want revenge, too? Thank God, she'd been able to eliminate being suspicious about Christine. It was silly, of course, that a doll could cement a friendship between two grown women and bring comfort for the loss of Lisa's family, but somehow, it helped.

"Was blind but now I see."

She did see now that she'd been wrong to keep the sheriff out of this, because they had not been able to force anyone's hand. It had to be settled here, not back in Florida where she'd be without Mitch's help and protection.

If she turned her head slightly, she could see Sheriff Moran, in full dress uniform, next to his car, just outside the cemetery gate. He'd come as a favor to Mitch and a kindness to Spike and had led the procession the short distance from the church to the grave. But she'd heard he was leaving for Talkeetna immediately after the burial.

Now that her head was clearer than it had been in the hospital, she agreed with Mitch they should get the sheriff involved. There was not much time left. Spike had said he'd fly them to Anchorage just as he'd flown them in, but she wondered if he'd be willing to take *her* anywhere.

The service ended, and, when she looked, the sheriff's car was pulling away. Some townspeople went up for final words with Spike; some walked quietly toward the gates. Those who had been invited to the lodge for a lunch reception headed for their cars. The lodge vehicles were parked close by. Lisa saw Vanessa and Jonas start for them, heads down, deep in a conversation Lisa would love to overhear.

And then she saw Gus striding toward the grave site from the back of the cemetery, and she grabbed Mitch's arm and nodded in that direction.

"He must have waited for the sheriff to leave," Mitch muttered. "He has every right to be here, but Spike's really on edge today." Before Lisa could say anything, Mitch moved toward Gus, just as Spike evidently saw Gus coming.

"Oh, my," Ellie said to Graham. "Not more trouble."

"Mitch will handle it," he assured her, and turned to Lisa. "You know I delayed announcing my selection for senior partner while you were hospitalized," he told her, taking her wrist as if to hold her there. His fingers snagged in the seagull bracelet Mitch had given her. She'd decided to wear it today for the first time in over a year, but she had a jacket on and Mitch hadn't noticed it yet. Holding Ellie with his other hand, Graham said, "I'd like to speak with you privately today before I tell everyone my decision."

"You realize some townspeople are coming back to the lodge for food after this?" Lisa asked.

"We'll find a time," he said, and they all turned their attention to Mitch, who stood like a referee between two fighters ready to go at it in the ring.

"This is surely not the place and time for anything but honoring Ginger's life," Mitch's voice rang out. "Spike, Gus is obviously here for that reason. Isn't that right, Gus?"

Glowering past Mitch at Spike, who stood much taller, though not as bulky as Gus, the man nodded.

"Spike, can you accept that right now?" Mitch asked.

Like Gus, he said nothing but nodded. By then the minister had evidently seen the confrontation and walked over to take Gus's arm and escort him toward the casket.

Lisa had overheard Jonas say earlier that people were buried pretty shallow in Alaska, probably because digging into the permafrost was a challenge. It was similar to burials in South Florida where the water table was near the surface. She'd never given it a thought before, but she realized now she'd rather be buried in Alaska than Florida. Who wanted water creeping up toward their coffin? Funny how so many things pointed to her living here.

"Come on, Lisa," Ellie said, gesturing toward Mitch's SUV. "You don't need to get overtired your first day out of the hospital, and I want to help Christine set up for the buffet. Graham, I'm really rather glad Mitchell didn't invite Gus to the lodge for the luncheon."

With a last glance at Ginger's casket and the bright rainbow of wildflowers gracing it—remembering the glorious Alaska sunset sky she'd seen with Mitch in the wilds and wishing she could see the dancing hues of the aurora—Lisa turned away. But she vowed anew not to turn her back on what had happened to Ginger or herself.

About twenty townspeople who had known Ginger or were Spike's friends mingled with the lodge guests near noon. Spike finally showed up. Mitch had been getting nervous since the near confrontation with Gus, but Spike said he'd just stayed to see the grave "closed proper."

Proper, Lisa thought. Nothing was proper about Ginger's death or two attempts on her own life.

For some reason, both Jonas and Vanessa were hovering so close to Lisa that she was starting to feel claustrophobic. Had they heard that Graham wanted a private word with her this afternoon, or were they really in cahoots to harm her—again? She couldn't live like this. She even took to guarding her drink and plate of food.

Maybe they had somehow learned she'd asked Mitch to put a call in to Sheriff Moran to ask him to come out when he returned to his office today. He'd be here as soon as possible, Mitch had said, but he was at the scene of a hit-and-run.

A hit-and-run, Lisa thought. She'd had two of those and she wasn't going to have another.

She was tempted to go up to her room to lie down, but she'd promised Mitch she would not be out of his sight, unless it was to talk to Graham, and then it should be in a fairly public place, like the patio.

When the locals finally left and Graham suggested they meet in ten minutes for a short conference, she surprised herself by suggesting they walk down by the dock. If, she thought, he'd had anything to do with pushing her in the river or trapping her in the sauna or with Ginger's death, that setting might unsettle him.

In the upstairs hall, Lisa told Mitch where she and Graham were going to meet. "Good move," he said. "I'll watch you from the back windows. That way I'll be here in case the sheriff phones or arrives, but I got the idea it would be later."

"I guess with all the time I've wasted waiting to call him in, I can't complain about a little wait now."

"And it's going to be busy here, so the time will fly, but I don't want you to tire yourself out. Christine suggested to me that, to keep Spike busy this afternoon and help him out, we all transport some items he wants removed from Ginger's cottage here to the lodge. Spike wants us to have some things and others will go to his place later. Ellic's going to organize it. As soon as you're finish speaking to Graham, come back in so I know what he said and I can update you on what's happening. And don't be shocked, whatever he says."

"He's not going to offer me senior partner, is he?" she said with a shake of her head and little snort. She propped one hand on her hip. "Damn, he is, isn't he? I'm getting so I can read your mind!"

"Then I'm really in trouble. Are you going to slap my face?"

"You're outrageous—and precious to me. What you told me in the hospital about loving me—I feel the same way, too. Not again, still. Mitch, look," she said, holding out her left arm so he could see the seagull bracelet. "I'm wearing it again."

He took her hand and turned the bracelet around her wrist, slowly, somehow sensuously, and whispered, "I wish we could get two ptarmigans on there, too—ones with feathered feet."

"I—it doesn't mean that. I don't know how we'll ever work things out, but if Graham's going to offer me that lofty and vaunted position after everything this week, he must be hoping to buy me off. Evidently he doesn't think my apparent string of bad luck will rub off on the firm."

"Hear him out. He may say something to tip his hand so that—"

"Lisa, you ready?" Graham called to her, leaving the huddle around Spike and Christine that must be the meeting over helping Spike this afternoon. Lisa felt good about that at least. Until the sheriff came, she'd pitch in and hope to smooth things over with Spike. Still, once the sheriff started questioning people, nothing might ever be smooth between her and her colleagues again.

"You want to just stand here or sit on the dock?" Graham asked Lisa as they stopped at the lakeshore. "You must be tired."

"I'm fine," she lied. "That little hospital stay was just what the doctor ordered."

"You're feeling flip today. Here I expected sadness—for Ginger, for leaving Mitch again."

"I do grieve for Ginger and Spike. For Mitch and Christine, too, for their loss of their friend. I guess I'm just mad as hell and not going to take it anymore about what's happened to me here this week."

"Despite your slipups, shall we say, I think it's brought out the best in you. And here I thought facing Mitch after he betrayed and deserted you would be the worst you'd have to handle here. Lisa," he said, turning to her, "your tough, resilient and determined qualities are just what Carlisle, Bonner needs in all its leadership positions."

She looked into his blue eyes. He stared back steadily, no wavering, no change of expression, despite a slight tic at the corner of his mouth. "Maybe you should be seated," he said and went over to sit on the edge of the dock with his feet on the shore. She sat, too. Spike's plane, still tethered to the dock, seemed to hover over them. "Lisa, this week of hardship has convinced me, and Ellie agrees, that we should offer you the position of senior partner."

Her eyes widened, and she had to fight to keep her lower lip from dropping open. It was what she had wanted desperately for so long, maybe partly because it had once been Mitch's. It was an offer she'd suspected was coming from talking to Mitch. Yet it was a shock to hear the words, especially after the chaos of the week.

But now the offer, even framed in such a flattering, supportive way, seemed sullied. Was it a bribe? Bait? Or, had this entire week been a sort of survival test, and she was the survivor?

"I didn't think you'd be speechless," he said. "It's not like you."

"I've changed this week."

"But for the better, or I would have named Vanessa or Jonas. They'd both kill for the position."

She narrowed her gaze at him. Had he meant to word it that way? Was he playing with her mind, as whoever pushed her in the river surely must have been, or was he innocent of such an innuendo?

"Graham, I know you will find this hard to believe but—"

"If you turn me down," he interrupted, his usually well-modulated voice rough-edged now, "you'll regret it."

"Do what you must, but, as honored as I am by your trust and support, I can't give you an answer right now. I hope that's acceptable, because I do not intend it as an insult to you or the firm. Considering what I've been through this week, I hope you'll give me a little time. I'm not even sure I'm going back with all of you tomorrow. I have to get a few things settled."

"Lisa, you have clients—important clients—who have been rescheduled once already. Settle things with Mitch, you mean?"

"Yes."

"All right—listen. I've offered to have him consult with the firm part-time. I think he's considering it. You come back with us tomorrow, see your clients, take a couple of days to decide about the senior partnership, then give me a yea or nay when you're in normal surroundings. Mitch has guests coming next week, but after that, I'll fly him in to discuss my offer—and you two can hash things out then. We'll help poor Spike this afternoon, then just tell Jonas and Vanessa the decision will be made later, because of the—the upheaval this week—and that they are still in the running, because obviously they are. And I repeat, we really want you to take this position, or I'd never allow a stall like this."

She nodded, thanked him for the offer and for being so understanding, then headed back inside the lodge, leaving him sitting stiff-shouldered on the dock. She felt like a coward that she had stonewalled him, not only about the fact she no longer felt she wanted his precious position, but because all hell was going to break loose when the sheriff arrived and heard what she and Mitch had to say.

She knew if Sheriff Moran dared to question Graham, his lawyers, and especially Ellie again, it was all over for her at Carlisle, Bonner, no matter what had just happened here.

"Just make sure," Spike told Christine as they stood by his truck outside the lodge, "that Lisa doesn't get near me. I don't care if they are all helping to move Ginger's things this afternoon."

"Listen to yourself," she told him, putting her palm against his chest. She was surprised to feel how hard his heart was pounding. The doctors had stabilized Lisa's heartbeat, but she was worried about Spike's blood pressure. "You nearly had a fight with Gus," she said, "and now you're at war with Lisa. Please, Spike, don't let Ginger's death turn you against folks who—"

"If I thought the sheriff had done a decent job looking into Ginger's death, I'd get him in on this again."

"Mitch called him. The entire thing may be reopened, but you can't let on. Lisa finally decided they needed official help—"

"I don't care if she's had it rough. She should have told the sheriff the second she got back to the lodge from her river rescue that someone pushed her in. Then he would have gotten on Ginger's case, too. I read there's like a twenty-four-hour golden period for investigations for murders."

"I think that's for kidnappings, not murders."

"Hell, you ought to know."

Christine felt as if he'd slapped her. She pulled her hand back from touching him. Tears filled her eyes. Spike hung his head, looked away.

"Sorry," he whispered. "I just can't stand it that Ginger died that way, and Lisa should have screamed bloody murder from the first. And the man you think can do no wrong should have filled me in right away."

"Maybe, but she and Mitch thought they could figure out who it was, but if it was public, they'd never know."

"Maybe they even thought I pushed her, trying to keep her away from Mitch. And see, you're defending him again—her, too. They hurt Ginger, hurt me. But I'm sorry I hurt you. See you later. I gotta lot to do."

24

Helping Spike in honor of Ginger was, Lisa thought, an appropriate way to spend time waiting for the sheriff. She was sad, for their activities emphasized Ginger's loss. And her stomach kept cramping over nervous expectation of the sheriff's imminent arrival. Maybe he would insist that she and the others stay behind for complete questioning. Or he might learn enough to make an arrest. Nervously, she kept twisting her seagull bracelet around her wrist.

She, Christine and Mitch were manning the lodge, storing items that Jonas and Vanessa, Ellie and Graham brought back in large vehicles from Ginger's cabin, where Spike was sorting through her possessions. Lisa and Christine put things away that were meant for the lodge. Most of Ginger's baking equipment was stored in the kitchen. They also made a pile on the front porch that would go to Spike's place later. All the activity meant that people—suspects—were scattered between the cabin and the lodge on the winding forest road.

Mitch was sticking close to the phone, waiting for the sheriff's call, or even better, his arrival in person. If anyone asked why Mitch wasn't helping to unload, Lisa and Christine were just to say that, since they had overstayed their reservation, he had to phone or e-mail future guests to be sure their travel plans were set.

"So where does this load go?" Lisa asked as she and Christine went out to meet Jonas and Vanessa. Jonas opened the trunk to reveal boxes of clay pots for plants and an array of garden tools.

"Spike said it's for the lodge and not his place. That's all I know," Jonas said. "At home or here, this kind of stuff's not my thing."

"I'll go ask Mitch," Lisa said.

She saw he stood away from the front windows but was looking out. She and Christine had orders to not so much as go to the bathroom without the other waiting outside the door. As Mitch had put it, "We're so close to telling the sheriff that I don't want anything else to happen."

Earlier, after Lisa had come back in from hearing Graham offer her the senior partnership, she and Mitch had huddled briefly in the back hall by the library. "Yes, he offered it to me, and I said I needed some time," she had whispered.

"Did you say you'd go back with them tomorrow?"

"No, but he insisted. He said he'd fly you to Florida soon about that consultant position he's offered you."

Mitch had hit his forehead with the palm of his hand. "Yeah, I just blew that off, almost forgot about it. No way that's going to happen."

"Another bribe? I have to think his offer to me was exactly that. And, if so, he's very adept not only at managing people but at hypocrisy and underhandedness. Which means he could definitely be the spider at the center of the casino-case web. How much did Graham want to have his own fortune, however he got his hands on it, rather than living in the lap of luxury because of his wife and her family's wealth? Maybe he saw a way to make big money, then got scared it would backfire and he'd be caught, especially when he had to take the case, then sabotage it so he couldn't be traced. We never could figure out how whoever tracked us and bugged us knew so much about our lives. He must have made a bargain with some devil, and got burned himself."

"Listen, sweetheart," Mitch had said, grasping her upper arms, "I'm going to keep a good eye on you until the sheriff comes—and hopefully for long after. But I told Christine that, whatever happens, before the sheriff arrives and hears us out, she's to stick with you. Promise me!"

She had promised him. But then she'd once promised to marry him, and that had been blown to smithereens. As far as she was concerned, that still had to be settled between them, but they had to get all this taken care of first.

Now, as she crossed the short distance to the

window where Mitch stood watching Jonas, Vanessa and Christine unload the car, she asked, "Nothing from the sheriff yet?"

"If I don't hear soon, I'm going to call his office again. They can patch me through to the accident scene. It must have been a bad wreck, injuries or fatalities."

Their gazes locked and held. *Injuries, fatalities...* She suddenly wanted to explode in tears, but she got control of herself. "Oh, I came in to ask you where garden pots and rakes and shovels go. I saw those tools in Ginger's shed when we were looking for her."

"In the boathouse for now, our general catch-all. Christine never goes in there, so tell her stuff should just be stacked along the west side to leave room for the boats and rafts when we put them away. I'll sort through it all later."

"Aye, aye, Captain," she told him with an attempt at a jaunty salute, when she actually wanted to just cling to him. She hurried back out.

The gardening pots and tools were piled by the porch, Jonas and Vanessa were pulling away, and Christine was on her way in, so they almost bumped into each other.

"I figured Mitch was in there, but I didn't want to shirk my duty of being your second skin," Christine said.

"You'll be glad to get rid of me."

"No, I really won't," she said as they went back out

and she hefted a box of pots as Lisa picked up a collection of rakes, spades and hoes. "At first I was afraid you would be bad for Mitch, but I see you love him, too—well, you know what I mean, not the same way I do."

"If and when I do come back here when this is all over, it will be to see Mitch, but you, too. I wish you the best with Spike once he can get past Ginger's loss. And I'm hoping our telling the sheriff I've been attacked twice will reopen the investigation of her death, so Spike won't be so upset. Oh—Mitch said all this stuff can be stacked up in the boathouse."

"Let's go."

They started to walk around the corner of the lodge. Lisa recalled Ginger peeking at them from here when Gus brought her and Mitch back from their river trek.

Mitch ran out onto the porch. "The sheriff was on his way, but had a flat tire just down the road about a half mile," he shouted, pointing in the other direction. "I gave him a quick briefing, and he was all ears. I'm not going to wait for one of the vehicles to get back. I'll just jog down to help him change the tire, or else bring him back here while we call for someone else to do it. You two stick together. I'll be back with the sheriff one way or the other in half an hour."

That was hopeful, Lisa thought as her stomach knotted again at all that was to come. Even if all these lawyers lawyered up at the sheriff's questions, no one would dare to try to harm her again. It would be like life insurance. If they all turned against her for bringing in the sheriff, she'd just have to find someplace else to work and live—maybe here?

They found the boathouse unlocked. Lisa had not been in it before, and it was obviously not familiar territory to Christine either. "Stack things on the west side," Lisa told Christine. "He said to leave plenty of space for boats later."

"Boats, kayaks, rafts," Christine said as she put the box of clay pots down, then shoved it farther into the corner with her foot.

Lisa liked the boathouse. It smelled of cedar and had big beams holding up the roof. It wasn't dark inside at all. Unlike the sauna, thank heavens, it was airy and light with a row of small windows over-looking the lake, though they were quite high up. She leaned the tools in the corner near the box of pots and said, "Either Mitch's uncle was tall or he built this for Spike. I have to stand on tiptoe to see out."

"I guess they wanted just the light, not the view. We'd better get the rest, a couple more loads, I think. The Bonners should be back soon with their next haul. We shouldn't tell them to go and pick Mitch and Sheriff Moran up, should we?"

"No way," Lisa said firmly.

As they started back to get another load, a shaft of sunlight slanting into the corner caught Lisa's eye. Something gleamed. At first she thought it was a spider web, since one laced itself behind the tools, and she thought of Graham. Mitch had said he believed Vanessa was first on their most-wanted list, but Lisa was picking Graham as the spider.

"What is it?" Christine stopped to ask as Lisa froze.

"The top of that spade caught my eye—not the reddish stain but something else."

Lisa went toward it, blocking out the shaft of sun. She lifted the spade, carefully. Moving it into the sunlight, she could see sticking to the reddish varnish on one side of the spade's handle several matted red hairs were stuck.

Christine bent closer to it. Lisa's mind raced. These red stains must not be varnish but blood.

"I guess," Christine said, "she could have cut herself working and gotten hairs stuck on it."

"No blood on her dock," Lisa whispered, suddenly feeling nauseous. "But the back of her head was hit hard. Vanessa knew she worked a garden and had been out to see it. She knew right where it was. She told me to look in the shed for Ginger, and if that's where this was, it doesn't make sense. Still, she could have—have hurt her, then set me up to find the body…."

"You think Vanessa is behind everything?"

"Mitch does—we're not sure. We have to hide this until the sheriff gets here."

"Lisa, we have to go get Spike so he's here when the sheriff arrives. We've got to tell him we've found something to reopen Ginger's case—strong evidence."

"Unless the Bonners have driven in, we don't have

a car to get to him, but then, I don't want them to think we're running for Spike for any reason. Ellie and Spike arranged who would be where today."

"Listen," Christine said, whispering now, "Ginger's boat is just outside, on the other side of the dock from Spike's plane. Spike's blaming you for what happened to Ginger, but I really think he should be here. We can take the motorboat and be to Ginger's cabin and back in just over ten minutes. We won't even go ashore, just shout to him to get back to the lodge. He can drive around while we head back."

"If Mitch finds us missing, he'll have a fit."

"We'll leave him a note, just saying we took a sandwich to Spike, in case anyone else finds it. Spike will be so grateful you found this extra evidence. Maybe it will stop his bitterness, because that's not like him. I'd give anything if he'd just be himself again, not so angry. I swear he's going to have a heart attack."

Tears welled in Christine's eyes. Lisa understood fearing for those you loved. And for Christine, after an abusive marriage, it must be so hard for her to trust another man, especially one who seemed to be losing control of himself lately. Yet Lisa desperately wanted Christine and Spike to be happy—and together.

"You do know how to run her boat?" she asked as she hid the spade behind two stacked barrels, then followed Christine outside.

"Sure, it's easy. Come on, twin joined-at-the-hip. Let's leave Mitch a note on the front door about taking a sandwich to Spike, and we'll explain the truth to him and the sheriff later."

They dashed inside while Christine scribbled the note. Lisa was elated about finding what could be a murder weapon. And to think Jonas and Vanessa had delivered it! That meant once again, she realized, that perhaps Vanessa had not hit Ginger over the head with it after all, or surely she would have spotted it and hidden it. As she and Christine headed toward Ginger's boat, she was grateful that the Bonners had not driven in with their next load.

Lisa sat in the prow and Christine easily started the old outboard motor. "Only twenty-five horsepower," she said. "An antique with a pull cord no less, but it was always old faithful for her. It's more like a plow horse than a racehorse, though."

It was indeed, as they plowed their way through the low waves toward the other end of the lake. Lisa thought of the day she and Vanessa had taken a rowboat across and found Ginger's body. Then her thoughts skipped to the day this all started, the day she and Mitch were going to take that red kayak to a picnic spot near Ginger's cabin. He'd saved her with that kayak, so it was sad they had to abandon it. And that day they intended to talk things out near Ginger's cabin, they had cans of ginger ale—how ironic. And appetizers Christine had fixed for what was to be their reunion feast while they tried to patch up their past. But instead of the appetizers, they'd ended up with fabulous wild blueberries and fresh salmon.

The motor sputtered at times. Its *putt-putt* barely drowned out the river's distant rumble. But Lisa was not afraid. She had good memories as well as the bad. Once they learned who had intended to kill her and why, she would learn to stride into the future without past losses haunting her ever again.

She heard another sound and looked back to see what was loud enough to carry this far. Christine turned to look back, too.

"Oh!" Christine cried. "I think the engine of Spike's plane is starting. Can you tell if the propeller's turning?"

Lisa shaded her eyes. "Yes, I think so."

"He must have driven in and seen us heading out and wants to get our attention, so we head back. We'd better go back. This won't turn on a dime, but hang on."

They made a small, slow circle, but the plane had left the dock and lodge behind. It was still revving up to taxi or take off. And, Lisa noted with increasing unease, it was making a path straight toward them.

25

Lisa's first thought when she saw the plane coming their way was that Spike had something to tell them. Maybe he'd found an item in Ginger's things that would be even more evidence than the spade.

Shading her eyes, Christine shouted over the increasing noise, "Maybe Mitch got back and was really upset we're out here on the lake. Spike might have brought a load around himself, and Mitch said, let's go in the plane and get them to come back."

"But wouldn't Mitch have just used his motorboat?"

Christine had brought them to a halt with the motor idling. It sounded as jumpy as Lisa felt. Christine said, "Maybe Spike's just moving the plane down to where it used to be, but he said he wouldn't. Or he's trying to teach us a lesson."

"Like what? This is getting too close for comfort. I don't think the sun's in his eyes and that he can't see us, but let's get out of the way!"

Christine turned them outward, but the plane adjusted its course. It did not seem to be accelerating enough to take off over their heads, but continued straight for them.

"This isn't funny," Lisa heard her friend mutter as she took evasive action once again. The plane was so close now its engine drowned out the rumble of the river and their own motor. "*Iah!* Hang on!" Christine shouted and made a sharp turn.

Rocked by the wake from the plane's pontoons as they passed within five yards, their boat nearly capsized. It rocked to one side then the other as Christine fought to turn their prow into the choppy waves.

"What's wrong with him?" she shouted and lifted one arm to make a fist at Spike as the plane came around again to face them.

For one instant, Lisa stared down into the roiling, blue-green depths of the lake, slashed by whitecaps pounding their boat. She fought her fear that faces would float to the surface, that she and Christine could be thrown in to join those drowned women staring up at them.

"It can't be Spike, it can't be Spike," Christine kept reciting like a litany. "Hang on, because we're too slow to make a run for it if he—if the plane—comes back, so we'll have to twist and turn."

Lisa realized they'd made a fatal error, maybe more than one. Nowhere in the boat was there a PFD. They'd been in too much of a hurry, hadn't checked, when Mitch said that was always a necessity. And she—maybe Christine, too—had made the huge mistake of trusting Spike.

Mitch wiped the grease and dirt from his hands with a rag the sheriff handed him.

"Where'd you learn to change a tire like that?" Mace Moran asked.

"Never have before, but I'm learning a lot of things since I grew feathered feet. Necessity is the mother of invention, remember?"

"One of Alaska's creeds. But your real talent's talking and working at the same time. Glad you finally filled me in about the attacks on Lisa. Pretty clever ones all right, made to look like she could have wanted to hurt herself, so Ginger's accident could be a setup, too. Let's get going, 'cause I got a few cages to rattle."

"I know you don't like having to deal with attorneys but—"

"But the law's the law. Now isn't it just like a couple lawyers to think they can solve a case that should be handed over to law enforcement? You don't see me trying cases in court, do you? I could get you and Lisa for suppressing evidence, obstruction of justice, at least on Ginger Jackson's death. I'm so mad that one of your fancy city lawyer friends thinks they can put one over on an Alaska sheriff that I'm about ready to spit nails."

He threw the tire jack and the flat tire in the trunk, where Mitch saw he had a lot of other police gear, including an assault rifle. He shuddered as the sheriff slammed the trunk closed. As they both got in the front seat, Mitch couldn't picture any of the lawyers from Carlisle, Bonner in handcuffs or being taken away in the caged back of this vehicle. *I've got a few cages to rattle,* the sheriff had said. At least Spike would rest easier when the investigation into Ginger's death was reopened. And Mitch and Lisa would finally get some answers so she could put the attempts on her life behind her.

Lisa and Christine had to shout at each other over the noise as the plane made another pass so close that one pontoon almost hit their boat. They got soaked with spray, and water washed in to swirl around their ankles. They would have been hit dead-on if Christine hadn't veered away at the last moment.

"I'll try to get us close to shore!" Christine shouted. "He must have snapped. Maybe when he saw we had her boat—"

"Can you swim?" Lisa screamed as the plane, sitting so high in the water that it seemed like a red sea monster risen from the depths, came at them again.

"I think we're gonna have to swim!" Christine shouted.

The sun glinted off the cockpit windows to nearly blind them before she managed a wild U-turn and gunned the boat toward the shore. Holding on with one hand and bailing madly with the other, Lisa looked back as the plane made another pass. She could see no pilot in it. Spike was tall, so his head would surely have been visible in that split second, unless he'd bent or stooped.

The plane pursued them. They were not near enough to shore for an easy swim. They were going to get hit hard this time. Shoving its white-crested wake ahead of its bulbous feet, the plane came faster, louder.

"Christine!" Lisa screamed. "Jump!"

They both jumped, even as the plane cracked into the stern of their boat. As it splintered and upended, Lisa dove, digging into the water with both hands, kicking hard, rocked and buffeted, going lower, down to escape the deep-riding pontoons.

Sounds were muted now, distant. The river reached for her again, then the seething wake of the cruise ship where her mother and Jani disappeared. Ginger floated closer, faceup, arms outstretched.

No. No! She would not be sucked under by this water or by nightmares. She did not see Ginger in this lake, did not see her mother's face or hear her voice, beseeching, begging, *Come to me, Lisa...come to me...*

After what seemed an eternity, Lisa broke the rocking surface of the lake with a huge gasp. Christine was a good distance off, stroking for the shore opposite from Ginger's cabin. Out of breath, exhausted when she'd told the doctor she'd do nothing strenuous, Lisa treaded water, trying to get some strength and time to think. Now, at least, as she saw the plane turn again and start back, she might learn if it was both of them Spike wanted to kill or just her.

Too soon, she had her answer. Again, the red plane headed straight for her.

"Damn!" Mitch said, as he snatched the note off the door.

"What's that?" the sheriff asked.

"It's from Lisa and Christine. Spike needed a break and came by to do a little work on something on his plane. He's going to be making taxis across the lake to test something, and Christine and Lisa are going with him. 'A tour of the lake without a boat,' Lisa's scribbled here—or Christine. Not sure who's handwriting this is. I can't believe they left when it might be Lisa's last day here."

"Not if I can get the ball rolling with a murder investigation and a double-assault case. Let's see if we can spot them on the lake, and if they get close, signal them to come in."

They went inside and walked across the great room to look out the back bank of windows. At the far end of the lake, the red plane was making all sorts of maneuvers.

"Kind of a thrill ride," the sheriff said. "Hey, I hear a car out front, so whoever's back, I'll start with them." They heard doors slam and hurried toward the front porch. Mitch frowned. He didn't like it. Something was really wrong.

Two vehicles had pulled up. Vanessa and Jonas got out of one, and Spike got out of the other.

Lisa was too exhausted to swim, but she knew she had to. She'd never make it out of the path of the plane at this pass, so she was going to wait until the last minute, then dive again. She wished she could leap onto one of the pontoons, cling to the plane as she had when she'd signaled across the lake that they needed help because Ginger had drowned.

Drowned. Drowned in this very lake now churned to chaos by this red monster coming at her.

"Swim! Swim! Move! *Lisa!*" Christine was shrieking from a distance.

The white-water wake pushed at Lisa by the pontoons reminded her of the river rapids. But no Mitch in a kayak to chase and save her this time.

She took a huge breath and jackknifed under, but was sucked upward by the pull of the water, when she had thought it would thrust her away. She wanted to shut everything out but she forced herself to open her eyes. Amazingly, above her head on the surface of the turbulent water, the plane slowed and stopped. Through a blizzard of bubbles, a pontoon rested right over her head, just yards away, a huge, bulky shadow, shutting out the light. Was the killer in it going to sit there until she surfaced and then try to hit her again?

Her first instinct was to surface—had to surface, out of air—and then swim away, but that's what the pilot was probably expecting. If she could just make him think that she was gone—drowned—maybe she could hold on for a ride near the shore and then make it in. Under the plane where she couldn't be seen from the cockpit was the best, the only, place to hide.

She swam up and gasped in air directly between the two red pontoons. Had the pilot hit Ginger over the head with that spade handle, then shoved her in to drown? Yes, it must also be the person who pushed Lisa in the river and somehow jammed that sauna door. Someone she knew, someone who feared something she knew.

Surely Spike hadn't killed Ginger. Graham and Ellie? Ellie knew how to fly, had been up more than once in this very plane. Ellie was short, maybe too short to be seen when Lisa had glanced through the cockpit window earlier. Had Graham convinced or coerced Ellie to fly Spike's plane to eliminate her and Christine, or was Christine just an innocent bystander? Surely, they could not have known the sheriff was coming. Or was Graham the one who had tapped their phones in Florida, and had also done it here? Oh, yes, Graham liked to tape-record things.

As Lisa had found a foothold on a pontoon the day she climbed on it to signal for help, she found a handhold now. Her seagull bracelet clunked against the metal, and she hoped the pilot had not heard as she hooked both hands over the back ridge of the right-side pontoon. There she rested, her head well above water, not even having to kick her feet while the plane idled, shifting slightly in a circle. If she could just convince the pilot that she was drowned, maybe she could slip away and make it to the shore. She couldn't see Christine now. Even if Christine had made it in, she'd be exhausted, and it was a long hike through thick trees back to the lodge for help.

"All right," the sheriff said, "everybody just sit down, and I'll ask the questions!"

At least, Mitch thought, Vanessa and Jonas sat instead of making all kinds of demands as they had at first. That had really set the sheriff off.

Spike was distraught when he read the note the women had left, which he said wasn't written by Christine. He finally perched on the edge of the couch before jumping up again.

"Sheriff, somebody's stolen my plane, and there it is!" he shouted, pointing at it hovering on the lake in the distance.

"Either of those women know how to operate the plane?" the sheriff asked.

"Not that I know of," Spike said. "You're gonna have to arrest me, sir, 'cause I'm going down there in Mitch's boat, and—"

"Now we don't know why Lisa and Christine left a note saying they were going with you, when they obviously didn't, do we?" the increasingly frustrated sheriff bellowed.

Mitch's mind raced. Spike was right. They had to get down to the other end of the lake because something was really wrong—and there was water all around again, as when Ginger died and in the attempts on Lisa's life.

"Lisa's finally lost it," Jonas muttered. "And I swear, Graham's going to pick her anyway," he added to Vanessa.

As if mentioning his name had summoned him, Graham came in the front door. "Why the sheriff's car?" he asked Mitch, ignoring the sheriff himself. "What's happened now?"

"Everyone's accounted for except Ellie," Mitch said to Spike, ignoring Graham's question and the sheriff's sputtering. "I'm with you, Spike, so let's go."

"What the hell's going on?" Graham demanded. "Ellie's upstairs, lying down with a migraine. I dropped her off here about twenty minutes ago, then took a final load to Spike's place."

"That's true," Spike said, edging for the back door. "Hey, Mitch, look at the dock. Ginger's boat's gone. They might have taken it instead!"

"Mr. Bonner," the sheriff said, "you go upstairs and check on your wife, see if she can come down here, okay?"

Mitch saw that Sheriff Moran's control of the situation was gone. What terrified him was that he'd lost control, too, and feared once again for Lisa's life. He ran out the door after Spike, and they raced for Mitch's boat.

26

The wash of waves against the pontoons, the scraping of her bracelet as she held on and the forbidding rumble of the plane's engine were the only sounds Lisa heard before distant shouts pierced her ears. Christine's voice? Yes, Christine shouting at Spike in the plane. Had her friend made it to shore? Lisa knew, however strong a swimmer she was, that she would not make it in, not after the physical setbacks of the river and the sauna. And now this— attempted murder by a plane, with who at the helm?

The plane's motor pitch went up. She leaned left and could see the propeller spinning faster, faster. The plane began to move forward. Had she convinced the pilot she was drowned?

She gave a garbled cheer when she realized the plane was heading back toward the lodge across the length of the lake. If she just held on—if the water being displaced by the pontoon didn't push her off— she could ride it nearly to the dock.

The plane plowed its way toward the middle of the

lake. She had no choice but to hang on and try to gauge when she should let go. To breathe, she had to lift herself higher out of the water and really hang on to the ridge at the top of the pontoon. It couldn't be much farther and then she'd let go. Mitch and the sheriff must be back to the lodge soon. They'd see her, come for her, if she just treaded water.

The plane continued to accelerate, the pitch of the propeller noise rising, humming harder. Dear God, was it going to take off? No matter where they were on the lake, she had to let go now. Gasping in a huge breath, she let go, but she didn't drop. As the plane skimmed the surface of the lake, her bracelet caught in the ridge of the pontoon and held her there, dragging her with it. To keep her wrist from being broken, she fought to put her other hand back up, holding on as her legs flailed free of the water.

The plane cleared the lake and was airborne. Lisa cursed the bracelet, but its clasp had never opened well, not even the night she'd wanted to throw it at Mitch for leaving her.

The plane climbed, then banked. She tried to pull her wrist free again; her hand had turned white.

Then it was too late, and she had no choice but to hang on for her life.

"Ellie's not upstairs anywhere!" Graham shouted at the sheriff as he ran out onto the lodge patio. Mitch had never heard Graham sound so panicked. He stood in his boat still at the dock. He had not started the motor because the plane had gone airborne. To his horror, Mitch craned his neck and saw Lisa hanging from one of the pontoons as it passed overhead.

"Where is she? I want the sheriff to help me find Ellie!" Graham demanded, then looked up and gasped as the plane went over.

Mitch shouted at the sheriff, "Get rescue people here ASAP! Cops, choppers, searchers!"

"That can't be, can't be," Graham was yelling.

"Spike," Mitch ordered as he grabbed two PFDs and clambered out of the boat, "see if you can find Christine out there somewhere!" He gestured toward the lake and ran hell-bent for the ridge between the lake and the river.

With Lisa hanging on, her wrist still snagged by her bracelet, the plane flew low over the tall Sitka spruce along the ridge between the lake and the river. She dared not let go with her free hand to try to open the bracelet. She imagined she heard Christine shouting, but it was just the whine of the wind and the engine, which blended with the river's roar.

Did the pilot know she was hanging on and was trying to scrape her off on the treetops, or did he think Lisa was drowned and was just escaping? Surely, the plane would not go low enough to slam her into the cliffs of the Hairpin Gorge up ahead, because that would mean destruction for the plane. Yet the pilot seemed to be on a lark, swinging along, almost as if it were some sort of joy ride. But as the cliffs narrowed ahead, flying this low would be impossible. So did the pilot intend to take the plane higher—or commit suicide?

She knew then it wasn't Spike, for he would know the lay of the land and the terror of the rapids and the falls ahead—unless he was so distraught over Ginger's death that he had, as Christine said, snapped. No, she thought she knew now who was at the controls, maybe the same person who had been at the controls of the law firm, of Graham, maybe of that casino scheme. But why? Ellie Carlisle Bonner had money, lots of it. And a husband and daughter she loved.

A husband and daughter she loved—the words snagged in Lisa's stunned brain. She knew she was going to die now, either by dropping onto the cliffs or into the river. Strange, how facing death instantly clarified some things. A husband and daughter she loved—surely, Lisa's own mother had been shattered when her husband deserted her. She'd become suicidal, thinking she was doing Jani a favor by taking her with her. And she'd tried to kill Lisa, too, and she'd been suffering from being left behind all these years, tormented by the loss yet grateful she'd escaped. Worse, she'd blamed herself for pulling free of her mother, but she knew now that she had not caused her loved ones' deaths. Too late to keep tormenting herself—too late to pull free from this plane. But now, strangely, all that wouldn't matter soon, because she couldn't hold on much longer....

The bracelet, which held her left arm tight against

the pontoon, reminded her of Mitch. She'd admired the seagulls flying free on the bracelet in the kitschy antique shop on Las Olas Boulevard in Lauderdale, and he'd bought it for her. He'd given it to her during a walk on the beach near Sunrise Avenue. Mitch—all the time they'd wasted apart when she could have been here with him, but now...

Lisa gasped when she saw that the plane was over the first part of the S turn in the canyon. This wasn't the way to Anchorage, the way to escape. Either Ellie meant to shake Lisa off here where she'd almost drowned before, or she intended to go down with the plane. Of course, Ellen Carlisle Bonner would not want questions, accusations, scandal. The one time she'd seen Ellie a nervous wreck was when the sheriff questioned her about Ginger.

So had Ellie hit Ginger with that spade handle and put her in the lake? No, this was all too unreal, all too—

The plane bumped and shuddered. Lisa's bracelet broke and fell away. Her wrist ached—imprinted with a seagull, deep in her flesh. If only she had stayed with Mitch, clung to Mitch. She fought to hang on as the plane slowed. It descended toward the frothing river and came closer to the cliffs of the narrowing gorge. Yes, Ellie, whether she thought she'd drowned Lisa in the lake or knew where she was now, was going to crash the plane.

As he ran toward the river, Mitch heard Spike speed away in his boat. Beyond the riverbank —just

as when Lisa was pushed in last week—the snowmelt
water raged. He squinted into the afternoon sun to
search the sky, then the river. Nothing. No sign of
anyone, not even a red amphibious plane. He could
have lain flat on the ground and beat his fists.

Vanessa and Jonas came up behind him, lugging
a single green kayak between them. "If you're going
after her again," Jonas said, "there's a paddle and two
PFDs in here."

Mitch just shook his head. He couldn't even manage to say thanks but nodded, then looked away with
tears blurring his vision of the river. Twice Lisa had
cheated death, but was three times too much to hope
for?

Graham came running. "You mean Ellie's up in
that plane?" He looked incredulous, more shocked
than sad. "I didn't even want her up there with Spike
again, so what's going on?"

If Mitch wasn't going to cry, he would have
laughed. His eyes still on the distant sky in the direction the plane had gone, he said, "You don't get it,
do you? It's hard to believe you're innocent but
ignorant of what she was doing."

"She's got her own plane at home! And was that
Lisa hang—"

"Ellie must have pushed her in the river last week,"
Mitch muttered as the sheriff joined them with a nod
that he'd sent for help. "Then," Mitch went on, "she
tried to kill Lisa in the sauna and make it all look as
if she was as crazy as her mother—suicidal."

"What are you suggesting? Why?" Graham asked, swinging Mitch around to face him.

"I assume to make sure Lisa and I didn't put our heads together to figure out you were behind the money laundering in the casino case."

"Me!" Graham roared, shaking Mitch. "It wasn't me, what—"

Mitch couldn't help himself. Sheriff standing nearby or not, he swung his fist and hit Graham squarely in the jaw to send him sprawling back on the grass.

The plane was going down. Lisa could feel the erratic but intentional flying. Poor Claire, Ellie's daughter, losing a mother who killed herself. The ultimate betrayal. Treason. A lifetime of regrets.

As they got lower over the river, Lisa realized she still had a choice. Go down with the plane or let go into the river. But she knew those killer rapids, their cold reach, what they could do.

The plane tilted to show white water under them and worse ahead. Ellie would never make it through these hairpin turns before the braided river began where the bears ate the salmon. Strangely proud, Lisa was glad she knew this land below…had seen this great land. It was over now. She'd let go and ride the river without Mitch, with no PFD, or go down with the plane….

As the plane twisted, perhaps tilted to make it through a turn of the gorge, Lisa let go and dropped,

dropped through an eternity of air into crashing water. Dreading it—the impact, the cold. Lisa and the salmon, struggling, struggling with the river, she thought as she hit.

Cold water slammed against her. She went under, but her feet hit the rocky bottom. She had shoes this time. She surfaced, made herself reserve her strength, didn't fight it. Yes, go with the flow, maybe get near something to grab before the falls...the falls...

As her head cleared the water, she looked up to see where the plane had gone. She saw it happen. Like a toy, not far downriver, the left wing clipped the cliff and it spun slowly, only once before it went down with a crack and a mammoth splash.

Lisa forced away the thought of Ellie in the water, trapped like her mother and Jani, like Ginger—like her now, if she didn't get out of this cold.

She was so exhausted but she bent her knees and tried to suck in a good breath now and then. Fingers getting numb already, like before. But she knew more now, about this river, her enemy, which had also, in a way, given her Mitch back and led her deeper into the heart of Alaska. She knew when to try to grab a rock and to pick a big one near the bank—if there was a bank with these sheer walls—to try to cling to.

Around the next swirling turn, maybe near the spot Mitch had pulled her out, a big tree leaned across the river rocks in front of her. No, not a tree trunk—the wrecked fuselage of the red plane with one broken wing still attached, reaching out into the brutal rush of river.

* * *

"I'll pay for a massive search," Graham was telling the sheriff as the first rescue vehicle from Talkeetna screeched up to the lodge. He had an ice pack on his jaw that Vanessa had brought after Mitch's fist took him down. It didn't stop Graham from still trying to give orders. "And Jonas here will be serving as my lawyer for now, and Vanessa over there as my wife's counsel."

Jonas frowned and shook his head. "I don't know, Graham. If you or Ellie had anything to do with Lisa's earlier injuries, I don't know."

"I'll represent you both for now, if that's all right," Vanessa piped up.

Rats off a sinking ship, Mitch thought, with Vanessa hoping to take over the helm. But he didn't care. He really didn't care about anything if he lost Lisa now— again. He ignored all of them as he jogged over to the emergency vehicle with the sheriff right behind him.

"How long to get a chopper in the air?" he asked.

"They're on their way," the driver told him. "But they can only fly surveillance over most of the area downriver from here."

"That's what we need. But they can hover and drop a rescue rope or basket. If they need someone to do that, I'll go down."

"If they haven't left the area," the sheriff said. "If we're in time."

Lisa knew she had only one chance to try to grab the wing and get out of the water and onto the wrecked fuselage. She could see and smell fuel spilling into the water and didn't want a ride through that. But what if the plane exploded? Would fuel ignite in this much moving water?

With the remnants of her spent strength, Lisa seized the strut of the plane under the wing that she'd used to haul herself up the day Ginger died, and held on. Water poured at, over and under the wing, and she had to climb to get to the split cockpit. The wreck of the plane was like a sieve, like the tree that had let Mitch rescue her not far from here.

Water pounded her back, but when she boosted herself slightly, it also thrust her upward as if a huge hand had pushed her from the river. Gasping for air, sprawled on her stomach across what must have been the copilot's seat, she grabbed on and held tight.

But the plane was shuddering as if it could be swept downriver toward the falls any moment. Should she let go and try to distance herself from this dead, broken ruin?

Then, Lisa saw the real ruin of a life sprawled and broken, the real monster, who had planned all the accidents, all the torments.

Trapped by her seat belt, Ellie was half in the pilot seat, half out. Her upper torso was pinned between the seat and the broken side window, through which a separate spray of gray water spewed.

Lisa braced herself, reached over and unfastened the seat belt, then hauled Ellie partway toward her like a limp rag doll. If she was dead, she'd leave her here, but if she was alive, she had much to answer for. Ellie felt cold, so cold. Both of them were so cold and battered.

Battered—Christine had fought back from being battered. Christine did what she had to do to save herself.

Lisa tried to pull Ellie closer, but her right leg was trapped between the back of her seat and the cockpit wall. What was left of the other side of the cockpit made a barrier to give some breathing space, at least for now, Lisa thought, as the entire plane shook and wobbled.

Leave Ellie or pull her out, whatever it took? Risk her life to get answers? Curiosity, the kind that killed the cat, kept Lisa there when she knew she should have fled the plane. Was Ellie jealous that Mitch hadn't fallen for their precious daughter, Claire, to become coheirs of the firm as Graham and Ellie had? Did she fear that Graham would be discovered as the spider behind the casino case debacle if Mitch and Lisa got their heads together again?

"Ellie!" she shouted and shook her shoulder feebly with one icy hand.

Ellie opened her eyes and groaned.

"Ellie, it's Lisa. Tell me why you tried to kill me. Tell me, and I'll pull you out of here."

"Too late. Can't tell. Don't tell Claire."

"I'm going to leave you here so I can tell everyone the truth. Claire is going to know how Graham managed the casino case scam to avoid being caught. She will be haunted by the scandal, the stigma, and by your murder of an innocent person and your own suicide. Believe me, I know."

"Too bad about Ginger, but—blackmailing me. For more money, because of what she saw."

"She saw you push me in the river?"

She barely nodded. "Graham had nothing to do with it."

"You mean *you* were behind the money laundering, then got caught or blackmailed by the bad boys who run such things?"

Lisa's teeth were chattering. She had to really struggle to enunciate. They were both shaking, and Ellie was turning blue and was bleeding from her chest and mouth, maybe from where she'd slammed into the steering wheel. But Lisa had to know. If Graham was not the spider, was Ellie? She decided to try something else. She was pretty sure she couldn't free Ellie's trapped leg and that this plane was going to be ripped away and thrust over the falls. Soon.

"Ellie, do you want to die?"

"Have to. It went wrong. Just a push—sorry. I had a headache. Graham dropped me off. I changed your note, went after you. Wanted you to think it was Spike, drown you."

"And drown Christine?"

"She—in the way. Like Ginger."

"When you took off, did you think I had drowned?"

Again, she barely nodded. "But when I flew over

the lodge roof—saw your shadow under plane. And everyone saw you—the sheriff there, so I had to die."

She wanted to slam the woman against the trembling wall, but she played her last card. "Ellie, we're both going to die, be swept over the falls. Who was behind the casino case money scheme?"

Ellie coughed up blood. "Merritt."

Merit what? Lisa thought, then realized what she must have said.

"Merritt?" Lisa demanded. "Your brother, Senator Carlise, was behind all that?"

"So proud of him, going far. Needed money, pay to play... Graham didn't know. You and Mitch last year—I had you bugged, followed. For Merritt, proud of him, going far, my own blood, going far..."

Ellie shuddered; Lisa, too. No, the entire plane was shifting. Lisa tried once more to free Ellie, but she'd gone limp. Going far, she'd said. Going far...

Lisa exploded out of the cockpit with sudden energy she didn't know she had. As on the day Ginger died, she clung to the top of the plane, just above the water, lifted herself up toward the roof to reach for a rocky ledge where the fuselage was wedged.

She held to the solid strength of the rock, of her memories of Mitch as the plane seemed to lunge downriver with a crunching roar.

27

Even after Spike's plane took off, Christine stood on the shore, horrified at what she'd seen. At first she'd been thrilled to see Lisa had not drowned, that she was hanging on to one of the pontoons of the plane. But when she'd seen her friend dangling with her legs thrashing, she screamed so loudly that she'd drowned out the snarl of the plane's engine.

She fell to her knees at the edge of the lake, sobbing. She hadn't cried when she'd shot Clay or when she'd been arrested, not even when his family and her people had turned their backs on her. She'd been devastated to think that Spike was trying to harm them with his plane.

But now she knew better. The man she'd come to love after she had sworn never to trust another man, after being helped by Mitch, would not have done that, no matter how distraught he'd been over Ginger's death. No, that had been Mrs. Bonner flying that plane, because she hated Lisa for taking Mitch from her own daughter. That must be it. The raven who was very clever but very crooked in this story was a woman who had seemed the best of generosity and graciousness.

Christine's tears mingled with the water of the lake where she knelt with her face in her hands. But she lifted her head as she heard the sound of the plane again. Could it be coming back? Had Mrs. Bonner not known Lisa was beneath it at first and was now going to put her gently down?

Christine wiped her weak-woman tears away and waded out into the water, looking up. No plane where she prayed it would be. No, it was a boat flying over the lake and a man with flame-red hair was in it.

Spike! Spike, searching for her. She screamed and waved, waded back to shore and ran along the bank in his direction, scattering a group of ptarmigan with their strange cries, but her shouting Spike's name drowned them out.

He headed straight for her. How could she ever have thought it was Spike in the plane?

The prow of the boat crunched into the shore. He was one big stride out of the boat when she threw herself into his arms and held tight.

"Lisa," she choked out. "Did you see her—flying?"

"It can't end well," he said, his voice breaking, too, as he picked her up, dripping wet, and carried her to the boat. He sat down on the front seat with her in his arms across his lap and held her so tight she almost couldn't breathe.

"It has to—all that they've been through," she said, her lips moving against the warm flesh of his neck.

"Us, too. I'm sorry I was so mad at her."

"Was it Mrs. Bonner who took your plane?"

"Yes. She must have killed Ginger. But no one's going to take you away from me."

"We have to go help Mitch," she said, lifting her head from his solid shoulder. "He's helped both of us—and if she's gone…"

"I know. Let's go."

He kissed her hard and set her down, then scrambled out to shove them off the shore.

It seemed an eternity as Lisa clung to a narrow ledge just above the reach of the river. She knew now who had tried to kill her and why. She was the expendable one of the two of them who had worked on the casino case, before Ellie and her contacts—maybe not Graham—had sabotaged it. Mitch was off in Alaska, but when Graham told her that Lisa might rise to become the next senior partner and they were going to the lodge, Ellie must have panicked. She'd laid plans to take advantage of any chance to make Lisa's death look like an accident. Lisa recalled that she had even known that police were scarce in this area. And Ellie knew all about Lisa's traumatic past, which she had played on.

Ellie must have feared that, after Lisa spent time reminiscing with Mitch, they might discover and blow the whistle on Ellie's beloved brother's scheme.

Ellie still might have wanted Mitch for her daughter and heir, so she asked Graham to try to get him back to Florida, even part-time, to set up that. After two tragedies—Lisa's and Ginger's deaths—Ellie may have figured Mitch would want to get away from the lodge. Graham's part in all this, Lisa wasn't sure, but he must have repeatedly asked them about the casino case because Ellie had urged him to be sure there were no bad feelings from Mitch and Lisa.

No bad feelings! Kind, refined Ellie was a murderer, clever but crooked!

Even as time passed, Lisa did not doubt Mitch would come for her on the river again. She took to turning her head upstream, looking for a kayak, though how he'd put in to help her here she did not know. Though she was trembling from the trauma and the cold, she held on, feeling strangely safer and much more at peace than she could ever remember.

This time, the rushing water had somehow washed away her guilt and pain over the loss of her mother and sister, a baptism, a blessing. But poor Claire Bonner. Poor Graham when all this broke, however much he knew of Ellie's desperate plotting.

But Lisa had survived, and was determined to yet. Another thing that kept her going was the desire to expose Merritt Carlisle, the real spider in the casino case. It would hardly be news that another person in power, a politician, had lied and "payed to play," as Ellie had put it. He'd needed a lot of money for that, laundered money.

And Lisa held on tight because, when all this was over, she was going to finally have time to settle things with the man she had never stopped loving and still wanted very much.

At last, when the sun slanted into the gorge almost enough to reach her and when the muscles of her legs began to cramp so that she could hardly stand and thought she might have to ride the river again, she heard a welcome sound, one that challenged the crashing rapids: the *whap, whap, whap* of a helicopter. But she couldn't see it, couldn't lean back or look up or move from her frozen position to lift her arms in the *V* that meant "Pick me up! Help me!"

The chopper hovered and soon a wire basket bumped its way down the rugged rock face near her. Carefully, she turned her head. Mitch! Mitch's face lit up through his tears, Mitch's arms outstretched, coming closer, grabbing her and hauling her in. Now she could cling to him, her own rock through everything.

"We saw the plane at the bottom of the falls!" he told her, shouting over the mingled sounds of river and the rotors. "But I told them, come back upriver! You didn't live through all that to be lost this time, not now that we've found each other again!"

She could only nod as they were lifted skyward over the Wild River and the land she'd learned to love.

Epilogue

Flashes popped in their faces as Mitch and Lisa left the Broward County courthouse in Fort Lauderdale. They had been through five days of grueling testimony against disgraced former senator Merritt Carlisle. The trial had also tarnished Graham Bonner, who had refused to let his daughter attend, so she wouldn't have her new law career tainted by the scandal. Lisa had longed to write Claire Bonner a note, urging her not to let her mother's desperate deeds and suicide ruin her life, but she knew it would not be accepted from the woman who had brought her family down.

Mitch pulled Lisa through the crowd of reporters into his lawyer's car and told the hired driver, "Take us down to A1A by the beach and drop us off near Sunrise, will you?"

"You sure? It's a raw, windy day, Mr. Braxton. It'll be deserted."

"Suits us. Besides," he said with a grin at Lisa, "I need to toughen the lady up with weather like that—

myself, too, after how long this trial has taken. We're heading home to Alaska soon." He loosened his tie. He'd had to buy an expensive suit for this, since he'd given all his old ones away, but he'd used it for their wedding, too.

If he expected Lisa to protest that they were hardly dressed for the beach with a February cold front coming through, he was mistaken. She just grinned, took off both her black pumps and jammed them in her briefcase. "Hey," she said with a little laugh, "to a Talkeetna mountain woman who swims Alaskan rivers for weekly exercise, a blustery day on a Florida beach will be a walk in the park."

"Thank God this is all over," Mitch told her as he gave his briefcase a quick kick. "I hate missing one long winter night of the aurora borealis."

"I'm considering following in the tradition of some of our lodge's Japanese guests who are hoping for a very fortunate child to be conceived under those lights," Lisa said with a grin.

They had been married for three months, a fact that had been dredged out at the trial as if the two star witnesses against the venerable former state senator and his brace of expensive lawyers were in collusion to smear his name somehow. But the Carlisles, Merritt and Ellie, had managed to do that well enough themselves.

"I've had a fourth call to join another law firm here," Mitch told her.

"That means I still have two more offers than you,"

she told him, with a quick poke in his ribs. "But I'm committed to a higher calling, namely, baking to help Christine with the food for our guests and taking over the ziplining in the spring. When I open up a law office in Talkeetna, it'll have to be worked around those things, but family and friends come first."

"Not to mention running the lodge, once Christine moves in with Spike."

They shared another silent smile, as they had so many times these last seven months. No way, now that they were back together, would they allow testifying in the courtroom here or in Anchorage about Ginger's death get them down. Christine had even found the strength to sit in that Alaska courtroom with Spike. They would be married this spring.

And Mitch's brother had attended Mitch and Lisa's wedding in Fort Lauderdale with his wife and kids and had promised to visit the lodge next summer, so there were miracles enough to go around.

The wind buffeted them as they got out of the hired car, waved it away and walked down the wide, deserted beach. Sand blew against their bare feet and Lisa tasted salt on her lips already from the frothing waves. But she felt so ecstatic she could have walked on the wild surf. Carrying their briefcases in their outer hands, they held hands and walked along the shore of the ocean an entire continent away from where they wanted to be.

"It took me a while to get something made," he told her, releasing her hand and digging in his briefcase. "I wanted to give it to you here since this is about where I gave you the other one."

"A wolfish look that day you first saw me playing volleyball here?" she teased. "Our first kiss?"

A cold wave washed in and swirled at their feet, but neither of them moved, despite the fact it soaked Mitch's trousers and slopped up her legs to wet her skirt.

"No, it's this, Mrs. Braxton," he said as he produced a heavy gold bracelet. "Last time I gave you a bracelet before the ring, so this time we just reversed it." He jammed his briefcase under one arm and moved to fasten the bracelet around her wrist.

At first she thought he had replicated the seagull bracelet she'd lost in the river the day the plane crashed, for she could see this had birds on it with outstretched wings. But she saw these were Alaska's state bird, the ptarmigan, and with feathered feet.

She blinked back tears as he closed the clasp. Yes, now that all the pain was past, she could live a rich, full life with Mitch and a family of their own in their blessed, beautiful Alaska home.

* * * * *

AUTHOR'S NOTE

This novel was inspired by a two-week trip my husband and I took to Alaska during the month of August several years ago. I was impressed by the land and its very independent people. More than once, someone I spoke with or interviewed explained why they love Alaska and would live nowhere else. I was surprised how many odd jobs Alaskans were willing to work to support themselves in the more rural areas.

We stayed in a rustic lodge near Denali Park that was partly the inspiration for Mitch's lodge. Bear Bones does not exist, but I based it on several small rural towns I saw. My husband and I have done white-water rafting in Colorado rather than Alaska. Still, although I have not kayaked on river rapids, it gave me a feel for the Wild River of the story.

For background information, I also used the cable-TV series *Tougher in Alaska* hosted by Geo Beach, and read numerous books on the state. Special thanks to Jonathan Krakauer for his amazing book, *Into the Wild,* especially for information on the gauging station by which Mitch and Lisa crossed the river. Another source for me was *Through Yup'ik Eyes* by Colin Chisholm, which I found so fascinating I had to tell part of the story through my fictional character Christine Tanaka's Yup'ik eyes.

I want to thank Dr. Julianne Moledor and Dr. Roy Manning for background information about the "too much sauna" scenes. And special thanks to sister author Carolyn Melvin, an attorney, for the vetting of my lawyer information in the book.

Talkeetna is a great town to visit, but if you want to do so virtually, information about it, the Mountain Mother Contest and Moose Dropping Festival are available at www.talkeetnachamber.org. The dates for these events may vary but are usually in July, not August, as I have set them in the novel.

And if you have any interest in seeing brown bears feasting on salmon, an excellent Web site, which includes photos and video, is Bob Arnebeck's www.geocities.com/bobarnebeck/dams.

The image of a drowned woman peering through water appears several places in the novel and was partly inspired by the painting which Ellie Bonner describes. If you would like to see John Everett Millais's beautiful and haunting painting, *Ophelia*, it can be viewed at www.tate.org.uk/ophelia.

Karen Harper

April 6, 2009

QUESTIONS FOR DISCUSSION

1. Have you ever participated in a team bonding experience? Was it effective? What did you learn about yourself and others?

2. Lisa and Mitch face the problem of two vastly different careers, locations and lifestyles. Can such problems be worked out for love? Is it the woman who is often pressured to make the big changes, and is that fair?

3. Lisa learns to love Alaska. Have you ever bonded with a unique place? Why?

4. This novel's two main female characters have traumas that haunt them. Have you known someone with such a burden? How can we overcome such devastating emotional shocks and losses?

5. Did Mitch handle his big change in life well, or did he make mistakes?

6. How early in the story did you believe Lisa had definitely been pushed into the river? When were you sure by whom, and how did you know?

7. The indigenous Inuit cultures of Alaska have some unique beliefs. What differences or simi-

larities do you see between the white culture and the First Nations people there?

8. The author was tempted to use a fourth quote to emphasize themes in this story: "Nature was here something savage and awful, though beautiful...What is this Titan that has possession of me? Talk of mysteries!...Who are we?" (Henry David Thoreau from *Ktaadn*) Going green and nature preservation are big topics today. How does nature impact your life and what is this mystery Thoreau alludes to?